LARGE
PRINT
EDITION

RANDOM
HOUSE

# HOTEL PARADISE

## MARTHA GRIMES

64,602

Published by Random House Large Print
in association with Alfred A. Knopf, Inc.
New York      1996

LIBRARY OF CONGRESS CATALOGING-IN-PUBLICATION DATA

Grimes, Martha.
   Hotel Paradise : a novel / by Martha Grimes.
   p.   (large print)   cm.
   ISBN  0-679-75879-8
   1. City and town life—Appalachian Region—
Fiction.   2. Hotels—Appalachian Region—Fiction.
3. Girls—Appalachian Region—Fiction.   4. Large type
books.   I. Title.
   [PS3557.R48998H68      1996]
   813′.54—dc20      95-49926

                                                      CIP

*Manufactured in the United States of America*
FIRST LARGE PRINT EDITION

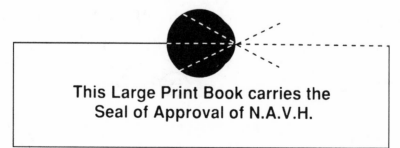

**This Large Print Book carries the
Seal of Approval of N.A.V.H.**

To the memory of
June D. Grimes
and Lillian F. Davis

and, of course,
to Will, Mill, and Walter

My feeling (no doubt hopelessly tinged
With how, were she here, her looks alone
Would resist my attempts to say these things)
That all of this was already lost, even then.
The Palace of Nowhere. L'Hôtel de Dream.
                                    *—Sherod Santos*

                    *from "Elegy for My Sister"*

# HOTEL
# PARADISE

It's a blowing day. The wind feels weighted and the air like iron. As I walked the half-mile to the lake this evening, I could hardly push against this heaviness that settled on me like a coat of snow.

I have been sitting on this low mossy wall for an hour, but I can't see the Devereau house, or if there is any light in it. The woods are so thick by the spring, they blot out the other side of the lake like ink spilled across the page I'm reading. This time I brought a book; I mean to wait, though I don't think he'll be back.

I wonder now if there are mysteries never meant to be solved. Or not meant to be solved to a certainty, for I do have some idea of what must have happened near White's Bridge. I've found out the answers to a lot of questions, but those answers pull more questions out of hiding, ones I never would have thought to ask.

I think I know how Fern died and who killed her. But I don't know why, exactly. I have to guess at the why. Even if I was absolutely sure, I would still not tell the police, not even the Sheriff. Some things mean more than the law. I have not sat through all of Clint Eastwood's old westerns for nothing. Clint doesn't always hound a rustler to his grave, not if there's a reason to let him off more important than a dozen law-abiding reasons to arrest him. Call it cowpoke justice. I hear people say "It's between me and my conscience," but I think it's awful risky to go by your conscience, for your conscience can be pretty leaky. I think Clint would agree.

Anyway. That was the decision I made this morning, not to tell the Sheriff, and it weighs mighty heavily upon me. What I discovered over the past couple of weeks is that what I think is a difficult decision to make is really a difficult decision to make. And what I think is hard and painful is truly hard and painful.

I guess that doesn't sound like much learnt, but I think it is.

## TWO

My mother is not a Paradise. Her grandfather (my great-grandfather) married into this family of hotel owners. And it really smarts my great-aunt Paradise that the Hotel Paradise does not belong to her a hundred percent. Because my great-uncle long ago got mad at everybody in the Paradise family, he made up some complicated will where the running of the place fell into my father's hands and upon his death, into my mother's. That is not to say that my mother *owns* the place. It is all extremely complicated, the legal ins and outs of the ownership of the Hotel Paradise, and always has been. My friend Maud Chadwick said thank God no one ever tried to go to court over it, because it would make *Bleak House* look like a parking citation.

Of course, my great-aunt insists she owns the Hotel Paradise. She's ninety-one years old, and "head" of the hotel in name only, for she doesn't do anything except keep to her rooms up on the fourth floor, playing cards and drinking, and complaining about what everybody else does. The work of running the Hotel Paradise is left to my mother and, now, to my mother's business partner, Lola Davidow.

Lola Davidow, who came on the scene only five years ago, said the name should be changed from the Hotel Paradise to the Spirit Lake Hotel. This was not unreasonable, since except for Aurora the Paradises are long gone from Spirit Lake; but when my great-aunt heard about Lola's idea, she raised such a ruckus everybody was afraid she might just come downstairs. My mother, being much more diplomatic than Mrs. Davidow, tried to appease my great-aunt Paradise by making her the Angel Pie my mother is famous for. Lola just grumbled, saying that it wasn't Paradise money that was keeping the hotel afloat (which was perfectly true), or the gin and whisky flowing (true again), but "the sweat of our brows" (true of my mother, not of Lola, whose own brow stays pretty dry).

I myself have to suffer enough brow sweating, working seven days a week waiting tables, besides having to put up with Lola Davidow and her horrible daughter, that I know what it feels like. Brow sweating and browbeating is a kind of treatment that I think just gets handed down from generation to generation. There is no one for me to beat up on, though, for I am only twelve, and the youngest of the family.

The Hotel Paradise is an old summer hotel set in ten acres of woods and really "ramshackle" without giving the appearance of being run-down (although the local fire department disagrees). My mother is too clever at sewing slipcovers and curtains to allow the hotel to go to seed. It is full of beautiful old furniture and huge fireplaces whose flames paint the slippery flowered chintzes and gilt mirrors in patterns of gold and rose. In late afternoons, nothing for pure prettiness can match the shafts of winter sunlight piercing the long windows of the lobby, or flooding through the rose glass of the music room and turning the keys of the upright piano to a pale gold.

The hotel is not located in the larger town of La Porte, but in a smaller village about two miles distant called Spirit Lake. At five thousand feet above sea level, the summers are warm and dry and clear and the winters cold and dry and clear. Plenty of sun, plenty of snow. From October through March in Spirit Lake there always seems to be the scent of snow in the air. I like that scent. The sky in winter is oyster-colored, and sometimes light appears like shied stones in water, bright and quick.

The "family" (for the Davidows, owing to the association, are becoming part of it) consists of my mother, my great-aunt Paradise, my brother Will, Lola Davidow, and her daughter, the awful Ree-Jane. And me, of course.

We children are not allowed to use shortenings: "Grandma," "Mom," "Mommy," "Dad," and such. It's as if we are meant to keep our relationship at arm's length, formal. Not that my mother—or my father, who's dead now—doesn't love me and my brother; but it's a kind of white-gloved, black-tie, swallow-tail-coated love that walks ahead and holds doors, not the sort that crashes through them. I'm not complaining; there are a lot of advantages to that distant sort of love: for example, you don't get knocked around and screamed at. But I thought it was stupid to have to wrap my tongue around "Great-Aunt Paradise," so to me (in my own mind, that is) she is just plain Aurora.

Long ago, Aurora Paradise took over the fourth floor of the hotel, a half-dozen catacomblike rooms, and established herself there. With a case of Gordon's gin and one of Johnnie Walker and a dumbwaiter, I guess she's content enough. The dumbwaiter was probably put in ages before for laundry, but Aurora uses it for pulling up the meals furnished by my mother, who everyone agrees is the best cook in the state.

From this you might think that Aurora lives peacefully with her gin and her fried chicken dinners, but don't kid yourself. Aurora Paradise puts me in mind of a black bird, a rook or a raven, the sort you see in pictures of the Tower of London, perched up there. Up there on the top floor, she thinks she can spread her black wings and cast a shadow over the whole ten acres. Not over me, though, for I caught onto her.

But Aurora Paradise can't outdo for sheer meanness the Davidow daughter, Ree-Jane. Of course, her name isn't really "Ree-Jane"; it's Regina Jane Davidow. I have always thought the name itself rather wonderful and am only sorry it belongs to her. But somewhere in some book, Regina Jane Davidow discovered a reference to a great French comedienne whose name was Réjane. So she christened herself with this French name and insisted that she be called by it. For some time, she refused to answer if anyone called her by her real name. (I rarely called.) Not only were we all to call her this, we were to give it the French pronunciation, which meant that the "Ré" was supposed to come "from the throat—no, the *throat*, the *throat!*" so that what came out was a sound caught between an *r* and a *w*. She kept giving me lessons, which I had no intention of mastering, in the impossible French *r* sound, by running her fingers up her own throat and emitting small growls that one of the guests' dog loved and tried to answer. Well, I've never seen a French comedienne, but there's one thing I'm certain one is *not*, and that is Regina Jane Davidow, who has as much humor in her as a cow in the rain.

Now, I'm sure she's sorry she ever found it, but back then she thought the name "Réjane" was really elegant, in keeping with her life plans, a name that fit all of the things she would one day become: a famous model, an American heroine living in Paris or owning a castle in the south of France, or the Countess of Kent in England. We had an argument about the Countess of Kent, for I assumed the countess would be married to a count. She always acts as if my ignorance is just the funniest thing in the world, and told me (snobbishly) that I had no idea of titles at all, and that, though the wife would be a *countess*, the man is an *earl*. I happened to be reading a book about vampires, and I asked, Oh, you mean like Earl Dracula? (That made her really mad.) So now there was to be added to her list of worldly accomplishments—that future structure, that brick shithouse she is always building in her mind—the role of famous comedienne, Réjane Somebody.

Well, it's dangerous to go making up names for yourself; you've got to be careful, for the change might stick in the worst way. That's what happened with Ree-Jane. It is of course such a totally unheard-of name that, naturally, the townfolks, who have never been tutored in the French pronunciation, assumed her name was "Rae Jane" and called her that. I admit this misunderstanding was mostly my fault, since I had no intention of hawking up that *r* sound and just went around calling her "Ree-Jane" to everybody in town. When they hear the "Ree," they translate it to "Rae," and Regina Jane Davidow has never been able to shake it. This infuriates her. It also infuriates her that I make such a big production out of calling her *Ree*-Jane, never forgetting to give that first syllable just that extra little push and, if I'm calling her down the length of the hotel halls, wail out that *e* like the place is on fire and we'd better get out: "*Reeeeee*-Jane, oh *Reeeeeeeee*-Jane!" She could kill me.

Unfortunately, any dumb fantasy Ree-Jane entertains about her future is fed by the pride of both her mother and (this is harder to understand) mine. That is what I hate, my mother's making me take a backseat to the Davidows. Ree-Jane is just enough older—four years—to try to lord it over me. I hope that any plots Aurora Paradise is cooking up include getting rid of Ree-Jane Davidow.

*　　*　　*

There are just two Paradises still living. Aurora has an unmarried sister named Alberta. She's like a carbon copy of Aurora, though a dozen years younger, and when the two are up there in Aurora's rooms, I like to sit on the landing of the third floor or, if I feel brave, crawl up a few steps farther to sit and eavesdrop. I sit in a pool of shadow with my skirt pulled down over my knees and listen. What I generally hear is a drone like bees around a hive, and then there might be a sudden clap of laughter, harsh and joyless, and then the drone again. The rumble of the dumbwaiter dragging their white-meat-only chicken dinners skyward serves as a kind of creepy music for the droning talk or shrieking laughter. When Aurora and Alberta get together the dumbwaiter is in constant motion. With her having to send canapes and dishes of olives and (when the fourth floor runs dry) pitchers of martinis up on the dumbwaiter, Lola scarcely has time for her own cocktail hour, usually taken in the back office. Poor souls looking for a room and under the impression we're running a hotel often get their comeuppance if Lola is into her fourth martini, the one that always seems to convince her the hotel is her castle, and she doesn't much like people swimming the moat.

I have always thought it speaks well of Lola that occasionally she's invited to join Aurora for cocktails. I suppose I could be mean and say that these invitations are extended only when Aurora's supply of Gordon's gin or Johnnie Walker is running low, but I'm not sure that's the case. There is something at times actually winning about Lola, a sort of blitheness which is a relief from the grinding work routine that my mother always follows. This is not to say my mother fails by comparison—good Lord, no. If she didn't have her work routine the whole place would collapse just as the fourth floor fire escape always threatens to do.

One of Aurora's rooms has a fire escape that she uses as a small balcony. Aurora and Lola Davidow sometimes man the balcony, joined occasionally by our chain-smoking, sixty-year-old desk clerk named Marge Byrd. Marge likes to keep a pint flask under the desk and takes nips from it when business either speeds up or slows down. The three of them sit up there on folding chairs, drunk as loons, hurling down greetings at arrivals coming up the drive. My mother naturally objects to this as unseemly, and so does Lola when Lola's not up there with Aurora and Marge Byrd. My mother comes out on the porch and then the driveway, looking. Finally, seeing Lola Davidow up there, her hand shading her brow, she calls up some kitchen emergency, real or made-up. The object of this is to let them know that she works while they play, and who can blame her?

So, Aurora can still continue as the "head." And I suspect that the visits of Alberta's are to be taken as board meetings, for the sister has a legal interest in the place also. When she shows up (always unan-

nounced) a couple of times a year, then Aurora has
family to join her out on the fire escape. Oh, how
they appear out there in their lavender and stiff lace
collars and buckled shoes as occasionally they look
down and wave!

Lola Davidow sometimes complains (because
she isn't invited, I'm sure) that they're getting rowdy
and maybe we should call the Sheriff's office. Of
course, she's only kidding, but I wish she'd go ahead
and do it sometimes because anything that could get
me within a stone's throw of La Porte's Sheriff could
only be good news.

## THREE

The county sheriff is the real bright spot in my life. His name is Sam DeGheyn and everyone calls him Sam, except I can't quite work up the nerve to do it. I call him "Sheriff" even in the privacy of my own mind. Since he has the important job of peacekeeping and, if it's needed, criminal chasing, I never want to appear to be wasting his time by hanging around the courthouse or interrupting him in his daily duties. What I do is help by watching for red flags on the parking meters or checking out cars parked where they shouldn't be—such as blocking an alley or sitting in a loading zone.

I keep my eye peeled for illegal parking so I can have something to report to the Sheriff. At one time I would have loved a horrible crime happening right at the Hotel Paradise—a shootout, maybe, with Ree-Jane in the crowd looking on from the porch, where she would then be sprayed by machine-gun fire. This would be a legitimate reason for calling the Sheriff. But that never happens.

The one time I honestly could have asked for police help, I didn't: that was the time I was left alone at the Hotel Paradise for two days while everyone else took off to escort the precious Regina Jane Davidow to visit a friend of hers. My brother, Will, was already off visiting his friend Brownmiller Conroy or he would have been left behind, too.

When I say "alone" I mean, of course, me and Aurora Paradise, but somehow I couldn't imagine Aurora coming to my rescue when the hatchet killer came. Imagine yourself as not even yet in your teens and alone in a ninety-eight-room hotel in dead winter. Imagine the possibilities for random noises—the creakings, the scrapings, the footfalls, the howlings in the woods, the owl sounds, the winds, the bats— and so on. Yet, I didn't think anything of it—I mean, I was *scared*, naturally, but I assumed this to be my lot in life. I had to send food up to the fourth floor on the dumbwaiter, and whisky. I was *not* to bother Aurora myself. She hated visitors. When the delivery was made, I would go to sit as close to the top floor as I could get so as to be near somebody.

I don't know how Sheriff DeGheyn came to hear about this, but he did. And when he asked me about it, with a look of honest concern, I was casual. Oh, I told him, *someone* had to take care of the hotel. The Sheriff just shook his head and mentioned words like "courage" and so forth that I couldn't apply to what had been my own quivering self sitting on the stairs, but I was immensely pleased. He told me he would have been happy to keep an eye on the place and even come in and have a Coke or coffee with me had he known, and if ever it happened again— but then he stopped and got a set look on his face and somehow I knew it wouldn't.

Soon after that, my mother asked me if I'd told

Sam DeGheyn I'd been left by myself, and I said no, of course not, which was true. The tight look on my mother's and Lola Davidow's faces told me that he must have given someone absolute hell. It was worth being in the way of Mrs. Davidow's terrible temper for a couple of days to know this. (The Sheriff is the only person in three counties who can bawl out Lola Davidow and get away with it.)

I was absolutely flabbergasted that I had managed to call up such concern in anyone, especially the Sheriff, for I was not used to someone's sticking up for me. I don't mean that if I was in real danger from illness or accident my mother wouldn't be *concerned*; but it's not wholly satisfactory to think you have to be mashed on the railroad tracks or get typhoid before someone cares. So the Sheriff's attitude made having to stay in the hotel alone an experience I wouldn't mind repeating, and I wished they'd all go away again. To work up that protective feeling in the Sheriff I would have wandered through the Transylvania woods with Earl Dracula himself for a week.

The Sheriff likes Teaberry gum, so I carry a pack in my pocket for when he runs out. He always seems to be running out, which surprises me, as he's a man with a good memory, hardly absentminded at all. But when he starts searching his pockets for gum and mildly cursing himself for leaving it back in his desk, I casually produce my pack. The Sheriff's smile is high-voltage, and he turns it on when I do this. I always tell him to take a stick for later, too.

Then, we'll walk along the pavement, the Sheriff with his citation book, me with my fund of knowledge about cars illegally or at least wrongly parked. People use five-minute zones and the La Porte library lot shamelessly.

Much of the time we share a comfortable silence on our curb treks. I love silence; I hate babble. Silence is a way of saying: We do not have to entertain each other; we are okay as we are.

The only place I have seen this at work is in a movie theater. Of course, there is the film up there as a wholesale "distraction," that's true. And yet, and yet . . . I like to look around in the auditorium lit just enough so that you can make out profiles and planes of cheeks, smiles or downturned mouths. Feelings show. And what I see then is little infant faces, child faces, tilted toward the screen, eating popcorn or drawing on straws in Pepsis and Cokes. When people are unaware they are being watched they look so innocent. Maybe I'm speaking of thralldom, of minds working together, a hush of lips, a hundred eyes all seeing the same thing and wanting the same thing (*"Oh, no! No! Don't go in that room; he's waiting for you, you poor girl . . ."*).

So the Sheriff and I walk in movie silence. The exceptional thing about him is that he never asks questions merely to fill a vacuum. "How's the hotel?" or "How's your mom?" never pass his lips. I imagine he's fairly certain that if the hotel collapsed and killed all the guests and help, or if my mother's eyebrows got burned in a grease fire, or if Lola

Davidow got her hand wedged in the cocktail-onion jar—I would mention it. No, if the Sheriff asks a question or makes a remark it means something. And because we can't always engage in meaningful conversation, we are sometimes silent.

On one such occasion, the Sheriff asked me if Regina Jane Davidow had got that new car Lola said she was getting for her sixteenth birthday.

"Yes," I said, glumly to his back. He was kneeling down checking the rust on the underside of the fender of Miss Ruth Porte's little VW. Miss Ruth knew nothing about cars, and Sam kept his eye on the VW.

"Is it a white convertible?"

Glummer still, I said yes, again. Imagine not only being able to drive, but having your own car, your own convertible to boot. Ree-Jane was all over town in it, showing it off. I had not been invited yet to ride. The Sheriff straightened up, put a nickel in the meter because you could just see the red flag was raring to go, and said to me, "I'll tell you something, and you can do what you like about it. You know that tavern—the El Lobo— outside of Hebrides?"

I frowned slightly. "I think so."

We continued on our walk. "Twice I've seen a brand-new white Chevy convertible parked outside it, sales sticker still on the side window."

That was Ree-Jane's, all right! How wonderful she should be in bad with the Sheriff, since she's so sure he adores her, although I have never seen evidence of it. I watched him then snap his citation book shut and jam it in his hip pocket. He did not look at all adoring of Ree-Jane Davidow.

"That place is strictly off limits to kids—"

*Kids!* He had referred to the future Countess of Kent as a "kid"! I could hardly wait to tell her.

"—to *anyone* under twenty-one years old." His look at me was very serious. "Now, I didn't go in and drag her out by her heels, which I should've. But if ever I see her there, I'll bust her. I'm telling you because you might want to warn her. Or not." He shrugged slightly. His eyes were expressive, but I couldn't quite read the message.

*Wonderful!* How wonderful to be in possession of this nugget better than gold, this warning to plague her with! Of course, I was casual about it, and merely said, "Um . . . I'll see what I can do." But roiling around in my mind as the Sheriff and I continued on our walk was a selection of great openings for the subject of Ree-Jane getting busted by the Sheriff. There was: "Oh, incidentally, I was talking to the Sheriff this morning, and . . ."; or "Sheriff De-Gheyn happened to mention to me that a white convertible . . ." Et cetera. Making sure I stuck in how the El Lobo was "off limits to *kids*."

It occurred to me that the Sheriff could easily have done the warning himself, as Ree-Jane has taken every opportunity to sit her ass on his desk since she's been picking up speeding tickets from one of the deputies, Donny. She sits on the Sheriff's desk like Lauren Bacall and tries to smolder.

I wondered why he didn't. Probably because he didn't want to embarrass her; the Sheriff is really nice that way.

# FOUR

Spirit Lake is a half-mile from the hotel, and I often walk down here and might even be the only person who does, aside from my brother, Will. I like to stop here at the spring and sit on the wall even when I don't have any particular reason for coming, as I have tonight. The place is overgrown now, the untended grass and weeds and trees choking the narrow road halfway around so that a complete circle of the lake is becoming impossible, even on foot. But it is still quite beautiful, at least I think so, and some of its beauty comes from all of the undergrowth and overgrowth, from its wild look.

The most important thing about Spirit Lake, or the most terrible, is that a girl drowned here over forty years ago. The girl was my age—twelve—and no one knows exactly what happened. They say she took a rowboat out into the lake and it must somehow have capsized. The boat was seen drifting in the middle of the lake one moonlit night, but the people who saw it thought nothing of it; they thought one of the rowboats at the boathouse must have come loose from its mooring. And then the girl was found. Her absence wasn't even reported until the next morning, and finally the family had to call the police.

Spirit Lake is small and partly covered with masses of water lilies and tall blowing grasses. Her body was found caught up in this water growth. Spirit Lake has always seemed mysterious, I think, and the drowning that no one could ever explain made it more so. No one back then knew why she had taken a boat out in the lake, especially at night, for her family said she had always been a little afraid of it.

Her family was made up of three aunts who lived in the only house near the lake, a large gray house built a short distance back from the lake's edge. There was no mother or father, only these sisters who all looked very much alike; yet she looked like none of them. Their name was Devereau, and her name was Mary-Evelyn. Mary-Evelyn Devereau.

I know all of these details because I have studied up on the case. Also, my own mother knew the family when she was a young girl herself, although she was older than Mary-Evelyn. I think my mother was about sixteen back then.

My mother was there when Mary-Evelyn drowned—I don't mean she was an eyewitness, but she was one of the many people who gathered down at the edge of the lake when the police were searching for the body. My mother actually saw them pull the body in from the grasses and water lilies, where it had lain near the bank, tangled and floating. Mary-Evelyn was wearing a white dress like a party dress; it had layers of ruffles all around the skirt and was embroidered with tiny flower buds of blue silk up and down the front. My mother, being good at sewing herself, noted these details.

And my mother knew the family from their

visits to the hotel; this was when the Paradises were still rampaging through it, including Aurora. Forty years ago, my great-aunt Paradise was probably just working up steam. Anyway, the Devereaus would occasionally drop in to have dinner. The dinners weren't nearly so good then, for my mother hadn't yet started doing the cooking. She is famous for her cooking. I have always been sorry she never got a chance to go to Paris and be famous in a place that's worth being famous in. The point about these visits, though, is that during one of them, which was a birthday party for one of the aunts, someone took pictures of all of them, and my mother kept one. So I know just what Mary-Evelyn looked like, and her aunts, just before she drowned. I keep the snapshot in a Whitman's candy box, along with some other objects I prize. My mother doesn't know I held on to it while she was rummaging through her snapshot collection, nor do I think she'd care or miss it.

I like to sit in the Pink Elephant (a cellar room below our dining room) and look up from my notebook at the shadowy wall where I can see on the pink stucco that darkness in imagined moonlight where the boat slowly circles and drifts, and I see Mary-Evelyn float and bob in the rushes, among the water lilies. Her body moves slightly with the current, like the boat out in the middle of the lake.

I see this in my mind and I feel like weeping; I think it is one of the unhappiest things I have ever heard. And I think perhaps Mary-Evelyn was one of the unhappiest girls who ever lived in Spirit Lake.

Just a short while ago I merely suspected it. Now, I know this to be true.

But I would take the picture out and study it and think about Mary-Evelyn Devereau. Her death puzzled me, and I don't understand why it didn't puzzle everybody at the time. I've written down a short list of questions which I keep in the candy box, and every once in a while I add another question to the list:

Why was Mary-Evelyn out at night?
Why was she in a *boat*, at night?
Why was she wearing one of her best dresses?
Why didn't they report her missing until the next morning?
Why was her body so far from the boat?

The police back then must have been dumb, for they never tried to piece all of this together. Oh, they asked the obvious questions: Why was she out at night in a boat? But of course everyone would naturally ask that question. It's just too bad that our sheriff now, Sam DeGheyn, wasn't around back then, for he could have solved the mystery of the death of Mary-Evelyn Devereau.

On Fridays, sometimes I accompany Mrs. Davidow when she goes into La Porte to do the weekend shopping for the hotel. She goes to town usually twice a week, on Mondays and Fridays, and it's understood between us that I can go with her on Fridays. It's a funny thing about Mrs. Davidow:

although a lot of the time she's like a tree across my path and makes my life a misery, there are these little pockets of pleasantness when we get on very well together—much better than she and Ree-Jane get on, and I think this is painful to her. So Mrs. Davidow and I ride into town, sometimes laughing about some crazy La Porte person or other, or maybe something one of the guests has done; then she goes about her grocery business with her long list, and I go about mine.

My favorite business is always with Sheriff DeGheyn. Sometimes we sit in his office in the court-house talking about one thing or another. Other times we might go into the Rainbow Café for a soda and coffee. But usually we walk around town, me doing most of the talking, the Sheriff doing most of the listening. And a lot of the talking for a long time has been about Mary-Evelyn Devereau.

I had put the questions to him about the dress, and the distance between the boat and the body, and a couple of other questions. Not all of the details of the body's discovery and the subsequent "investigation" (if you can call it that) were told me by my mother; most of them I got from going back into the archives in the *Conservative* offices. Mr. Gumbel, the editor-in-chief, thought it quite unusual that someone my age would be interested in an almost half-century-old death, and made a lot of tired jokes about me becoming an investigative reporter. No, I told him, I didn't want to be a reporter and work for *The Conservative*. That's Regina Jane Davidow (I told him) who wants to be a reporter, but she says she's going to write for the *New York Times* or some other fabulous paper, and she's going to be a foreign correspondent. I said all of this about Ree-Jane, of course, just to see what Mr. Gumbel would say, because Ree-Jane had written some tiny little thing once and Mr. Gumbel had accepted it for publication. He had accepted it when Lola Davidow got him drunk (and herself also) one night and foisted it on him. Well, it didn't take up much space buried there in the back with a lot of advertisements for the feed store and so forth. But if there was one person who knew the limits of Regina Jane Davidow's writing ability, it was Mr. Gumbel. And he snorted down his nose when I told him Ree-Jane was going to be a foreign correspondent. She'll get as far as Hebrides, was all he said.

But he was very helpful in showing me where to look for reports on Mary-Evelyn. He remembered the drowning, but vaguely, as he was young himself, about my mother's age. The longest report I could find was a triple-column with a picture of Mary-Evelyn at the top. The reporter's account didn't tell me much that I hadn't already heard. There was a detailed description of Spirit Lake and the dock, but I figured that was just to take up space. (*The Conservative* has never been known for the originality of its reporters.) The picture was of a pretty but very sad-looking girl with silky hair in a beautifully sewn dress. I was tempted to take this account to put among my other valuables. I looked around to see if anyone was watching, and no one was, for no one else was around. I guess they had better things to do than hang around watching me. But as Mr. Gumbel had been so helpful, I left the account where it belonged. I know Mr. Gumbel wondered why I was so all-fired interested in it.

The Sheriff, I know, wonders why, too. But he gives me credit for having a good reason. And he always gives a lot of thought to my questions. On Fridays, as we work the meters on Second Street, I talk to him about Mary-Evelyn. And he takes off his visored cap, wipes his forearm back over his fore-head, and fits the cap on again, all the while slowly chewing the Teaberry gum I've given him. The Sheriff has the bluest eyes I've ever seen. They're baked blue, as if they've been fired in a kiln. "That's really a possibility," he'll say, of some point or other I'm making about Mary-Evelyn. He'll say it as he pulls out his spiral notebook and makes a note to himself.

On this particular Friday, we walked on, slowly. Up ahead, Helene Baum, the doctor's wife, was plowing towards us. Towards the Sheriff, I should say. Helene Baum was La Porte's biggest trouble-maker. She always had some complaint about some-one or something—a person, a dog, a cat, a bench by the bus stop. Probably, she'd just seen the parking ticket we'd left under her windshield wiper. The Sheriff took my arm and we walked across the street to continue our parking-meter ticketing on the other side.

Helene Baum crossed the street too. Walking

behind us was a wall of Friday shoppers, and they blocked us from her view just long enough for the Sheriff to grab my arm again and pull me into the nearest door. It happened to be our favorite place, the Rainbow Café.

The Rainbow is owned and operated by a woman people just call "Shirl" who is well known for her ways with customers. You get the same impression from her as from Lola Davidow, and that is that their places of business are private residences and the customers are more like intruders. Between Mrs. Davidow and Shirl there is no love lost, especially since Shirl outright stole my mother's recipe for Angel Pie and sells it right and left. I'd love to see Mrs. Davidow and Shirl duke it out right there on Second Street.

The person I especially like who works in the Rainbow is Maud Chadwick. Maud Chadwick is the sort of person you don't mind seeing when you don't want to see anyone. And a lot of the time I don't want to. (Mrs. Davidow tells me I'm "moody," and I always think that's pretty funny, considering the source.)

The Sheriff really likes Maud Chadwick, I can tell. They are a lot alike underneath, although on the surface very different. Maud appears to be quite shy, except with a very few people like the Sheriff and me. But since I'm only twelve, I suppose she can feel fairly easy around me. Kids like her. She doesn't have that uppity manner that most adults put on for children.

I have always thought Maud Chadwick has a kind of pixie look, like the fairies in my old *Peter Pan in Kensington Gardens* book, which I don't read anymore, of course, but I sometimes look at the silvery-blue illustrations, just to see if they are as I remember them. As I said, Maud has that sort of look. Her eyes are wide-spaced and her mouth hooks up at the corners in an expression like a little kid's. Maud is the only adult I call by a first name, for I have received strict instructions from my mother not to use adults' first names. But since Maud waits tables (something else we have in common) and has to wear a little name tag on her dress, it's only natural that everyone uses her first name—just as they called Shirley "Shirl" and Charlene "Charlene."

There are hand-lettered signs tacked up on the wall of each wooden booth, instructing the customers how many have to be in a party before the booth can be occupied. These signs seem to change constantly, depending on Shirl's mood. Most of the time, three people are needed to occupy one booth. But two people are permitted to take up one of her precious booths if she's in a good mood. At one point when she'd been on a real rampage there had to be four in the party to get a booth to themselves. And *one* person, well, occasionally some poor soul who doesn't know the rules tries to sit in a booth *alone*, and that's the last you ever see of him or her. That's the truth. Shirl is always saying around the cigarette dangling from her mouth that she isn't about to play host to the homeless of La Porte.

But there are days when Shirl has to be absent from the Rainbow for one reason or another. She does her shopping in Hebrides two or three times a month, and regular as clockwork has her appointment at the Prime Cut (a poor name, I always thought, for a beauty shop). When Shirl isn't there, Maud Chadwick always lets me have a booth to myself. On days when I figure Shirl isn't going to be at the Rainbow, I take my notebook with me into town. I often walk the two miles from the hotel into La Porte, sometimes accompanied by Ree-Jane. Once in town, Ree-Jane goes off looking for new worlds to conquer, maybe going into the other beauty parlor (the Hair and Gone) for a makeover, and comes out looking like an ad for Day-Glo; or sometimes she drifts into the courthouse and the Sheriff's office.

As for me, I slide into a booth, usually the one at the back of the café, and set up shop. I sit there writing, sometimes about the people at the counter when I finish with the ones in my head. At some point, Maud will walk back and set a bowl of chili before me. Oh, that chili! I cannot explain its appeal to me, and I'm sure any real chili expert would find it much too watery and bland. I tear the cellophane from the cracker packages and crumble the crackers all over the surface. I don't think I would like this chili if I ate it at the hotel, or at school, or anywhere else except sitting in a back booth at the Rainbow.

And I love the booths, too, despite the signs. They're made of dark wood, the entire booth, including the table between the high-backed benches, backs so high I can't see over the top, so that if someone approaches, or I want to check out something, I have to peer around the side. I guess that adds to the island-like isolation of the booth, and I like that.

I also talk to Maud about Mary-Evelyn Devereau and the whole odd story. Maud isn't a native of La Porte, and even if she were, isn't nearly old enough to remember the Devereau business. Yet she shows a lot of interest. Sometimes she sits with me in my booth and has a cup of coffee and a cigarette.

"Don't you think it's kind of funny the police were notified at six a.m.?" Maud asked once.

I thought about this for a moment, sipping my cherry Coke. "Well, I guess that's when they found out she was gone. Or wasn't back."

"Does anyone check to see if you're in bed before six a.m.?"

"No." I didn't bother to add that nobody checked to see if I was in bed at six, nine, or midnight. "But why would they lie to the police?"

The question had no answer, of course, and Maud knew it, and we both sat in silence and reflected on it: Why would they lie? The "they" in question were the Devereaus, the aunts with whom Mary-Evelyn lived. People had known very little about them; a lot that got gossiped around was pure speculation—stories have a way of growing up around women living alone as they did.

One thing that people did know—because they could hear it—was that they loved music, especially opera, especially *Tannhäuser*. Marge Byrd told me this. Marge is knowledgeable about music, although she hadn't been well acquainted with the Devereaus either, having been about the same age as my mother back then. And now, I supposed. But even as a little girl she'd been steeped in music, for her family was very musical and she inherited this inclination. I have always envied those who, because of their upbring- ing, inherit a love for art or music or books. All I inherited was good breeding. Oh, my mother likes to read a lot, so I like it too. But what my brother and I were brought up to cherish was not Wagner or Mozart or Shakespeare or Rembrandt, but Emily Post.

Anyway, Marge let me have a few of her old records to play on the ancient wind-up Victrola I had found up in the garage. I would sit in the Pink Elephant playing *Tannhäuser* and the aria sung by the Elisabeth character and picture the house at Spirit Lake when the Devereaus all lived there. The lake gray and cold, a mist swirling above it or rising from it, and no sound except for the faint slap of water over the little falls off to the right, and all of it informed by the voice of whichever of the sisters (I have since found out there were four, not three) had a voice singing Elisabeth's song from *Tannhäuser*.

Or else I walk the half-mile to Spirit Lake, stand there, usually at dusk, and hear the music in my mind. The aria from that opera drifts from the great big gray-shingled house and floats along the surface of the water, weaving in and around the water lilies and the tangled grass in which (I can't help this) I often see the small figure of Mary-Evelyn floating.

I find all of this eerie and frightening and spectacular—the empty house, the misty cold lake, the music. It is plain spectacular. I have a strong imagination.

"Unlumbered by reality," Sheriff DeGheyn says to us. "The two of you." He was speaking of me and Maud, for Maud occasionally joins us on our meter-checking mornings and walks along.

"Completely unlumbered by reality," the Sheriff says again.

But I think he's wrong, for I feel very lumbered by it. It plain weighs me down.

# FIVE

"If we had to be concerned about *reality*, there wouldn't be much point to *imagining*, would there?" Maud said, more or less answering for both of us, on that particular day which found the three of us on the curb while the Sheriff wrote a ticket and stuck it on the mayor's white Oldsmobile. The car was a foot over into an alley, not really blocking it, but still making it a slight obstacle for a truck to make deliveries to the five-and-dime. The Sheriff didn't answer, since it wasn't really a question and Maud loved to suck him into pointless arguments, I knew.

"Do you think it's haunted?" I asked, largely of her, not him. No notion appeared too outlandish for Maud to entertain, which is one reason I like her. I was speaking of the Devereau place. I don't believe in hauntings, but I thought it might introduce the Devereaus into our conversation.

"What isn't?" she asked, as we stopped before a meter.

The Sheriff looked at her and shook his head. "Oh, for God's sake."

"Hauntedness is pervasive," she said. "I feel full of windy places, like a flute." She stood by the curb, holding her elbows cupped in her hands. She seemed pleased with how she'd put that.

The Sheriff made a strangling sound. He was

slotting a dime into the meter where Miss Ruth Porte's black VW was parked. " 'Like a flute.' "

"You wouldn't understand, of course," said Maud, as we walked on.

I smiled. I love to hear the way they razz each other, something they don't do with anybody else. No one talks to the Sheriff the way Maud does; everyone else was either in awe of him, like me, or a little afraid of him, like Mayor Sims and that car dealer over in Hebrides.

It was the car dealer's baby-blue Cadillac we were standing by now; the red flag was up on the meter. The Sheriff stuffed a ticket behind the windshield wiper and we passed on.

Maud and I, on these little excursions, enjoy fitting out certain townspeople with imaginary histories, histories that the Sheriff occasionally attempts to bring in line with the reality the two of us he said were "unlumbered" by. Which is why his answer to my question about the Wood brothers surprised me.

The two of them, Ulub and Ubub, were sitting on the bench outside of Axel's Taxis. The bench is meant for Axel's Taxis' customers, a place where they can wait for the next taxi to come. There are only two taxis, Axel's and the one driven by his employee, Delbert. We'd been talking, Maud and I, about how we never actually saw anyone *taking* Axel's. Axel would pull out with no fare in it and it would come back with nobody in it. Except for Axel, of course. The Wood brothers sometimes sit on the bench and watch Axel and Delbert come and

go, and when the taxi isn't there, they watch the rest
of us come and go. They are sometimes joined by
Mr. Nasalwhite, who doesn't like to talk much either,
except to tell the Woods (and passersby) that he's
the King of Bohemia. Usually, the Woods have
breakfast in the Rainbow Café, then the morning
stint on either this bench or the one outside Britten's
store in Spirit Lake. Then it's lunch in the café, and
the afternoon bench-sitting. The Woods report to
benches the way other people report to jobs. They
sit in silence (for they rarely talk) and watch the
world of La Porte go by.

The Sheriff got them talking on a couple of
occasions, and Maud kept after him to tell her what
on earth they'd said, but he never did tell her. I had,
on this occasion, asked him about their names—
Ulub and Ubub. "Somebody told me they got them
from license plates. But they must have *names*."

"Uh-huh," said the Sheriff, who was searching
his pockets for a dime. The red flag was up on Bunny
Caruso's pickup. "Ubub is for Useless Big Bob and
Ulub is for Useless Little Bob. You got a dime,
Maud?"

"What?" I asked, puzzled over these names.

"He's making it up," said Maud, digging in her
pocket and bringing out a dime. She always had
change because of the tips she got.

"No, it's true," he said. He slotted the coin into
the meter and turned the handle.

"You're making it up," said Maud again, with
absolute confidence in her verdict.

She's always accusing the Sheriff of "making it up," and once in a while I think maybe he does, with her, so that she can never be absolutely sure when he's telling the truth.

"I could see you doing it, I could *see* your mind making it up, just in that pause while you thought up something that UBB and ULB could stand for."

"UBB" and "ULB" are the first three digits (or letters) on the license plates of Ubub's and Ulub's twin pickup trucks. That's where whoever started calling them by those names got the idea, as far as I know.

The Sheriff didn't answer Maud; he just went on inspecting and then kicking the tires of Bunny Caruso's truck, and I could tell Maud was really irritated because he wouldn't say anything. Indeed, she looked so frustrated, I thought she just might cross over to the bench and ask Ulub and Ubub.

"Well, they are kind of useless," I said.

"Don't listen to him; don't pay any attention to him at all. He makes up half what he says." She spoke as if the Sheriff might be some wayward play-mate who could lead me astray.

We walked on down Second Street, and Maud seemed to be in a snit, which I thought was really funny, since the last person in La Porte I could imagine being in a snit with was Sheriff Sam DeGheyn.

I decided to break into this mild fuming of hers by reintroducing my topic. "Do you believe a place can be haunted?"

"No." "Yes."

They answered in unison; I don't know if Maud said yes because she believed it or if it was just to get his goat.

"Nobody's lived in the Devereau house since Mary-Evelyn died, have they?"

"Not that I know of," said the Sheriff.

The thing was, though, that he and Maud hadn't been around then, and anything they said was guessing.

"Marge Byrd said she heard really weird noises coming from the house one night."

"Probably vagrants. Some people don't pay attention to No Trespassing signs. Donny said he had to chase some people out of there once."

Donny is deputy sheriff. He isn't very smart or good-looking, but he thinks he's both in his uniform. Ree-Jane hangs around the courthouse to impress him, too, when the Sheriff's not there.

"A person who dies in a state of misery has been known to come back and haunt the place where he dies." Maud looked as if she were about to.

"I think you mean a person who's suffered a violent death," the Sheriff said.

She stopped walking. "No, I mean a *miserable* person, like me. And you."

The Sheriff's beeper had buzzed just a stroke before she said "And you," which I bet was an afterthought, that she wanted to make him hesitate and wonder just before he had to answer his beeper. (I always think a person must be very important to have a beeper, anyway.)

"Me? Just because you're—oh, never mind. . . . Donny?" he said into the beeper.

Donny's voice rasped over the beeper, saying something about an accident out on Route 6—the Lake Road, we called it, although I think its official name was Splinter Run Road. It sounded like Donny was talking about the Silver Pear Restaurant, but since he always got a little hysterical over police business it was hard to tell. Also, it was hard to hear; it was private police business, but I cocked my ear anyway. Maud was looking off towards the railroad tracks as if she couldn't care less.

I asked the Sheriff what a "domestic" meant and he said it generally had to do with a quarrel—altercation, fight, trouble—inside a house. He left, and I asked Maud who lived at the Silver Pear. She said it was owned by Gaby and Ron von Gruber, but she couldn't imagine them having an altercation. They both wore silver pompadours and were tall and thin like pussywillows.

We were walking back to the Rainbow Café, Maud having taken her lunch-break time to walk up and down Second Street with me and the Sheriff. I asked her if she'd ever eaten at the Silver Pear and she said yes, a couple of times with Chad. Maud was divorced and Chad was her son and she told me this rather sadly. Chad had gone off to school and I knew she missed him. But at that point, the sadness of adults was a subject I did not want to think about too much; I didn't want to believe, I think, that they actually suffered. Their world was supposed to be different. *If* they suffered, they must have efficient ways of dealing with suffering that were totally unknown in my world. That was one of the advantages of being an adult: you could neatly package unpleasant and painful feelings, wrap them up, toss them on a delivery truck, and send them to be dropped off here and there along Misery Mile. Not like me. Not at all. I had to endure my bad feelings.

"Was it good?" I asked, after this turnover of thoughts of Maud's possible unhappiness. I meant her meal at the Silver Pear.

"No. The food was good, I guess, but the portions were minuscule. They have this *nouvelle-cuisine* type of French food. 'New' cuisine isn't really food, it's the illusion of food. A carrot curl, a sprig of escarole, a triangle of smoked fish in a puddle of pink sauce. Your mom's such a much better cook it hardly bears mention."

I filed that compliment away to tell my mother, as the Silver Pear is always being held up as the smartest restaurant within fifty miles. "But it's the favorite place with the lake people," I said, hoping she'd continue talking about how bad it was, so I could amplify the compliment.

This lake I spoke of is an entirely different lake from Spirit Lake. It's on the other side of La Porte, and the lake people are a race apart: rich, handsome, tan all year, living in fabulous houses, and when they're not swimming and boating they're skiing. Maud herself lives in a little house by the lake, but on the near side, the unfashionable edge.

Maud said, "If the Hotel Paradise were just five miles closer to the lake, you'd be overrun with business."

Business, our business, has not been good. Spirit Lake is pretty much a has-been resort, a little village that once depended on its railway station for tourists and has seen a lot of them. Now Spirit Lake suffers a lot because people no longer depend upon trains; they drive automobiles and can whiz right through Spirit Lake on their way to somewhere else. There used to be over a half-dozen hotels; ours is the only one left now.

As Maud and I walked past the window of Prime Cut, we could see Shirl in there looking like a drowned rat. Since she hadn't gone under the dryer yet and still had to have her hair rolled by Alma Duke (the owner-operator), I knew she wouldn't be back in the Rainbow for at least another hour. Often she got a manicure too. We stood outside the window and waved at Shirl. She pretended not to see us, as she probably didn't want to let on anyone had seen her in this state.

I mentioned to Maud she'd probably be in there another hour and asked if I could sit in a booth. She said yes, of course, and that she'd have a cup of coffee with me, since she hadn't had her lunch yet— that is, she added, "if I won't be interrupting your writing."

Now, that's what I like about Maud and the Sheriff. Neither of them assumes that because you're twelve years old you have nothing to do but twiddle your thumbs until the movie opens. I was, actually, going to the theater on First Street after this hour in the Rainbow. I loved movies. I especially love the Saturday matinee, when they always try to show a western, like those spaghetti westerns, they call them, with Clint Eastwood; or an adventure, or a comedy— in other words, something not overlumbered with sex scenes.

The Orion movie theater is where you can find me any Saturday afternoon at the two o'clock matinee. Mr. McComas, who owns it, is a nice, middle-aged man who pinch-hits for any one of his employees if the person gets sick. A lot of the time, he takes tickets inside the door. There's an official ticket seller and taker, but I think Mr. McComas likes to do it so he can hang around the theater, for I have a suspicion he just loves movies, and that's why he runs it in the first place. Other times, he shovels popcorn into the thin, tissuey cylinders that are stacked inside the machine in all of their different colors. This popcorn is popped right there and is the freshest, hottest popcorn around. It's sometimes hot enough, having jumped right out of the metal popping canister into the cone, that it just misses scorching my fingers.

There are two aisles and one screen that slants in slightly, to the left. The screen has always been a puzzle. It doesn't interfere with the viewing, really, once your eyes get used to it, but the customers do seem to favor the left-hand seats that put them into a squarer relation with the screen. As for me, I like that slanted look, and will usually sit on the right side, eating my hot buttered popcorn from one of those blue or pink cones and thinking life really might be worth the trouble.

All I knew about sex was that to have a baby, you had to get "poked" by a man (someone I knew told me that in third grade), but the nature of the "poking" was very cloudy in my mind. I at first thought it had to do with "cowpokes," which made it interesting, though even more puzzling. I ate my popcorn more slowly and thoughtfully, thinking this over.

Except there really wasn't anything to *think*. And there certainly wasn't anybody to ask. It would be impossible to ask the Sheriff; I'd have been mortified. Maud would have been a possible informant, only I was so embarrassed by a *lack* of knowledge that I couldn't ask. God only knew it had been bad enough when I'd started my periods, and although I suspected that had something to do with the whole picture, I still didn't know what. All I knew was that *that* was painful to the point of screaming, and if that was what sex was like, forget it.

## SIX

My favorite store sits next to the Orion movie theater. It's called Candlewick and sells nothing but candles and candleholders. Before Miss Flyte took it over, it was a hardware store. Now, instead of rakes and leaf bags and fertilizer, its big plate-glass window holds large displays of candles on a dark velvet cloth. The candlesticks are brass, marble, wood, ceramic; tall, short, squat, square. Metal ones soldered to hold a dozen candles, and pottery ones from Mexico painted in astonishing colors. I can stand before this window for long stretches of time, amazed that candles and candlesticks can be so fascinating.

Miss Flyte always keeps a few artificial lights flickering to imitate candlelight. On certain occasions, such as Christmas, she removes the cloth for safety's sake and lights every candle in the window. From a distance, all you can see is a black window and all of those flickering lights.

Miss Flyte "does" (as she puts it) weddings and funerals. It's easy to tell a Flyte wedding. It isn't simply that there are a lot of candles burning; it's more than that. Flyte weddings have a mysterious, dreamy quality, a kind of fairylike atmosphere of crystal wings and moon dust and pale colors melting into one another, rainbowlike. Naturally, a good deal of it has to do with the effects of candlelight, but I always think the glow is more than this. There is something of a blessing given about a Flyte wedding. (Her funerals I steer clear of.)

Miss Flyte refuses to "do" anything else. "Weddings and funerals and nothing in between" has always been her motto. The "in between" occasions are things like dinner parties and birthday parties, like the huge birthday party at the home of one of the lake people, with caterers and ice swans and a five-piece band, which Miss Flyte turned down. Her refusal only made her more of a plum and a prize. The lake people, being rich, think they can buy anybody, but they can't buy Miss Flyte. She even gets invited to take her candles to New York City and Cape Cod and other fancy places to do dinner parties. The more she refuses, the more insistent people become. It would really be a feather in your cap to get Miss Flyte.

But it is more than that. The town's social climbers, like Helene Baum, are always trying to imitate her. They can't, of course. For it isn't enough just to have a hundred candles burning. Only Miss Flyte knows how to fix and arrange them, where to put the tall ones, and where the tiny ones; where to sit them and where to hang them. Nobody else has the touch. Miss Flyte is a master of light.

Next door to the Candlewick, and run by another old lady, is a little gift shop. They are friends, Miss Flyte and Miss Flagler, and nearly every day have coffee or tea and buns together in one shop or the other. Both shops have side doors facing each other,

and so Miss Flyte and Miss Flagler can slip across
the narrow alley between and have their mid-morning
coffee or afternoon tea. I'm a customer of both, and,
although I'm twelve and they're both up in their
sixties or seventies, we still have something in common. I don't know what. But somehow sitting in
Miss Flagler's kitchen, near-to-dozing over my tea
or hot chocolate, I can see the days wearing us away,
we three.

Miss Flagler's gift shop is tiny, a mousehole
called the Oak Tree Gift Shoppe. I cannot figure out
how she scrapes by, for she rarely seems to have
customers in her shop. There's just the single tiny
room for merchandise, shelves of little porcelain soap
dishes, delicate cups and saucers, china and glass
animals, linen handkerchiefs, and a display case of
silver jewelry, pins and bracelets and necklaces.

She might have her private source of money,
for she never seems to be wanting for anything. Her
clothes are good. She always wears one shade or
other of gray silk or bombazine, with a white linen
collar or jabot separate from the dress so that it can
be washed. And the dress is always covered with a
cardigan, a gray cable-knit or brown cashmere. The
cashmere is my favorite; it's the color of foxes' fur,
golden-reddish-brown, which she always wears with
a strand of pearls.

Inside the door of the Oak Tree is a silver bell,
set to tinkling by the movement of the door, and this
will bring Miss Flagler from her rooms in the rear,
through the drapery that divides the living quarters

and the shop. Although I sometimes think she regards the "shop" part of her life with distaste, she is always decorously polite. She is remote, but pleasant. My mother calls her "the last genteel maiden lady," and I think this an excellent description. With her cat named Albertine, and her comfortable kitchen with its smell of cinnamon and ginger, I imagine there are worse lives than Miss Flagler's. It is true that her life must be muted and lacking in gaiety, but I do not put a high price on gaiety, having seen too much of it when Aurora Paradise and her sister get out on the fire escape of the Hotel Paradise.

I am sometimes invited to share their morning coffee or afternoon tea (oh, those fresh cinnamon buns!) and could think of them as just putting up with me, but I don't. For some reason I feel at home with old ladies, as if I wear, in my ancient twelve-year-old soul, pince-nez and cardigans.

We sit on turquoise and buttercup-yellow painted wooden chairs (that have me revising my notion of a lack of gaiety in Miss Flagler's life) pulled up to the white kitchen table. In winter we are warmed by the black cast-iron stove into which Miss Flagler shovels fresh coals. She has a gas stove, too, but she swears by the cast-iron for even baking. My mother does too, so I take Miss Flagler's word for it. The buns and biscuits always come out of the coal stove, and my cocoa is heated in a pan on one of the iron cylinders on top. There's a big white GE refrigerator she said can run circles around "these skinny new ones." From a pantry off to one side, I can sometimes hear the noisy thumps of a Bendix washing machine that sounds like it's in agony.

I love the cocoa. But I have a problem trying to get the skin off the top of the steaming surface without appearing rude. I usually just blow it back and drink quickly as my close-up eyes watch it drifting towards my mouth. Or I "clumsily" drop my paper napkin in the cup and that sops up the milk skin. If there's a marshmallow engaged in this sopping up, that makes it frustrating, for I especially like the melting marshmallows.

We sit and sup and they ask after my mother, who they greatly admire, and after Lola Davidow, who they admire far less, and after Ree-Jane, who they don't admire at all. Misunderstanding my made-up name, they call her "Rae Jane," an error I have never corrected, knowing how Ree-Jane hates it. I think it balances out the injustice of my being confused with her and called "Janey" sometimes. It's simply infuriating to be overshadowed by a girl who appeared on the Hotel Paradise scene only five years before, and canceled out my existence.

Miss Flyte and Miss Flagler never make this mistake. They know who I am and that the Hotel Paradise has little to do with the Davidows. But Ree-Jane goes around telling people that her mother "owns" the Hotel Paradise, which makes me absolutely furious, and I tell my mother it does, but she has never done or said anything to correct this mistake; she simply tells me to never mind.

Of course, one reason Miss Flagler and Miss

Flyte like having me there is that they're gossipy—
and why not?—and like to know what's going on
in Spirit Lake, mainly in the Hotel Paradise with
Aurora living up there at the top. Aurora has always
been (they say) "a bit of a wag," which I think is a
nice way of saying she's crazy as a coot.

Miss Flyte and Miss Flagler are both of an age
to have come in contact with the Devereaus and with
Mary-Evelyn, Miss Flyte being sixty-three and Miss
Flagler (I was surprised to find out) seventy years
old. That meant both were young women in their
twenties or thirties when Mary-Evelyn died. Yet their
memories are vague on that count. Miss Flagler
remembers "a little red-headed girl with a faraway
look" who was always beautifully dressed, if a bit
peculiar. No, Miss Flyte corrected Miss Flagler; it
was those aunts of hers who were peculiar. One of
the aunts was a wonderful seamstress. Sewed for a
living, and had made Miss Flagler a dress once of
organdy and silk. It had been quite the thing (Miss
Flagler said, and Miss Flyte agreed) to own a Devereau dress, for she had been the best dressmaker in
the state, and this was back when dressmaking was
commonplace. Now, one could go to Hebrides, perhaps, to the Emporium; or one could travel even
farther to Camberwell, which is La Porte's equivalent
of a nearby "city," to a shop called the Europa, owned
by Helen Gay Struther. She supposedly does her
buying in Europe. But it is doubtful any dress in the
Emporium or in the Europa is the equal of a Devereau
dress. Miss Flagler's dress had been ice-green

organdy, with a silk lining. She had worn it to a
garden party, which she described to me as "all
white": white dresses, white suits, white pumps,
white roses, white-iced cakes.

I was momentarily carried away, or carried
back, to this fairy world of garden parties and
organdy dresses. I have personal experience of neither. I try to picture Miss Flagler moving airily
around in her ice-green organdy, a punch cup in one
hand and a plate of tiny sandwiches in the other. The
color sounded both cool and delicious. I decided it
must be the color of Albertine's eyes.

Mary-Evelyn had attended the party in a Devereau dress, of course. She had been handing around
plates of small sandwiches. A really pretty little girl,
Miss Flagler had said, in a pale yellow dress.

With a faraway look, I added to myself. I was
glad she'd been at the party, for when I picture Mary-
Evelyn, she is always by herself—at the lake's edge,
maybe; or behind one of those high dormer windows,
pushing back the curtain, looking down. On what, I
don't know. So it was nice to think of Mary-Evelyn
at a party, even if it was a party of adults, and she
was apparently there to hand around plates of cakes
and sandwiches.

Why were they thought to be peculiar? I wanted
to know, and asked Miss Flagler.

Well. Miss Flagler didn't actually know. It was
all what she'd heard. A look passed between Miss
Flagler and Miss Flyte, as smooth as passing a plate
of junket.

That there was some sad secret attached to Mary-Evelyn and her aunts I had long known. The Sheriff didn't know anything about them, as I said before. If he had known, he would have told me, especially since whatever people might have said about them could easily be some old bits of rumor, gossip without any foundation that had floated down over the years, passing from generation to generation, growing and diminishing, shooting out new little leaves here and there, far from its original root.

Miss Flyte could not really add much to the picture, except to note that Mary-Evelyn had no friends to speak of, none her age. I asked how could she have, since it was known that she didn't go to grade school in Spirit Lake, or anywhere else; she had private lessons from tutors. I took the defense of Mary-Evelyn upon myself.

My mother had not said anything about Mary-Evelyn's "peculiarity," so I wondered if Miss Flagler was merely being overly delicate in not telling me some unsurprising detail she had picked up about her. Unrepeatable bits of information usually have to do with sex, a subject I know next to nothing about; I'm only dimly aware, even, that it is a subject. I suppose I know on some uncomfortable level of my mind that the occasional Saturday-matinee scene (that might slip past the watchful eye of Mr. McComas) involving the embraces of the actors are not going to stop with hugs and kisses; still, I don't know into what country these folks are headed. I feel embarrassed and somehow forsaken by them, leaving

me there in the dark popcorny musk of my seat (that
I slide farther and farther down into) while they travel
where I cannot follow. I don't know how a person
can live for twelve years and come up blank on a
subject that is on everybody's mind for most of the
waking day and all of the sleeping night. That I can
remain ignorant of it goes to show what I feel to be
my "operating room" life: white and sterile and into
which people come gloved and masked and silent.
That might sound peaceful and quiet (it certainly
sounds clean) if you forget the scalpels. A lot of the
time I wander around feeling doped up, but appearing
alert. Too alert, some people might say.

Which is what Miss Flagler might have felt, as
I refused to let that "look" that passed between her
and Miss Flyte pass on into the land of lost looks. I
pressed Miss Flagler for details. What was "peculiar"?

Well, Miss Flagler said, pouring out some more
cocoa from the jug and adding a big marshmallow
(an act I took to be some harmless bit of blackmail),
Mary-Evelyn had not seemed a very affectionate sort
of person, not very loving; no, she did not seem to
love many things.

The definition of "peculiar" appeared to be getting further away from us. What things did she not
seem to love?

Miss Flagler nibbled at her lower lip, as if she
should be able to produce evidence of the charge of
"peculiarity." Mary-Evelyn, she told me, had a cat

that died. She didn't feed it, it was said. And the poor thing died.

Then we all turned to look at Albertine, sitting in plump state on the white table, as if we were consulting her on the consequences of withholding her canned milk. But I was astonished by Miss Flagler's news. Even if some townsperson—daily woman or handyman—could have reported this tidbit, I couldn't understand why Miss Flagler didn't seem to take in the obvious implication of what she'd said. When I had this thought, something gave way and sank within me, leaving me overwhelmed by sadness.

If the cat died, no one else fed it, either.

## SEVEN

The implications of this I didn't even want to consider. Yet I knew I must if ever I was to understand what happened to Mary-Evelyn Devereau.

I recalled that Marge Byrd had said one day when Ulub (or Ubub) was raking leaves around her yard—slowly and thoughtfully, like the Woods did everything—that one or the other or both of them had done yard work for the Devereaus. For several days I watched Ubub and Ulub on their various seats and benches—the Rainbow, Axel's Taxis, and Britten's store—before finally deciding to tackle them.

As long as I can remember, I have never seen anyone conversing with the Woods, not beyond a friendly "hello," or maybe a playful punch on the shoulder and a "hi." The two of them can hear all right, because they respond with words or grunts, though Ubub is, I think, more vocal than Ulub. They aren't twins and don't even look much alike, one being tall and lanky, the other squat. I'm pretty sure Ubub is the tall, thin one because he is Useless Big Bob—UBB.

I see them on the flaking green bench provided by Britten's store, used by two or three old men who occupy it in the morning, until the afternoon shift of two or three old men comes to relieve them. They're the bench regulars, and the Woods sometimes swell their ranks, making the green bench a tight squeeze. It was my intention to advance on Ubub and Ulub some afternoon when they might have the bench to themselves, as occasionally happens.

The bench sitters' outlook, from the front of Britten's, is over the highway, where they can watch the cars and trucks race by, watch the whole excited world going about its business. Also, the bench is near the spot where the First Union Tabernacle bus stops to let off people coming in from Cold Flat Junction. It makes two stops, one at Britten's and one across the highway and up on a rise where there is a camp meeting tent. There, the First Union Tabernacle members gather to sing songs and (I guess) spread the word. Anyway, when the people get off, I can sit and watch with as much interest as the others, for I'm always on the lookout for a Tidewater.

Cold Flat Junction is eighteen miles from Spirit Lake, and that's where the Tidewaters live. I have strict orders from my mother to have nothing to do with the Tidewaters, which means I'm fervent in my bench-sitting on the days when the Tabernacle bus drives in. I hoped for at least a look at Joleen or Toya Tidewater, or perhaps one of their brothers, because my mother is so determined I shouldn't. It's another mystery, except in the case of the Tidewaters it's more of a case of lips sealed, not a lack of knowledge. I think it's Toya who is supposed to be the worst (which means, for me, the best) girl in the family, so I know sex must have a lot to do with it, as it does with everything else.

The La Porte police spend a lot of time over in Cold Flat Junction, so Sheriff DeGheyn knows all about the Tidewaters. Not that the calls necessarily have to do with them, for Cold Flat Junction is home to a lot of off-limits people, and my mother knows about them all. I am to stay away from it altogether.

Toya Tidewater (nearly thirty by this time) had waited tables at the Hotel Paradise ten years ago, when I was but one or two years old, so, of course, I don't remember her. (I often wonder what my baby eyes and ears took in.) My mother would sometimes drive her home. Even now, Lola Davidow goes to Cold Flat to get eggs; that's what a number of the families do there—they keep laying hens or make rag rugs. There's nothing else to do in Cold Flat except go to the one bar, Rudy's (which provides the Sheriff with most of the phone calls), or sit in the one diner.

Cold Flat Junction does have one thing, though—its railroad station. For the town is just what its name says it is: a junction. Yet why Cold Flat Junction is home to this truly beautiful and elegant structure, I don't know. There are vague guesses at the reason. It was once an important intersection, people say. But that's like answering the question with the original question. Why was Cold Flat Junction an important intersection? La Porte, only fourteen miles and one stop away, is a much larger town with a nice old station. But it's no match for Cold Flat Junction.

There is nothing there that would cause people

to get off, and, consequently, to get on. It's just that sort of wrack-and-ruin place that people always want to escape from but never have the means to do it—Cold Flat being what it is. There's not much money in chickens or rugs. So it all goes around in a circle. And Cold Flat Junction *is* cold, away out in nowhere, unprotected by mountains or surrounding trees. The temperature drops and the winds get high and howl out there.

Marge Byrd guesses that the reason for the handsome railroad depot was that the biggest and most elaborate of the hotels in Spirit Lake was owned by the railroad company, and that once it had been thought that Spirit Lake would expand for miles around, back when it really invited business. But Marge's reasoning does not really solve the mystery of the railroad station, for it looks as if it went up long before this hankering after expansion on the part of the railway people. And how was Spirit Lake going to expand for eighteen miles, anyway?

On egg-buying days, I never get to go to Cold Flat. I sometimes hint around to Lola Davidow, saying I'd be happy to help with carrying the eggs, or anything else. But Lola (usually delighted to say I could do what my mother said I couldn't) never takes me up on it. Ree-Jane gets to go, however. And the only reason Ree-Jane wants to go is because she knows it sticks in my craw. She knows how interested I am in the station and the Tidewaters and comes back talking about both (though I know she doesn't give a damn about the station and wouldn't know a

Tidewater if she fell over one). And she leaves the car and walks in that careful way she has of showing herself off, up the front steps of the hotel, and there's never an egg in sight. Her mother has to carry the eggs.

What I did, then—and this was extremely daring—was to go to La Porte one day and hop on the 1:53, whose final destination was so exotic I didn't even bother longing to go there. I only wanted the next stop. "Hop on" was the right phrase because I had to make a quick jump while the conductor's back was turned and he was looking down the line of cars. For the fifteen-minute ride, I walked the aisles, moving from one car to the next, searching intently for my seat beside the adult who had paid my fare. That's what the conductor must have thought, for he didn't question my expense-paid trip. There are advantages sometimes to being really young. People ignore you.

The Junction was the next stop, and there I hopped down. No one got on and no one except for me got off.

I stood for a moment in the rush of wind stirred up by the train rumbling off down the track and looked around at the depot. It was huge and constructed of winey-colored brick with a cupola-like tower. Despite the years of exposure to coal dust and cinders, it seemed incredibly clean, and so did the platform. And I could see its dark and cool interior was also unblemished, or appeared to be. A lot of polished mahogany and maybe oak or pine benches, all unlittered.

As I was debating entering the station to inspect it more closely, a girl—a young woman, really—came out. Her look slid right off me as if we met like silk and satin, and was perfectly indifferent in a place where there's probably so little going on you'd think a stranger might cause a look to snag, at least. It either goes to show how uninteresting my presence is, or that she was mightily preoccupied with her own mission. I wondered what it was. She had no suitcase and was not dressed for travel, at least not for far. She wore a cotton dress, sleeveless, except for the small wings of material that hung off the shoulders in little gathers. The dress was a washed-out blue, so pale it was almost white, the color of dawn. It had a heart-shaped neck and ties at the side that pulled the waist in when tied in the back. I guessed she was twenty, or nearly, but not more than that. After standing awhile, looking up and down the track as if she were wondering where the train was, she turned and sat down on one of the platform's benches. She was carrying nothing except what looked to be a small purse.

I didn't want her to see I was staring at her, so I pretended to be studying the train schedules with some fascination where they were tacked up under glass. I knew the La Porte–Cold Flat Junction run, and knew there wouldn't be another train until late afternoon (4:32, to be exact) for I naturally had to plan my return trip. So what was she doing here? After a few moments of schedule reading, I just looked at her quite openly, for she obviously didn't care that I was there. I didn't exist for her; she didn't care about anything but what was out there along the horizon.

The reason I noticed all of this was because she was so pretty. Beautiful, I guess, with hair so fine and pale blond it looked like milkweed in the sun and eyes the color of Spirit Lake itself, dark gray that I knew would shift around depending on the slant of the light.

I wondered what such a girl was doing in Cold Flat Junction. In type, she resembled none of the people I'd seen getting off the First Union Tabernacle bus, for they all seemed heavy in the face—"coarse" is what my mother would say—as if some potter had stopped the wheel too soon and left the features a little rough and lumpy, unfinished and unrefined. They all looked, no matter what the age or sex, as if they were in need of a potter to finish the job— even the kids. But maybe they weren't really representative of Cold Flat; maybe that's just what the First Union Tabernacle does to you after a while. Anyway, this girl with the milkwood-colored hair sat quite still, her feet flat on the platform, her head turned and looking down the line, down the tracks, off to that horizon from which I had just come.

I remember the sky. It was especially, well, *white*, a thick, milky kind of whiteness with nothing at all suspended in it. It was like a giant page from which the print had faded, unreadable and opaque. I am not a very observant person; I do not note the barks of trees or patterns of leaves or wings—stuff like that. My mother knows every flower that ever bloomed, and Marge every bird that ever warbled. I myself am flower-blind and bird-deaf and it's a good thing Nature doesn't depend on me to write it down. Yet, I will never forget that sky. Nothing moved up there in that vast whiteness, no shred of cloud, no drifts of swallows, no sickly stillborn moon left over from the night before. The horizon was a blurred gray line and that was where she looked. The sky was like a judgment, but I could not think upon whom.

In the other direction off to the right there looked to be a few businesses. I made out a big red-and-white Esso sign, what looked like a general store, and another I thought that said "Diner." It was there that I made for. It wasn't as short a walk as it looked, because the emptiness of the landscape played tricks on the eyes. I was inside the Windy Run Diner within another ten minutes and letting the metal and glass-louvered door suck shut behind me on its tight spring.

Here I did excite a little bit of interest, for the row of heads at the counter turned and there were a couple of nods, a few vague little smiles. Probably they assumed my parents were getting the car filled up over at the Esso.

When the waitress slapped down her book of checks on the counter (a signal for me to order, I guessed), I said I'd have a Coke, really wishing like

anything that I could order coffee instead with some
authority, even though I didn't much like coffee.

If I had any plan at all in mind, it was vague.
I must have thought that if I sat amongst the townfolk,
they'd all be jabbering away about the people who
lived there and I'd surely overhear something about
the Tidewaters. But they didn't and I didn't. Sitting
to my right were two old men as silent as the grave;
the only sound coming from there was the click of
glass against china as they shook enormous amounts
of sugar into their cups. The woman on my other
side was chewing gum with short breaks to puff in
on her cigarette and push her thick glasses up her
short nose.

The waitress (who wore a little badge like
Maud's, only hers said "Louise Snell" and "Prop.")
was pleasant and asked me, "Where you from,
sugar?" and I lied I was from over in Comus, another
thirty or forty miles beyond. I figured Comus was
big enough that she wouldn't be surprised she'd
never seen me. Besides the Tidewaters, I really
wanted to know who that girl at the railroad station
was, but had no idea how to set about finding out.
It was fairly easy to introduce the Tidewaters into
the talk, though, since I knew their name. So I said
I had a friend who lived in Cold Flat and that her
name was Toya Tidewater.

Now, given my mother's fearsome look and
compressed lips whenever she mentions the Tidewaters, I was prepared for wild eyes and sharp, intaken
breaths all along the counter. Nothing like this hap-

pened. The old man at my right brought up some phlegm in a disgusting way, but just kept right on looking at his mirror reflection as if he found himself tantalizing.

Louise Snell called down the counter to a truck-driver type named Billy and asked where Toya lived, and was it that little gone-to-ruin place along Swansdown Road, and Billy answered back, nah, that was the Simpsons' place, and the Tidewaters lived out Lonemeadow way. Well, this was immediately contradicted by the woman on my left, who said there wasn't no Tidewater lived there, least not now, and Billy must be thinking about old Joe and he was dead. Billy got kind of surly, probably because this woman was telling him he was wrong, and yelled up the counter that maybe old Joe was dead, but that don't mean none of his *folks* didn't live at the end of Lonemeadow. At one of the chrome-and-Formica tables marching in a row down the length of the place a man and woman were sitting and they jumped right into this argument, telling both Billy and the woman they were wrong, that the Tidewaters moved last year over to Dubois—or at least *some* of them did (the man said to the woman, rather timidly). The argument over where the Tidewaters lived pretty soon expanded into guesses about all of the Tidewaters themselves, and who was whose kid, and which one went off to work in Comus, and which girl married someone named Mervin. Names broke and crested atop the waves of conversation ("Mattie Mae" . . . "Abraham" . . . "Joleen") and on and on, so

that the original question about Toya got completely
forgotten and so did I. I just picked up my check
and walked over to the cashier, a thin boy reading
a comic book and muscling his nose around a bad
cold, and obviously not a Tidewater fan, for he barely
looked at the money, and at me not at all.

Outside on the narrow walk beside the highway,
I wondered what to do. I could, I supposed, take a
look at this Lonemeadow Road (if I could find it),
but I still wouldn't know if the people living in the
end house were Tidewaters, since no one in the
Windy Run Diner had agreed upon that point.

The diner, as I said, is one of the few businesses
at the Junction; the train tracks ran at an angle a little
farther past, cutting across one of the two "highways"
(not much wider than wide roads), and as I stood
there, looking off in the direction away from the
station, I could see and hear the next train (probably
a freight train) coming along. I walked up the road
a bit, a little closer to the tracks, for I have always
loved trains, the mournful sound of them, and guess
everybody does. As it clattered on by, the conductor
looked out, saw me and waved. I waved back. I felt
strange, for I would imagine he took me for a resident
of Cold Flat Junction, assigning to me a new place,
a new identity.

I walked back up the road, aimlessly, seeing
no one except a woman coming out of the door of
a house set quite far back from the road, coming
out and tossing dirty water from a pail and going
back in.

A short distance later I came to a small school-house of white clapboard. It was the sort you see represented in paintings in the same way village churches are—bell tower, steeple. School didn't seem to be in session, which was peculiar, as it was only May. I never pay much attention to school holidays, as I usually have to leave school wherever we are most winters to return to open up the hotel in spring. There were still a few kids at the other end of the schoolyard shoving a ball through a basket and dribbling away. And there was one girl standing behind a chainlink fence, doing nothing but staring out, one hand locked in the fence and the other holding a sort of tube against her face which I recognized, as I got closer, as pick-up-sticks. She was simply staring out. I mistook her attitude as interest in me, but I was wrong, for she was looking right past me. Everything about her looked washed out: her jeans were faded; her eyes were a queer clear gray, without depth; her skin was pale; her hair looked rinsed in Clorox. There was this disturbing colorlessness to her, as if she were a piece of the Judgment sky.

Knowing pretty much I wouldn't get an answer, I went up close to the fence and asked her if she knew where the Tidewaters lived. Her fingers moved, curling and uncurling in the webbing of the fence, but she did not reply. I leaned against the fence and put my hand up there too, curling my fingers in and around the metal as she was doing. I don't know why I did this. But it worked almost like a secret sign, and she asked me if I wanted to play pick-up-sticks in a voice as small as any I've ever heard. I said sure, even though I think I am a little old for pick-up-sticks. (I have always had a secret liking for the game.)

So I walked to the end of the fence and through a gate, and we both sat down on a grassy verge and let the colored sticks fall on the concrete. She held them in a bundle and released them, letting them lie where they fell. She was very good at this game, better than I was. It's not a hard game, but it takes concentration and patience and coordination, for you have to be careful when lifting one stick with another that you don't touch a third. She was able to lift, without touching, half the sticks in one turn. I managed about a half a dozen, and then she picked up the rest. After a game, she put the sticks back in the tube. I left. She never did tell me her name; for all I knew, she could have been a Tidewater.

Beyond the school sat a post office. It was a gray cinderblock building with an American flag drooping high on its flagpole. I thought how stupid I'd been not to come here first off: the post office would clearly know the whereabouts of the Tidewater family. Or families, for there appeared to be more than one.

The light inside was fluorescent, unshadowed and kind of unearthly. Facing me was a wall of those metal boxes you can rent so that any mail you receive is completely secret and private. Our post office in Spirit Lake (much cozier than the Cold Flat one) has these boxes, only ours, instead of having a metal door, are half metal and half glass; they are very old, antique probably.

My brother, Will, and I used to have the heady job of picking up the mail. We would walk the long boardwalk that started at the tennis club building and ran parallel to the highway, through trees and shrubbery, all the way down to the railroad station and the post office. We would take our time about the mail route. After we left the post office, or before we went there, we would sometimes go to Greg's and get an Orange Crush and a Moon Pie (his friend Brownmiller's favorite combination, and I often think we ate this in honor of him, as if he were a war hero or something, when actually he only lives a hundred miles away). Then we would set our pop on the pinball machine and Will would just about tilt it nearly to death and was good at winning free games (though not as good as Brownmiller).

But that was years ago and time past, and Lola Davidow started driving down to the post office; sometimes Ree-Jane does it, especially since she got that new convertible car. Ree-Jane, God knows, isn't about to *walk*. So the mail route became one more Davidow takeover. It means that on the rare occasions when someone writes to me, Mrs. Davidow or Ree-Jane gets to see the letter first; worse, they get to tell me who it is that's writing. It's discouraging, for by the time I get my letter, it seems used; it is drained of that bewitching power unopened mail has. And, of course, if Ree-Jane picks up my mail, she is totally unmerciful. She would never just leave it at the desk or hand it over. No, there has to be a big production staged about the sender and my relationship to her or him (if "him" it's always worse); that, or she might open it "by mistake," thinking it's from a prospective guest who wants to make a reservation; or sometimes she even "forgets" to give me my letter and it doesn't turn up for days or even a week. By the time Ree-Jane gets finished with my poor letter, it's almost as if the ink is worn away. Certainly, the excitement of receiving it is.

So I have always wanted to rent one of those little metal boxes; that way I could receive my mail in total privacy, for my eyes only. It was always a high point in Will's and my day when we could look through the glass and see the white envelopes slotted in there, along with the occasional blue or official-looking tan one. My brother and I would take turns spinning the combination.

Sometimes we would be given money to buy stamps, and I thoroughly enjoyed that, for it allowed me to talk to the postmistress, Miss Crosby, through the arched window opening, which is the only vantage point for seeing into the "back" room and the great swell of letters and parcels on the table. Through this window, which has a flat wooden door she can slide down, Miss Crosby dispenses stamps and change and, up to a point, information. When she is "off" for lunch (tea and a tuna sandwich and some selection of Hostess cake) or has to go out on an errand, she can shut the window—bang the window, sometimes, when I was asking too many questions. Actually, Miss Crosby will sometimes keep the window shut if she does not feel like exposing herself to the outside world; no one has any way of knowing if she's back there with her cup of tea and Hostess cupcake, hiding. I think hers must be the most enviable job in the world, back there with tea and Twinkies and all of that mail.

But here in Cold Flat Junction, the post office was a more efficient-looking and businesslike affair. The counter that ran half the length of the small room would leave whoever was behind totally exposed. Except there was, this day, no one behind it. No sounds came from the inner room, and nothing moved except the ceiling fan, making its slow, faintly whistling rounds.

I supposed the person could be using the toilet, so I waited. I read the Most Wanted posters and mused about the lives of the two men pictured there. One of them was named Drinkwater, which definitely caught my eye. The other was named Waters. But they must have been related, probably brothers, for they looked so much alike, and one or the other of them had simply shorn a syllable off or added a syllable in some infantile attempt to change the name. They really did look alike. Then I dimly remembered having seen other posters and *they* all looked pretty much alike, too. I made a mental note to ask the Sheriff why this should be. Why did all Most Wanteds seem to have dark hair and spidery little mustaches that slanted down to the corners of their mouths? And small, beady eyes. I stood with my hands clasped behind me, rolling on the balls of my feet, reading about these men. Armed robbery, both of them. Robbery was pretty boring, except if you went armed, which I guess made it more interesting. I shot both of them with my thumb and finger.

Still, no one appeared to take my order. There was a rack of postcards of places like La Porte and Cloverly and the Cold Flat station and the church. I selected the station and the Tabernacle ones. My plan was to buy two stamps to make my presence here reasonable and then to ask casually about the Tidewaters. The Drinkwaters (I was sure they were brothers) made this even easier, for I could laughingly tell the postmistress (or -master) that I had nearly died looking at the poster, thinking the name was *Tide*water. This wasn't, but could easily have been, true. But clever as this story was (cleverer, I was sure, than the Drinkwaters would be when they got caught), I was unable to put it into action, for no one appeared, even though I hung around for another ten minutes. It was no way to run a country. I put two dimes on the counter and pocketed my postcards and left.

Then I stopped on the walk outside and pulled out the postcard, wondering once again how I could be so dumb. The First Union Tabernacle, of course! The minister or reverend or whatever he was would not only most certainly tell me where the Tidewaters lived, but also what they were like. Just from reading his expression, I would probably know if they'd all gone to hell, or were regular churchgoers, or whatever.

A church steeple rose in the distance, and since I saw no other churchlike building, I hurried towards it. Just then, a bell tolled. I took this as a sign that I was on the right track. I walked on and listened to the tolling and then realized what it had tolled: four o'clock. That didn't give me much time until the only train I could take came through. It would be impossible even to walk as far as the church and get all the way back to the station.

Defeated, I turned and trod back.

And never a Tidewater had I seen.

## EIGHT

When the First Union Tabernacle bus was letting off its passengers on this Sunday, I looked for the girl I had seen on the station platform. Ever since I had seen her there, it had bothered me the way she seemed not to fit in Cold Flat Junction. It was like suddenly being pulled out of a fantasy in a movie house when someone walks in front of the screen and casts his shadow over the actors there. But I did not see her, so I guess she wasn't of the First Union Tabernacle faith.

The bench outside Britten's store was occupied on this particular day by the same old man, who always had a wad of chewing tobacco he pulled at the way I do at taffy and who always wore a faded blue railroad cap. After I'd left Britten's with my box of jujubes, I sat down at the other end to wait for Ubub and Ulub. The old man looked over at me, probably thinking that something really interesting might be happening today since there was this new person on the bench. Of course he'd seen me, as I had him, a hundred times before, going in and out of the store, but this seating arrangement must have struck him as novel. He said, "Evenin'," though it was still afternoon. I imagine he probably had his dinner around four o'clock, like so many old people who tend to get up really early—dawn, I'd've bet—

and go to bed the same way. I smiled at him and said "Hello" and that was our conversation.

We sat there counting cars, me eating my jujubes, him chewing his tobacco, until finally the Woods came along down the narrow gravel path beside the store. They went in, but came out soon, both with bottles of Nehi grape. They both nodded and smiled, and I did too, getting up to give them their regular seats, but Ubub told me, "Knit dow, knit dow," which I guess was "Sit down," for he patted the air downward with his palm. I sat next to the man in the railroad cap, and Ubub sat next to me with Ulub on the end.

Now we were four. I offered my jujubes around and they all took only one—not much if you know jujubes. Ulub waited to see what Ubub was going to do with his jujube, and when Ubub put it in his shirt pocket, Ulub put his away too. The man in the railroad cap had not put his teeth in that day, but he gummed the jujube around, mixing its fruity taste with the Mail Pouch tobacco. You've got to be careful of jujubes if you've got teeth, for once one gets stuck in a crevice it's like cement. I once told Marge that the dentist in town should use jujubes for fillings.

The three of them seemed very pleased I was there, as we sat with our candy and pop and Mail Pouch, and I did fit in pretty well, I thought. I have always been rather unusual in this regard—that I take on the coloring of whatever I'm experiencing at the moment and blend in with it. Sometimes I think I could be used to plug up holes in things with this way I have of becoming where I am. I like to think this is a compliment to myself, but I'm not sure.

Anyway, it was nice to know that just my presence created an enjoyable novelty for them. The Woods knew who I was, because they lived in a frame house in a muddy quarter-acre across the road from the back driveway of the hotel. They had also done a few odd jobs around the grounds. Our regular handyman, Wilton Macreedy, doesn't like them and calls them "retards" and "idiots." As far as I'm concerned there is no bigger idiot than Wilton Macreedy, who's a drinker and spends a lot of time over in the El Lobo Bar and Grille that the Sheriff wants Ree-Jane to stay out of. It's located between Hebrides and La Porte, and Wilton Macreedy drives his ancient Ford pickup over there and starts fights. He's mean and has a jealous nature. You'd have to be really poor in spirit to be jealous of the Woods, but that's what Wilton is.

I didn't want to call them "Ulub" and "Ubub," for I wasn't sure but what it might offend them. I didn't think they were both named Bob, so I sat there trying to figure out how to address them. Well, of course: "Mr. Wood" would be the proper way. So I asked Mr. Wood (Ubub) if he could think back forty years or more, and was it true he and (I nodded towards Ulub) the other Mr. Wood there had worked for a family named Devereau that lived in that house out on the lake. The house where no one lives anymore.

"Len seh," Ubub said. "Duen-rwoh." He knit his brow with the effort. I would like to have told him that the way he pronounced the "reau" in "Devereau" made me want to take him right along to the hotel and have him say hello to Ree-Jane. He was made to order for pronouncing that crazy French name just the way she said. Imagine, Ubub Wood, the only person who could really pronounce "Réjane"! I tucked that away to tell her.

When Ubub was saying this, Ulub was watching him intently and making lip movements in imitation of Ubub's. Then Ulub nodded several times, and Ubub nodded, too. Ubub expanded on what he'd said: "Wuhwr da aw un suahmu."

I moved these sounds around in my mind for a while and decided he'd said something about "one summer," and then deduced it was "*worked* one summer." I asked him if that was right, and again he nodded his head eagerly. Ulub smiled at his brother's success.

It might have been better to ask things that could have been answered yes or no, but I wasn't sure exactly what I wanted to know (except about the cat), and, anyway, that struck me as a little insulting. Ubub clearly didn't mind trying; therefore, I shouldn't either. Then I thought of a question that might really tell me something.

"Did you like them? The Devereaus?"

Both of them shook their heads immediately and fiercely. "Nah!" The syllable exploded from Ubub's mouth.

"How come?" I asked, noticing the tobacco chewer was leaning forward, elbows on knees and hands clasped before him, rapt, wanting to know, it appeared, the answer.

Ubub looked up at the sky, stretching his long neck, and scratching it, as if he were turning over in his mind the best way to phrase what he wanted to say. Finally he said, "A din tah." Ulub nodded his head in vigorous agreement with his brother.

"A din tah," I repeated mentally over and over, trying to figure it out. *A din tah.* I was fairly sure "A" was "They." "A din" must have been "They didn't." But "tah"? What was "tah"? I hated for Ubub to think I hadn't understood him, so I tried to make it sound as if I were just meditating over the implications of the words, and not the words themselves.

"Hmmm," I said, myself studying the sky, "so they didn't . . ."

"Tah. *Tah*-eh—" He tried but couldn't get out what I bet was some consonant.

"Talk!" I said. "Talk?"

Again, both nodded happily.

"Mr. Wood, you're saying the Devereau sisters didn't talk?"

Nod.

"To you, you mean?"

Shake of the head. Both heads. No, they didn't mean exactly that.

"Nuch . . . N-uhn . . . En-itch Uhu-er." Poor Ubub. He was trying so hard to be understood.

The old man beside me was frowning as hard

as I was over this exchange. He scratched the stubble of gray hair beneath his cap, resettled it on his head, and said, "'Each other.' Ain't that what you're sayin'? They didn't talk to each other?"

Ulub and Ubub seemed incredibly grateful to him, nodding eagerly.

"They didn't talk to each *other*?"

Enthusiastic nods. The old man looked mightily pleased and spat out a long stream of tobacco, as if he'd earned the right.

It was a little like playing charades. I wanted to ask, Why not? Why not?, but I doubted the two of them would know, even if they could have expressed it.

"You mean you never heard them talk to each other?"

"Nah du war—" Ubub's face started working, his tongue trying to form sounds that wanted to stay locked within his mouth, slipping around, getting no purchase, like a climber trying to find secure footing on a glass mountain.

Everyone watched in suspense; we couldn't help it.

Finally he blurted out, "Mur-rah."

And Ulub nodded.

Ubub added: "Uh-uhv-win."

Mary-Evelyn! I thought, at the same time the old man slapped his knee and exclaimed, "Mary-Eva!"

"Mary-Evelyn," I said. "You're saying that the sisters *never talked to Mary-Evelyn*?"

Both of them looked at me, at the old man, at each other, nodding all the while.

"But—" I was stunned by this news. Stunned. In whatever my mother (or anyone) had told me about the Devereau sisters, never was there any suggestion that they were "abnormal" in any way. My mother never said anything about the sisters' not being able to talk, or anything like that. They came to the hotel, all of them together, or in pairs (never alone, apparently), and with Mary-Evelyn. They must have ordered their food or conversed with the other guests, just like anybody else. So it wasn't that they *couldn't* talk, but that they *wouldn't*.

By this time, I had got up off the bench and was standing in front of the Woods. Maybe I could understand Ubub better if I watched his face. "Didn't you ever hear them say *anything* to Mary-Evelyn?"

Emphatically, Ubub shook his head. So did Ulub, and not, I thought, just in imitation of his brother. No, they had never heard them say anything to her. Then Ubub offered: "Nu-ee th-thun uh uhn ee." Ulub turned to Ubub and they both nodded, confirming this statement.

And the old man, who'd edged closer to them and was now Official Interpreter, again mouthed Ulub's word forms and exclaimed: "Funny! They thought it was funny." He meant the Woods did.

Both nodded and grinned at him.

I knew the Woods didn't mean funny "laughable," but funny "strange." To me it was worse than strange; it was scary.

"But you were only there a short time," I said. "Maybe they just didn't want to talk in front of strangers. Or something."

Ubub considered this, bringing his long, oil-begrimed fingers to his forehead. But he had set his face to a certainty and was shaking his head. He made small, grunting noises and then looked upwards, closing and unclosing his small hands. He had the look of a person who meant to throw a tantrum at God, and I can't say I blamed him. (I knew all about tantrums.) Then he lowered his head, as if he were in disgrace. (I knew all about disgrace, too.) Ulub simply put his hand on his brother's arm and patted him into a sort of dark, frustrated quiet.

I thought how awful it would be to be speechless (though I imagined some people—Lola Davidow chief among them—wouldn't mind too much if such a fate befell me). And since I was pretty sure the Woods neither read nor wrote, how it would be to have no means of communication excepting if they found someone, or some occasion when someone really wanted to understand them, such as this one.

Yet the two of them together (and they were never apart) seemed almost pleased with things. I've always thought it dumb, really dumb, to comment on other people's happiness—that is, whether they were or were not happy—but the Woods had an air about them as if they *were* more or less happy. Such as when they would be eating their lunch in the Rainbow, listening to the regulars at the counter kidding around, and they'd smile as if they were included in all of the buffoonery. And, naturally, they liked the Rainbow because Maud was there, and always insisted on waiting on them; she wouldn't let Shirl do it because Shirl teased them—Shirl could bury a lot of nastiness underneath a quirky little smile (and even that smile looked mean, I thought) and pretend she couldn't understand what Ulub or Ubub were pointing to on the menu. But Maud would tell them the specials and tell them if anything was particularly good that day. They really liked that, being treated like anybody else, and sometimes would ponder over their order, but they always wound up pretty much with the same thing: hot roast beef sandwich and mashed potatoes and gravy.

I wondered, too, if their memories might not even be better than the rest of ours because they could keep them clearer, so to speak, and depended on them more, and were much deeper into their own thoughts than others were. They weren't clouding over their memories with a lot of talk.

I said to Ubub, hoping he would understand that I had understood him, "You don't think—you think they never talked to her. To Mary-Evelyn."

Ubub raised his head, nodding and looking happier. Then he added: "Uf Mur-ur-ah tahn nu-uhn ah-ah-ahnwur."

This was truly inscrutable. I mulled it over, frowning deeply. I think the "uf" must have been "if." So I said, "If Mary . . ." They nodded, encouragingly. But what was "tahn"? "Talk," maybe. "If Mary *talked . . .*"

Heavy nods.

But I couldn't get the rest. The old man was thinking deeply and finally said—he was really incredible—"No one answered. Ain't no one answered her, right?"

The Woods were almost gleeful, both of them. "Yuh, yuh," said Ubub.

"So if this Mary-Evan person talked," the old man went on with authority, "nobody talked back, nobody answered her." He spat a stream of tobacco again, wiped the back of his hand over his mouth and looked at his shoes. "That poor little girl must've had the blue devils."

"What's the blue devils?" I asked.

Mr. Root pursed his lips, thinking. "Some call it the *de*-pression, like. I call it the worst kind of misery. Misery's misery." Then he was silent, as if he knew.

## NINE

I should have known better than to tell anyone about my exchange with the Woods, but I was so wrought up about what I'd discovered that when I got back to the hotel, I did. It was during Sunday dinner.

We were at the "family table" in the rear of the dining room. Mrs. Davidow, Ree-Jane, Will and me, and, off-and-on, my mother, when she didn't have to dart through the swing door into the kitchen, her dinner getting cold all the while. She had so much to do at mealtimes that she often ate her dinner standing up in the kitchen.

Lola Davidow certainly didn't have to eat standing up; by dinnertime she was usually so "oiled and lubed" (as Will put it) that she couldn't stand up straight, anyway. That night she was eating her steak. Filet mignon, her diet food. She's always going on grapefruit-and-steak diets, which sounds all right until you throw in the pitcher of martinis. The rest of us were eating fried chicken, including Ree-Jane, except she always gets white meat. That's understood, and one of the waitresses had got a real tongue-lashing from Mrs. Davidow once because she had made the unforgivable error of putting the white meat in front of *me* and serving the chicken leg to Ree-Jane. The plates were exchanged, but not before I got my fork prongs into that chicken breast and wrenched out a big bite.

This is an ongoing argument for me. It makes me absolutely furious. I wouldn't mind at all taking turns about the white meat, but to have Ree-Jane always get the favored part of the chicken was unbearable. Neither would I mind so much if my mother didn't *own* that chicken, so to speak, for it's she who's the Paradise part of that "family table" (you can bet Aurora always gets white meat of chicken), and not the Davidows. Of course, Ree-Jane just gloats fit-to-kill every time fried chicken appears on the menu.

No matter how often I point out this favoritism to her, my mother won't do anything about it. She always says that guests prefer white meat, and she has to make sure she holds some back in case a party orders it. Well, I said, if that's the point, then it should be held back from Ree-Jane, too. Why make a fuss about such a little thing? is always my mother's fuming response as she bangs around the pots and pans preparing to shut down for the night. She can't stand all of this "dissension," she keeps saying to me. All she wants is some peace and quiet. Well, I say, all I want is some white meat of chicken.

But this particular dinnertime I didn't care much about the drumstick I was eating (much to Ree-Jane's disappointment, I'm sure, for her gloating went unattended), because I was too excited about what I'd found out.

". . . And they said her aunts wouldn't talk to her. Isn't that horrible?"

At the other end of the table, Ree-Jane was laughing, heaving with silent laughter, and I assume had been all during my account. I felt my throat tighten. "What's so funny?"

The laughter now was audible. The words came out, broken a little: ". . . can just (har har) *hear* it now. I can (har har) *hear* it. You (har har) and the Woods (har har) mumbling and grunting . . ."—and here she made some disgusting sounds intended to mimic Ulub and Ubub.

Her mother shook a little too, with laughter. I will say that Lola Davidow didn't always back up her daughter in Ree-Jane's nastier moments. Actually, I don't think Mrs. Davidow was a nasty person; Ree-Jane was. But Mrs. Davidow was pretty "lubed" tonight, and I guess laughter came easy to her.

Even Will joined in, sucking up to them. That really made me angry, and I flashed him a razor-sharp look. He knew he was being mean and stopped and said, "Well, sometimes I can understand them. Big Bob I can understand sometimes."

By now my mother's famous chocolate cake had been served and Lola Davidow (her diet officially forgotten) was raising a large forkful to her mouth. She said that the Wood boys were probably imagining all of it. "It was over forty years ago, how could they remember? I don't think they can remember what was around the corner they just turned." She was mashing her fork against the chocolate crumbs on her plate.

My mother was at least taking my story seriously, although she questioned my conclusion. She said, "I don't see how the Wood boys could say something like that." She had appeared briefly with her coffee cup in hand. "The Devereau sisters were very social once they got going, once they got into company."

"But what about when they were out of company?" I insisted.

Ree-Jane, who was eating the chocolate icing but not the cake, put her two cents' worth in. "Well, why do *you* care? If it all happened forty years ago?"

I ignored her and asked Mother, "When they brought Mary-Evelyn along with them, did you hear them talk to her?"

"I can't remember. But I'm sure they must have or I'd have noticed."

"Why? Adults don't pay much attention to kids. And you always said Mary-Evelyn was really quiet. So maybe she didn't say anything herself that would give one of the aunts a reason to answer her. So maybe that's how it was, and it wouldn't have stood out as peculiar."

"You'd be a lot better off," said Ree-Jane, licking the back of her fork, "trying to get to know some *living* girls your age instead of *dead* ones." You could tell how clever she was.

She meant that I had no friends. That dreaded

subject is always rearing its head. It isn't technically
true, for I do have friends when school's in session,
but school is often somewhere else, for in the winter
months we close the hotel, or all of it except for
Aurora's rooms in the attics, where she warms herself
with her gin reserve and a portable heater and Marge
Byrd to see that she gets meals. (Why the hotel is
still standing when we return I can't imagine.) When
they get on this subject of me and my friends, they
all yammer at me, sometimes even Will, and it's
terrible.

So I was determined to keep the subject on the
Woods, and said, "What about her cat? She had a
cat that died . . . in strange circumstances." I didn't
actually know that, but said so anyway. "Miss Flagler
said. Miss Flyte said so, too," I added, though she
hadn't.

"Really, I wish you wouldn't have anything to
do with the Wood boys," said my mother, who was
still standing there with her coffee cup.

"And Gertrude Flyte is crazy as a bedbug; don't
you have any friends you can go around with instead
of sitting in that shop talking to old women?" said
Mrs. Davidow, dragging that topic back.

No one asked me what the strange circumstances were; no one was interested; no one found
my news fascinating. It's always like that, it seems
to me: whenever I express excitement over something, or even pleasure, whoever or whatever caused
it is discredited (another "dis" word, my life being
full of them, it seemed) and criticized, or, worse,

made fun of to the point where I feel shamed by my own enthusiasm.

Like the wedding reception Miss Flyte had been engaged to take charge of for one of the McIntyre girls. The mention of Miss Flyte was a red flag to both Mother and Mrs. Davidow, for they had both been furious over this McIntyre reception. My mother had fumed and fussed out in the kitchen, making the ribbon sandwiches that were so pretty and popular, cutting wafer-thin slices of cucumber for the cucumber ones, and painting another delicate white rose on the four-tiered cake with a pastry tube. Anyone can put a few damned candles around, she had said. She was incensed that somebody *else* was to supervise an affair that she was well able to handle herself, and in a domain that was hers exclusively. *Almost* exclusively, for of course Lola Davidow had to have her say, and though she usually disagrees with my mother on principle, whenever there is a slight, real or imagined, to the Hotel Paradise—and to have somebody for whatever reason being hired to boss a party held in the Hotel Paradise was definitely a slight!—Lola would certainly agree with my mother. Lola Davidow considered the Hotel Paradise even more her domain than my mother's, although she neither made ribbon sandwiches nor baked cakes. But she did make a heady sort of champagne punch. Anyway, Mrs. Davidow's say was that Gertrude Flyte was a worse thief than William Archibald (vice-president of the First National Bank and its best customer, having taken a lot of the depositors' money), the way she overcharged; well, did we know what the McIntyres were paying her for "lighting up" this reception? She'd heard one thousand dollars. Since that was almost as much as they were paying for the food and service and use of the big hotel dining room (one hundred people at twelve dollars a head), they were both highly insulted. And neither did they like me pointing out that they would be saved a lot of work and trouble with Miss Flyte having to do all of the "arranging" of things—tables and flowers and, of course, candles. The thing was that the McIntyres wanted my mother's cooking and Miss Flyte's decor. Mrs. Davidow had her revenge by upping the charge per head for the McIntyre party to thirteen-fifty.

She also had her revenge by making unmerciful fun of Miss Flyte and her candles. During the back-office cocktail hour, she would put the stub of a candle on her head and sit there, giggling, until it fell off. After four or five martinis, she was usually in a very good humor, and the candle was the height of it. It doesn't make me proud to have to say that I would laugh along with her, as it was such a relief not to have her mad at me. But I felt like a traitor to Miss Flyte.

So by the time the wedding reception rolled around, they had pretty much worn away my enthusiasm. The dining room looked beautiful when Miss Flyte finished. Light streamed, winked, cascaded in all sorts of subtle ways, reflecting off the little gold and glass attachments she pinched around the candle tops, doubling the effect. Yet as I looked at it, the light seemed to drain away; the whole elaborate setup seemed silly; the candles were no more than flickering wax. For I was seeing Lola Davidow with the candle on her head and hearing my own laughter.

I have always tried to curb my enthusiasm, for I know if I don't, someone else will. And if you do that, eventually there's less and less you feel thrilled about. But when it came to Mary-Evelyn Devereau and what the Woods had told me, I *had* to talk about it, and with the same old result, only worse this time. For once again Mrs. Davidow was "leaving."

I had "talked back" to her; I told her that she didn't know anything at all about the Woods, that she'd only come to Spirit Lake five years ago, so how could she say they didn't remember? And I said all of this in a determined manner. The result was (it always was when I talked back) that she would leave, and leave immediately. She threw down her napkin and clattered up from the table, jumping the dishes and spilling the water glasses, and my mother hurried after her, cajoling all across the dining room.

I was in disgrace. Dis-grace, perhaps the saddest of the "dis" words. Out of grace, fallen from grace, lost grace.

## TEN

I sat in the Pink Elephant with my head lying on my outstretched arm and my hand making slow loopy doodles in the notebook, and letting the uproar proceed without me. Mrs. Davidow would be either packing or still threatening to pack. Ree-Jane would be in a fix of indecision (though decision was out of her hands, anyway), not wanting at all to go with her mother. Why would she? If she wasn't living exactly high-on-the-hog at the hotel, she still had a white-meat-of-chicken kind of life. Even though the Davidow absence would continue only for a day or two, three at most, the leaving still had the weight of forever, a catastrophe for my mother.

For some time I sat this way, my head on my arm, looking sideways at my notebook, as if I hoped the notebook would give me enough energy to write in that afternoon's revelations. To raise my head seemed too much effort, and I just let my eyes move slowly around the room, taking in whatever they could. The room had pink stucco walls and a low ceiling, and it was the ceiling I was seeing most of from this lopsided angle. I saw a spiderweb I hadn't known was there. Given the cold pink stucco it was not surprising spiders might home there, for the Pink Elephant was something like a cave. From the web, a medium-sized spider dangled, motionless. I wondered if spiders got weary. And that made me wonder if the whole insect world, and by extension the *animal* world, could get "weary." Tired, yes, but *weary*? Weariness was more like your *feelings* giving out. I watched the spider, dangling up there in the shadowy darkness, for signs of industry, and saw none. Of course, the thing was that insects and birds (for instance) couldn't really afford to be weary, for they had to be always on the lookout, so to speak, and had to move quickly just to survive. I remembered the afternoon I'd been sitting on the porch watching the hotel cat hiding and waiting in the flowerbed near a berry bush the birds liked. For an incredibly long time, the cat was frozen there among the mari- golds, tense and patient, before it finally sprang and a cloud of wrens rose in the air. It did a pirouette, nearly a full circle, way up in the air there above the berry bush, and gracefully batted down a bird.

Wow. I inspected that "wow" to see how much energy was in it, but there wasn't any, so it was not yet time to raise my head. The spider hadn't moved, either, and I wondered if it had its eye on a fly droning around up there. The insect world rolled on, oblivious to weariness, I guessed.

The Pink Elephant was directly below the dining room and the window right behind the family table. The window was open, as was the door to the Pink Elephant, open a little, and I could hear voices grow- ing weaker, growing stronger. There was a lot of to- ing and fro-ing going on up there, and raised voices, notably Lola Davidow's, she having apparently returned—probably with a fresh martini instead of a suitcase—angry and arguing. I knew I would have to apologize, and I closed my eyes and did not care that my arm was asleep by now. Apologizing is hard to do even when you're wrong, but when you think you haven't done anything, not really, except just *disagree*, well, having to apologize is horribly humiliating. But I would have to, and depression settled over me.

Does it come, this depression, when you first know the hopelessness of your situation, the way, perhaps, a convict on Death Row knows it? (The term was always written with capitals, as if it were a hotel.) You hide from yourself the fact that the hopelessness comes from something that can't be changed. It's like a switch was thrown at some point to change the train's direction on the railroad tracks. And you're going to end up wherever the track takes you and see whatever is along the line—and only that. You might be sleeping in your seat or just reading—not paying attention, anyway—when the switch is thrown and the train takes its new direction. Asleep and unaware that something horribly important had happened and that you don't have any control over it. With my other hand I felt around for my Whitman's candy box, pulled it over, and pushed the lid from it. I drew out the snapshot of the Devereaus, standing outside the hotel with the porte cochere as a backdrop. There were three Devereau sisters and Mary-Evelyn. I held it close to my eyes and studied it. Mary-Evelyn was standing in front of her aunts and she looked ... I don't know ... *apart* somehow, as if she had nothing to do with the picture taking, as if she wasn't really there.

I could have been imagining this and decided to raise my head and get a better view. All of the aunts were smiling stiffly at the camera, arms held awkwardly at their sides. Usually, when children stand for snapshots with grown-ups, the grown-ups are almost always putting their arms around the kids, pulling at them, strongarming them, clasping them— generally mauling them around, for they love to have the kids in these little pictures and want them to do something the kids don't want, like smile, or stand up straight, or be petting the dog, or something. Yet here, not one of the grown-ups so much as laid a hand on Mary-Evelyn's shoulder. They stood there, the three, with silly useless smiles, staring directly at the camera, not noticing Mary-Evelyn.

It was as if she were *invisible*.

Why didn't they touch her, and why didn't they talk to her?

For I still believed what Ubub and Ulub had told me, no matter how much my mother and Mrs. Davidow put down the whole episode.

I sat there for another little while in spider darkness. Then I decided I might as well go on up and apologize.

# ELEVEN

We weren't, as I've said, permitted to bother Aurora Paradise. If even Lola Davidow was skittish about the fourth-floor stairs (except for the rare occasions when she'd been invited), then certainly we young ones would hardly brave them. Aurora had no interest at all in me or Will, we being nonspecific Paradises. If she wouldn't grant that my *mother* had any claim on the family, then Will and I could pretty much count ourselves out as Paradises. At best, we were leftover Paradises.

My impression of my great-aunt Paradise is of a gnarled gnomelike creature, something that might be happy living under a bridge and popping out to mistreat travelers. Her old-fashioned dresses of gray silk and black wool didn't actually brush the ground, but they didn't miss by much, either. She wore her hair pulled back and tightly coiled.

*So.* The next morning, after the guests had been fed my mother's shining yet greaseless eggs over easy, and the kitchen had been vacated, I set out bottles and blender and went to work. I poured and measured, measured and whirled, dropped in ice cubes, made the blender grit its aluminum teeth and grind away, whisked in a drop of food coloring, and when it was in the tall glass iced with granulated sugar, stuck in a fruit assortment speared on a skewer.

The result was very handsome, and I left the kitchen pleased with myself.

I carried it on a small black enamel tray, decorated with a brilliant green dragon breathing fire. My mother's strict dining room rule was that anything that went into the dining room went in on a tray and never, *never* in one's hands! I wouldn't have been surprised if she'd meted out some old Oriental punishment, like cutting off the offending hand, as I had heard that Japanese princelings would do to servants and pickpockets back in the old days. Yet the tray rule was perfectly understandable, not merely a rule all hotels should follow but (according to my mother) a matter, simply, of breeding.

Despite whatever Aurora might say about the superiority of the Paradises, my mother, in terms of good breeding, could have run circles around her or anyone else.

I carried my tray and glass through the late-morning silence of the hotel, hiked up the stairs, stopping on both landings to screw up my courage. Instinct told me that there was only one way to succeed with Aurora: do not hesitate; do not back down.

She was sitting in a dark green wicker rocking chair, one of the porch chairs that my mother was always complaining were being stolen. There were two more in the room and I knew there were a couple out on the balcony. Against one wall leaned several faded paintings in oil and three others hung askew on the

walls. Two steamer trunks stood open and rich-looking clothes hung in them. I guessed she was using
the old trunks in place of a wardrobe. She herself
was wearing her long-sleeved gray silk dress and
fingerless crocheted gloves, also gray and decorated
with brittle little sequins that winked in the sunlight,
very pretty for a ball, perhaps, but not what you'd
expect for a morning on the fourth floor. She wore
a brooch at her lacy neckline of a blue so deep you
could dive into it, and I wondered if this was a star
sapphire. I knew nothing about jewels, and was never
likely to, my jewelry prospects being limited.

Next to her chair was a table on which were
set out items for her entertainment. There was a Bible
that looked scarcely used, and a deck of Bicycle
cards that looked like they'd been put through a
wringer. There were walnut shells, three of them,
and a dried pea.

She stared at me as if I were being born in front
of her, and perhaps I was. I cleared my throat and
held out my tray. The glass glistened, its tiny tracks
of moisture shining in the late morning sunlight that
streamed through the tall window. We made a pretty
picture, I thought, me and the pink-tinged drink, for
I had scrubbed my face and brushed my hair. "I
brought you something."

Naturally, she was speechless (I expected that),
not with gratitude but with total surprise at this unre-
quested visit.

"Aunt Aurora—"

"Do *not* call me 'aunt.' I am *no* relation of

*yours*. Oh, *I* know who you are." She said, as if I'd been trying to keep my identity secret. "You're the Graham girl."

"What should I call you, then?"

"Nothing. And I won't call you anything, either. We'll both be nameless. With any luck, we'll both disappear. Who made *this*? That Davidow person? This drink"— she had reached out and taken the glass and was holding it up to the window light, where the sun painted both her hand and the glass a lovely daffodil yellow—"is poisoned." She smiled an unpleasant smile. Her lips were thin and slightly blue and snipped off words like scissors.

"I made it. It's a special drink."

"I'm already dying, you know." Her thin lips smacked a bit over this news and her eyes narrowed to see how I would take it.

"I doubt it," I said calmly. I was feeling strangely steely. It must have been being in the same room with her.

"Here!" And she thrust the glass towards me. "Try it out on the dog."

I looked around behind me to see where it was.

"No, no, *you*, you idiot. It's what the kings did, to see if their food was poisoned. They tossed some to their dogs."

There was no arguing with her; I took it, sipped, and refused to cough, for all that my throat burned and my gullet flamed. But the taste, after these moments of fire, was nice and sweet from all of the fruit.

She retrieved the glass and held it, saying, "I'd better wait to see if you collapse and writhe on the floor."

I stood and she sat in silence for perhaps half a minute.

When I didn't writhe, she said, "Very well." She took a drink, smacked her lips a few times, considered. "Not bad. *Interesting*. What's in it besides the gin?"

"Well, there's Jack Daniel's and Southern Comfort and pineapple juice and some apple brandy and—" I stopped, remembering my mother's rule to never give out a recipe without adding to it one or two ingredients that weren't in the mixture, so that if the other person made it, it would taste wrong. She'd learned that after Shirl at the Rainbow had got the recipe for her Angel Pie and started selling those pies as her own creation. When Shirl had tried to wheedle the recipe for her famous chocolate cake, my mother had told her to be sure to add a handful of cold coffee grounds.

"And strong tea." Thinking of the coffee grounds, I added. "*Used* tea. That's important."

Aurora frowned. "That's peculiar to put in."

"I know. But that's what gives it the nice tart taste." If anything gave my drink its tart taste it was three jiggers of gin.

"What's it called?" She pulled the liquid up the straw.

Names crowded my mind from *Joy of Cooking*, my mother's personal bible—Gin Sling, Singapore

Sling, Gin Fizz, Zombie—the last being the best, but not original. Then I remembered a chief ingredient was Southern Comfort. "Cold Comfort," I said, feeling clever.

Aurora looked totally surprised and suspended drinking for a fraction of a second to actually congratulate me. "I never would of thought a Graham had any imagination."

"Some of us do," I answered smartly. Since there were only the three of us, that left Will and my mother up shit creek imagination-wise. But I was careful not to smile, or to register any sort of pleasure in this visit, knowing that if I did, she would probably tell me to get the hell out. So I waited.

She studied me for a while, her eyes traveling over my face and frame as if she were sizing up some item she couldn't make up her mind to buy. "You play poker? Gin rummy?" She grabbed up the tattered pack of playing cards, cut them quick, and snapped the two halves together in a lightning shuffle. There was in Aurora the strong hint of the card shark.

But I wasn't to be put off. "No."

"Wait until you're old and forgotten," she said, slapping down a card. "Then you'll be glad of cards."

This pitying description of herself was laughable. "You're not forgotten. That dumbwaiter must come up here a dozen times a day." I was getting reckless. "And you wouldn't be alone if you lived downstairs with the rest of us." I hoped she wouldn't take me up on this. She paid no attention; her hand was straying back over the table, the card forgotten, on to the several items there set out for her entertainment, and came down on the walnut halves. "We can play this, penny a point." She slid the dried pea under one of the shells and gave me a wily look. "You guess which one it's under." Expertly, she whisked the shells around. "Guess."

The thing was, on the table sat a large bowl of walnuts, and these shells had been cracked open, the nuts eaten. "You can't play it with real shells," I said. "Because they're all different." I pointed out the broken off end of one shell, the blackened line that ran down another. "It's like playing poker and having an ace of hearts in there from a pack with a different design on the back. People would always know who had that ace."

She said nothing, just sat there waiting with her lips clamped together.

"The pea's under this one," I said with a sigh as I touched the shell.

She shook her head and with a grim little smile said, "No, it isn't."

Well, it was. But she wasn't going to lift the shell to prove it, and when I started to protest she swept shells and pea off the table into her palm.

She said: "For someone that wants something, you don't seem to be willing to work for it."

"Who said I wanted something?"

"You wouldn't be up here bribing me if you didn't." Her hand in its sequined gray mitt curled around the Cold Comfort; it made me think of a snake, its flashing scales, coiling.

"I only wanted information."

"*Ha!*" The syllable exploded, flung upwards as if through the ceiling, as if she were challenging an Archangel with an "I told you so! Didn't I tell you?"

"It's just something nobody remembers anything about, much. My mother only remembers a little—"

The "Ha!" hit the ceiling again. "Your *mother*, she's not a Paradise! And that Lola Davidow—they think they can steal my hotel out from under me! Well, *I* have my plans to stop *that*, don't think I don't!"

"What plans?"

Her eyes were bright as the sequins on the mittens as she gouged the bottom of her glass with the straw, the way I like to do with sodas. Right then and there I had an overpowering desire for a chocolate ice cream soda with whipped cream and a maraschino cherry. I told myself when this Aurora ordeal was over, that right after lunchtime, I would walk into La Porte to Souder's Drug Store. Mrs. Souder used real whipped cream on her sodas.

I clutched the black dragon-painted tray as Aurora leaned towards me out of her green wicker chair, stirring up motes of dust and light and sending out whiffs of rosewater and lavender. The closer I was to her, the sweeter the air became, a whole potpourri of scents. I had expected a fouler air, I guess, something rank and nasty you'd associate with old age and a wasting body and a mean mind, something smacking more of fire and brimstone.

"My *plan*, Miss Smartypants, is to burn the Hotel Paradise to the ground, if it don't combust before I get around to it!"

Involuntarily—for I had meant to stand my ground, no matter what—I took a step backwards. "When?" My first thoughts were not for anyone's fate, but to get my belongings out of the Pink Elephant.

"At my con-ven-i-ence, of course. It'll be like Manderley! I'll go down with the hotel! I'll be out there on that balcony"—and she waggled her hand towards the window— "laughing fit to kill! I'll be the last thing to go! Anyway, that's my plan," she wound up in a completely normal tone of voice.

"You'll be the *first* to go if you're out on that balcony, it's so rotted."

"Oh, don't be so goddamned *literal*! Here"— she brandished the empty glass— "scare me up another Cold Comfort."

I didn't take it. I stood there resolute and said, "I will if you tell me about the Devereaus."

Her forehead clenched in a deep frown. "You mean the ones lived over by Spirit Lake?"

"Yes." I relaxed a bit. At least she hadn't thrown the glass at me. Seeing I wasn't reaching for it, she relented and set it on the table. But she stared at it as if by sheer power of will she'd raise the bit of liquid in the bottom to brimful.

"Tell you *what* about them?"

"Whatever you know." I didn't want to qualify this by mentioning Mary-Evelyn's death.

"They were all touched. Especially Isabel Devereau. Though maybe that made her less cold-hearted than Louise. Well, craziness is to be expected if you have all those sisters living together. If I lived with *mine* I'd be stark raving. And there was the young one, Rose Souder."

Rose? My mother hadn't mentioned a Rose Souder. "You mean she wasn't a Devereau?"

"Oh, she was, far as I know. She was a half-sister. Her mother was related in some way to these trashy Souders around here."

I thought of Souder's Drug Store. Old Mrs. Souder didn't strike me as "trashy" at all. But I didn't want to say so and have her arguing all over the place and bringing in other Souders to prove her point. I said, "My mother didn't ever mention a Rose Souder Devereau."

"That's because no one talked about her. She was the black sheep."

Those words stilled any nervous shifting I'd been doing, standing there with my tray. "Black sheep" was a phrase that always got my attention, since I thought probably I belonged to that poor flock. "Why? What did she do wrong?"

"Made trouble." Aurora had put back the walnut halves, the dried pea under one, and was playing the trick on herself, since I wouldn't cooperate. Her bony hands whisked the three halves about the table's surface. "She played the piano, though. She played and that crazy Lillian, or Isabel, sang. You could hear it from down the road."

"What kind of trouble?"

Now she was sitting back, staring in frowning concentration at the shells, ready for another round. She looked up at me from under penciled-in eyebrows. "Where's the pea?"

I guessed I'd have to play the stupid trick. "This one." Anyone else would have been clever enough to choose the wrong walnut shell. But I had no patience with this sort of thing. We both knew where the pea was, and I couldn't pretend *I* didn't, even if she could. I don't know what it was about me that made it so difficult to go along with harmless deceptions.

Her mouth cracked in her version of a smile. "No it isn't."

"It is too." I reached out my hand to prove it and she smacked it, smarting the knuckles.

Then she removed the pea, at least I suppose she did, since she shielded the operation with her hand. And, still keeping the shells blocked from my view, she hid the pea.

It was just plain silly. "Wait a minute! The whole idea of this trick is to show the hand is quicker than the eye. That doesn't work if I don't see where the pea's put at the very *start*."

But she was paying no attention to my objections, just shifting the shells quickly about. "Which one?" Her tone was triumphant, as if she'd really bested me this time.

I didn't even care where I pointed, and she

clapped her sides several times, *whack whack whack*, and cawed with laughter, as if she'd just done the cleverest thing in the world. "Wrong! Wrong! It's *this* one!" This time, of course, she raised a shell-half to reveal the traveling pea. Satisfied now that she'd finally got me, she pushed them to one side, picked up her glass, and gurgled the straw.

But I refused to knuckle under. "What about Rose Devereau?"

"Who?"

Impatient, I said, "Rose Souder *Devereau*. You didn't tell me why she was a black sheep."

"Ran off with Ben Queen." Now, she had the Bicycle cards in her hand and was snapping them.

I was rooted. Here was another name totally new to me. *Ben Queen*. I nearly licked my lips, tasting these new names that seemed as delicious as the Souder's soda I was hankering after. New names I could search for, since my investigation into Mary-Evelyn's strange death had pretty much stalled.

Even without my asking, putting the cards down for solitaire, Aurora said (but it was clear it was to herself), "Ben Queen! Now wasn't he the best-looking man I ever did see! Women'd line up all the way to perdition and back for a chance at Ben Queen. I think he took a fancy to me; it was him taught me how to play cards, poker especially." Her hand ruffled the pack of cards, as if it too had a memory. "I was a *little* older than Ben Queen—" Cagily, she looked at me. "He mustn't have been much more than twenty

or twenty-one—or else I might just've run off with
him myself, even if those Queens was crazy. I wonder
if he's still alive? Be in his sixties by now, I guess."

Did she think she'd taken me in with that age
business? If he was sixty now Aurora would be thirty
years older than Ben Queen.

"Well, they wouldn't let him come to see Rose,
those crazy Devereau sisters. Never set foot in that
house. Probably thought the Queens wasn't good
enough for the Devereaus. Ha! But men like Ben
Queen, they always find a way in. So Rose ran off
with him." Aurora stopped a moment to study the
walnut shells. "Then there was the scandal."

My eyes bugged out. "The scandal?"

She gave me a sly look. "Never you mind, miss.
It was over in Cold Flat Junction, anyways."

I sighed. She was making it up, I suspected.
"Do you remember Mary-Evelyn?"

She frowned. "Who's she?"

How could anyone forget, who'd been around
then? "She drowned. She was the youngest of the
Devereaus."

She shut her eyes, apparently thinking. "Oh,
*her*. That child they pulled from the lake. Sad business." She paused and then was back on the subject
of Ben Queen. "Probably he's dead. People like Ben
Queen don't live long. They burn out. Cold Flat
Junction people, the Queens."

Cold Flat Junction! My mouth dropped. And I
had been there only a few days before, my one and

only trip to Cold Flat. So here I was with *three* bits of fresh information: Rose Souder Devereau, Ben Queen, and a connection with Cold Flat Junction. I decided I shouldn't push my luck with Aurora, and picked up the glass and said, sweetly, "Would you care for another?"

"Well, don't mind if I do, now you mention it."

I ran down the stairs, glass and tray in hand, praying it wasn't yet time for my mother and the others to be filing into the kitchen for lunch preparation.

My luck held; I couldn't believe it. The kitchen was as empty as a tomb and I quickly dragged out the Jack Daniel's and juice and Southern Comfort and tossed everything into the blender with a cube of ice, and, while it whirred, thought about my new information.

Carefully, I checked out the dining room to make sure no one was around, and then walked through with the glass on the tray, the drink looking even prettier than the first one. It was certainly more potent. I had a heavy hand.

Through the dining room and next through the music room, where I stopped and looked at our upright piano.

Rose Devereau and Ben Queen.

Into that splintered picture of that fatal summer, I could fit two more puzzle pieces. I placed the piece that was Rose into place in the Devereau music room, sitting at a piano. My inner ear composed some sort of watery music line, trembling up and down the keyboard.

Ben Queen, a wild card apparently in every sense of the word, I pressed into the dark and smoking wood that surrounded Spirit Lake.

# TWELVE

Between Spirit Lake and La Porte runs a dusty country highway, a two-lane road that's used mostly by local people now, since another highway was built that bypasses Spirit Lake. The land on both sides is flat and windy, with breezes stirred up by passing cars. In the distance you can see bands of dark evergreen trees where the woods begin. Sunlight sifts through these burnt-looking acres of faded grasses and Queen Anne's lace, which I had always spoken of as a flower until Ree-Jane told me it was "weeds, just weeds," quick to de-beautify anything I love. And I wonder: why is it that a growing thing that springs up of its own accord and in surprising places must be "just a weed"?

I pass this sea of Queen Anne's lace and those fragile, starry-looking weeds called puffballs, whose white filaments I can make vanish with one breath. The puffballs make me think about God, something that my mind doesn't dwell on much; I wonder if our souls are like the white threads of the puffballs and if God is the breath blowing them around, making them vanish. Would these almost invisible filaments finally curl and die like daisy petals pulled away from their source of life? I frowned over my comparison and thought it probably didn't hold up. Finally, I stopped breathing at the puffballs, for I thought I was taking unfair advantage; they are too much at my mercy, and it seems childish and mean to pick wildflowers at all, much less pick them apart. So I let the puffballs alone and merely admire them and the Queen Anne's lace, especially on my circuits of Spirit Lake where Queen Anne's lace grows in profusion and puffballs line the rutted and overgrown road.

Ree-Jane sometimes walks the two miles with me to La Porte, but only at those times when she can't finagle the money out of her mother for the taxi fare. As it's a somewhat lonely two miles I am glad of the company, even hers, even though she turns her cold eye on anything that I like.

But this particular day, after supplying Great-Aunt Paradise with her second Cold Comfort and then doing my waitress work, I had the road pretty much to myself. During the two-mile hike to town I was passed only by a couple of rusted-up pickups, Billy Clutterback's snout-nosed Studebaker, and Axel's taxicab, going the other way, empty except for Axel. My stomach was pleasantly full of my lunch—*dreamily* full, I should say, for lunch had been my mother's ham roll slathered in cheese sauce, one of my favorites, but a dish that my mother thought little of, saying it was tossed together from leftovers. This ham roll consists of ground-up and seasoned ham spread onto pastry and then rolled and sliced into big pinwheels. Across this she pours a rich sauce the color of marigolds from the cheddar cheese and the mustard. My mother doesn't give a second thought to such lunch dishes, even though the pastry melts on your tongue and the sauce is satin-smooth. To her way of thinking, this ham roll is such an old peasant dish she hasn't even bothered making up a name for it. Not like her Angel Pie or her Chocolate Feather Cake. Oh, that ham roll! That cheese sauce! I actually patted my stomach as I walked along, for it was the home for this wonderful mix of textures and flavors.

Despite this lunch, I was still making straight for Souder's Drug Store as I came to the edge of town and continued along First Street. I bypassed Candlewick, the Oak Tree Gift Shoppe, and the Rainbow, and even the county courthouse, in my relentless pursuit of the chocolate soda.

There were three drug stores in La Porte; Souder's and Frazee's had more marble and mahogany than Sparks's Walgreen. In Sparks's, you ate at a Formica countertop in a double-horseshoe loop; it leaned more towards sandwich lunches and waffle breakfasts than towards ice cream sodas and sundaes. Souder's was hemmed in between Prime Cut (Shirl's favorite beauty salon) on the one side, a narrow alley; then Betty's dress shop on the other. The salon and the dress shop always seemed to be bathed in a milky light, while Souder's stayed dark and almost cold inside. Also, it now had the distinction of a tie to Mary-Evelyn because of the Souder connection.

Here there was another little bell just like Miss Flagler's, jangling over the door, and as I took my seat at the counter, I wondered if Mrs. Souder could

give me any information about Rose Souder Devereau. The trouble was, there were so many Souders
around that it hardly seemed worth the trouble of
trying to get old Mrs. Souder to remember whether
there was a Rose in her arm of the family. And Mrs.
Souder was pretty deaf, too, which would have made
it really hard even to get the question across to her.

The wooden-bead curtain back in the shadows
clicked and clattered as old Mrs. Souder came
through it, twitching like always. I never have known
what's wrong with her; whatever it is affects her
head, which jerks to the side as if someone is pulling
a string fastened to her chin. Mrs. Souder doesn't
seem to like young people (like me); probably we
make her even more nervous.

But if anyone should be nervous, it should be
her husband's customers. He's the pharmacist, and
his hands suffer from the same nervous disease as
her neck. When Mr. Souder measures out liquids in
slender vials, the beaker stutters against the glass. I
always think the colors of these medicines are amaz-
ing: the globelike bottles standing along the wooden
shelf in front of him range from springwater-clear
to purple, aquamarine, and chartreuse. When the old
B & O train charges through town, it sets the shim-
mery liquids jittering, just like the Coca-Cola glasses
and ice cream dishes shiver on the tier of glass
shelves.

I always have a chocolate soda with chocolate
ice cream. I try to make myself order something else,
but never do. The chocolate ice cream tub, just about

everybody's favorite, is usually half-empty, bits of cream crystallizing around its sides. On this day, I inspected the various tubs, heaving my chest across the marble counter to do this, thinking I would choose something else—maple perhaps, its surface undisturbed, so that my scoop would make the first creamy dent—but no, I was a slave to that chocolate.

I ordered chocolate-on-chocolate as Mrs. Souder stood there with the ice cream scoop already raised and ready to fall. She was surprisingly generous with her scoops, putting two into the ribbed glass rather than the one you got at Frazee's. I watched the composition of my soda with the concentration of an addict.

A tiny, long-handled ladle deposited a ribbon of chocolate into the bottom of the tall glass, and this Mrs. Souder topped off with a dollop of milk. This was followed with the first scoop of ice cream, then a brief fizz of water, a lot more chocolate sauce, more water frothing up, and then the second scoop of ice cream, followed by another brief fizz of water that bubbled across the surface. Then Mrs. Souder drew artful circles with the whipped cream spoon, forming a small iceberg of topping. A maraschino cherry was the last ingredient, and Mrs. Souder let it drop down into the whipped cream. The cherry juice bled into the white cloud, the same way Mrs. Souder's bright lipstick bled over the edges of her thin mouth.

I always thought this lipstick rather brave of her, for she was quite old, with tissue-papery skin, delicate and very white, but that was probably from lathering on the Pond's powder that they sold in the store.

Mrs. Souder is a silent and unfriendly old woman, but I think she is rather proud of her ice cream artistry. She looks as if she enjoys holding the chocolate-sauce ladle high over the glass so that the sauce forms swirls and dribbles ribbons; she enjoys making those high white peaks with the whipped cream and then displacing the peak by the drop of a cherry. As she comes to the end of these maneuvers, her grumpy silence gives way to the hint of a painstaking smile, the barest raising of the corners of the mouth. In her tea-colored eyes is an expression almost of delight, quickly extinguished if she sees me watching her. And it makes me wonder if Mrs. Souder, who seems as far removed from people my age as anyone can be, and who is sharp with us when she isn't silent—if during the ice-cream-soda composition, she is remembering her own childhood, maybe spent right here in Souder's Drug Store, maybe even sitting on one of these very same stools, for I believe she has lived in La Porte all of her life. This makes me feel some sort of kinship with Mrs. Souder, and feel I should be able to picture myself as old as she is, but I can't. It's too difficult to see that far into the future. Beyond my own imagined wedding day to various people (the bridegroom changes a lot, depending on my mood), my future is a blur.

So I drank my soda slowly while I turned on the wooden stool, looking over the familiar interior, and the gray backs of the items in the window—a cardboard cutout of Vitalis hair cream, another of Pond's cold cream, two deep blue bottles of Evening in Paris toilet water, a sunburst of various styles of hairbrush. As if it were an artwork hung for years in some museum, the window never changed, and I could see the thin coating of dust on the blue bottles and the dust mouse caught behind the Vitalis cutout. The only sound in the silence was the ticking of the regulator clock on the wall. The interior of the pharmacy was dark and cool in the way that only marble and mahogany are dark and cool.

The quiet was shattered by the talky entrance of Helene Baum, the doctor's wife, followed up by two other women, the mayor's wife and Mrs. Dodge Haines. They're some of Helene Baum's followers, for she always seems to be trailing women in her wake, talking back to them over her shoulder. She has deep-dyed red hair and always wears yellow, that day's yellow being a sweater over a tweed skirt. She also wears harlequin-framed eyeglasses with a dusting of rhinestones across the top that are really awful. The three women went chattily to one of the little ice cream tables, Helene Baum pausing long enough for me to acknowledge her. She never says hello first. With her raspy, nasal voice, I always feel she's going to file me down like a fingernail. I think she's a mean-minded person, going around town cut-

ting people apart so that Dr. Baum can sew them up
again. And she thinks that being the wife of La
Porte's chief doctor gives her social standing.

To have a social standing in La Porte isn't easy,
since no one's really rich or well connected or a
member of some swank family like the Rockefellers.
When it comes to sheer staying power, probably the
Paradises have been around longer than anyone else.
Even the Grahams (of which I'm one) have been
around a lot longer than Helene Baum. I know it just
kills her she never gets asked up on the balcony on
those days when Aurora is feeling sociable. And it
must be especially maddening to her that Mrs.
Davidow gets invited, since Lola is, in Mrs. Baum's
mind, a Johnny-come-lately.

As I was scraping the last of the chocolate from
my glass (and trying to ignore the nasal ordering-
around of Mrs. Souder by Helene Baum), I wondered
how long Dr. Baum had practiced in La Porte, for
he must be in his fifties or even sixties. Could he
have been a doctor here at the time of Mary-Evelyn's
death? No. That was forty years ago, and he'd hardly
have been out of school, even if he was in his sixties
now. Then I suddenly remembered Dr. McComb,
who was quite elderly and who *had* been around La
Porte for fifty or even sixty years.

I let the long-handled spoon clatter into my glass
and wondered why I hadn't considered this before:
that some doctor or other had to sign a death certifi-
cate, or something like that. I had heard my mother
talk about Dr. McComb; he collected things—flow-

ers, or butterflies, things like that. I frowned. "Horti-culturist." That was the word. He had written articles for magazines on the flowers and wildlife around this area. He probably knew a lot about weeds, too.

I took another couple of turns on the wooden stool, pushing myself with the toe of my shoe. And while I did this, I considered what I knew of flowers and butterflies. Not much. What I was turning over in my mind was how I might come by a butterfly (or a flower) that Dr. McComb would like to add to his collection. That would get him to talk to me. If I could talk to Dr. McComb, I might be able to ask him about Mary-Evelyn. Why had I never thought of this before in my search for information? Probably because Dr. McComb is no longer seen much around town, for he gave over his practice to a younger doctor, the one Helene Baum was always warning people against.

It was she whose voice cut through my mental butterfly-catching, ordering me to stop turning because the stool squeaked and it was very annoying. The other two women looked at me with crimped, disapproving lips, and though I didn't have the nerve to keep the exercise up, I did manage to push off just once more with my foot and sail around, taking in the plate glass window. As I whizzed around, I got a glimpse of a person outside studying the window display. I had the impression of a face all shadows; then as I sailed around again, the sun struck her back and fuzzed her hair and her body. It was as if she were wrapped in a gold cocoon. Perhaps it was all that thinking about butterflies that put this into my mind.

When I finally slammed to a stop, she was turning away, but I was almost certain it was *her*, the one on the railroad platform in Cold Flat Junction. And then I saw her profile.

It was definitely the Girl.

# THIRTEEN

She disappeared from the window.

I would have run for the door, but I had always been taught to restrain myself. Never jump from your chair but rise and walk slowly to wherever you're going. I remembered years before sitting at one of the small, scarred tables in the children's room of the library and reading in a book of poems about a girl named Jenny who always jumped up out of her chair to kiss the person who wrote the poem. I remembered my eyes filling up, my whole *body* filling up with tears, it felt like, and not being able to keep them back. My head was carefully bent over my book and the tears dripped down on the pages. I wanted to be Jenny.

Since I had already paid for my soda, I could have run lickety-split for the door. In fantasy, I jumped from the stool and rushed outside and grabbed her and asked, "Who are you? Who are you?" Inside of my cool exterior, I'm pretty much a Fourth of July fireworks person: feelings flaring, shooting, wheeling, sizzling, or just popping; or, on the down side, falling, sinking, plummeting with almost equal energy. Outwardly, though, I'm exceedingly careful to remain cool and even dry, like a person without body fluids—no spit, no sweat, no tears. What I've picked up is that it's important in this life not to appear too enthusiastic about anything, as if in that way you can avoid disappointment. It was superstitious thinking. And it doesn't work, either; the disappointment is always just as bad.

So by the time I strolled outside, she had vanished.

Desperate now, I did run. I ran in the direction she'd been aiming, down to the corner, looked one way towards the railroad tracks, then quickly turned the other way and collided with the Sheriff.

"Did you see her?" I was breathless.

"See who?"

I was searching the sidewalk beyond him. Empty—at least empty of her. "You *must* have passed her. She couldn't have gone across the tracks, because the barrier's down. That freight train's coming. So she must have gone up the street there, the way you just walked. . . ." The Sheriff just stood there like a wedge. "Maybe she went into the five-and-dime—"

*"Who?"*

"She's blond and really pretty. I don't know how old she is. Around twenty, maybe." I was dancing up and down on the balls of my feet now, trying to look past him, right side, left side.

"Hold *on*, for Lord's sake!" He brought his hands down on my shoulders, stilling me. "Now, what's so important about this girl?"

I didn't know, only that she *was* important. I dodged down under his arms and made a beeline for the five-and-dime. She could have gone in any of the stores along this street, into the dime store, the haberdashery, the hardware store on the corner, or any of the others. I figured a stranger would most likely want a dime-store item, perhaps a toothbrush or maybe a lipstick.

There were four aisles and I walked them all; she wasn't among the two dozen people in the store. Unfortunately, the dime store had a lot of distractions. I stopped to leaf through one of the comic books hung in the metal racks; I stopped to review the latest in lipstick shades, deciding on a pale, peachy color—that is, if I wore lipstick, which, naturally, I don't. Deflated and disappointed, I walked out into the cold sunlight and the Sheriff was still there, leaning against a parking meter. He was talking to Bunny Caruso.

Now, Bunny Caruso belongs to that mysterious band of local people I had strict orders to stay away from. Like Toya Tidewater. And there were others: there was Gummy John; there was a tall old man with silver hair whose name I could never remember; and a few others. In other words, all of the weird or fascinating people. Bunny Caruso, though, was *absolutely* to be avoided, whereas some of the others, like the Woods, got tossed in for no particular reason (and when they worked on the hotel grounds, it was all right to talk to them). It seemed to me that anyone who was different was also thought of as dangerous. It was the boring people, the nasty people, like Helene Baum, that I was supposed to bow and scrape to. Naturally, I balked.

I wasn't told *why* I was to stay away from
Bunny, and because of this I of course assumed it
had something to do with sex, that subject I knew
even less about than I did God and puffballs. My
notion of "sexy" was pretty foggy, but Bunny never
did strike me that way, for she's kind of thin in build,
though her face is extremely pretty. I heard that there
were always men hanging around her little place on
Swain's Point, and I was never, never to go near her
house. This was a commandment I broke at the first
available opportunity, which was one day when I
helped her carry her groceries from Miller's to her
beat-up pickup truck and she invited me home to
have lunch with her. I had seen the little delicatessen
cartons sticking out of the bag, and I was only too
happy to accept. Miller's cole slaw is almost as good
as my mother's.

We bumped along in the pickup for several
miles with Bunny chattering away amiably, and for
the life of me I just couldn't imagine what was supposed to be so dangerous about her. She had an
innocent-looking face, completely absent of makeup,
and goldish russet hair cut boy-short, except in back,
where it curled over her collar in a little switch. If
anything, Bunny struck me as being a farm girl,
someone I could easily picture out in the fields in a
broad-brimmed hat, picking something—corn,
maybe. But then I preferred the vision of acres of
waving wheat and the sound of threshing, and so she
threshed.

Bunny has a strange accent—strange, that is,

because I can't place it. It isn't southern, nor is it mountain. The *a*'s draw out and the *u*'s disappear, so that "I can't figure" becomes "I cain't figger." The harshness of the accent is softened by her voice. She has the softest and most musical voice I think I've ever heard. Her voice makes me think of the low winds rippling the sea of wheat, a sowing sound, a threshing sound.

That day was the first time I'd ever seen her house, and it was really interesting. It was full of mirrors; whole walls were mirrors. And there were a lot of candles; there must have been more than two dozen bunched around. I asked her if the house had been done by Miss Flyte, and she said no, she couldn't afford Miss Flyte, but she'd gotten some ideas from the candle shop. The mirrors, she'd said, were to make the room look bigger, since the house was quite tiny. We ate all of the cole slaw and tuna fish and stuff and then went down to sit on a rock that was only slightly above one of the lake inlets and stuck our feet in the water. Bunny liked to talk and I liked to listen, mostly to the sound of her voice. She also had a butterfly net and sometimes we chased butterflies, or, rather, because we were too lazy to move from the rock, we'd just sweep the net in the air if one happened to fly by. I visited several times after that.

One of my fantasies after my visit was to have, one day, a farm where Bunny and I would live. Perhaps this farm would be in the miles of fertile land called Paradise Valley (a name that I think had to

do with God and Heaven, and not Aurora Paradise). I
pictured Bunny out there in our fields in her big
straw hat and blue gingham, picking whatever needed
picking, and, of course, threshing. (My knowledge
of crops and livestock went the way of God, puffballs, and sex.) In my fantasy, Bunny and I would
spend a lot of time with our feet in the stream, skip-
ping stones and watching dragonflies and swooping
down on butterflies.

And out in the fields, I would wander through
the stalks—of corn, perhaps—followed by farm
dogs. Occasionally, cats would leap up out of the
tall grass and bat at butterflies. Bunny worked the
wide fields, but I do not know what I contributed to
the farm running. Not much, apparently. After all, I
was in the hotel business.

"You scoured that place pretty well," said the
Sheriff, nodding towards the dime store.

I didn't answer him; I said hello to Bunny and
included her in our search for the Girl. "You must've
passed her," I said to the Sheriff, letting him know
that he was, after all, the Sheriff and should know
about strangers in town and what they might be up
to.

"Who?" asked Bunny, looking from me to the
Sheriff. I think she really likes the Sheriff, but then
who doesn't? I felt a twinge of jealousy.

I told her about the Girl, but not everything, not
about me being in Cold Flat Junction. She frowned
a bit, shook her head slowly. "I cain't remember
seein' no'un like that."

In this way, she's like the Sheriff, and like Maud Chadwick, too. She gives things her deep consideration and doesn't brush you off or ignore you. I ponder this sometimes: how three people who are so different can be so much alike. And then I ponder: but *are* they so different? *Are* we all so different from one another? For I naturally include myself in this little band of my favorite people.

When the Sheriff suggested stopping in the Rainbow, Bunny took a step backward, as if it weren't for her to be included in the likes of such festivities. I told her come on, but that only made her more anxious, clutching her tiny shoulder bag to her waist.

I asked the Sheriff, after she'd walked off to her pickup truck, why people seemed to object to Bunny Caruso.

"They don't like the way she lives, I guess."

We were doubling back towards the Rainbow Café. "But she just lives with her cat in a little house on Swain's Point. It's neat and perfectly respectable." ("Perfectly respectable" was a favorite phrase of my mother's, usually meaning the person didn't have much else going for him.) "It's just like other houses, except for the mirrors—"

The Sheriff suddenly stooped to tie his shoelace, so I couldn't read his expression when he said, "Sounds like you've been there."

He rose from his kneeling position and we walked on. Things just slipped out of me when I talked to him or to Maud. I certainly never intended

to tell anyone I'd visited Bunny's place. "Once I
was. Or twice." I sighed and told him, "I'm not
supposed to even *talk* to Bunny. My mother told me
not to. I think it's silly. Bunny's really nice."

We were nearing Souder's again, and I saw
Helene Baum's Cadillac parked one door down in
front of Betty's dress shop. Naturally, she drove a
Cadillac, maybe thinking that car was better than the
mayor's Oldsmobile. Hers was buttercup-yellow. I
supposed she was still in Souder's, telling the other
two how to live their lives. As we drew abreast of
the Cadillac, the Sheriff stopped, and I was hoping
the red flag was up in the meter. But it wasn't. What
he was looking at was the front end of the car,
nosed a foot or two across the alley entrance. The
Sheriff considered this for a moment and then (I
liked to believe as a result of the power of my
inward urging) he drew his book of tickets from
his rear pocket, clicked his pen, and started writing.

I danced a little jig by the meter and grew even
more excited to see Mrs. Baum marching fumily out
of the drug store and bearing down on us. She must
have seen what was going on through the plate glass
window. Me, she ignored, of course.

"What are you doing?" she demanded.

"Afternoon, Helene," was his only answer, as
he politely touched his fingers to his cap.

"I *said*, what are you doing? I'm not overtime!"
She rapped her knuckles on the meter as if bidding
it to verify this.

The Sheriff just kept writing. "No, but you're blocking the alley there."

Elaborately, she measured the distance with her two hands. "Don't be silly. Even a truck could squeeze through there."

The Sheriff ripped the pink ticket from his book and held it out to her, smiling. But she brushed his hand aside. So he placed the ticket securely under the windshield wiper, saying, "You know, if Doc Baum was doing bypass surgery on me and didn't open up the artery all the way, but just shrugged and said, 'Oh, well, there's room enough so the blood can *squeeze through*,' I guess I'd be kind of upset." His smile was dazzling. "See you around, Helene."

And the two of us walked off. I should say I *danced* off, heady with delight, drunk with the Power of the Sheriff's Office! I looked back and Helene was standing there going up in smoke.

"How about that Coke, now?" the Sheriff asked.

The chocolate soda was lying heavy on my stomach, or heavy on the ham roll and cheese sauce and a side order of baked beans. My mother made no bones about the beans coming out of a can, which surprised everybody, for they tasted homemade. "Doctored" was what my mother called these vastly improved canned vegetables. As far as I was concerned, my mother should have run a vegetable hospital, the way she took hold of limp, pale, unhealthy-looking green beans and peas and cabbage and with her seasoning and a little wrist action had them walking through the swinging doors looking like they'd spent all their days in the sun and never even seen the inside of a can.

Now, standing in front of the Rainbow with the Sheriff, I decided, no, I couldn't get another thing down on top of all the things I'd eaten in the last two hours. Even I had my limits. And there was also my recent brainstorm about Dr. McComb and his butterflies and wildflowers. I was eager to go to the library.

"Do you know Dr. McComb?" I asked the Sheriff.

"Some. Why?"

I was still turning it over in my mind, that he might have been the doctor who had to pronounce Mary-Evelyn dead. "I guess he must be really old. He must be sixty-five, at least."

"More like eighty, I'd guess." Behind his impenetrable sunglasses, I couldn't see his eyes. But his mouth smiled. "It may surprise you, but there are people that don't think sixty-five's really old."

"Is eighty?" I thought I should check, in case I was stepping on toes here. The Sheriff might have had an eighty-year-old relation.

"Yeah, I'd say eighty's old."

"Where does he live?"

The Sheriff looked somewhere off beyond me and nodded. "Up there on Valley Road. He's got an old house, a big Victorian house, at the top. It's not exactly woods, but his house is in the middle of a lot of trees and undergrowth. Pretty isolated place. Why? You thinking of visiting him?"

Sometimes the Sheriff annoyed me with his mind-reading. So I didn't tell him. I just shrugged the question off and said I was going to the library, and thanked him very much for offering to buy me a Coke.

The Abigail Butte County Library was a place even more necessary to my sense of well-being than Souder's Drug Store. I have no idea who Abigail Butte was, nor why the library was named after her.

It was not that I was "bookish" or a great reader; I read, but not widely (as my lack of knowledge about nearly everything should show). I just loved the quiet of the library, the fact that people spoke in whispers as if someone were ill or dying. Why I liked that kind of atmosphere, I don't know.

Except for the children's room, which was off to one side, everything else was in one big room: the counter where the head librarian checked the books out, the several tables where people could sit and read, a number of easy chairs for the same purpose, and, of course, the shelves. I loved to amble through the shelves, feeling entombed, hidden, thinking myself invisible and impossible to find.

Today I visited the section on gardening and then realized that was too general. I could have asked the librarian, Miss Babbit, who had never changed in all of the years I'd observed her (though it's true

my actual observing years weren't more than seven
or eight), but I would ask for information only as a
last resort. It was my belief that libraries, being
stuffed as they were with encyclopedias, dictionaries,
card catalogs, and a hundred ways of looking things
up and a thousand books to do it with—that it was
really giving in just to ask.

I checked the card catalog for "butterflies," then
went back to the shelves and pulled down several
books. I checked the pocket cards for Dr. McComb's
name and found "L. W. McComb" written in three
of them. Now, I didn't know if "L. W." was the
McComb I was interested in, but I could, of course,
ask Miss Babbit if he was old Dr. McComb. I thought
he must be; I didn't think there would be two
McCombs that interested in butterflies, not unless it
ran in the family. And also, the dates that L. W. had
checked them out were years ago, not last week,
which would also suggest Dr. McComb, since I imagine he would long ago have exhausted the resources
of the Abigail Butte Library.

So I settled down to read. I understood very
little of all of the technical description, but I did
enjoy the pictures in full color. I simply had no idea
there were all of these species of butterfly, my mind
having formed only a vague notion of them as fluttering wings, pale yellows or orangeish, or speckled
and dark-banded. That shows how observant I was.
But here were butterflies to be displayed on black
velvet, like jewels: emeralds, aquamarines, rubies.
They were really quite breathtaking.

For some moments I sat, frowning into space and trying to call up one subject I really knew a lot about. I knew nothing. My mind wandered over every conceivable category but came up blank. I certainly knew how to eat my mother's cooking, but not how to *cook* it. I looked at my hands, since my mind was a total loss. Did they have any knowledge? They couldn't cook, sew, play the piano, plant seedlings, carve wood. . . .

I was wasting my life. And I certainly wasn't going to get by on my looks. For a while, I sat there gluming away and searching my mental dictionary of "dis" words. "Dis-consolate." I guess it meant "dis-consoled." That was me. I sighed.

Then, continuing to turn the colored plates, I suddenly remembered there was a section on local points of interest, like the lake (the big one) and woods and parks, and any events that might be coming up. This La Porte shelf also housed books and articles by local people, especially local poets, or people who thought they were poets. (Even I, whose reading matter never extended very far beyond Nancy Drew and the local paper, could tell the poetry was awful.) And then I found what I wanted: a thin book about rare species of butterflies made up of several essays or articles by various men—teachers, professors, or men with advanced degrees—and one of them was Dr. McComb.

His particular article was a description of unusual butterflies that he knew about in our county, ones that he and his net had gone investigating, seeking out specimens in different areas. He wrote about the woods over by Comus, about seventy or eighty miles away; Paradise Valley, right across the railroad tracks beyond Spirit Lake; and Spirit Lake itself. This was better than I had ever expected to find, for already there appeared to be a bond between Dr. McComb and me, both of us searching out things connected with Spirit Lake. I had taken the little book back to my table, and as I sat there with my chin in my fisted hands, reading with heavy concentration, I had the queer feeling that Dr. McComb and I were supposed to meet. If I were a more dramatic-type person, I might even say *destined* to meet.

I really liked the way that Dr. McComb wrote: it wasn't at all like the writing in the books I had just been trying to read, dry as twigs and kind of superior, as if the scientists expected everyone must know Latin, and as if they disliked even to use the common term "butterfly." No, Dr. McComb wrote about his search for the "White Lace" (which is what he had named this butterfly) as if it were a story. He wrote:

> *It is the most elusive butterfly I have ever come across in my nearly fifty years of observation. I took up my position some distance back from the road, settled in my canvas chair for upwards of two hours and, although I saw many specimens of the West Virginia White and one variety of the Eastern Tailed Blue, I saw nothing of the*

*White Lace, so named because it reminded me of the Queen Anne's lace that lined the road, for its wings were edged just on the inside by tiny apertures, bare pinpricks through which light shone and gave this particular butterfly its luminous, gossamer appearance.*

*Recollecting I had seen it before nearer the lake, lighting on a dandelion stalk, I inferred that water must attract it and moved my "camp" (my gumboots and glass) in amongst the peaty grasses and stood in the shallow waters there for upwards of an hour. . . .*

In water for an hour! I can't even stand still for five minutes without scratching.

*. . . I was at last rewarded by the White Lace appearing suddenly, settling again on the milk-weed. I am sure it lit there for a full two minutes, slowly beating its wings. . . .*

Why, I wondered, didn't he net it? But he didn't. It sounded almost as if he had some kind of respect for this butterfly that he didn't have for the other kinds.

That very afternoon when I got back to the hotel, just before I had to get the salads ready for dinner, I set about finding something to use for a net. I would have borrowed Bunny's net, but she wasn't around. Then it struck me as strange that Bunny Caruso, the

outcast, was the only other person I could think of
who had this strange sort of connection with Dr.
McComb, for she was the only one I could think of
who ever bothered about butterflies around La Porte.

## FOURTEEN

I'm not sure why I chose the early morning for my search for the White Lace; the butterflies around Spirit Lake might not even be up yet. I suppose I had some vague idea that all excursions like this one should be undertaken at inconvenient and difficult hours, self-sacrifice being necessary for success (as it usually is, I've noticed).

In line with Dr. McComb's description of his own outing here, I stood watch near the edge of the lake, but not *in* it, as he had done, for I had no gumboots, only rubbers. I hated these rubbers; I hated being forced to wear them on rainy days to school. But I was glad for them that morning. I shivered in the knee-high grass, cold and dew-clammy, gripping my pool skimmer and a flat vegetable drainer I'd taken from the kitchen as I squinted through the white mist rising from the water. The butterfly box I had made with holes and with a window of plastic wrap sat a little ways away, by the roadside.

I figured I had a good hour before I had to be in the dining room setting syrup pitchers and jelly dishes on the tables. Vera, the hotel head-waitress, would be surprised to see me there before she was, for I think she prided herself on being up before anyone except my mother, who was always up at dawn and down in the kitchen making biscuits and rolls. It was best not to think too long about those biscuits (hot, small, the color of early-morning sunlight) as I stood with goosebumps covering my arms and legs, for thinking about the biscuits only led my mind wandering through the highways and byways of breakfast in general. Clouds of omelettes, corn cakes soaked in syrup, sausage, eggs over easy. I've eaten in restaurants where "eggs over easy" came to the table like they'd really lived a hard life, shriveled and brown-edged. Not only would my mother never *serve* such an egg, she would not allow an egg with a broken yolk to leave the kitchen. They had to be perfect, which also meant nongreasy. I've seen her apply a hanky to the barest trace of grease, and considering she cooked them in butter, the grease itself was pretty high-class. Those eggs absolutely glowed on the white china plate. Just about everything my mother cooked had its equivalent in cloth: silk (scrambled eggs); satin (fried eggs and cheese sauce); chiffon (omelettes and lemon pie). Even the pancakes felt like cashmere; I know this because I held one against my cheek once and it was soft and comforting.

Light began to penetrate the trees and the goldenrod and steal across the ivory carpet of water lilies at the far end of the lake. Soon the boathouse, midway, rose up from its comforter of fog. The four small boats that the summer people loved to row around in were tied to the dock pilings and floated there, motionless. It wasn't a large lake, probably no more than a mile or so of shoreline—although I thought "line" possibly the wrong word, for there didn't seem to be a clear break. Land stopped; water started. Nothing resembling a beach or a rocky shore existed. The peaty land became marsh, became water.

There was something in the half-light and half-dark that made me stop thinking of eggs over easy and corn cakes and how delicious and durable they were, and instead I began to wonder about my surroundings. In the light that was mostly shadows and a silence filled with faint twitterings I began to feel as if the world were coming awake for the first time— as if the dawn were not a repetition of the one yesterday or the day before, but something totally different. Of course, this was ridiculous; what would I know about previous dawns, not being an "early riser"? (Vera could certainly testify to this.) I sighed and stopped trying to philosophize and looked across the lake.

There sat the old Devereau house in its thicket of trees and shrubs. It was a way back from the lake and only two of its gabled windows, a chimney, and part of the high peaked roof were visible, in addition to patches of lattice-like porch railing visible through the pines and oaks. In a little stand of pines and largely hidden by them was a weathered gray statue that looked like the figure of a woman. It was hard to see from this distance. I thought the little statue strange, for it seemed a romantic thing for the Devereau sisters to have standing there, looking out over the lake that way.

One reason the house was difficult to make out

was that it was not painted white like most of the summer houses, but gray. Neither dark nor light, but a strange woodland gray, like the trunks of trees around it, which caused it to melt into its surroundings. Even I, who knew it was there, would have had a hard time picking it out had it not been for the sun making silver scabs of the gable windows.

The Devereau side of the lake was so overgrown, had suffered the crash of so many storm-struck trees, that the narrow dirt road that circled the lake, and which was fairly walkable two-thirds of the way around in each direction from where I stood now—this road disappeared into undergrowth, all but impassable on the far side. I know because I tried it several times. Each time I got a little bit closer and then was turned back, either by boggy, marshy land which I was afraid might be quicksand (too much time spent with Nancy Drew), or by strange noises—howlings or slitherings of imagined coyotes and rattlesnakes (too much time on Saturdays with Clint).

What I needed was for somebody to go with me, but there was no one. Even had a dozen people been dying to make the trip, there were very few I would want to share it with. I had asked my brother, Will, who had said he would, "sometime." But "sometime" hadn't rolled around yet, and I wondered why, as it would have been a real opportunity for him to make up all sorts of lies about snakes and so forth and scare the pants off me. I had even thought of asking the Sheriff (who, in addition to being smart and able-bodied, also had the advantage of being able to shoot, if it became necessary). But I was much too embarrassed to ask him; he thinks I'm too taken up in the death of Mary-Evelyn, anyway.

As I allowed myself to reflect pleasantly on the Sheriff hacking our way through hanging vines and branches, an object flickered just out of my line of vision. I turned to see a butterfly lighting on the tip of a pussy willow. It wasn't a White Lace, but it was quite pretty, large and brilliantly blue. Slowly, I drew the little library book from my pocket and turned the pages to see if I could find its picture. It sat there, swaying and waiting, giving me a chance to identify it. I found a picture which looked very similar, one of a species of blue butterflies called a Spring Azure. It shone in the pale sunlight. My gaze lifted ever so slightly from the page and roamed the lake water, where light was spinning in tiny waves stirred up by a fresh morning breeze. Across the lake's surface, insects skimmed the water in little furrows—dragonflies, I guessed, and water beetles.

The blue butterfly flicked itself away as I was debating reaching down for the pool skimmer, which I had dropped in the grass to take up the book. I sighed and waited some more. I would have liked to see, if not the famous White Lace, some other butterfly that Dr. McComb had described as rare in these parts. As I was thinking of the Mourning Cloak (the "Camberwell Beauty," a name I thought just wonderful, and wondered if it came from Camberwell or nearby), a little shower of what looked like copper coins lifted from the brambles by the roadside. Too far away to net, of course. I checked my book and decided they were just that—Copper butterflies.

In the next half-hour or forty-five minutes, several different species of butterfly glided over to check me out, some of them lighting, as the Spring Azure had done, on a tall blade of grass or pussy willow. I wondered what the tiny ones were, the clouds of pale yellow ones tinier than my little fingernail. It was hard to think of Dr. McComb killing and sticking pins in these specimens because of what he had written and the way he had written it.

And then I saw a large white butterfly dip, bank, curve around, and come to rest not far from me. I held my breath as I leaned closer, carefully, to see if its wings were riddled with tiny holes. No, it was just one of a variety of white butterflies. I stood and watched, not once bringing the pool skimmer or sieve into play, and knew I wouldn't, not if I stood here all day, for it just didn't seem right, somehow. The butterfly just rested there, unaware that I had its fate in my hands. Actually, it probably wasn't in all that much danger; I never have been well coordinated.

As I looked away from the butterfly and over the lake toward the Devereau house, I thought I surely must be seeing things.

For there she stood, the Girl. Away across the lake. She stood there in that dawn-colored dress with her moon-colored hair as if she were simply looking out over the water in the same way I was. As if she were looking at me. I dropped the net and the sieve in the water and actually rubbed my eyes. But when I looked again, she was still there, only farther back, half-hidden now in a little stand of ash and drooping white willows. In a way, she blended with them. Finally, she turned and walked back towards the house. I could see her for only a few steps, for the trees hid her. How long did I stand there looking at the opposite shore and the Devereau house? I don't know. I did not see her again.

In a way I was glad that I was nearly late for breakfast and that it was time to get back to the hotel dining room and go through the boring round of butter plates. It was one of my prebreakfast chores to carry the bowl of butter pats around and jab each with a fork. The butter was ice hard and always stuck to the prongs, and I'd have to shake to loosen it— jab and shake, jab and shake. At times I would sooner have got the butter out of the cow.

Oh, but then, of course, there were the corn cakes and eggs over easy to cheer me up as I plodded the hard dirt road. As I walked along in the blue-gray of seven o'clock, it was cool, almost cold, almost fall weather. And with fall, there would be *buckwheat* cakes! My mother's buckwheat cakes are beyond my power to describe. But I can see them in my mind's eye—brown-veined, crispy-edged, and just the right degree of sour.

I am not Catholic or of any particular creed, but I cross myself whenever I think of those buckwheat cakes.

## FIFTEEN

I kept the butterfly box, which I'd made from a small carton that once held Hunt's tomato sauce, for I had gone to a lot of trouble making the plastic-covered window, and I might be able to use it for something else.

After two helpings of corn cakes and a pitcher of maple syrup at breakfast, and several extra meatballs with my spaghetti at lunch, I decided I needed the exercise and walked the two miles into town and out the other side of it, on the road that led to the golf course and country club. The Sheriff had said that Dr. McComb lived on Valley Road, and that is where I headed.

I had called him before lunch to make an appointment to see him, telling him I wanted some information on butterflies, and he had sounded really nice. The minute I mentioned my mother and the Hotel Paradise, he had sounded truly delighted to see me, for he remembered me as a baby. I hoped that I wasn't going to be compared, at my present age, with how I was as a baby. Babies never seem to live up to their reputations.

On the other side of La Porte, I took Red Bird Road for about a half-mile until I came to a fork, where Valley Road began on the left. I passed only one dwelling, not a house, but one of those mobile homes made permanent by building a couple of steps and putting up an awning and plastic goose families. There were no real houses along Valley Road, not until the end of it, where Dr. McComb lived. His name was painted in white on a mailbox that sat atop a wooden pole.

The house resembled ones I'd seen in travel books about England. It had no porch at all, so that the land came right up to the door, which was surrounded by tall grass and lavender-blue gladioli, and the house looked as if it had sprouted right up from the ground. It looked a little mysterious, the sort of place Nancy Drew might stumble on when she was nosing around at dusk with her flashlight.

I walked up a path overgrown with grass and my favorite weeds—Queen Anne's lace and puffballs— and knocked on the door. I waited for some time, but no one answered. Dr. McComb had told me to come any time today, so I was sure someone was at home, unless he'd got to be like the old people in Weeks's Nursing Home who couldn't remember what they'd said five minutes ago. Eighty was pretty old; even the Sheriff agreed with that.

I knocked again, harder, and found the door opening. Should I walk in? Yes, I should, for he had probably left it open for me. He must be around, somewhere, out of hearing range.

Inside it was dark, the way the Orion movie house is dark; out of the shadows I had to blink up the shapes of chunky chairs and shawl-covered tables. It was chilly, too, much chillier than it was outside, where the sun was like a spotlight. It was almost as if I had walked from one season into another, spring into autumn. I preferred autumn; I always had. Summer had so much effort about it—all of that shouting on the beach, or smashing at tennis balls; or the big lake beyond La Porte churning in the wakes of speeding boats; or the flowers by the hotel porte cochere standing tall and bright, and birds swerving and screeching, and bees as loud as buzzsaws. Everything exaggerated, soundwise, colorwise. Everything exhausting, right down to sunsets streaming colors like flags. In the house here it was quiet and cool, and I was grateful.

Still, I wondered about such a reduced temperature for a man as old as Dr. McComb. Miss Flyte and Miss Flagler always seem to need to have their living quarters several degrees warmer than was common, and like to say their blood's thinning out. They wrap themselves in sweaters and shawls, and Miss Flagler on some days even opens the oven door "to take the chill off." Secretly I envy them their warm and muffled life, for it is saturated with stove smells, of molasses and dough and that wonderful bitter dipping chocolate that often perks on one of the burners.

Often I just sit, cocoa in hand, my eyelids drooping, and with the cat on the low shelf above me gently chewing my hair. Sometimes I even doze off, my chin dropping onto my chest. Once my hand slid the cocoa cup from my lap and spilled the cocoa all over Miss Flagler's linoleum. The two of them just pooh-poohed my embarrassment and my apologies, saying it wasn't any trouble, heavens to Betsy, it was only old linoleum. It's strange, I think, for me to enjoy these teatimes. For it's "no place for a twelve-year-old" (the voice of my mother) who "should be 'out'" (the voice of Mrs. Davidow, sending me to any place I didn't want to go) "making friends my own age" (the voice of Ree-Jane).

It's as if I were doing something shameful in enjoying the company of these old people. I wonder about all of the ones in Weeks's Nursing Home, where I sometimes go to take a cake or Parker House rolls that my mother has made for them (my mother being quite charitable). I know that some of them are miserable, for they weep; some are angry, for they shout; but there are others who seem content to sit and stare out of windows. These have the settled look of fallen and heaped leaves and appear to me, in their thin robes and slippers, to be almost comfortable, and I imagined myself leaping into their laps as I might have leapt, when I was younger, into a great pile of leaves. These were only fancies, and probably dumb ones, for everyone told me how pitiable these old people were and how dreadful it would be to grow old and have to go live in Weeks's Nursing Home. I could certainly understand why Mrs. Davidow wouldn't want to, because I never see any bottles of Southern Comfort or Gordon's gin around. I said to Mrs. Davidow one day when she was driving us to the nursing home to deliver my mother's cakes and rolls that I didn't see why there shouldn't be a

cocktail hour at Weeks's Nursing Home. It would
make a lot of them a lot happier, and what difference
did it make if you were a raving alcoholic at age
ninety? And we drove on, in almost jolly fashion,
to talk about how brilliant it would be for some of
the patients there; how Helene Baum's mother-in-
law must be missing her old fashioneds before dinner
(for she certainly wasn't missing Helene, said Mrs.
Davidow, and we laughed fit to kill), and how much
more elegant Ruth Baum would look with a tumbler
of bourbon in her hand.

Around Dr. McComb's dark living room I
drifted, dry and leaflike myself, touching things just
to touch them: the lace antimacassars, the silver-
framed photos collected on a side table, the dark
wood of the doorframe and the piano, the fringed
silk shawls, the heavy drapes, the wallpaper itself,
which was cool and damp, patterned with wide bands
of leaves. Yes, it was an autumn room, no doubt of
it, and I felt as I did in Miss Flagler's kitchen, or
walking through the candle forest of Miss Flyte's
shop, I felt we were all those drifting leaves, slowly
falling, settling. I plunked a few keys with two fingers; I played the first bar of "Clair de Lune," which
was all I'd learned in my piano lessons with the local
teacher. I'd take lessons for a few months, then stop;
then I'd start up again a year later. I never learned
anything more complicated than a few bars of "Clair
de Lune." After my piano playing (which I hoped
might bring Dr. McComb—where was he?) I moved
over to have a good look at a tray of milk and

doughnuts set beside the easy chair. I sat down— *sank* down, really, in cushions that felt stuffed with clouds. I looked at the plate and decided it had been left either for Santa Claus or for me. I picked up a doughnut, studied it, decided it was store-bought (not that that was a sin), and used it as a sort of binocular, the hole serving as lens, for looking through at the portrait on the far wall. It was a grim-faced woman who looked like she'd really give them hell if she ever landed up in Weeks's Nursing Home. And she didn't look like she needed a drink, either.

I munched the doughnut around the edge and the white powdered sugar sifted down onto my shirt front. Then I had a drink of milk and polished off the doughnut. The other one was cinnamon, and I decided to save it in case I might be here for a few days waiting for Dr. McComb.

I dusted the powdered sugar from my shirt and wondered if maybe this offering of food might be a trap—not for me, but for Dr. McComb's archenemy—and that it was poisoned. This was really arsenic powder I was flicking from my chest. I decided that if the sugar doughnut was poisoned, I might as well eat the cinnamon while I still had my wits about me, and started in on it, with sips of milk in between chews. I thought perhaps this was Dr. McComb's way of letting me know he'd be late and to make myself comfortable. It was very unusual for an older person to go to this kind of trouble for a child. Dr. McComb must fit into the category of Miss Flyte and Miss Flagler, then. Sitting in that cloudlike chair and with two doughnuts and a tall glass of milk inside me, I began to feel sleepy. It wasn't until a hand was on my shoulder that I realized I must have fallen asleep.

The hand that shook me awake, and pretty roughly too, was at the end of a long black sleeve that did not belong to Dr. McComb, for it was a woman's face that I looked up at. The face was sharp with nose and cheekbones, and the black hair strained back from it into a coil, as if it, the hair, were responsible for the backward tilt of the head. This face looked down at me disapprovingly, to say the least. Its expression was not exactly angry, but very fierce. I thought maybe they were *her* doughnuts and milk I'd just eaten.

"Oh. Hello," I said, rubbing my face awake.

But she did not answer; she kept her lips sealed together and her hands clasped in front of her waist. She was wearing a black dress that looked as if it would really appeal to Aurora Paradise. It reached nearly to the tops of her black shoes and had a high neck. A smothering sort of dress.

She took the chair opposite me as if she were settling herself down for talk, unpleasant as that might be.

Since she still said nothing, I began. "I've come to see Dr. McComb. He knows I'm coming." I was a little defensive.

She didn't answer, she just turned to look at the fire as if I hadn't spoken, as if I weren't there at all.

Then I thought, Well, maybe she's totally deaf, but I decided that wasn't the case when the clock struck and she turned towards it, listened to it take forever to chime the hour of three, and then turned her gaze back to the fire. There was nothing I could do except to join her in watching it.

Who could she be? No one, not the Sheriff nor anyone had mentioned Dr. McComb had a wife or a sister. She could be a housekeeper. But would a housekeeper just sit down in the living room like this in the presence of a stranger? Yet, she fit the role of housekeeper; she looked like Mrs. Danvers in *Rebecca*. Acted like her, too, as if I were the new mousy person come to stay and she was jealous as all get out. I ran this script through my mind but didn't get anywhere with it, because I was me, and I was twelve, and no one was going to be jealous of a twelve-year-old, much less me. So we sat and stared at the fire. At one point she picked up the poker and gave a half-burned log a few quick jabs and then sat holding the poker beside her like a cane. I would have preferred she put it down, but she didn't.

And then, as if her whole mission in life was just to come in and wake up any strangers that might be hanging around the living room—she left. She just rose, smoothed her skirt, and walked out without so much as a glance in my direction.

I sat still in my easy chair, frowning. I couldn't imagine what I was to do. Go away, probably. I was just sighing myself out of the chair preparatory to

doing this when an old man appeared in the doorway.
Dr. McComb, it must be. At least I hoped it wasn't
any more of his relatives.

"There you are! I was wondering."

*He* was wondering? But I didn't argue because
I was really glad to see him. "Hello. I've been sitting
here. I didn't know where you were."

"Henhouse," he said, looking around and patting his pockets as if he were searching for new-laid
eggs.

He wasn't as old-looking as I expected. If Dr.
McComb was eighty or more, he was in awfully
good shape. He was about medium height and build
and had white hair and a moustache and a complexion
that was fine and petallike, of the sort I was used to
seeing in Weeks's Nursing Home.

I was suddenly embarrassed by my appearance.
I was conscious of my skirt being too long, long like
an old lady's, and my brown "corrective" shoes being
too big and chunky. And since Dr. McComb was a
doctor, I suspected he could see into me, see all of
my organs floating around in whatever murky liquid
they lived in, and see through my eyes to my brain
and figure out my little butterfly scheme.

Dr. McComb smiled, though, and greeted me
as if he had known me a long time. I quickly told
him about the white butterfly I'd seen. And I told
him I'd read his article (which was very good, I
added), and that I often went down the road to the
lake, for butterflies were my main hobby, and when
I had seen this particular butterfly I wondered if it

could possibly be the one called White Lace. After I told him all of this I was out of breath. I talk hard and fast when I'm lying.

He asked me a couple of questions, thought over my answers, and then said, almost sadly, no, he didn't think so, that the one I'd seen sounded like—and he said a long Latin name that I couldn't understand.

"Oh," I said, pretending I knew exactly what that was, and trying to sound disappointed.

"If you're a collector too, you might want to come with me now." He looked back through the open door. "There's a painted lady out there I've been tracking. I'm sure you'd like a glimpse of it. I've got a net you can use, too."

Outside, his smile implied such confidence in my being as interested as he was, that I felt ashamed of myself, and accepted the butterfly net with more enthusiasm than I felt. I followed him through the square of bright light framed by the side door and out into the backyard. But it couldn't really be called a "yard." For one thing, there were no visible boundaries—the weedy land stretched away as far as the woods. Except for the area right outside of the door, through which a rude path had been worn, there was no sign of any pruning, mowing, or cutting ever having been done. Even the grass beside the door was shin-high; when we got twenty feet farther, it was up to my knees, then nearly to my waist. I had the sensation of walking from dry land into deeper and deeper water.

In among the other weeds were masses of verbena, black-eyed Susans, coneflowers, Queen Anne's lace, thistle, in addition to all of the small and large fruit trees, oaks, and drooping willows.

"We don't cut the grass or trim the hedges or deadhead flowers here; we wouldn't want to disturb the butterflies' habitat, or the birds' either. So we leave the vegetation alone. Over there's the bright patch, see? I've got my nectar plants in there; I've got my Indian blanket, my verbena, and my butterfly bush. They like weeds, too—milkweed, joe-pye weed—"

"Like Queen Anne's lace," I said, knowledgeably. Had Ree-Jane done me a service? Even if she had, she'd never meant to.

Dr. McComb nodded, wiped his neck with his handkerchief. "Mostly I've got nectar plants."

"How do they drink?" Then I realized too late that was something I should know, given they were my "hobby."

"They taste through their feet."

Well, I couldn't help it. I just whooped. I thought maybe he was kidding me, but he said no, no, that was the absolute truth. Through their feet. I looked down at mine. What if it was my *feet* that got to taste my mother's ham rolls and cheese sauce? Or the Angel Pie? My feet instead of my mouth? For once, I was pretty sure God knew what he was doing.

\*   \*   \*

It was vegetation all right. Now I'd progressed inward to where the buffalo and blue grass, the vines and weeds were just about to my chin, and one patch—more butterfly bushes?—into which I'd stepped too quickly, was almost over my eyes. As I stood thrashing about at the tall stalks that grazed and tickled my face, I heard Dr. McComb call to me.

"You there? Hey?"

I thrashed around a bit more and held the net up above my head, like a flag. I emerged, if not into anything like a "clearing," at least into growth that wasn't higher than my waist.

"There you are! Find anything interesting?"

I hadn't been *looking* for anything, but I didn't want to sound unemployed. After mentally racking my brain, calling up a quick succession of colored plates from my library book, I said—tentatively, of course—"I thought maybe I saw a Ghost Brimstone."

He snorted good-naturedly. "Around *these* parts? I don't think so. You see those down in South America, mostly."

Trust me to pick the wrong country. "I only said I *thought*." I was getting peevish.

We had moved forward through this jungle and were now walking slowly along a dirt path. It was only about a foot wide but it looked like civilization to me. I made several sweeps with the butterfly net, awfully grateful to Bunny Caruso that she'd given me some experience. I probably looked pretty well-trained the way I could flick my wrist and whoosh the net around.

A few stops and starts farther along, I said, "When I was at Spirit Lake—"

"*Sssssshhhh!*" Dr. McComb stopped, squinted into the hazy distance, his rather thick white eyebrows making a little shelf when I looked at him in profile. Since his *ssssshhhh*ing was loud enough to wake the dead, I didn't see why he bothered. And anyway, butterflies didn't have ears, did they? They couldn't actually *hear*, could they? He started whispering, the barest murmur. "Look along the path there amongst the marigolds. About two o'clock from where you stand. That's a Little Wood Satyr, bet you anything."

"Ummmm," I said. That was pretty noncommittal.

"What do you think? Is it?"

I managed to nod and shake my head almost simultaneously. Fortunately, the butterfly spread its wings and made a drowsy exit, giving him a better look. No, he decided it was not a Little Wood Satyr, thus relieving me of declaring it one thing or another.

"They patrol, you know."

"Who does? You mean Little Wood . . . ?" I managed to have a coughing spell.

"For females."

I had no idea what he was talking about, so I mumbled agreement. We moved along in silence then, for a few feet. Above the dogbane patch, hundreds of tiny butterflies, white and yellow and no

bigger than my fingernail, floated in such an unbro-
ken cover they might have been white mist and yellow fog.

"Look at them all!" I exclaimed.

It was Dr. McComb's turn to say *"ummmm."*
Then, "Dainty Sulfurs, maybe."

I marveled at the cloud of Dainty Sulfurs.

"It's the milkweed that grows out here. They
love that."

"I guess there's none of that stuff around Spirit
Lake, is there?" I said, prompting him. "At least,
I've never seen any at Spirit Lake." But he said
nothing, just stood there looking sleepily at the blan-
ket of butterflies, and I went on: "Did you go to
Spirit Lake again to look for the White Lace?"

"Umm. Several times."

"It's too bad they let the lake get so run-down,
isn't it? It's kind of swampy now; well, you'd know
that, if you've been there lately." Again, he didn't
answer. I looked at him, the way he stood on the
walk, stock-still and hoped he wasn't going into a
coma. "I saw pictures of Spirit Lake like it was a
long time ago. Forty years, maybe. When it wasn't
so overgrown. There was a boathouse. Well, there
still is, but it's mostly a ruin." He didn't comment.
"Yes, it's mostly in ruins now. Oh, I guess you could
still take one of the boats out. The boats are still
there. But I guess they'd spring a leak." He blinked
and blinked his eyes slowly as I talked, leaning a
little into the dogbane, as if he might pull them
towards him, the butterflies, like a coverlet, and just

lie down there and go to sleep. "There's a house the other side—"

"Devereau," he said suddenly, and to my surprise, as he slowly brought his net around, skimming air. There was a beautiful specimen, rose and lavender and the deepest blue, poised on a hollyhock, that I hadn't even seen. He'd been tracking it with his eyes. But it flew off just as he was about to bring the net down on it. He sighed, heavily.

"Gee, that's too bad. That's really too bad." Now, of course, I'd have to pump the Devereau talk up again, like a deflated balloon. This was work. Dr. McComb stood staring into the blue-gray distance, braced for a sighting, a discovery. I really wasn't sure why I had to be so cagey. Why, if I wanted information, didn't I just flat-out ask for it? Maybe I thought that if there was information I shouldn't have—that is, some kind of knowledge that my mother or others thought I shouldn't have, then I was obliged to weasel it out of people. "It's a nice house, the Devereau house, only it's gone to seed. I wonder why no one lives there now. It looks like no one's *lived* there for, oh, maybe *forty years*." I glanced at him to see if that number got a reaction. But he hadn't flinched, or moved from his combative, hunter's stance, net held to his side like a shotgun, as if he meant to shoot them instead of net them.

I was trying to think of another approach when he surprised me by saying, "Probably because of the Tragedy."

My eyes opened wide. I was thrilled, stupefied nearly, by such a direct reference to the death of Mary-Evelyn and even more by its being so named: the Tragedy.

"The Tragedy?"

"Little girl drowned."

"She drowned? How?"

He turned now to look at me. His round glasses were suddenly stabbed by rays of sunlight and transformed to silver discs. "She was your age."

Involuntarily, I stepped backwards, feeling my legs crowding into briars and raspberry patch. The air that had seemed so thin, clear and blue, thickened. All of the tiny sounds—cicadas, crickets, gently sowing grasses—came together, thrummed.

I started to say, "My—" but my throat was thick too, my vocal cords stiff and strained. The field, the henhouse, the weeds and flowers, and Dr. McComb himself all seemed to have shifted in some weirdly sinister fashion. He was still looking at me, the discs of his glasses like bright ice. I thought the only person I had ever seen look friendly even behind black-mirrored glasses was the Sheriff. I swallowed, hard. I wished he was here.

But just as quickly, the day tilted back, righted itself as Dr. McComb shoved his glasses atop his head and snapped up his binoculars. "Ah!"

The backs of my legs, my calves, felt laced with bramble and thorny pricks as I moved out of the patch to hear Dr. McComb swear softly that, no, it was only a common cabbage white. I was glad; pursuit of the rare variety would have meant working up the death of Mary-Evelyn all over again.

"You said she was drowned?" I had to remind him.

He nodded.

I chewed the inside of my mouth. "Gee, and she was only twelve?"

Dr. McComb nodded, but said nothing else, until after a few moments he said, "Well, time for a cup of java. Want some?"

Disappointed as I was that I couldn't keep the subject going, still I was pleased that he thought I was old and sophisticated enough for coffee. "Sure," I said, with a "why not?" shrug.

We retraced our steps to the house, he whacking absently at tough, brown stubble; me, thinking over how to reintroduce the subject of Mary-Evelyn. I followed along towards the kitchen door, a door whose sill was lost in another tangle of vines and Queen Anne's lace, as if this end of the house was sinking into the soft earth.

Retreating from the dense sunlight of the thickets and fields into this cool, shadowy room—the kitchen—I had to squint things into existence once again. The aluminum-handled refrigerator door, the white enamel stove on its curved legs were identifiable in the gloom. But other objects—like the kitchen table, the ladder-back chairs—I had to blink up, finally, to make them out. I came up with big chests and a small one, and an old icebox, and against the far wall what I think was called a Welsh dresser, on which I could see rows of plates and cups, and as my eyes adjusted to the kitchen's grayness, I saw they were the Blue Willow pattern.

I was sitting on a stool by the white kitchen table as Dr. McComb puttered around, getting out the Pyrex coffee maker, measuring water and Maxwell House. And in this kind of dim, dull light, where objects were not clear-cut, but the lines of things were muffled, like sounds, I had the jolting thought that I would never find a proper place, a place that was my place, and that I could look and look and I could settle down here and there, but it would all be only a dream. This shocked me, absolutely, because the Hotel Paradise had *always* been "my" place— my family's, and my family was, of course, mine. I belonged to it. But now I didn't feel I belonged to it or to any place, even though I had always walked the dusty old roads of Spirit Lake and the two-mile highway into La Porte, and I wished right now my shoes were held down by mud, thick hands of mud fastening me down. Earth holding me to earth.

But look! Look how easily the hands unclasped, how easily the Davidows had come and laid claim to it all—my hotel, my walks and roads, my past. My present.

Was that *possible*? I heard the refrigerator door open and shut. No, it wasn't. None of that belonged to the Davidows any more than to me. That moment outside when Dr. McComb had turned his bright, icy spectacles on me, I thought now that inward eyes, not mine, were picking up something on another wave length and that I had resisted this, shoved it back because it was too frightening, had swept some knowledge away like cobweb paste in front of my eyes. For some reason, all of this brought to mind the old store in Spirit Lake. Not Britten's, not the bustling one that everyone bought at, but the small dark one on the other side of the village, more of a ramshackle house really, owned by an old lady who must have decided she could earn a living by selling basic supplies—nothing fancy like Britten's, with its separate meat counter (and even a butcher, one of the Brittens), or its big see-through crates of cookies, or its glass-topped counters of penny candy. No, this old store was dark and spare, its shelves nearly empty, just some cans of soup and beans. The brightest thing in it was the rows of Wonder bread. The loaves shone in their white wrappers. Shadows and gloom and glimmering Wonder bread.

And then I thought of Ree-Jane's bright lipstick, her crayon-colored clothes (faded colors by the time I got them), and that party dress my mother had made for her, yards of tulle with rainbows of sequins tossed all over it. And I wonder now, does life really need all of that cheap, bright adornment? Or is it better to have the plain, spare room with its glimmering Wonder bread?

I heard thunder gathering in the distance, and in a moment drops of rain slapped the roof. At the window, light drew down like a blind and nearly vanished altogether, leaving the kitchen in greater gloom, and yet increasing my feeling of well-being. I did not quite understand why, rain and shadows generally being associated with sadness and misery. So to think better, I looked down at the floor. I'd have closed my eyes, only Dr. McComb would have asked me, "Why've you got your eyes closed?"

I let him move about the kitchen, whistling under his breath, as I thought of the henhouse, the chickens ganged up inside, pecking, ruffling feathers, or sitting fatly on straw, maybe laying an egg or two (however they did this), despite the rain now belting the rooftops and the thunder really bellowing. Weather didn't give them cause for comment. Rain, sunlight, ice, spring. I guessed the chickens noted it and acted accordingly. I bet they didn't even bother to leave the dirt yard and go in. Without even thinking how stupid the question was, I asked Dr. McComb.

"Some do, some don't," he answered, setting down empty mugs and a plate of brownies. Then he moved off again to the stove.

This struck me as both a sensible answer and a sensible mode of behavior. You got in out of the rain or you didn't, depending on how you felt about rain. Dr. McComb had apparently taken my question as matter-of-fact and answered in kind.

I turned to the window, squinting rather than looking straight, for in that way I could project better what was in my mind, which was filling up with weather. The old store, the kitchen gloom, Spirit Lake: they all shared something. There was a secret hidden in them, some secret of lostness. I saw the

Girl. I thought of her that way: the Girl. Through my half-shut eyes, I saw Spirit Lake, the rain pocking its gray surface, the wind ruffling its edges, rocking the carpet of water-lilies.

The Girl.

I saw her standing there on the opposite shore, just standing, arms straight down at her sides, her hair that strange color of the moon. Her dress was very light, glimmering like the enamel stove here in the corner, or the Wonder bread in the bare store. She had been sitting on that railroad platform, too, empty-handed, except for the small purse clutched in her fist. And then again on the sidewalk in La Porte, in her flower-sprigged cotton dress: nothing but what she held in one hand. It was as if she had no possessions at all; and far from seeming sad to me, it struck me that nothing held her down to any time or place. She seemed weightless.

"Are you in a trance or having a fit or what?"

I jumped at Dr. McComb's voice. "Huh?"

"Your eyes are squinted shut and your lips are moving. Here, have a brownie."

He shoved the brownies toward me. They were very rich-looking, dark dollops of icing in their centers. "I was just thinking," I said coolly, looking for the brownie with the most icing. But Dr. McComb grabbed it first.

"Huh!" The grunt sounded as if he didn't believe me. He poured coffee into the thick white mugs. I would have liked the Blue Willow cups better, but probably they saved that china for special occasions. Yet, I doubted that there were many "special occasions" celebrated in the McComb house. That brought back to mind the strange woman in the living room. Where had she gone? Who was she? I did not ask, because I didn't want to leave the Devereau business, but even more because I figured if Dr. McComb wanted her noticed or mentioned, he'd do the mentioning himself. Maybe she was an embarrassment to him. Maybe he didn't even know she was around. That sounds crazy, but I've come more and more to suspect people just wander around and into your life (or your house) without prior notice, that they just pop up on the walk or in your doorway. A face at the window—whose? Life is just so disorganized and crazy it hardly bears saying.

I didn't really want to mention the Girl, but I remembered his reply to the chicken question and decided he could probably be trusted not to ask me the usual one million questions that grown-ups generally reserve—"What makes you ask that?" "Why do you want to know?" "Who told you that? Did anyone tell you that?"—for any kid asking anything the least bit unexpected.

"Did you ever see anyone over at the Devereau house on Spirit Lake?"

He shook his head. He was eating around the edges of his brownie, saving the icing for last.

"Well, I did."

"You did?" His old forehead pleated neatly in

surprise. "But how'd they get around to that house? Must have had to cut through all of that under-growth."

I sipped my coffee and added another two spoonsful of sugar. "Well, someone did."

"What was he doing?"

"She. Nothing. Just standing there."

"Maybe it's one of the real estate agents." He frowned.

"I don't think so."

But he wouldn't let the idea go. "Maybe it's that bum Henderson. Only, you said 'she.' "

The nice thing about Dr. McComb was that he didn't tell me I hadn't seen anyone. Nearly any other adult (except for the Sheriff and Maud) would have told me that I probably saw something else and just *thought* it was a person. A cow, maybe?

Dr. McComb was still talking about the real estate agent. "That bum Henderson got back there a couple years ago in his goddamned Cherokee Chief and hacked out a kind of path because he was looking to sell it. What a shyster, what a slime bucket! Ought to lock up people like that. You know him?"

I shook my head and sort of flowered in the light of his assumption that I was capable enough to have had dealings with La Porte slime buckets. And to listen to swear words without flinching.

He polished off the icing-middle of his brownie, licked his fingers, slurped some coffee. Then he went searching around the kitchen and came back with a dish and a half-smoked, shredded cigar. He started to light up, stopped, said, "Mind if I smoke?"

As if I were used to people asking me if I minded—no one ever had in my living memory—I casually waved my hand in a "go right ahead" gesture. I was interested in the last brownie on the plate, but didn't want to be a pig. He pushed the plate toward me. I took it and munched.

Thoughtfully, watching the smoke eddy around him, he said, "Wonder who it was. This woman, you said?"

"Yes."

"What did she look like?"

For some reason, I didn't want to say. I frowned. Why didn't I want to tell him? "She was too far off to see—I mean, enough to tell her features."

He smoked. I ate the rest of my brownie. The silence was pleasant, like the little silences in Miss Flagler's kitchen. The clock ticked. There was no cat, though. Then I said, "Maybe she's a Devereau."

Dr. McComb said, "Haven't been any around here since that inquest. Sisters all left. And they must be dead by now."

"Rose wouldn't be. She was young then."

He frowned as if he didn't much credit that idea. "Rose Devereau. Yes, I do vaguely remember her. Rose Souder, her name used to be." His frown deepened. "So how do you know about her?"

"My great-aunt Paradise was telling me about her."

Dr. McComb gave a sort of sighing laugh. "Aurora Paradise."

The way he said it and shook his head you would have thought "Aurora Paradise" was cause for all of the world's confusion. He said it again, laughing again.

I said, "When the Tragedy struck"—the capital still sent a pleasant little chill down my back—"I'd have thought she'd have been around." I put my brownie down.

"Yes, you'd have thought. I wasn't their doctor and I hardly had anything to do with the Devereaus. No one ever mentioned any relations living other places."

"Who was the doctor?"

"Well, there was Dr. Jenks back then."

"Was he doctor to most people?"

"Uh-huh."

"I guess he had all the patients. I bet it's hard to get people to switch doctors." I remembered Aurora yelling around about some "new sawbones" who came to see her once.

"Certainly is."

"How come you had to go when they found her instead of Dr. Jenks? Wasn't he the police doctor?" I couldn't remember what the Sheriff had called that kind of doctor.

"Well, he wasn't in town that night. Had to go see to some sick family over in Hebrides, as I recall."

"So she drowned."

His cigar had gone out and he was trying to

puff it alive again as he nodded his head. It looked pretty shredded and awful.

I slid down in my chair and tinkered around with my coffee cup and hoped I sounded casual. "It's kind of funny. I mean, her being twelve and being out in a boat *alone* and *at night*." I looked at him.

"Who said it was at night?"

"You did. You just did."

"Oh." He picked bits of tobacco from his lip.

Into the silence, blue shadows fell and moved, graceful as sheer curtains, across the window behind him. How long had I been here? "It's kind of, well, funny. Strange." The clock ticked; I looked over at it. Five-thirty! I would have jumped out of my chair if Dr. McComb hadn't said just then:

"I thought so too." He cleared his throat. From his voice and his expression I could tell he felt really uncomfortable.

So I kept fast to my chair, and I didn't say anything, for he had drawn into one of those quiet inward-looking silences that grown-ups sometimes do when they're sizing up the past. I did not speak.

He cleared his throat again. "Yes. I thought so, too. Thing was, just like you say, *why* would that little girl be in that boat? It didn't make any sense. No sense at all." He shook his head. "But what could I say? What could I do?" Dr. McComb was not really asking me these questions; maybe he'd even forgot I was there. I did not speak. "Well, the three of them—the older sisters, Rose being gone—they just . . . *hung* over me. I mean, they just stood there, by the lake, all wrapped in those dark shawls and capes and . . . hung over me. You didn't know the Devereau girls." His chin fell slowly, nearly to his chest. And for a moment he seemed to be more my age than his own. Slowly his pale eyes fastened on me and then blinked as if he were bringing my face into focus.

I shook my head. I did not speak.

"It was a long time ago." He turned over the spoon by his cup, turned it again and again. "The only other person who said he'd been around that night, near the house, was Alonzo Wood. Do you know him?"

My eyes widened. The clock struck off another quarter-hour like it knew I was going to catch it, for I would not be back to get the salads ready for dinner. But even if that B&O freight train had been rushing right through the kitchen wall, with Vera engineering, you couldn't have pried me away from my seat. Not for anything. *"Who?"*

"Alonzo. Call him something really silly, like Ulab, or something."

"Ulub. Ulub and Ubub. The Wood boys? *I know them!*" I had seldom been so excited in my whole life.

"Well, Alonzo said he was there. I mean, that's what I *think* he said. He'd've been, oh, maybe in his early teens back then. And his brother, the tall one—"

"Ubub, they call him. I'm not sure about his name. Bob, it might be."

"Where'd they ever get those ridiculous nicknames?"

I was fidgeting so much, with the anxiety of
waiting for information, you would have thought I
had to pee. I didn't want to waste time on nicknames.
"From their license plates."

"*License* plates?"

"It was a joke, sort of. The letters were all but
the same. But go on with your story." He was looking
now at his wristwatch and I was afraid he was going
to tell me to get out, to go back to the hotel and do
my waitress work. That was silly.

"Well, Alonzo, or *U*-lub"— he shook his head
to let me know how he disapproved of the nickname—"came around to see me. They both did. I
guess the brother—Robert?—was older and he was
sort of backing him up. You know, lending him
encouragement. It seems Alonzo was near the lake,
or near the house, that night, and he told a different
story."

I was still as stone. But when he stopped talking
I was afraid he'd stopped forever. "Go on. What'd
he say?"

Dr. McComb looked at me and smiled slightly,
as if this was some kind of checker game and he'd
just run roughshod over my reds or blacks. "Well, I
don't know. I couldn't understand him."

"*What?*" I nearly shouted it at him. How could
he smile over missing such important news? I just
couldn't believe it.

"If you ever talked to him, you'd know what I

mean. I was patient enough, and his brother kept trying to interpret for him, but that's a case of blind leading blind, you know."

Then he must have sensed my disappointment. Really, I thought I could cry to think that someone knew and yet it was locked inside of him. Dr. McComb said, "But I did write down some of it. In a notebook. Do you want to see it?"

I was astounded. Did I!

Dr. McComb left the kitchen and I heard him in the living room and it sounded as if he were frenziedly tossing things around. In a few moments he was back. "You're the only person who's ever seemed at all interested. Maybe you can make something of it."

Speechlessly, I nodded as he put the notebook down on the table. It was a plain school notebook, one of those with a mottled black-and-white cardboard cover and a white square for putting in your name. "You mean I can take it with me?"

"Uh-huh, if you want. Thing is—what difference could it make now? That's forty years ago. Hardly anyone around now who was there then. Aurora Paradise, maybe."

"Ulub and Ubub," I said, as I stroked the notebook, cool and smooth under my hand.

# SIXTEEN

*When the leaves fall, you can see—*

The notebook wedged inside my thin jacket, I made it back to the hotel in record time, because Dr. McComb very kindly drove me. I thought he drove very well for a man of his years; his hands didn't even shake on the steering wheel. I asked him please to drop me off at the end of the drive, as I really didn't want to answer a lot of questions about where I'd been, and so forth. Not that there was anything wrong with where I'd been, or that my mother wouldn't approve, but I just didn't feel like answering a lot of questions. He understood.

The notebook under my mattress and my white uniform on, I ran down the stairs and into the dining room, where Miss Bertha and Mrs. Fulbright were already seated solid as rocks, dinner having begun a half-hour before. Vera was whisking through the dining room, her tray of water and rolls held nimbly on her fingertips. The tray hid my quick entrance from view.

I went to the salad table. Fortunately, Mrs. Davidow wasn't around in the kitchen. Mrs. Davidow always could find the time to rant at me; my mother, however, counted herself too busy to waste much time bawling me out beyond the knife-like look she gave me which cut me dead—or at least down. She was preparing pork chops for browning in the buttery pan sizzling on the stove—browned and then baked with apples and onions. Cutting bits of bone from a pork chop with the cleaver seemed to sluice off the anger she felt for me as it went *whack* through meat and bone, as if she were saying, "This chop showed up—" *WHACK!*—"when it was supposed to—"*WHACK!*—"because this chop is dependable—" *WHACK!*

I tried to ignore the cleaver by concentrating on what was left to do at the salad table. Anna Paugh had completed about a dozen salads, so there weren't many more to make. On the iceberg lettuce I arranged tomato quarters, a green pepper ring, and an onion ring. There was a little dish of black olives sitting beside the crock of French dressing, and I decided to be a little creative and carefully cut the olives in half and placed the halves dead center. This green, red, and black palette I thought quite pretty until Vera appeared, slipping up to my elbow and picking each olive half off the salads, onto which she spooned the French dressing for her customers. Then she whisked over to the main table and deftly called out her two orders before she spun out of the kitchen with her tray of salads. Vera stirred up breezes in her brisk turns and pauses. She might have been a ballet dancer, only she wasn't pretty enough.

Although the salads were not to be "dressed" until the diners chose their salad dressings, I decided to adorn three or four of them with my mother's Roquefort-dressing-without-equal. I know there are

people who hate Roquefort cheese dressing. But they
have never tasted my mother's. It is the picture of
simplicity: Roquefort (well, blue cheese, as times are
hard) and oil. Just those two ingredients. The trouble
is, most people (like Helene Baum) don't know how
to put the two together. The dressing is like velvet.
I capped the salads with it and replaced the discarded
black olive halves, studding them atop the glossy
white dressing. I finished them off with just a powder-
ing of paprika. They looked quite lovely.

Mrs. Fulbright and Miss Bertha were my dining-
room charges. Miss Bertha was difficult, and cheap
to boot. Vera always knew where the tips were. But
her dinner companion, Mrs. Fulbright, was as sweet
as could be. She wore black voile and was ancient—
she might have been even ninety—and she knew
Aurora Paradise and would always ask after her, as
if Aurora were in some foreign place rather than
upstairs.

Miss Bertha reminded me of a silver snail, with
her gray hair worn in a bun, a gray dress of some
shiny stuff that reflected light like rain, and a corset
like a shell. Her small body seemed hard and com-
pact, armored against the world. She had a really
mean streak. Of course, she could hardly hear at all
and wore a hearing aid big as a fist with a battery
that was always running down. About the only thing
that didn't have to be repeated to her a hundred or
so times was the whistle of the passing B&O train.
So after several tries of telling her what was out in
the kitchen for dinner and having her say "What?

. . . what? . . . what?" I'd just yell. Naturally, that would bring Vera fast on her feet and she would later report the incident to my mother, saying, well, *she* had no trouble at all taking Miss Bertha's order, and no one paid any attention to me saying, "Of course she could, because I'd just yelled out 'PORK CHOPS OR MEAT LOAF? PORK CHOPS OR MEAT LOAF?'" or whatever happened to be out in the kitchen on a given night. No one ever paid any attention to me.

Will and I were always getting lectured on How to Treat the Aged. It was really irritating. My argument was that the aged had been around for decades longer than me and they should know by now that life was really tough. Whereas *I* was only twelve and had yet to learn.

I argued. Will smiled. Will would just stand there with his bright brown eyes agleam for all the world as if he just adored these lectures and was soaking up *every* word, when I knew he wasn't paying the least bit of attention. His way was to pretend life was just great and then go away and do what he wanted, which included things like going to Miss Bertha when no one else was around and pretending, by moving his mouth, that he was talking. She would get really hysterical about her hearing aid—pounding it, shaking it, and so forth—until Will would calmly take it and give it a little punch or something and then start talking in a slightly louder tone of voice. Miss Bertha thought Will was the Miracle Worker. Most people did. Sonny Smooth.

Instead of the two dozen guests expected, there were only ten or twelve more who showed up, and they all came in fairly close together, so I was able to break away earlier than usual. After my own wonderful dinner of apple-onion-laced pork chops and mashed potatoes, I retrieved the notebook from under my mattress and carried it down to the Pink Elephant, where I burnt the candle at both ends, as the saying goes.

The notebook was wonderful.

It was full of strange utterances, as if the story had been told by someone in a cave, the words coming through some tunnel in the rocks, distorted by twists and turns. There were a lot of cross-outs, some scattered words and phrases that Dr. McComb had managed to make out. But mostly it was like an indecipherable code.

Indecipherable until now, that is.

*When the leaves fall, you can see—*

But see what?

*—minnows swimming light.*

Was Ulub talking about the lake? Was it minnows swimming in the lake? That didn't make any sense, either.

I had taken the big flashlight from the drawer

beneath the front desk where Mrs. Davidow kept a few tools. Down in the Pink Elephant, I lit what stubs of tallow candles there were, dropping their wax in the saucers and drawing the saucers right around the notebook. I spotlighted the words with the flashlight's beam. Its top was nearly as big around as a car headlight, and it was heavy to hold. But the candles were too low and guttery to shine across the pages, so the flashlight would have to do.

And I had to remember: this was not only Ulub's stumbling account of what happened (*what* happened?), but it was his account in combination with his brother's equally difficult speaking problem, and then strained through Dr. McComb's understanding of both Ulub and Ubub, for it was he who was deciphering the words. A shadow of a shadow of a shadow.

I refused to be discouraged. Carefully, I read every word—or maybe I should say every *marking*. Words failed Dr. McComb at certain points and he tried to put in sounds, like little grunts across the page, and sometimes left blanks. There were also a lot of cross-outs. So that

> *When the leaves fall, you can see minnows swimming light*

really was set down

> *When the leaves fall, you can see ~~minahs minds~~ ~~mends winds~~ minnows swimming ~~lake like~~ light.*

It was not long, the notebook story, not much more than three pages, and it stopped abruptly, as if they were all tired out, the three of them. But after a while there were not so many cross-outs, not so many grunts and blank spaces. This was not because Ulub had finally grown a silver tongue, but it seemed like Dr. McComb had got caught up in his story and just supplied words that sounded like what Ulub was saying without all of the agonizing over them or trying to make sense out of them. Although the "minnows" passage certainly made precious little sense. I read on through a rush of images and sounds that I could make nothing of, except to note their movement and color.

The word "raft" ended it so abruptly I felt as if I'd stumbled and fallen, as if my foot had hit a boot scraper and dropped into some dark doorway.

I went back to the first sentence and the cross-outs. What I thought was that the words crossed out must *sound* like what Ulub and Ubub had said, and Dr. McComb had been looking for a meaning in the sound so he could put down actual words and make some sense out of them. They *didn't* make sense, of course, so there were cross-outs.

"Minnows" I was sure didn't mean tiny fish, nor had Ulub meant anything like fish. The crossed-out words were "minahs," "minds," "mends," and "winds." "Minds" was probably changed to "mends" as that was nearer the sound. But there was an "o" sound too, so that's where he'd gotten "minnows." I looked at "winds." I thought about that. I tried to be Ulub, pouting up my lips, and hearing an "m" and seeing how close it might sound to a "wuh."

My eyes snapped open. Windows. *Was it "windows"?*

> *When the leaves fall you see* windows *swimming light*

Oh!

> *When the leaves fall you see windows* swim in *light!*

Could Ulub have been *looking in through a window*? But that made perfect sense. For Ulub and Ubub worked around the Devereau house, raking leaves and pruning and stuff during the day, so it was certainly possible that Ulub might have gone back at night.

I was truly excited. For if I began with the fact that Ulub had been peeking through the windows of the house, and had *seen* something, then other details might fall into place. I sat there with my head in my hands, staring down at the page; the candles flickered wanly and the old flashlight, brilliant as a sun at the start, was now weakening, its batteries dying, I supposed. I shook it, but that only made it fade more. Light was being leeched away, sucked into the shadows that were growing like thick heavy vines up the Pink Elephant's stuccoed walls.

Oh, if only Mr. Root had been there when Ulub and Ubub told this story!

Well, he wasn't, so I would have to make do with what I had. And what I had to remember was that this tale was important enough to make the Wood boys actually tell it to Dr. McComb (who they were probably even more afraid of than other La Porte people, given his "position"). So there was no doubt that it was worth getting to the bottom of.

But it was more like the bottom of a dream. For it read, not like a waking experience, but a dream one, where images tangle together and meanings pile on top of one another like a row of cards in Aurora's solitaire game.

I had the notebook. And I had Ulub. And Mr. Root, the translator. And I could put questions to Ulub, who could at least nod, or say no or yes, or some version of them.

But then I wondered: Should I put poor Ulub through this? Bring it all up again when maybe all the Woods wanted to do was forget it—maybe already *had* forgot it? I ran my hand over the cool black-and-white cover, thinking. Curiosity, I guess, won out. But it was more than just curiosity: I had to know what had happened to Mary-Evelyn.

I snuffed out the candles and sat in what was left of the dying light of the flash. The flashlight pointed its dim ghost-circle at the wall and in my mind I saw the Girl again as I had seen her that morning. Was it only that morning? It seemed so long ago.

Anyone would have said to me that I'd seen a ghost, and laughed. Would a ghost appear walking along Second Street in La Porte? There was just something so *substantial* about Second Street, where the Sheriff gave out parking tickets.

If I hadn't been so sleepy, I think, I would even have come down here to the lake, like I did tonight. I think I wanted to look across its flat blackness, wanted to see if the Girl would be there. Wanted to see her moonbright hair glimmer, like Wonder bread, in the dark.

## SEVENTEEN

You would think that the very first thing I'd do the next morning would be to take the notebook straight up to Britten's store and look for Ulub and Ubub. But I didn't. First, I wanted to talk to the Sheriff, for I was uncertain about making Ulub relive all of this, as it might be painful to him.

Anyway, the *first* thing I always did in the mornings was to get down to the kitchen at seven o'clock and see to putting the syrup pitchers on the tables. It was always cold in the dining room before my mother got the stoves going full blast, especially if you were carrying a bowl full of ice and butter around. Even Vera, although she would not stoop to such a chore, and who was always black-uniform-perfect, would sometimes wear a dark cardigan as she whisked around the dining room, checking the tables for syrup and meanly hoping I hadn't done my job.

The other girls, like Anna Paugh and Sheila, would come later, Sheila looking disheveled, like she didn't know what struck her and like she'd just this moment risen from bed and yanked on whatever was lying around. It was hard to blame anybody for acting dislocated and wandering in with a "Where am I? Where am I? Is this hell?" expression. To have to deal with Miss Bertha's hearing aid in the early-

morning cold was not my idea of fun, either. Since
the breakfast menu was much the same from one
morning to another (except French toast sometimes
replaced pancakes, as it did this morning)—eggs any
which way, bacon or sausage, toast or biscuits—I
thought sometimes Miss Bertha was just doing this
to me on purpose, making me repeat and repeat items.
But my humor would always improve when I remembered that I myself was soon to be the recipient of
some of my mother's powdered-sugar French toast
and spicy sausage.

This particular morning my mind was occupied
by things more important even than French toast,
and I raced through the serving and then polished
off my allotment very quickly so that I could take a
taxi into town. I called Axel's Taxis to pick me up
about halfway up the drive, because Ree-Jane was
up early for once and would undoubtedly want a
ride, with me paying, of course. The dispatcher told
me Axel would be there right away, but of course it
was Delbert, not Axel.

The Sheriff wasn't in his office, and Donny told
me he thought Sam was over at the Rainbow Café.
I found him there, standing near the pastry counter
talking to (of all people) his wife. It was bad enough
not to find him simply walking around town, patrol-
ling things, occasions when I could speak to him
quite privately; but that he would be with his wife
was a blow. Though he wasn't "with" her, they just
happened to land up at the Rainbow's pastry counter
at the same time. I knew that she came in a lot to

buy pies (I had heard she couldn't cook) and that's what she was apparently doing, for even as I watched through the window, she picked up one of Shirl's big white boxes and left.

I entered, thinking about her.

She was dark and flashy-pretty (for her age). Someone had mentioned she was "of Mediterranean extraction," whatever that meant. Some time before, upon hearing this, I had gone to the Abigail Butte County Library and opened their massive world atlas to look at the Mediterranean Sea and the countries around it. There were a lot. I decided Florence De-Gheyn was Italian. Miss Flyte said no, she's Greek. I wondered about this. Of course, I could simply have asked the Sheriff, but I didn't want him to think I was all that interested. I don't know why some casual question such as "Is your wife Greek?" would sound overly interested, but the Sheriff could sense things other people never noticed. So I studied Florence (as if she were indeed another country) from afar.

This morning, as I walked into the Rainbow, the Sheriff was moving back to the Reserved booth, where he stood now with his cup of coffee talking to Maud. I asked Charlene for a cherry Coke, and stood thinking about Maud and the Sheriff for a few moments. Far more than wondering about Florence, I wonder about the Sheriff and Maud. She is always bickering at him. This amazes me. And he seems, almost, to like it; as a matter of fact, I sometimes wonder if some of the things he says to her aren't meant *just* to get her to bicker. Like the time, last

winter, she made some passing comment about wanting to go ice skating on Spirit Lake. He told her
some story about no one skating there, and everyone
being afraid to go near the place. Because I had
written down a lot of the conversation (as I often
did so I could recall what they said to each other),
I remembered this:

He said, "Axel Spiker's cousin went out there
and disappeared. Nobody ever saw him again until
one of the Spirit Lake people looked down and there
was this shadow under the ice. Frozen over."

"Axel doesn't *have* a cousin."

Given what had happened to the supposed
cousin, I thought her answer not to the point.

"Maud, you don't know whether he's got one
or not; you're just contradicting for the sake of it.
Don't you remember that ad in the *Conservative*
about the Spiker reunion last year? There're so many
Spikers in these parts, they have to take out an *ad*
to get the word out. Of course he's got a cousin."

What was wrong with them? I wondered. I
wanted to hear more about this shadow under ice
and they were arguing about whether Axel had a
cousin or not.

"It was in dead winter," the Sheriff had gone
on, "and Axel's cousin had gone all by himself,
skated right out to the center, and fallen through. End
of February they found him—perfectly preserved.
Imagine."

I didn't want to. The Sheriff was making it up,
I knew; for I know how thick the ice gets on Spirit

Lake. Everything around Spirit Lake gets thick in winter. Ice, snow, air, sky. When we were little, Will and I would skate out to the middle with only our heavy socks on. The whole lake was like milk; you couldn't see anything beneath its surface. I bet it was frozen straight down to the bottom. Will would take a rock out there and hammer it on the surface (not the smartest thing to do) and nothing would happen. It would gash the ice a little, sending out hairline cracks, but it wouldn't go through.

Whenever, in winter, I hear the Rainbow's juke-box play scratchy winter songs, usually sung by Nat King Cole, I think of Spirit Lake. The words of these songs are pretty stupid, for it doesn't look "wonderland"-ish. It looks unearthly, as if it doesn't belong on this planet. Words cannot possibly fit the experience of Spirit Lake. But, then, words usually don't fit any experience.

I like to walk to Spirit Lake in my boots and my cap with ear flaps, heavily gloved and coated. Such a heaviness of snow lies here that I sometimes think it will collapse into itself, the whole scene. On days when it's nearly dark at five o'clock, I stand here as the snow gets slowly deeper, thinking that snow falls at Spirit Lake as nowhere else. That's what I imagine. Straight down it falls, thick and windless, burdening the smaller trees to what looks like breaking point and turning the hedges into round white walls. The stubble is so thick with hoar frost, I can nearly skate across this icy grass itself. Thin rails of ice lace the trees and coat the spindly branches in transparent bluish sleeves. I know there are colder places on earth—Alaska, for instance, and the Poles—snowier and icier, but I don't think anyplace could have the wintry *feel* of Spirit Lake. Maybe because it is small and enclosed it feels completely shrouded. Winter's home, I say to myself, standing here in the dreaming stillness, with my face so cold it must look finely crazed and cracked, and my white fur eyebrows, while the snow falls and falls straight down. If ever winter has a home, its home is Spirit Lake.

They were bickering now, or at least Maud was. The Sheriff was telling her not to do something and that would make her want to do it all the more, or *pretend* to want to do it. They stopped in the middle of their argument to greet me, as if they were really happy to see me back here. It made me feel quite warm and welcome. Maud slid over in the booth so that I could sit beside her, even though the seat opposite was empty. The Sheriff remained standing with his cup of coffee.

Maud said to me (excluding the Sheriff), "I'm going to walk to Hebrides." She smoked her cigarette with a smug look.

Before I could say something like "But it's too far," the Sheriff told me she'd been making a big deal about this since before I came in. What Maud wanted was for him to give her a ride in the police car.

Maud said, with that put-on sweetness she used

around the Sheriff, "You'd think, wouldn't you, a *friend* might give you a lift that would only take maybe fifteen minutes to drive." She did not look at him.

"Take a cab. Axel can take you," said the Sheriff.

"Axel never takes anybody," I said. "Delbert would, I guess."

Maud was too busy being annoyed with the Sheriff to note that. "What is so precious about your official vehicle? Don't tell me you never use it for private purposes."

"I *will* tell you. I never use it for private purposes. I won't loan you my gun to shoot at the moon with, either."

That the Sheriff walks around with a weapon on his hip gives him a gritty celebrity that no one else in the whole of La Porte has. In my mind, I could see myself with this gun, slowly drawing a bead on Ree-Jane. There's a sheriff over in Hebrides, but he's fat, with a beer belly and piggy little eyes. I would hate to have my life depend on being saved by him. The gun was at the Sheriff's side now, its grip showing out of the dark brown leather holster. He was lethal as God.

"Take the bus," the Sheriff said.

There's this local bus that runs between La Porte and Hebrides and Lord knows how many house stops along the way. It's dark green and rusted out. You'd have to be desperate. As I think he well knew.

"You must be crazy," Maud said, tapping ash

into a metal tray. "It stops to deliver milk and eggs and to pick up people's mail, for God's sakes." Then she turned to me. "Do you want to walk with me? We can stop at the Stoplight Diner near Hebrides and have lunch. Or dinner."

"Don't pay any attention to her."

Actually, crazy as walking all the way to Hebrides was, I would have liked to walk there with Maud. "I have to wait tables at lunch."

She sighed. "Doesn't Lola Davidow ever give you a day off?"

I noticed that she carefully didn't include my mother in this complaint. "No." It was true, too. Oh, they would, I guessed, if there were some kind of personality-improving emergency, like if I was taking posture lessons, or if some movie producer wanted me. Except for that, I work three meals a day, seven days a week. "What do you want to get in Hebrides?" I asked her.

"Nothing." The Sheriff answered for her, smiling ever so slightly in that way he does when he's trying to keep a laugh back. It was strange: With everyone else (like me), both of them are kind as kind can be. They seem to *know* what you are feeling, and what will hurt or annoy, and are careful not to do so. But not with each other. It's very puzzling, and that's why I wonder about them.

"Oh, yes, I *do* need things. I want to go to the Emporium. I need . . . something dressy."

I could tell from the way she paused that she hadn't even thought about what she wanted to go to

Hebrides for. The Sheriff was probably right. He usually is.

" 'Dressy' for what?"

"I'm not sure that what I want a new dress for is actually your business." She said this with great deliberation, slowly moving her hand over the Formica tabletop, as if wiping off crumbs and ashes.

"Is it for Alma Stuck's funeral?" He did not crack a smile.

She stopped in her imaginary-crumb gathering and I could sense how it irritated her that what he meant was all she had was a kind of funeral popularity. Nobody was asking her to dinner or to a movie.

Then she resumed her wiping motions. "Of course, I know *you* never go, but you *do* recall the Red Barn has dances sometimes?"

"Yes, I do recall. Donny and I—and most of the state troopers—are usually over there trying to keep the peace." I watched the Sheriff set down his cup and fold a stick of Teaberry gum into his mouth before he said, "So who're you going with? Dodge Haines? Axel Spiker?"

Maud smoothed down her dress. "You don't know him, so don't bother guessing. My break's over. Goodbye." With this she rose in her dignified way, patted my shoulder, and walked off. He watched her go, kept watching as she walked behind the counter and was taking Dodge Haines's loudmouthed order, and then Carl Beddowes's nasal whip of a voice—the Sheriff was smiling one of those glorious smiles, the leftover part of which he turned on me.

But even leftover, it gave me the kind of feeling I guess I should have when I look up at the new stained-glass window in church. The smile is more dazzling by far.

"Come on. Let's see if Helene Baum's meter has a red flag up."

I gathered up my notebook and the two of us walked out of the Rainbow. I noticed how Maud's eyes slued around to watch him go.

I was surprised how sad they looked.


At the last tally, the Sheriff told me as he wrote out another ticket for the yellow Cadillac, Helene Baum had twenty-three unpaid tickets, and he had warned her (in writing, to let her know he meant business) that if these tickets were not paid, the Cadillac would be towed. I can see her still, fingering her double strand of pearls, just fuming with anger, her red hair looking almost tipped with sparks (for I remember she'd just had it colored in the Prime Cut), and yelling "Harassment!" at him, following us for more than a block.

Helene Baum had threatened many times to get Mayor Sims to fire the Sheriff, which was ridiculous, of course, because he was so popular, though not with the mayor himself (who I always thought was jealous, and who Maud told me was afraid of losing the mayorship to Sam one fine day). Maud said Sam DeGheyn was absolutely untouchable. She said this with the sort of pride that seemed all at odds with the bickering tone she adopted around him. Like I said, I wondered about them.

Today, he calmly wrote the parking ticket and carefully affixed it under the windshield wiper, where it stayed glued against the glass still damp from the Cadillac's weekly bath over at the Brush-Up (a name I always thought might have been better for the Prime Cut than for a car-wash).

"Twenty-three," I said, amazed.

He nodded and stuck his ticket book in his back pocket. We walked on, with me sort of riffling the notebook, holding it out in front of me.

Naturally, he asked me what it was I had there, and I told him, at first in what I hoped was a slightly bored tone (since I liked to be casual around him), but growing more and more excited as I went on.

He stopped. "Are you saying that Ulub and Ubub were at Spirit Lake that night and saw something?"

"Yes. Yes. See—" And I pointed out the passage I had worked so long on: "minnows swimming light."

He frowned, but not in disbelief, I thought; more in a study of the page.

"The trouble is, I can't figure it all out," I said, and he nodded. "And what I was wondering, do you think it would be okay if I took the notebook and went and asked the Wood boys themselves?"

Thoughtfully, he held it and looked up at the sky of that blameless blue you sometimes see in religious paintings. "Talking to the Woods isn't the easiest thing in the world, you know." He shook his head a little as he returned to studying the page. " 'Minnows swimming'?"

I told him what it meant. I didn't want to spend hours standing on Second Street and filling him in on every word I'd translated. "Well, Mr. Root can."

"Who?" He frowned.

"Mr. *Root*. He's good at figuring out what people say." But this wasn't the point, was it? "What I'm wondering is whether Ulub will be—" What was the word? What was the word Dr. McComb had used?

The Sheriff just stood there waiting for me to finish. I was really getting impatient with him. "You know . . . like in those movies where a doctor or someone makes the person remember something horrible and the person goes kind of crazy?" It occurred to me then that I might not be as concerned about Ulub's welfare as I was about my own.

The Sheriff unzipped a fresh pack of Teaberry gum and folded a stick into his mouth. He said, "Oh, I don't think that really happens in life. If something in the past is that traumatic—"

"Traumatic," yes, that was the word everyone in town seemed to know but me.

"—I think what happens is, the person just can't remember. Refuses to remember."

"So even if I read to him from the notebook, if what happened is too traumatic then Ulub won't even recall it?"

"That's what I think." He still had his head bent over the notebook. Then he looked at me. "It happened so long ago, though. Everyone's forgotten it, as far as I know."

Testily, I said, "Dr. McComb hasn't."

"How'd you and Dr. McComb ever get on this subject?"

It was my turn to look up at the blue sky. "Oh, it just came up."

"Uh-huh." He handed the notebook back to me. We started walking again. "Mary-Evelyn Devereau." He said the name almost under his breath as he stopped to check the parking meter before Miss Ruth Porte's car. Only five minutes left, and she was probably in the Rainbow having her lunch. He slotted a dime in and turned the silver crank. "I wonder if Aurora Paradise knows anything. You ever ask her? She'd be easier to deal with than the Wood boys."

"Well, she isn't. Anyway, she lies about stuff. It's hard to tell what's true and what isn't. Like Ben Queen."

Tammy Allbright was sashaying towards us, lathered up in her usual ton of Pond's lipstick and Maybelline eyeshadow. She smelled a fright, too, probably took a bath in Evening in Paris. She'd stopped us and was giggling all over the Sheriff, batting her Maybelline eyes and biffing him softly with her fist. It was really disgusting; I wonder he could stand it. But he just smiled and asked her about her family.

He turned to me and said, "Who?"

I was looking after Tammy Allbright's fat rear end. "Who what?"

"Aurora told you about somebody."

"Ben Queen, his name is. Or was. He was a real ladies' man." And I gave the Sheriff what I hoped was a look full of meaning, trying to hint that if he didn't watch out, he might go the way of Ben Queen. Except I didn't know what way that was. "Aurora—I mean my great-aunt Paradise—said that one of the Devereau sisters ran off with him."

"Hmm." The Sheriff was hunkered down now, checking a tire on Bunny's pickup truck.

I chewed the inside of my mouth, wondering why I wasn't telling him what I had told Dr. McComb about the Girl. Was it because Dr. McComb had actually had a part in the Mary-Evelyn story and the Sheriff hadn't? Or was it more because I was disappointed that he wasn't more interested in investigating her death himself? *He* was the policeman, after all.

So I held on to my special bit of information.

## EIGHTEEN

Before I could go to Britten's store, I had to get the bread plates ready for lunch, which meant another round of the dining room at eleven-thirty. Lunch ran from noon until two. Sometimes, the Hotel Paradise seemed like an endless succession of meals. Not that I was criticizing the guests who ate all of these meals, considering my own interest in what was now coming out of the oven on a huge cookie sheet: ham pinwheels. I quickly moved over to the stove to check the pot simmering there and make sure it held cheese sauce, although I knew it did. I just wanted to lift the lid of the double boiler and dampen my nose with cheesy steam.

When I was six, I had to memorize this poem about my heart leaping up when I saw a rainbow. No rainbow could make my heart leap as much as when I beheld those ham pinwheels and smelled that cheese sauce. It was an added piece of luck Ree-Jane didn't like them, or it might have been another white-meat-of-chicken contest. Ree-Jane wouldn't stoop to eating "leftovers": leftover pastry and leftover baked ham. Leftovers! Couldn't she see the shining brown glaze on that pastry, made by whisking a little brush dipped in egg white over it? And that cheese sauce so full of sunlight? Leftovers! I just told her "leftovers" should be good brain food for her. Ree-Jane didn't understand this; she just looked at me out of her blank blue eyes. I never saw anyone with emptier eyes in my life.

So with expectations of this tantalizing lunch, I perked up a little, zipped a little faster around the tables, and even had a pleasant smile for Miss Bertha, as I tried to sell the ham pinwheels. In her loud voice she kept asking What was I talking about? no matter how much I repeated or went into detail; and since "Spanish omelette" was the other thing on the menu, I had to hang around Miss Bertha's table for a long time. Finally, she said she wanted eggs with cheese sauce, and I couldn't get her mind off this track, and finally went into the kitchen to tell my mother. Vera gave me one of her starchy looks, as if I were trying to play a practical joke on Miss Bertha. Lola Davidow (who was hanging around the kitchen drinking Bloody Marys) thought it was howlingly funny and laughed until she was wiping away tears. My mother, though, simply shrugged and whipped up a cheese omelette for Miss Bertha. When I presented this pretty dish to her, Miss Bertha actually beamed. And Mrs. Fulbright, who never put my mother out, actually requested one too (if it wasn't any trouble). Miss Bertha beamed even more, thinking she had brought about the discovery of a new dish.

Full of a double order of ham pinwheels and cheese sauce, I lugged my groggy self up to Britten's store. I had decided not to take the notebook, although I hated giving up what authority it seemed to lend me. Did I think that upon seeing the book, light would dawn in Ulub's eyes? That all of that night would come back in a rush?

They were sitting there on the bench in front of Britten's, Ulub and Ubub and Mr. Root, too. They seemed to be looking out for something or someone, and upon my approach the three of them smiled and waved. So I was the thing they were all waiting for, and that brought me up short because I'm not used to having anyone waiting for me with that look of expectation, or delighting in my coming.

Ubub and Ulub slid apart, making room for me to sit between them. This left Mr. Root on the far end of the bench, but this position appeared to suit him fine, for he could then lean forward, forearms on knees, and survey the three of us as if he had been appointed a sort of referee or deputy placed there to oversee our meeting and make sure each of us understood and was given a fair shake. In some way, I guessed this was true. He still wore his blue engineer's cap, and he touched its brim in a little salute as I came up to the bench. He had put in his teeth today, perhaps indicating the grave importance of our gathering, although none of them had known I was coming to gather with them. And then it struck me that they had simply assumed, after the drama of two mornings ago, that that meeting was certainly not the end of it. I would be back. This really pleased me.

During the few moments we were arranging ourselves on the bench, I wondered how to approach the subject of the tale in the notebook. As usual, I was not one to put the question directly. I told myself it was because directness scares people off or shuts them up. The real reason is probably that I like dragging things out because I don't want them to end.

Then came a surprising turn: Ubub had taken from his jacket pocket a little bunch of papers— newspaper clippings, as I soon saw. One of them was the very same triple column with picture that I had read in *The Conservative* office and had refrained from stealing. But Ubub had other clippings, too; it looked as if he had them all. And a couple were from the *Star-Times* in Cloverly, a thicker and more citified newspaper. He handed them to me, nodding hard.

There was a difference between his front page and the one I had read: all around it, someone (one or both of the Woods, I guessed) had drawn little things, such as flowers and roundnesses which I took to be their versions of woodland creatures. Certain of the statements in the story were underlined in similar colors. I guessed this clipping must have been decorated with crayons. What surprised me more was that I had gone along thinking (probably with the rest of the town) that the Woods couldn't read, couldn't do anything that required a glimmer of intelligence. Now, I was ashamed of myself; I had simply assumed that the difficulty they had speaking must mean they couldn't do anything else—read, or even think properly. I told them I had never seen most of these clippings.

"Duh nu en oo eh um." Ubub said, tapping the longer account.

Mr. Root pursed his lips and looked at me to
see if I understood. I scanned the first and last para-
graphs and knew what he'd said. "Nothing new . . .
in them." Ulub and Ubub nodded. "It's the same as
what's in the *The Conservative.*"

Both of them smiled, nodding even harder. Mr.
Root nodded too and gave a grunt in agreement. I
liked the way Mr. Root interpreted; he did not butt
in with his version. He waited to see if I was stumped.
Of course, it did occur to me that Mr. Root himself
could have sometimes been stumped and hoped I
wasn't. But, anyway.

I read bits of the longer account just to make
sure no clue appeared there; I read the whole of
the three much shorter follow-up pieces. And then I
realized: the clippings themselves weren't as signifi-
cant as the fact that the Woods had *collected* all
of these pieces and had underlined certain parts. I
fluttered the newspaper pieces before them. "I bet
this isn't really what happened, is it?"

Both of them exclaimed at once, shaking their
heads hard, Ulub pounding his fist against his knee.
I was surprised at how small his hands were.

"Is it these parts you've underlined that are
wrong?"

Said Ubub: "Um oh em."

" 'Some of them?' " But I was saved from inter-
pretation, because Ubub was tapping his finger
against one passage. "'Lonzo sah—"

It was interesting he could say "Alonzo" so
clearly. I thought maybe I could make it easier on

all of us if I told them about Dr. McComb and the notebook and asked them if I had figured out some of the passages correctly. But then I thought that might make them shy, knowing I had their halting account written down. And also that it was kind of insulting.

This passage said that according to Miss Isabel Devereau, Mary-Evelyn had gone to bed around eight o'clock and that's the last she (or her sisters) had seen of the girl.

All the while I read this out, Ulub was shaking his head so hard I thought it would fall off. "What did happen, Ulub?" Too late, I remembered his real name was Alonzo, but he didn't seem to mind the nickname at all and was used to it. Ulub looked at his brother and even at Mr. Root, as if asking permission to explain.

Ubub, with a gracious little movement of his hands, gave place to Ulub, as it was the younger brother who had actually been there. Mr. Root nodded, too, even though he never knew a thing about all of this until the other day.

Well, I was nearly holding my breath, waiting, despite the fact I knew it would be a long time between the utterance and the understanding. He said:

"Ah uz eh uh oods. Ah, ah, ah—" He was wrenching his head to get the word out.

I had worked out certain key sounds both from listening to them several days ago and from the notebook. I knew that "ah" was "I" and that most of the "eh" and "uh" sounds were like prepositions and articles. "Uh" was almost always "the." So as he talked I translated what little I could. "Ah uz eh uh oods" must have been "I was in the woods." That, after all, made sense.

"You were in the woods," I said.

"Es!" He nodded. "Ah uz eh uh oods cuz ah neft aye irk un aye kippers un ent bah to geh um."

I frowned and scratched my head and looked at Mr. Root, who seemed frozen in place he was concentrating so hard. I could make out "cuz" as being "because" probably, but "neft aye irk"? I was stumped.

Mr. Root suddenly looked up and said, "You was in the woods and *went back to get something*?"

Ulub nodded furiously. "Ah neft aye irk. Uh irk un aye kippers!"

I thought hard. So did Mr. Root, who had his eyes squinched shut and was maybe trying out different sounds with his tongue. Ulub and Ubub looked from one to the other of us, waiting.

"You left *work*?" Mr. Root was so pleased he'd figured out something he ignored the fact Ulub was shaking his head. He snapped his fingers. "You was doin' yard work. . . . *Clippers!* You went back to get your *clippers!*"

Ulub nodded, but he still was waiting for Mr. Root to untangle the "irk." It was the first time I'd ever realized Ulub could be willful. I thought it a good thing, being somewhat that way myself.

Clippers and an irk . . . "Oh, for heaven's sakes!

A *rake*, is that what you left, Ulub?" Well, it really was like a quiz show, the way we applauded one another, though I thought Mr. Root looked kind of put upon because he hadn't gotten to "rake" first.

Something occurred to me then, and I asked, "You ever go back there, Ulub? Either of you?" Well, it wasn't hard to tell by the quick glance at each other that they had. "Oh, don't look so guilty. *I'm* the *last* person that would ever criticize going where you're not sup—" It was just sinking in that they went there still.

And then it came to me, my brilliant idea: We could all go to the Devereau house.

The scene of the crime—assuming there'd been one. I guess I hadn't thought of this before because I just assumed the way was impassable. That wasn't quite true, not if that real estate agent managed to get there a while back. No, I'd been thinking it was impassable for *me*, that's all.

The Devereau house. In my mind I pictured it on the other side of the lake, a house by itself, the color of fog and drifting there, insubstantial as fog.

"We could all go," I said. "We could go to the Devereau house and—investigate!"

They all stared at me.

"Why not? You two"— here I looked at Ulub and Ubub—"you've done it; you know the way. And Mr. Root looks like somebody that'd be good in an emergency!" I'm not sure that he did, but he certainly perked up when I said it.

The three of them were exchanging looks, giving little nods of the head, or scratching behind an ear, but it was clear they were all falling in with the idea.

Without a thought for his speech difficulty, Ulub was the first to ask, "En?"

"When?" I liked it that I was expected to give the go-ahead, or not give it. That made me, for once in my life, the leader. I chewed the corner of my mouth, thinking: it was mid-afternoon, and if we went now it would only give me two hours until dinnertime. That included the traveling time from Britten's store, which was probably a mile from the lake, and then the half or three-quarters of a mile back to the hotel, where I had to be by six o'clock at the latest, and that didn't include time to make the salads.

I said this aloud, shaking my head. "I've got to make the salads and put the butter plates around."

They all looked at me in a wondering way. Well, it must have seemed like a strange barrier to adventure—salads and butter plates. I explained as how these were two of my waitressing duties and that I had to appear by five-thirty to carry them out.

The thing was, of course, that *after* dinner it would be getting on to dark and I didn't much want to be in the Devereau woods tangled up in trees and vines in the dark. But the days were lengthening now in May, so that it didn't get dead dark until near eight o'clock. I traded off the dark with the dinner deadline and thought I'd rather take a chance on spookiness than on the lethal looks of Vera and Lola Davidow if I showed up late.

I stood there scratching my elbows and pondering. I said, "I could leave early; I might be able to get away around seven, and that would give us time, wouldn't it? I mean, until nighttime? I could meet you down at the lake. Say, near the boathouse." I knew at this point we had practically no reservations for dinner and that my tables, Miss Bertha and Mr. Gosling (a salesman and regular guest), would be in at six and six-fifteen or -twenty. I could be well away by seven. If I had to, I would just disappear.

They all looked at me and nodded.

We were a team.


Thus, I appeared in the kitchen that evening early for once, even before Vera. This really annoyed her, I could tell, when she finally breezed in through the kitchen screen door. I was at my salad station by five-fifteen, arranging little Bibb lettuces in individual salad bowls. I sprinkled them with chopped-up egg and black olives and striped each one with pimiento. I was in my artistic mode again.

Salad art with the Bibb lettuces annoyed Mrs. Davidow. She took the position that a whole Bibb lettuce was a display of generosity and elegance on the part of the Hotel Paradise, and nothing more should be done with the Bibb lettuces except for adding French dressing. To spend more money (egg yolks, olives) on each portion was going overboard. She'd spoken to me about this before when she'd caught me making faces on the Bibb lettuces, with olive rings for eyes, pimiento mouths, and egg-yolk curls. This sort of thing just drove her to distraction, which is why I did it. But a lot of the time, she'd made so many trips to the martini pitcher, the Bibb lettuces could have talked back to her and she'd never have cared.

I whistled as I worked, making an olive cross on Miss Bertha's salad, hoping that might help to Christianize her. On Mr. Gosling's lettuce I sprinkled another spoonful of egg yolk and partially hid it between two of the pale leaves, just in case Lola or Vera might come along and try to scoop it off again. He loved hardboiled eggs. Then I realized: if I was going to meet them at the lake, I would miss my own dinner! While my mother was out in the office I inspected every pot and pan on the big stove to see if I was missing any of my favorites. The big roasting pan was full of freshly fried chicken pieces, as usual (and as usual, short on white meat); two thick filet steaks were arranged on a plate, marinating in something winey; lobster tails were arranged on a cookie sheet, glazed with some exotic mixture. Only the chicken could possibly be aimed at my gullet, and not the white meat, so I'd only be missing a leg or a thigh. I sighed heavily, though, when I saw the steam rise from a double boiler of mashed potatoes, buttery, mealy clouds of them. I took one of the tiny white porcelain dishes from the shelf, the small

vegetable dishes in which the potatoes were often
served, scooped out two big spoonsful, and then
neatened up the surface in the steaming pot, adding
a curl on top.

After making a well for a butter patty, I trans-
ported my dish back through the small kitchen, where
Paul was sitting. Paul was the dishwasher's boy. She
came some nights to help Walter out when there was
a dinner party. She was washboard thin, with a broad,
flat face. I guess you could say Paul resembled her,
except her face was so nondescript, it was hard to
see it duplicated anywhere else. Paul was slapping
back pages of a comic book that was lying in front
of him upside down on the table. It was understood,
of course, that Paul (who was seven or eight) still
could not read. But I thought it was really interesting
that he could not look at pictures, either. He grinned
a lot, but he hardly ever talked. This was probably
because his mother boxed his ears nearly every time
he opened his mouth. His mother had got the idea—
not really surprising—that Paul was not to speak
when in my mother's kitchen. Actually, I thought
this pretty smart of her.

I guess just to be ornery, I reached over and
turned the comic around, telling him (in a superior
way) that it was upside down. He grinned. When
Paul grinned, he looked exactly like the boy on the
cover of *Mad* magazine, eyes dopily close together,
face splattered with freckles. He grinned and turned
the comic upside down again, and kept on slapping

the pages back. I knew Paul wouldn't tell about my dish of mashed potatoes.

There was an extra party of six (the Baums) scheduled for seven o'clock, and my heart sank when my mother said I'd help serve. But Vera did not really want me to help and insisted she could "handle" the table by herself. She knew Dr. Baum was a good tipper and had no intention of sharing with me.

They sailed in early, just as I'd finished clearing off Mr. Gosling's table, Helene Baum in her butterfly eyeglasses and bright yellow chiffon dress, the doctor in a black turtleneck, and all six of them drunk as lords. Seven of them, really, for Mrs. Davidow was steaming in at their head, rouged and corseted and reminding me of those carved ladies riding high on the bow of a ship, like the one in the John Wayne movie I'd seen not long ago. Mrs. Davidow often more or less invited herself to sit down with guests she'd been having cocktails with, wedging in her own filet and chair to make one more at the table.

Vera was looking really disapproving, her nose rising nearly off her face because they were too far gone to appreciate her superior table waiting— mostly, though, because Dr. Baum might forget to leave an extra-large tip. I was afraid she'd change her mind, seeing that I was free, and press me into service.

So, to make sure that didn't happen, I disappeared.

# NINETEEN

It was seven o'clock by the time I drew close to the boathouse, and the three of them were standing there, waving at me. The Woods had on their heavy black peacoats. Mr. Root was wearing only a thin denim jacket, but I bet he had on long johns underneath his clothes. Up here in the mountains at five thousand feet it could still get cold after the sun went down.

Ulub had a flashlight and a pair of rusty old scissors, for some reason. Mr. Root was carrying one of those old oil lanterns that had me imagining him walking along railroad tracks, swinging it to signal a train. Both flashlight and lantern reminded me that night would fall. I looked up at the sky, as if looking up there would somehow change the quality of light nearer the ground. It looked to me like daylight, though I would have to say not like full daylight. Gradations of light were pretty much lost on me; I was more attuned to ham pinwheels than to nature. Mr. Root also showed us the box of kitchen matches he'd brought, in case we ever wanted to make a fire—another unpleasant reminder that we could be out after dark. He also had one of those curved knives that I think is called a Bowie knife; it was pushed down in a leather holder which he wore rather importantly on his belt. Ubub was wearing a back-pack. I wondered what he had in it. Before we set out, we all turned and looked reverently at the house over there, mist-colored, black windows like eye sockets.

We walked the rutted dirt road to the spring, passing the boathouse with its narrow wooden board-walk and peeling white paint. We passed the grove of maples and that single birch tree I love. This little spring is about a quarter of a mile around the lake, and here we stopped for no particular reason except that the spring is usually the final destination for anyone walking by the lake. It always has been for me, and Will, and for my father, when he walked us down here. There's an old metal pipe jutting out from a little rock alcove. And someone at some time made a large, round, shallow pool in this resting place and lined it with quite beautiful tiles, glazed and brightly colored and painted with fish. The pool is fed by the spring and the spring by the lake.

We four sat down on the low stone balustrade and passed around the tin cup that is always left in the alcove, which looks as if it had been fashioned especially for this cup. Anyone who wants a drink can place it beneath the pipe to catch the water. I wonder a lot about this cup: I wonder who put it there, and if that person meant to hide it; I wonder how it could stay here year after year and nobody steal it; I wonder if it has rested there the whole length of people's lives, and if it will be here after I die. We passed the cup along, one to the other, until we'd all had a drink. When it came round to me, I hurriedly wiped the rim before I put it to my lips. As we were passing the cup, I asked them about what we might expect in there among the trees and in the dense brush. On my way here, I had turned many possibilities over in my mind, rejecting bears and panthers, but not at all sure about snakes, spiders, and wolves.

Mr. Root bit off a plug of tobacco and offered the rest around as he pondered my question. Ubub accepted some tobacco, but Ulub preferred a stick from the packet of Teaberry that I usually carried around for the Sheriff. I decided to chew a stick myself, as everybody else was chewing. After turning his tobacco into black spit, he said, "Ain't no wolves, no. Fox, maybe. Rabbits, most likely." He scrutinized the narrow road beyond us, where it disappeared into the dark. "Milk snakes, for sure."

I wondered what a milk snake was, but didn't want to stay on the subject of snakes. I assumed it wasn't dangerous, or Mr. Root would have said so.

Ulub was nodding. "Uh cah," he said, snapping the rusted shears as if they were crocodile jaws.

Everyone looked at him, frowning. And he repeated the word, straining to add the final sound. "Cah-aa-aaa-ud."

Cahd? Cud? "Cat!" I exclaimed triumphantly.

Ulub looked at me happily, nodding.

"Ah, he means one of them feral ones," explained Mr. Root, probably a little annoyed I'd beat him to "cat." "Feral, yeah. I seen one a them."

I had a feeling he was guessing. Actually, I

was a little disappointed that they weren't full of knowledge of what might lie ahead in the woods. I guess I figured the Woods' talking problems and the way they lived alone would have improved their relations with animals and nature. As far as I knew, Ulub and Ubub had no family at all; it was only themselves who lived in a ramshackle wooden house on a road up beyond the hotel. Mr. Root, I think, lived on the other side of the national highway that bisected Spirit Lake. There was some idea that the people on the other side from the Hotel Paradise were higher on the social ladder and had more money than the people on the hotel side. This was not a view my mother held to, of course. Though there might have been a few more big Victorian houses on the other side, it was true, there were also a lot of crackerbox houses and trailers. So it looked all one to me, the ramshackle rich and the ramshackle poor. I thought most of us were really ramshackle middle-class. Spirit Lake was definitely way above Cold Flat Junction with respect to upper-classness, though.

We all sat there chewing and looking at the road ahead where it burrowed in among the trees and tall grasses, with nobody making a move to get up and follow it. No matter which way you approached the Devereau house—by the spring side or by the dam side—the way became what I'd told myself looked to be impassable. But then, I asked myself, how would the Girl ever have turned up on the other side of the lake? I did not like to think of the alternatives. Especially the one that said she hadn't—that she hadn't been there at all.

Maybe that's why I said nothing to them about the Girl, or about her appearing over there, for it would just mean a lot of questions that I couldn't answer, and didn't want to, anyway. It was something I seemed to want to keep to myself. I was gripped by a feeling I could not name. It wasn't fear, for there was no rush in my veins or sudden dropping of my stomach. It was more like a terrible sadness. It was not deep dark at this time in the evening, not even movie dark, for light tunneled through the dense black pines, filtered through the leaves of the maples. Light's gray dust sifted across the dead black leaves of more than one autumn. Rainwater lay pooled in old tire tracks, and the road narrowed even more where it was hemmed by bracken and spongy mosses and overrun with vines and dead branches. We all made a single file, me being sure I was between two of them. All the while I kept my eyes peeled for signs of the Girl. I honestly think I must have expected she would drop bread crumbs behind her. Sounds, tinny rustlings in the dead leaves, the short, cut-off bird calls—all of them came at me sharp as a knife edge. Something flashed above and Ubub tried to tell us what it was; something dashed away and Mr. Root said, "Rabbit."

It was Ulub who we had decided should lead the way, since this had been his route on the night in question. This route was a little bit shorter than the one around the other side of the lake, where the stone dam had been built. It was nothing but a small rubbishy pile of cemented bricks and flat stones worn smooth from people walking across it. At one end was a crumbling gray stone pillar.

So Ulub led, occasionally snapping his shears. From his backpack, Ubub had taken out a small axe with a broken handle and used it to flail away at dead limbs and hanging vines. Mr. Root seemed to enjoy thrashing through undergrowth. But, raising my hand against some tangled vines before me, I thought the axe and scissors might really not have been necessary, for in many cases the growth was so old and fine and brittle it took little more effort than sweeping away spiderwebs. It was deceptive. You'd see before you this intricate drapery of vines and twigs that from a distance looked impregnable, and yet, once upon them, you could push them back with a stroke.

Up ahead, Ulub had stopped in front of an oak tree and was running his hand across its trunk. He motioned us over and I saw that carved into the bark was a rough heart. Beneath the heart were hewn the letters AL.

AL. It made me smile. For this was before Ulub started being called by his license-plate letters, and I remembered Dr. McComb had said his name was Alonzo. It made me smile to think of Ulub being an Al. I wondered, too, if the heart was just for him; there was no arrow through it, but I supposed Ulub's heart had often been pierced.

Except for the birds' twitters and the soft plop-
ping of occasional pine cones, it was all deathly
quiet. It was really like walking through something
dead, a dead landscape.

Something slithered across my instep. Prepared
for a milk snake, I squinted my eyes nearly shut and
looked down. But it was only a lizard, a very small
one, now nestled in its camouflage of leaves.

My tongue moved in my mouth, searching for
the flavorless wad of gum, before I remembered spit-
ting it out back there among the vines. Yet my tongue
still moved. A strange emptiness came over me, and
I wondered what would happen to a person whose
thoughts trailed away, whose mind emptied out. Who
had nothing in his mouth, or in his stomach or in
his mind, a sieve through which everything had
leaked out, just as on the ground the light-confetti had
leaked through the branches overhead. I remembered
those gangster movies where the one with the
machine gun would tell later how he made a sieve
out of so-and-so, blood spewing everywhere. I
looked down at the light-droplets fallen through the
webs of branches and imagined light leaking out of
me like silver blood spewed across the leaves. What
I longed for was another helping of mashed potatoes.
I knew I was not actually hungry, for it had been
only an hour since I had eaten, and yet it felt like
hunger. Hunger or this huge emptiness. I felt faint-
hearted. It was a better word than "cowardly." Can
your heart swoon or sleep? Run away? Hide? The
lizard dashed away and woke me from this fantasy,

and I saw the others had gone on, and were stopping long enough to get Ulub away from another tree—another heart, I supposed.

We went a little distance, no longer filing along, for what there was of a path was either covered by leaves and twigs or was not even there, and maybe never had been, and what we'd taken for a path was just an old rut in the ground. So we were separate and divided, as if we each had our separate thing we were looking for, but all moving in the same direction. I was closest to the lake, about twenty or thirty feet from its edge. I could catch only glimpses, through the thickness of the brush and the hanging branches and the trailing bend of a willow. Light was turning to nickel, and that made it harder to see the water. I was taking some heart from the silence around me. It could not be penetrated by kitchen sounds or by the rattle of a martini pitcher or by Vera's waspish commands.

I squinted to see what I could of the lake, fast disappearing in the disappearing light. And I thought of my father. This was my father's lake, for he came here often, to the boathouse and the spring. To fish for fish that I guess he always tossed back. I do not remember much about my father. I do not think about him much. Other people have come to this lake and gone away, fewer and fewer over the years, almost no one now. But my father seems to hover here still. Finally we came to the edge of a clearing, and then the clearing itself, and then there was the house. To me it was like coming upon a familiar dream-place, one I'd seen again and again in my dreams. Here it was now, in person, in the flesh.

Slowly we approached it. Mr. Root stopped so that he could light his oil lamp, for it was close to eight o'clock now, that period of lavender light that signals approaching darkness. It was the time when drivers will switch on their lights, even though you can still see clearly. But drivers like Lola Davidow become uncertain in this light. It is always a relief to me when adults are uncertain, for most of the time they claim they're so right. So Mr. Root grew a little uncertain and lit up his oil lamp. It looked friendly, the small flame spurting in its glass cage.

We paused around back to look at the small porch where a screen door listed, the top dropped away from its hinge. This was the rear door to the kitchen, which we could tell was quite large, for it was still the same room around the next corner, where we stood looking in through a long window with old, watery glass.

Then we rounded another corner and looked in through the same sort of window to what appeared to be a living room or front parlor. Its most prominent furnishing was a grand piano. Against the walls were bluish blobs of old overstuffed chairs and a sofa. There were round tables covered with dark cloths. Ulub now went into an act, waving his arms and trying to talk, his excitement making talk all the harder. He was pointing to the piano and then running back around the side of the house and pointing to the kitchen. We tried to quiet him down a little, and

I decided we should go into the house and let Ulub show us what he meant. This is what we did.

Nothing seemed to be locked up, including the back door to the kitchen, and I wondered how the house had kept itself together all of this time and free of squatters. For there were no signs that people had attempted to take it over, nothing except for stubs of candles stuck on little plates. Bread-and-butter plates, my wide experience with them told me. Yet, even they could have been left behind by the Devereau sisters, along with their furniture. I wondered if they had taken flight suddenly. Probably not, though, for no one had ever mentioned their leaving in that way. No one knew where they had gone, either, or if they had gone together.

Mr. Root brought out his matches and lit the two candles on the kitchen table, for it was growing dark and of course there was no electricity. The table was a lot like Miss Flagler's, white porcelain, only this one was chipped in a lot of places and dark patches showed through. The four chairs were painted wood. Ulub, still in his pleasurable excitement, gestured for us to follow him into the parlor.

Atop the shawl covering the closed lid of the piano sat three more candles, and Mr. Root went to work again with his matches. He didn't waste them, lighting only one and picking up the other two candles to hold their wicks against this lighted one. They were still stuck to their dishes, rooted there in candle-wax drips. The room was eerily illuminated now, and the clumps of chairs and sofa sprang into greater relief. There was a big fireplace with a marble mantel, in front of which sat two dark horsehair armchairs with little lace antimacassars, stiffened with age. Several round tables of varying sizes—one behind the sofa, a larger one more or less in the room's center, two smaller ones beside chairs—were all cloth-covered but absent of photos or knickknacks. Had they held such things, the room would have looked much like Dr. McComb's sitting room, I was surprised to see. Except that his seemed warmer and more friendly. Well, of course it would be; his had been lived in for all of the forty years or so that this one had been vacant. I could not make out the colors of the wallpaper very well, but the pattern was of vines and weary-looking flowers, petunias maybe. One portrait hung against the wall by a sideboard. It was the only picture in the room and I went to inspect it. The Devereau sisters when they were children, that's who the three girls in it must have been. Four girls, really, for in the center and below their chin level was another little girl, the youngest in the portrait. The three sisters ranged around her were unmistakably sisters, for they all had the same squarish faces, long brown hair, plaited or loose, and straight-lipped, solemn expressions of people about to be baptized. But the fourth was blond and had a round face and an almost merry look. Pale blond.

I had to shake myself out of thinking it might be the Girl. Time seemed to be melting, running off like a stream or a river, for, of course, she could not even have been born at the time this picture was taken. I figured that the Devereau sisters were probably in their early teens here, but could have been younger, for children always looked pinched and solemn and old in pictures back then. My mother certainly did. If what Aurora Paradise said was true, this blond girl must have been Rose.

Ulub's arm wavings and guttural words were distracting me, and I turned to see him sitting on the piano stool, punching a finger on the keys and saying something like "Ee wah may-en," and then he'd punch some more keys.

Ulub kept saying this—"Ee wah may-en"—and Mr. Root had his face screwed up in a terrible act of concentration. Finally, he snapped his fingers: "She was playing!" And when Ulub nodded his head vigorously, Mr. Root slapped his thigh.

"Mary-Evelyn was sitting here playing the piano when you looked through the window?" I nodded to the window nearest the piano, where it was still light enough to see the place where we had been standing out there, looking in. Ulub nodded again, yes, yes. Then he rose and beckoned us to follow him back into the kitchen, where he sat down at the table and pretended to pick up a fork or a spoon and raise it to his mouth. Back and forth from ghost plate went the ghost fork. He also wore a rather dumb expression, which he meant to mean this was not his face but another's. One of the Devereaus, of course. And then he moved to another chair and changed his expression, and then to the third chair. Ulub was taking all of the parts. In silence we watched him making his rounds of the table until he got the bright idea of having *us* play the Devereau roles.

"Hit own, hit own."

It was clear enough he meant for us to "sit down," so we pulled out the white-painted chairs, but hadn't actually sat before Ulub was pulling at each of us, at our arms, plucking at sleeves and rearranging us. We all wondered about this—I know I did—why Ulub thought one or the other of us was more one or the other of *them*; but we let him have his way. Me he sat at the table's head, and I wondered which tormentor he had me down as, and whether she was worse or better than the other two. Ubub and Mr. Root sat solemnly, their hands folded before them, awaiting further developments. Ulub smiled a rare smile and continued, clapping his two hands against his chest and pointing into the parlor. "Ah on in air." Here he made little waves with his hands, patting the air before him. He was going to play the piano, I guessed correctly. Ubub applauded me. It was like charades.

Ulub pointed to each of us. "U cuh nin nen ah caw"—and here he gave a short yell.

No one knew immediately what he meant, so it was up to Mr. Root and his concentrated efforts. He made Ulub repeat the phrase twice. Both of them looked equally pained until finally Mr. Root, slapping his thigh again, said, "You going to call to us. We got to wait here until you call us in, right?"

Ulub beamed and nodded and left.

"Hell," said Mr. Root, "he ain't hard to understand. Don't see the problem, myself."

In another moment, an awful raucous noise filled the air as Ulub pounded on the keyboard. Ubub (I could see) was about to rise and protest when a silence as full as the sounds had been came over the room. This was followed by muffled movements and then a cry or call which we took to be his signal. We rose and went through the door to see Ulub, not at the piano, but on the other side of the wall, standing there as if glued to the wall directly beside the kitchen door. I was first in the room, and he pulled himself away and ran back to the piano, where he started crashing around on the keys again. I doubted Mary-Evelyn had played that way.

He beckoned us over and, by means of more gestures and grunts, got us to stand in a semicircle around the piano and stare at him. When Mr. Root started to say something, Ulub furiously put his finger to his mouth. We were apparently not to speak; we were to look at the shamed Ulub—or Mary-Evelyn, sitting there with bent head and laced fingers staring at her shoes, or the floor.

I remembered what the Woods had said about the Devereau aunts not talking to Mary-Evelyn. What she must have been doing was merely listening outside the kitchen door, listening to conversation just to hear others speak. I remembered too my mother's saying what a "silent little girl" she was, carrying glass plates of tiny canapes around at parties, never saying anything. She had run back to the piano when she'd been discovered.

Ulub was saying something to Mr. Root that sounded like "autumn, summer."

"Aw noo un-ner."

Mr. Root looked really perplexed, and Ulub repeated it two or three more times, all the while pointing at the piano keys and rippling his fingers up and down the air above them.

"All through dinner!" said Mr. Root, brightening. "All through dinner! That's it, ain't it?"

Now everyone nodded as if all of our fears had been confirmed. I said, "Mary-Evelyn was to play for them all through dinner, and if the music stopped, they'd go check on her."

Almost ferociously, Ulub nodded.

I bowed my head. I found it truly hard to believe—not Ulub's story, but that such a thing could happen.

I wondered if it had been a ritual thing, Mary-Evelyn playing the piano while they ate their dinner; if it was her penance that she must entertain them (though I doubted they took much by the way of "entertainment" from it) all through dinner.

Ulub spoke again: "Ee ride."

Ubub and I looked at each other, and Mr. Root listed forward a little, as if this could help him in his deciphering.

Ulub said again, "Ee ride, ee *ride*." Seeing then that no one was getting it, he screwed up his face and started to shake with dry sobs.

Mr. Root exclaimed, "She cried! That's it, ain't it, Ulub?"

Having made us understand, Ulub stopped heaving and nodded.

I said, "And her aunts, they just stood around and watched her?"

Again he nodded. Ulub looked truly unhappy.

No one said anything then. I guessed, looking around at our faces, no one wanted to. Gathered around the piano this way with our heads slightly bent, and looking down at our shoes, it was like a prayer meeting.

I could think of no yes-or-no question to ask and finally resorted to: "Then what happened?"

Ulub's knitted cap was in his hands and he kept kneading it and pulling at it. He said, "Ah ot n-n-aared." He looked down, sad or shamefaced, or both. On a small breath, he brought out what sounded like "raft" or "heft." And then a short barrage of words uttered so quickly no one, not even Mr. Root, could make them out. "Ah end ome."

I thought about the "raft" word. It had been the last word entered in the journal. "Raft." Could it be "left"? And then, Ulub said, he "went home."

Mr. Root, warming his hands under his armpits and chewing away at his tobacco, said, "Ulub was scared."

"He left and went on," I added. I was sure Ulub, seeing as much as he did, must have seen more. Must have seen the awful end of it. How disappointed I felt! And I realized that Ulub must have felt my disappointment, too. I also remembered, then, that this happened forty years ago and that Ulub was probably a teen-ager or less—my age. If it had been me—well, there was no use thinking about that, for if it had been me, I wouldn't have had the nerve even to come here in the first place, much less hang around watching what the Devereaus were up to. Maybe what Ulub had spurted out at the end had to do with someone seeing him. Maybe one of the Devereaus had seen or heard something out here and come to investigate. And Ulub had run home. *I'd* surely have run; you wouldn't have seen me for dust. I thought Ulub would feel better if I told him that. I put my hand on his arm. "You were really brave, Ulub. You were only a kid, anyway. If it'd been me, you wouldn't have seen me for dust."

He surprised us then by saying, as he pointed in the direction of the lake, "Ah ame mack, ah naw um awken roo toods."

Ulub had gone back to the lake! So there *was* more! More even than he'd been able to get across to Dr. McComb—another chapter that I had been hoping for. I listened to his broken words so intensely I think I must have stopped breathing. We all leaned slightly toward him. I said, "Ulub, did you see *more*?"

He nodded vigorously and said, "Ah uz ovr nere." And he pointed again.

"You mean the other side of the lake?"

Mr. Root was just a little miffed at my appearing to take over as translator. He dragged up on his belt and said, "You mean it was after you run away home and come back again you seen something?"

Pretty much what I had said, but I kept my mouth shut.

Ulub said, "Ey gum ith amps, awken."

Mr. Root was stumped on that one and so was I, so it's a good thing there were props sitting around. Ulub took Mr. Root's oil lamp and held it high; then he took one of the candlesticks and shoved it in his brother's hands and said something that Ubub seemed to understand, but we didn't. Ulub led and Ubub followed as they walked slowly about the parlor, holding their lights high.

I was open-mouthed at this little bit of dumb play. When I got my wits back, I said, "You mean that the Devereau sisters went out and walked through the woods with something like oil lamps?"

Ulub nodded. "An nanduls."

"Lamps and candles," said Mr. Root quickly, like he was a contestant on one of those TV quiz shows, making sure he answered first. He pulled up his belt again and repeated, "Lamps and candles, that's it, ain't it, Alonzo?"

Ulub nodded and waved his arms. He seemed almost happy, maybe because he'd finally got something off his chest.

I slowly shook my head in astonishment. Then I asked him, "Ulub—what about Mary-Evelyn?" I knew the answer before he told me.

"Ee uz tast un." Here he picked up the lamp

again, handed Ubub his candle, and then pulled at my arm. "Et nine, et inine!" As if I were a stuffed doll, he positioned me behind Ubub.

Having regained his control over the Ulub-language, Mr. Root said with authority: " 'Get in *line*,' that's what he's tellin' you!"

I did; I followed them slowly around the parlor. After circling it once, Ulub grabbed up another candlestick from a side table and shoved it at Mr. Root. "Et nine!" He pushed Mr. Root between his brother and me, then looked us over to see if we'd do. I never realized how bossy Ulub could be, but I felt it to be a good thing. We circled the room at a slow and creepy pace, the three Devereau sisters and me, Mary-Evelyn.

In my mind's eye I saw them out there, dressed in black (though they probably weren't), and little Mary-Evelyn, in her fussy white dress, following. I could barely hold this image in my mind, it seemed so desolate.

Mr. Root asked, "Now, where was them three old witches goin'? Was they takin that poor child around to the *boathouse*?"

*Yes*, I thought, that's where they were taking her. It was just too awful to be believed. I hung my head as if I had had some part in this punishment of Mary-Evelyn, as if I shared the blame.

So Mr. Root became official questioner. "So where was you, Alonzo? Near that boathouse?"

Ulub shook his head. "Uh ring. Uh *ring*."

Mr. Root said to us, "Says he was at the *spring*."

The spring was only a short distance from the old boathouse. I took a step toward Ulub and asked, "What happened then?"

Ulub had picked up his cap from the piano top and was wringing it in his hands. He kept his eyes on the floor, unwilling to tell us more. He said again, "Ah not narr-ared, narr-ared." Ubub moved over to him and put a big hand on his shoulder.

This time I knew what he'd said—that he got scared. Who could blame him, watching that black procession with its sinister, flickering lights? But he did not say he ran from the spring, so I asked him what he saw then. I was upsetting him, and I certainly didn't want to. His tongue would move to try again; I could feel the words wedged like cement between his tongue and his teeth, and his throat must have locked up over telling the rest of that night. He was too discouraged, or probably too shamed. Here he had finally got people who would listen to him, who honestly *wanted* to listen to him, and he must have been feeling he had let us down.

I myself felt ashamed and moved to put my hand on his shoulder, as Ubub had done, in comradely sympathy, and said, "It's okay, Alonzo. It really is. It's as it should be."

Now, where on earth had I come up with that? "It's as it should be"? That was not the way I talked; that was not the way anyone talked except maybe Father Freeman trying to convince some poor farmer whose crops had all withered away that there was a place for that withering in God's plan. I fooled around with this idea of God for a moment. Then I had what I later would call a "moment of clarity." It told me: yes, it really *was* as it should be. The silence forced on Ulub by the awful collision of throat and tongue, that was "as it should be." It was almost as if Mary-Evelyn had come back to say to the Woods: "I'll tell you what happened; I'll tell you because you won't tell anyone. But it will make me feel better for telling it, and you for hearing it." They were in a way alike, Ulub and Ubub and Mary-Evelyn, for they were all three bedeviled by silence. Silence had been Mary-Evelyn's lot in life; it was her punishment, not for things she'd done, but for just being *her*. I could guess at half a dozen reasons for them hating her. It's very easy to find reasons to hate someone; all you needed was the will to do it.

I gazed up at the ceiling and said, "Let's go upstairs; let's each take a different room."

We trooped up the staircase, whose banister was listing and rotted. We looked in each of the rooms until I decided the small one must have been Mary-Evelyn's. It looked like a child's room, with its blue-painted furniture. The other three went into the larger rooms and all of us poked around.

The small one was at the front and was the room I had seen from the other side of the lake, the one with the dormer windows that overlooked it. This must have provided the very best view in the entire house, and I could only guess that Mary-Evelyn had been given it because it was the tiniest room. Also, there were people who probably thought a view over Spirit Lake wasn't exactly a prize.

The single bed sat between the two windows, covered with a spread. It was an iron bed, painted white. A narrow chest of drawers was blue, the wooden knobs painted along with the rest of it, as if someone couldn't be bothered removing them. A little table beside the bed was also blue. An old rocker sat in the corner, with a faded flowered cushion, and there was a big dark wardrobe, the kind we had at the hotel, for only modern houses had actual built-in closets, which were boring. Wardrobes were much more interesting, because they came in all shapes and sizes and different woods, some with beautiful mirrored doors, and the coat hangers rattled and clinked when the doors were opened. Better for hiding in, too.

I opened this one and was surprised to see clothes hanging there. Dresses. There must have been eight or nine; all of them probably had been sewn by the Devereau aunt. They were fine material and beautiful. There was a deep-blue taffeta one with a full skirt. I touched its folds and thought of the Waitresses.

Except for opening drawers there was nowhere to look. I struggled to open one of the windows and succeeded and crawled out on the narrow balcony, realizing only after I stood there that what I had done was foolhardy, for the balcony could be rotted like the banister, could be dangerous like the one outside of Aurora's rooms. But nothing gave. It seemed very secure. Still, I sat on the windowsill with my rear pushed more than halfway into the room, just in case there was a sudden wrench and lurch.

It was dark now. In the time between the parlor and the bedroom, the sky had changed from that beautiful plumy dark to ink. The moon was up and looking like one of the china plates my mother serves dinners on. It was cold and hard and white like that. It hung there right over the lake, which looked as sheerly smooth as a black ice rink. Rivulets of moonlight moved across its surface. It was interesting, being here and looking over there, for I had never seen my side—meaning, the now-other side—of the lake before. It was interesting looking at all of the objects that I was so used to seeing from a different angle.

Ulub's tale certainly said a lot about what Mary-Evelyn's state of mind must have been; it was information any policeman would want to know. I sat there balanced on the windowsill, in the dark, and half-hearing (but paying no attention to) the calls of Mr. Root and the Woods, coming from below. I think I was searching the opposite shore for the Girl. My eyes roved, mistaking any sudden movement to be her: moonlight playing on the sculpture of rocks by the dam; the sudden illumination of a plank in the house; the birch tree bending in the wind. These objects in another moment revealed themselves to be normal and ordinary. I thought of the faded brown photograph on the wall, the young blond girl there in front of the much-younger sisters. Then I thought of my one picture of Mary-Evelyn, my mother's snapshot, with the Devereau aunts standing behind her.

It was not my father's lake any longer. Mary-Evelyn haunted it.

# TWENTY

To look at me, or even to listen to me, you wouldn't think that my life is a succession of terrors. "Blue devils" is what Mr. Root calls it. I try hard not to let this show in my face or my voice; I try to keep calm. Oh, I don't mean the sort of terrors that include being led away in early morning to be lynched, or stumbling in the dark and sliding down a sheer rock face without finger- or toeholds, or waking to see the smoke fingering my doorsill. Not those kinds of terrors. I'm talking about things like this: the face behind the steamed-up window of the Greyhound bus and a hand waving when the bus pulls away, both face and hand disappearing in the steam and the distance; or being out in the woods or the field calling and calling for a dog or a cat you haven't seen for two days; or Lola Davidow in one of her snits. Things like that. I don't, of course, always feel this way; I can bury the fear or push it back if, say, I'm eating buckwheat cakes or ham pinwheels or even the Rainbow's chili, or if I'm down in the Pink Elephant scribbling, or eating popcorn in the dark of the Orion, or doing meter checks with the Sheriff, or sitting in the Rainbow talking to Maud. So there are many things that toss a veil over such terrors. But the blue devils are always there, I think, underneath the surface, ready to jump out.

In this state of mind, everything stands out sharply. I can sit in the Rainbow, in my booth, and look at the row of faces seated at the counter and see each one surrounded by a fine line, each head scalped by light; or see the trees beyond the window out there looking cut away from the sky, each separate and severe; or when someone plugs money in the jukebox and Patsy Cline sings "I Fall to Pieces," well, Patsy does, piece by piece. It's like hearing prisms shiver in a chandelier, shards of glass on glass.

The blue devils. I'm glad Mr. Root gave me the words for it.

My mother told me that once my father got run over by a train. I do not know if this story is God's truth, and I'm inclined to doubt it, but what my mother says happened is that my father got his foot caught in the middle of the track and the train was coming. According to her, he had so much presence of mind that he managed to lie down between the rails, longways, and hold himself perfectly straight and pressed against the ties, and the train just passed over him. I don't think it was a whole train, or a passenger train. It might only have been a slow-moving caboose (though you'd think if that were the case, the engineer would have seen a person lying there). I find it hard to believe that anyone would have that kind of courage or command over his feelings that he could stop struggling to pull his foot out and just lie down. But that's what my mother says. A lot of mornings I wake up and feel that I have my foot stuck in the railroad ties while another day is bearing down.

It's the blue devils I got when I heard the police had found a woman dead in Mirror Pond, over near White's Bridge. A blond woman.

And it was Ree-Jane who told me all about it (as if she knew), who said she'd heard it from "Sam" (as if she knew *him* better than I did).

To have Ree-Jane be the one to carry this news was utterly horrible. Anyone, *anyone*, else would have been better, even her mother, even Helene Baum. The only thing that saved me was that Ree-Jane knew nothing about the Girl, and so she couldn't taunt me about this dead blond woman possibly being somebody important to me. Which she would have done out of jealousy that she didn't know her, too, but even more out of plain meanness.

I held myself together and pretended I was bored until I could get away from her and out to the porch. There, I went around the corner at the very end, where I couldn't be seen. I sat down in one of the dark green rocking chairs and cried.

The blue devils, for sure.

Finally, I wiped my eyes and took some action. I would go into town, to the courthouse, and try to get some clue as to the dead woman's identity. I walked the two miles into La Porte, walked boldly up the courthouse steps, and stopped in the open door of the Sheriff's office. He saw me and smiled and said hello, and so did I. That's all I said: "Hello."

I stood there in the doorway, frozen. I felt ice-locked. I could tell there was a lot going on, for I'd never before seen Donny, the deputy, act so busy. The Sheriff gave me a sort of quizzical look, as it was rare for me ever to show up in his office, and I suppose it was. Now, of course, if the dead person *was* the Girl, I knew that he'd want to know what I knew. But that was of no concern to me at all; I couldn't care less if I helped out the police—not even the Sheriff, for once. All I wanted was for it *not* to be Her.

Just a couple of questions could put me out of my misery: Exactly what did she look like? What was she wearing? But I couldn't ask these questions. I mumbled something about checking the meters and turned on my heel and left.

The next day would bring the weekly edition of the *Conservative* and more details. It would draw me like a magnet and make me want to look away, both at the same time. On my walk back to the hotel, I asked myself the important question. This question was, of course, Why did it matter so much that the dead woman might be the Girl? I reminded myself that I had seen her only three times, and each time for just seconds, and that I had never spoken to her. How did I know but that she was just a ghost only I could see? (*Just* a ghost?) I didn't know anything at all about her. I saw her on a railroad platform in Cold Flat, and I saw her walking along Second Street in La Porte, and I saw her across the lake. The first two times she might have been doing what anyone might. But not the third time, no. For no one ever went to that old unoccupied house across the lake. No, the third time I saw the Girl was something totally different. She was somehow connected to the story of Mary-Evelyn Devereau.

So I had come back from the courthouse and the Sheriff to sit on the porch again, around the corner where no one would be likely to see me. After I wiped my face on my sleeve so I could see straight, everything had that terribly clear, icy-edged look of separateness. Each tree lining the dirt path that stretched down to the highway stood out in stark relief instead of just blending into two blurred lines as they usually did. Each looked cut away from the background, as if separated from the sky.

Why did the world, I wonder, take on this look of separateness when bad news came my way?

## TWENTY-ONE

I think there are people who feed on other people's discomfort and fear, really *feed* on it, like vampires. They get their sharp little teeth into your big juicy fear and enjoy sucking away at it. And they can smell blood, too. They can follow that smell to its source— *oh, it's you, is it?*—Sniff, sniff. Mmmm. And then *chomp!* Since people like this are completely insensitive, it always amazes me how they can sense somebody else's trouble. I guess the technical word for this is "sadist." When it comes to Ree-Jane Davidow, I'd use plain old "mean."

I could not hide from this special talent of hers; that is, I could not hide my feelings. My feelings seemed to hum along electrical wires, showering visible sparks. I think there was always a slight vibration that made the air crackle when I passed through it. So perhaps I'm giving Ree-Jane too much credit for having some sixth sense when it comes to me. This misery-making talent of Ree-Jane's was never practiced on Will, I'd noticed. But then a lot of people never did anything to Will. For one thing, he was a boy, the only male in the "family." For another thing, he was good-looking and he was smart. They say brothers and sisters are always fighting and making life miserable for each other, but not Will and me. He played a lot of tricks on me (since I was really

gullible), but we got along practically all of the time.
I wondered what we would be like when we were
old and gray—if I lived that long, what with Ree-
Jane around.

Yet, at the same time I think I'm really good
at covering up. This is a complete contradiction, but
I still think it's true. The way I turned into a Popsicle
when I went into the courthouse. The Sheriff couldn't
tell I had the blue devils; nobody could. I was cold
and stiff from head to toe. My lips hardly moved.
Funnily enough, this made a lot of people think I
was unfeeling. So I'm back to Ree-Jane's peculiar
ability to read me, even though I do not think I'm
an open book.

And that's what she was doing the next day
when I was sitting, again, on my corner of the porch,
knowing that the weekly newspaper was out but too
afraid to go in search of it. Well, of course, I didn't
have to, for Ree-Jane strutted out to the porch wearing one of her Helen Gay Struther outfits from the
exclusive Europa boutique. My mother said Ree-Jane
was spoiled by being so indulged by Lola Davidow.
Helen Gay Struther was one of those who gained a
lot from Mrs. Davidow's indulgences. They would
not lower themselves to shop anywhere else; they
would buy only from "Helen Gay" (a big woman
who wore lots of purple eyeshadow and chunks of
clattering gold jewelry).

Ree-Jane smoothed out the tiny-pleated skirt of
her two-piece blue silk dress. In my T-shirt and faded
shorts, I was no fashion match for her. After she

made a big display of her expensive dress, she then made a big display of the paper, shaking it out as if it had dustballs all over it, and she pretended then to be really surprised by the account (although it was clear she'd already read it) of the finding of the dead woman.

Before she even opened her mouth, I knew what she was up to. I knew she'd sensed in her vampire-bride way (though it was hard to imagine even a vampire marrying Ree-Jane) that I didn't want to read it or hear about it. Even though I had not let on yesterday, not even for a second, that I minded. I had gone right away into my Popsicle mode, my face expressionless as ice, my body stiff. But she knew I didn't want to know. Why couldn't I run away? Just get up, say "Excuse me," and take off? Probably for the same reason I was *capable* of becoming a robot and emptying my face of expression. You can't be able to do that at the same time you're screaming inside, and also be able to jump up and run away. Don't ask me why.

So I sat there staring straight ahead at the double line of tall oak trees carved against the sky, as Ree-Jane read the story. Suzy Whitelaw (the paper's star reporter) had written it. I knew because she'd given it a title: "The Mystery of Mirror Pond." It made me grunt with disgust. She thought she was a big-time writer; she'd written a mystery that nobody on God's green earth wanted to publish, although Suzy kept hinting her "agent" was after a huge "advance." Ree-Jane and Suzy were always yakking around about their writing, when I knew Ree-Jane had never put pen to paper since her measly little piece for the newspaper. They believed they had something in common, despite the big difference in their ages, Ree-Jane being not quite seventeen and Suzy Whitelaw being thirty or forty. A huge difference like that probably doesn't matter when two people just want to suck up to each other.

So here I was not only having to listen to the facts, but having them come at me from someone who couldn't write by way of someone who couldn't read. If I had heard it from the Sheriff, see, that would have softened whatever blow was coming. At least I'd know that he wasn't trying to give me pain just by telling me. Or even if the death could have been reported by Mr. Gumbel, in his straightforward style, that would have taken some of the awfulness away from it. But no, I had to get it in the worst possible way. I felt doomed. My whole life was like this.

Ree-Jane cleared her throat and read:

" 'The Mystery of Mirror Pond.' The moonlit tranquillity of the little expanse of water by White's Bridge known as Mirror Pond was broken on Tuesday night—"

I relaxed enough to gag. One reason was because she was reading in the most singsongy, stagy voice she could manage. Ree-Jane also wanted to be a Broadway actress.

Ree-Jane looked up over the paper, really irritated, and asked sharply, "Well? What's wrong with that?"

"It's not tranquil. Mirror Pond's dirty; it has slime on top. The moon couldn't shine on that pond, not even with one of those big emergency road flash-lights."

"Oh, for God's sake! Don't be so damned *lit-eral*!" Ree-Jane loved to swear at me.

"Suzy Whitelaw's supposed to be reporting a death. It should be literal." I rocked; this argument was helping to reduce my fear.

"Well, what do *you* know about reporting or writing?"

"More than Suzy Whitelaw, but that's not say-ing much."

Fuming, Ree-Jane started to slide from the porch railing, saying, "Listen, do you or don't you want me to—" She stopped.

I rocked, feeling almost happy. She stopped because she didn't, now, know what to do. If she marched off in a huff, she'd lost an opportunity to make me miserable. It must have been a real problem for her. Making me miserable won out, and she went on:

"—was broken on Tuesday night by the grisly discovery of the dead body of a woman as yet uniden-tified. When questioned, it was determined by Sheriff Sam DeGheyn that this woman was not—"

Quickly, I put in, "That's not even good gram-mar. It's a dangling modifier."

The paper came down again. *"What* is?"

" 'When questioned, comma, it was determined.' " I wasn't sure if it was, but Ree-Jane couldn't contradict me, for English was my best subject; I always got A's. Nothing was Ree-Jane's best subject. I'm so much better in school than Ree-Jane, it's pathetic.

So she was stuck with "Who *cares*?"

"Well, I do. I want my news brought to me by someone who can write good English."

"You think you're so smart!"

Smug as I felt, I winced. *"You think you're so smart"* was something I hadn't said since second grade. That's what we all said then when we couldn't think of anything really clever and cutting. "You think you're so smart! You think you're so smart!" I could still see me, hands on hips, leaning into the wind or the swings, yelling at Twinkie Petri, who yelled it right back at me. "Yeah? Well, *you* think you're so smart!" And here was Ree-Jane, supposed to be going to college next year, just yelling like Twinkie Petri. I felt pretty powerful, because now she was getting mad at me and completely forgetting the newspaper account.

"All I said was, it's a dangling modifier." I rocked and scratched my elbows. Then I took a chance and said, "Go on."

"Why should I? You keep interrupting with your smart-ass comments." She sounded really shrill and must have known it, for she changed her tone. "Writing is an ART."

Whenever Ree-Jane talks about it, I always hear the word as if I'm looking at the blinking neon sign on top of the greasy spoon between La Porte and Hebrides. The owner's name is Arturo, and he's an Italian, which he thinks makes his eating establishment classy, but it's only an Italian greasy spoon. The neon sign used to spell his name, but the "URO" must have burned out, so he's left now with "ART." And that flashes off and on again with the other word, "EAT," so the sign over the cafe goes ART—*blink*—EAT—*blink*—ART—*blink*—EAT.

"You still have to punctuate and spell right," I said, as I watched the sign blink on, off, on, off in my mind, and felt comforted.

"Oh, don't be *stupid*! Artists are interested in great issues, like Love and Beauty and Death and . . . so forth. They don't have to walk a line between *spelling* and *punctuation*," said Ree-Jane, in her most sneering tone.

"Tell that to a tightrope walker."

"Don't be stupid!"

She was exhausting her store of insults. But I had managed to completely get her off the subject of the dead woman at Mirror Pond. I was proud of myself.

"Here's this Tragic Death, this poor soul—"

Ree-Jane concerned with poor souls? I raised my eyebrows.

"—who might have shot herself—"

*Shot herself?* I stopped rocking. If that was so, the person could not be the Girl. She would not kill herself. Why was I so certain of that? Because she was searching for something, and it wasn't death. Don't ask me how I knew that. My mind went back to Cold Flat Junction and that railway platform, and her sitting there, and her standing up, searching the distance up the track and down it. Standing there in her pale cotton dress and with her long, light hair, she was so . . . lit up that she seemed like the line of oaks (now beginning to melt back into their background) carved away by light from everything around her. This feeling I get when the blue devils come over me of things separating and pulling away might sound frightening. It isn't, actually, for what I seem to be looking at then just has very sharp outlines, as if before, in my normal state, I see things a little fuzzed over, kind of all blending into one another. But when the fear comes over me, I see differently; things become separate and more themselves. It isn't frightening; it's a sort of comfort. But now the oaks were melting back into the sky, for I knew the danger was over. Now Ree-Jane was too taken up with her ART argument.

I was still thinking of the neon sign, ART—*blink*—EAT, and thinking that cooking was as much an art as anything. I sat there hearing her words, like wasps, circling and mostly dropping dead, but kept my distance by filling up mentally with more of that day's lunch—chicken pie. My mother's chicken pie had no equal, anywhere. The pastry crust alone proved that (she was famous for that crust), for it was light and flaky, gold streaked with brown. But the thing was, my mother's chicken pie had *chicken* in it, big chunks of white meat (so even I got white meat then) in a gravy that wasn't that watery stuff you get in most chicken pies, but was creamy and had that sagey, peppery seasoning that took you back to Thanksgiving. . . .

"What are you smiling that silly *smile* for?"

"What? Oh. Chicken pie." I had just started in on the succulent dice of potatoes, and the peas and the tiny onions, which I guess was too far from Tragic Death for Ree-Jane's comfort.

"I'm talking about writing and art and you're thinking of *food*? No wonder you're fat."

I wasn't fat. I didn't bother contradicting this. "Well, didn't you have some chicken pie for lunch?"

Preening, showing off her supposedly wonderful figure (which it wasn't), she said, "I never eat lunch."

"Poor you." The bits of deep-orange carrot, the silvery little onions . . .

"I don't think *only* about food."

She didn't think about anything. "But what I was considering," I said, "was, well, cooking's an ART." I sat there in the dark-green slat-back chair, rocking with even more energy, knowing we were so far from Mirror Pond we could have been on a desert island. What a horrible thought: Ree-Jane and me on a desert island.

She was having a little problem, for she actually couldn't *criticize* my mother's cooking. Everyone seemed to get almost deathly honest and awed when

it came to my mother's cooking. I frowned, thinking
this over. It seemed a little strange. But it was true.
Perhaps even I had missed some important point
about my mother's cooking. That was hard to believe,
considering.

"Well, okay, your mother's kind of an artist,
okay. But that's not what I'm talking about."

I decided to change the subject (which had gotten changed three or four times already) again, and
drive the final nail into the vampire bride's coffin
by giving her an opportunity to show off and brag.
"Why're you dressed up, incidentally? That's really
a pretty shade of blue." I'd heard her tell Will she
was going out.

"I have a date." She looked off into the loaming
(I was thinking in poetic terms because she was
trying so hard to look dewy and dreamy) and added,
"You don't know him."

No surprise, since I didn't know anybody, particularly boys. And of course she wanted to make it
seem that there were so many "known" boys interested in her that she had to have a whole new category: the Unknowns. "Where are you going?"

Here she extended her hands behind her head
and lifted up her blond hair as if it were angel's
wings. I loathed that gesture. And Ree-Jane's hair
seemed to do a lot of color changing, sometimes
lighter, sometimes darker, which she explained in
summer by saying it was "sun-streaked." Well, there
were also spring and autumn—meaning, I didn't

think the change was seasonal. "Probably to the Cliquot Club."

"I thought you had to be twenty-one to get in there." I said it because I knew she wanted me to.

"*I* can *always* get in. Perry knows me."

Perry was a man in his thirties who slobbered around lots of women, but I didn't think Ree-Jane was one of them. "Oh," was all I said. I was smiling down at the newspaper, now lying forgotten on the porch. I said a few more things about the club, really boring, until she finally got the idea she'd sucked whatever blood she could on this occasion and dragged her blue dress off the porch railing and left.

For another while, I sat there contentedly rocking, looking at the lines of oaks that were fuzzily back in place, mixing with the sky and other trees and mossy ground and gravel. Of course, my eyes fell more than once on the paper, but I was strangely untempted to pick it up and read. For possible bad news is just as much of a magnet as good. Although I still didn't know the identity of the dead woman, although nothing had really changed, somehow the power of the facts to kill me had been weakened.

I had found out nothing more except for that "possible" suicide business. No details about where she'd come from, no physical description at all. Except she was blond, and blond could mean anything.

Just look at Ree-Jane.

# TWENTY-TWO

It was a small victory, shutting up Ree-Jane, but that still left me with the problem of finding out just who had died in Mirror Pond.

*The Conservative* was lying there near my feet, a corner lifting and fluttering in a gust of wind. What I wanted was to find out in easy stages, a little here and a little there—a shred of truth, a pack of lies, a jumble of information I could choose bits and pieces from and put them together and see the answer to my question when I was ready to see it. Suzy Whitelaw's drippy story should have satisfied this need; but no, any newspaper account would still have too much truth in it for comfort. But not nearly as much as the blare of truth that would come from the Sheriff's mouth—and I was amazed by my foolhardy visit to the courthouse yesterday morning. True, I'd rather have heard it from him, but the "it" I wanted to hear might not be the "it" he was going to tell. And the trouble was, I could not let on by so much as the flicker of an eyelash that I would be devastated if he said something like "a young girl, real young, pale blond hair, wearing a sprigged cotton dress." I would actually turn into the pillar of ice I was coolly pretending to be.

Then came the question Why? Why would I turn into a pillar of ice at the discovery?

I couldn't answer that.

What I wanted, then, was a kind of *slanted* truth, and I turned over possible sources of undependable information. There was Ulub and Ubub, not because they were undependable but because I couldn't understand them. Probably, they hadn't heard about the dead lady. I got the impression they didn't keep up with the news in *The Conservative*, and since most people didn't talk to them, they'd have no way of knowing. Unless from Mr. Root. Then there was Britten's store, where a lot of old-timers gathered, so each one could prove he knew more than the others. There was Miss Flagler, too. She was much more fearful than Miss Flyte, I'd noticed, and certainly would be of dead bodies. She always tried to pretend they didn't really happen, or that there was a happier explanation, and so made such details out to be better than they were. She might even bring the dead lady back to life again by saying, "Well, she was probably just concussed after all that, and they must have taken her to County General." "But the paper said 'dead,' Miss Flagler!" "Oh, pshaw, you know you can never believe anything that Whitelaw woman tells you."

The easiest of all of these at the moment would be Britten's store as it would take only five minutes to get there. I was about to set out when a car came crunching along the drive, and I figured it was Mrs. Davidow's station wagon, bringing her back from town. The wagon bumped along, spewing up gravel bits, horn honking as she rounded the corner (as I eased down in my chair so she wouldn't see me) and coming to rest under the porte cochere. She always tapped on the horn to let people know she was back so we could start up the marching band and throw confetti, but it was mostly a signal for Walter to come and get the groceries. I always thought that was pretty funny; she could have waited on the wind as soon as Walter to carry the grocery bags. Eventually, Walter would get there, but no use honking.

Steps on the porch stairs, and the screen door banged. I heard her calling out for Walter.

Her first stop would be the kitchen, for she would be buzzing with news for my mother. Mrs. Davidow loved her role of Messenger. Sometimes, I pictured the hotel as one of those out-of-the-way castles back in the Middle Ages, where huge beamed doors were flung open and a messenger nearly fell off his horse to rush in with news for the king. In many ways I like this fantasy, for it makes me feel the hotel is its own place, surrounded by water, connected to the rest of the world only by a drawbridge which can be lowered or raised when we see fit. So what I realized was that with the paper out today, she'd come back absolutely full of all the news about this dead woman. There is no better source of questionable information than Mrs. Davidow; she loves her role as the person coming from a distant country so much that she can't help making a bad thing worse or a good thing better with a lot of little odds and ends either left out or put in just to make her story better. Thus, if I heard some detail that confirmed my worst suspicions (*"pretty," "young," "a stranger"*), I might be able to ignore it.

After these trips to town, Lola Davidow always heads for the kitchen, where she sits on the salad table and smokes cigarettes while she shares with my mother that day's takings of gossip, and my mother would be standing as always between the long work table and the cast-iron stove, cutting up vegetables or cutting circles in biscuit dough, smoking too, and listening. It's a familiar scene. When I am not busy criticizing them for a hundred different heartfelt sins, I almost admire them. For they are making the best of things. They certainly aren't making money.

Knowing where she was going, I followed her. When I banged through one of the swinging doors between dining room and kitchen, Mrs. Davidow was perched as always on the big white porcelain table where at dinnertime I put up the salad bowls. The table was blessedly clear now of everything— a clean slate—except for the crock of French dressing that always sits at one end, aging and being added to when it gets low. Half an onion steeps in the crock; a red swirl of paprika floats on top. It is, of course, the best French dressing in the universe. The kitchen was blessedly free of Vera, who always butts into their conversations, correcting them for truth. The only other person was Walter, standing in the shadows at the far end of the room with the big industrial dishwasher. Mrs. Davidow was telling him to go out and bring in the groceries, and Walter nodded, but just kept wiping at a cookie sheet. Naturally, I didn't want anyone to think I'd come to *listen*, so I purposefully moved to the French dressing crock, lifted the lid, and peeked in. As it was my responsibility to keep an eye on the dressing level, no one paid any attention to me. Anyway, I put on a busy frown, twirled the ladle around, and made patterns with the paprika. Then I added some oil. I wanted to think it was a compliment to my skill that no one questioned what I was doing, but I knew that wasn't so, since it would be hard to ruin the French dressing, there being no exact ratios of one thing to another. This is another thing that amazes me about my mother's cooking: there seldom are. And one day it struck me that this was real ART-EAT, in the full Arturo sense—that an artist simply *knows*. It might appear that the person was haphazard, tossing a little paint here, a little paprika there; but no. The artist has such a feeling for what he is doing that little measurements are built into his mind and eye and hand. That's the way I explained it, and with this thought I lightly tossed a sprinkling of paprika and a teaspoon of sugar into the dressing.

I was also lightly listening. Lightly, because what I wanted to do was partly remove my eardrums from unpleasant news and partly open them up to what I wanted to hear. If I'd had Miss Bertha's hearing aid I could have fiddled it around. What I did was to enter a kind of dream world where I could raise and lower a sort of theaterlike curtain between Mrs. Davidow's words and my hearing. Like a filter.

Mrs. Davidow was perched in her usual way on the salad table, her stocky legs crossed at the ankles and swinging slightly. She smoked and talked. My mother smoked and listened. I added salt to the crock and stirred and heard her words muted as in a dream or in memory.

*. . . a stranger, probably not even one of the lake people.*

Well, I already knew that no one had identified her. I decided to go to the icebox and look in. Now she was talking about actually having bumped into "Sam" in the Rainbow Café. That stopped me in my intention of making a Black Cow with Coke and vanilla ice cream, as it would be too complicated a procedure. Instead, I quietly slipped out a small pitcher of iced tea and went to the cupboard for a glass.

*. . . said it was really strange, she must have walked across White's Bridge. Where was she going?*

Lola Davidow, lady dick. My mother said something about she didn't see why that was important either and then told me to put back the pitcher of tea. As I did this, Mrs. Davidow was answering:

*To meet someone? She might not have gone there on her own.*

Dreamily, I carried my iced tea glass towards the dish drain, walking between Mrs. Davidow's swinging feet and my mother's dicing knife, too close to their voices to blunt the hard edges of their words.

By the time I got to the drain table, where we waitresses dump trayloads of dishes for Walter to stack up, I was out of waking danger, back into semidreaming. The state was helped along by Walter, whose motions were always dreamlike, and who was wiping a big platter, cradling it like a baby and slowly dragging the dishtowel around it. He told me "Hello," a nasal, sort of tongue-stuck sound, as he gave me his wide, rubber-band smile. Walter was always in a good humor, always working at his many jobs, always in shadow, as if he carried a bag of shadows to take out and put on.

"Sam said there were tire tracks. A pickup truck, probably. Four-wheel drive."

My mother said, "Mirror Pond. I wonder why anyone would get killed there. Or kill herself. It's miles from anywhere."

That was true enough. But then I suppose if you're going to kill somebody, you'd want a miles-from-anywhere sort of place. The map in my mind of the local geography was about as dependable as directions from a blind man. I knew Mirror Pond and White's Bridge were somewhere north of Spirit Lake; that is, if you went as the crow flies from the Devereau place, you'd come to White's Bridge and Mirror Pond, near it. But this was miles I was talking about; it was too far to walk.

For I had decided, listening to my mother and Mrs. Davidow, that I simply had to see it. It was the murder site. I didn't think the Sheriff would see fit to give me a ride in an "official vehicle." That's what he called his police car when Maud asked for a lift to Hebrides or somewhere. "Sorry, I can't ride you around in an official vehicle." And she'd say, "Ride me around? Like I'm Miss La Porte or someone? I'm not asking to 'ride around.'" Of course, the Sheriff only said it to get her goat.

Nor was Mrs. Davidow about to give me a ride, not unless she got so curious herself about the dead woman that she'd want to go there and would want me to go with her. For some reason I seemed to make her feel more secure, as if I were riding shotgun. I didn't understand this.

Absentmindedly I had picked up a dishtowel. Wiping dishes could sometimes help my concentration. Now there was, of course, Ree-Jane's white convertible. Only, Ree-Jane went with it, and although I could stand to humble myself and beg her, having to take her along would ruin the trip.

There was Axel's Taxis. I had enough money to pay for one for all that distance; the trouble with that was that Delbert would broadcast all over La Porte that he'd driven me to Mirror Pond. Then I suddenly thought of the Wood boys and their old pickup trucks. I wondered if they were up at Britten's right now.

I heard Mrs. Davidow saying: . . . *there was no identification on the body, there was nothing in the pockets of her cotton dress, Sam said . . .*

The pockets of her cotton dress . . .

Painful as it was to smile, I returned Walter's smile and picked up a salad plate while the word "pockets" . . . "pockets" . . . "pockets" wheeled in my mind. But then, I told myself, pockets in a dress were pretty common.

 . . . *or in her handbag* . . .

Like a freight train, those words rushed towards me! Her *handbag*! One of the things I had noticed about the Girl was that she didn't carry a *handbag*. She was here, she was there, she was in places (such as the railway platform) where you would have thought a woman would have brought a handbag with her. But the Girl carried only a small purse not much bigger than her hand. Would such an article be called a "handbag"?

Was my argument kind of weak? I leaned against the dishwasher. Walter wondered, was I sick?

I wasn't, I told him.

But then I thought: Mrs. Davidow is telling my mother what she says the Sheriff told her. Immediately, some of my fear returned, for the Sheriff would never have taken Mrs. Davidow into his confidence, and that's the way she was making it sound. Probably, a lot of what she was reporting to my mother was her own invention, although she might even think these details were received from the Sheriff. So I could be pretty much back where I was before.

I tossed down the dishtowel and headed out the back screen door.


Neither the Woods nor even Mr. Root had taken up their positions yet on the bench outside of Britten's.

It was occupied by an old man, who sat with legs crossed and arms wrapped so closely around himself his hands nearly reached his back. He was bent over as if in pain, but all he was doing was leaning forward and squinting off across the highway at (I guessed) something interesting to him that I couldn't see. He wore a black-and-white striped cap that gave the impression he'd either been a convict or borrowed the hat from one. I didn't know him, but then there were a lot of people in Spirit Lake I didn't know.

Just as I expected there would be, several old-timers had taken up their stations in Britten's long narrow room, the canned goods shelved along one wall, the candy and cigarette counter along the other, where the cash register was and the large containers of loose cookies. The men were talking to one another across the expanse of the room. I thought it would be simpler for them to stand together, but they only did that if there was something juicy to chew over.

Well, today there was, for not ten seconds after I'd walked in, one of them brought up the subject of Mirror Pond. Another of them replied, "That there woman the po-lice found, well, I never did hear nothin' like that."

Then they seemed to be pulled together, the four of them, as if by a magnet. They made a small circle near the meat counter at the rear, where Mr. Britten's son, also the butcher, was leaning his chin on his folded arms and listening, so that he could put his two bits in.

I stood before the candy-display case looking

at the lineup of Butterfingers and Necco wafers and keeping my own ears open. When I left the kitchen, I remembered I'd want some money, so I crossed the grass to the other wing and went up to my room to collect some of my tips. I took a dollar in change along, which I jiggled in my fist whenever Mr. Britten looked my way, just to let him know I was here on business and not to loiter like some other people I could mention.

". . . stranger . . ."

I was tired of hearing that word; it was pretty settled in my mind that she was a stranger. But then came a contradiction.

"Ain't what I heard. . . . [*mumble*] said she was from one of them ritzy places the lake people own. . . ."

My hopes soared. If that were the case, it couldn't be the Girl.

"Hell *no*, that ain't right. They tol' me"— and here a stream of tobacco juice got aimed at one of the spittoons Mr. Britten kept around—"she be from over to [*mumble, mumble*]. . . ."

Strain as I did, I couldn't hear. So my stomach churned again. Now they'd all lowered their voices, so I just went ahead and studied the candy display. The penny candy had gone up to two cents some time when I wasn't looking. I especially liked the paper-wrapped hard ones with the melty centers and the fruit from which each took its flavor stamped on the white wrapping. Then I heard, much to my delight:

". . . Hebrides. You hear that, Bryson? That that woman's from Hebrides?"

He was addressing Mr. Britten, a fairly useless task, for the storekeeper didn't seem to like talking much. Mr. Britten grunted and adjusted his specs, thick black-framed ones that went with his black hair. I think he's rich and owns a lot of property around. Mildly relieved—for the Girl, I would bet, was from Cold Flat Junction, if from anywhere around here—I went on looking at the Fireballs. I loved Fireballs. Some were dark red and some were a glowing orange color that I'd never seen anywhere on this earth except in a Fireball. The voices were rising and falling, too difficult to hear from the candy counter, so I moved back and to the left to take up a position nearer the meat counter by the shelves of canned goods. There was a single wooden rocker in the corner, and one of the men had sat down in it to shout his opinions up at the others. I pretended to be inspecting the baked beans, the Heinz and Campbell's, knowing that Mr. Britten would be over to ask me what I wanted. I couldn't walk in and just fool around like the adults did; I was expected to take care of my errand and move out quickly. The hotel being probably his best customer, I thought he should treat me with at least as much respect as he did these men. Well, here he came, making me lose out on some of their talk, and I told him I was trying to remember how many cans my mother told me to get. He just annoyed me to death by telling me the hotel always got the big ones, the "institution-sized" (as if anyone could tell me anything I didn't know about my mother's baked beans). I told him, not this time, this was something different. He moved away, suspicious. Mr. Britten always had that look, like someone was going to rob him blind.

". . . you thinkin 'bout Louella?"

"Looks just like her, from what Donny said."

*Donny.* He was deputy sheriff! *Louella.* I stiffened and kept staring at the rows of canned beans, Heinz and Campbell's.

"*Hell* it does. Why, I seen her not three days ago!"

"Well, you mighta see'd her, Bub, but three days ago ain't two *nights* ago, and the way Donny said it, she looked just like Louella. You know—" this was directed to the others—"big girl, lives over to Hebrides." He spat.

*Big girl.* I was so still and breathless I could have turned into one of the cans of baked beans. That would never fit the Girl.

Another one they called "Jeepers," who had a high, raspy voice, claimed not ever to have seen Louella, and who the shit was Louella?

Mr. Britten told them to mind their language.

They mumbled apologies and kept arguing.

"Lives over t'*Heb*rides. I *tol'* you. Louella Smitt."

"You mean *Ella*? *Ella* Smitt?" said Bub, who spat more tobacco towards the spittoon with complete disdain. There was another of my "dis" words.

Bub went on, scoffing. "Now, that there's completely crazy. Ella's baby-sat for the Kramers next door going on three years. Now, why'd she be out to White's Bridge middle of the night, I'd like to know?" He folded his arms hard across his chest and chewed away as if that settled things.

Knowing I couldn't just look at the cans all day, I made a move and grabbed some Brick Oven beans off the shelf, all the while wondering how this Bub person was making a connection between baby-sitting for the neighbors and being out around White's Bridge, as if the two things couldn't possibly happen to the same person. I just shook my head over the Brick Oven jar (the best beans except for homemade) and wondered if I should bother with this source at all, that maybe it would be better to go out and look for aliens. Maybe Mr. Root was outside on the bench by now; he was kind of pig-headed, but at least he could add two and two.

They had hooked me with the so-called report of the deputy sheriff (and I knew Donny would gossip all over the place about a case, whereas the Sheriff would be forever tight-lipped); but everything else they said being pure guesswork (even more than Lola Davidow's), I could hardly credit either "Hebrides" or "big girl" as reliable. So I was about to return the jar to the shelf and go buy some Fireballs when the door opened and brought in a pleasant gulp of cool air and a big man with a square jaw, wearing a quilted jacket too short in the arms. He marched in as if he meant to straighten things out, but I guessed he always looked that way. As they greeted him—"Hey,

Jude," "'Lo, Jude"—as if he were more or less their leader, he slapped a dollar bill by the register and told Mr. Britten he wanted a pack of Luckies. He stood tearing off the cellophane and Jeepers called over in his whiny voice what Bub and the other one were arguing about, and did he read the paper that morning?

"You mean that body in the pond out there at White's Bridge?" He lit up his Lucky and snapped the match toward the spittoon and sauntered towards them. "Yeah, a course I read it."

"Luke here says it's Louella Smitt."

He just snorted as he exhaled smoke from his nostrils. "Why in hell you think that?"

I stood there, quiet as could be, holding the Brick Oven jar. The one named Luke I could see wasn't happy with this new addition, for he had up to then had an edge because he'd come up with a name.

"Heard it over to the courthouse," replied Luke.

"Hear a lotta things at the courthouse that ain't true," and Jude laughed as if this were one of the funniest things. The others laughed, too. Then Jude asked *how* over at the courthouse.

Luke sort of mumbled around and then he finally said, "Sally."

Sally was one of the secretaries. So he hadn't heard it from Donny after all, and I knew I'd been right to doubt everything he'd said. This didn't make me happy, though; I would rather have believed it was this big girl, Louella Smitt.

Again, Jude scoffed and yanked Jeepers's cap down over his eyes, as if he were the one who'd said it was Sally. I hated people who messed about that way, yanking and pulling at other people. I bet this Jude was a grade-school bully.

"Well, it sure's hell ain't any Louella what's-her-name. It's Ben Queen's girl."

I froze.

*Ben Queen.*

Here was truth, sure as God made little green apples, and I knew it, and it just about took my breath away. I knew it because I had never heard the name "Ben Queen" in my entire life until Aurora Paradise said it only a few days ago and here it had come up again for the second time in my life. It was as if that name was coming at me from off a far horizon, like the twister coming across the Kansas plains to carry off Dorothy, or like the train bearing down on my father.

*Ben Queen.* And besides, Aurora Paradise had brought up that name in relation to Mary-Evelyn Devereau, and I knew the Girl had something to do with that family. This was clear, else why would she have been over there, across Spirit Lake?

Looking my way.


I had to get out of the store when this Jude person started talking about the bullet wound, for it could quite possibly be what I didn't want to hear. I was pretty scared by what I'd heard so far. Making my way to the door, I was stopped by the voice of Mr. Britten yelling to me I should have brought that over to the register so he could put it on the Hotel Paradise account.

I was still holding the can of Brick Oven baked beans and saw nothing to do but just continue on out the door, calling back some vague apology.

Mr. Root was there, sitting on the other end of the bench from the old man in the convict's cap. They weren't talking, just staring off in the direction of the weathered wood-frame café up the incline on the other side of the highway, as if they were considering maybe going over and getting a burger or a soda. When I walked up and said hello to Mr. Root, who gave me a big grin, the old man in the cap slowly rose, as if he were plagued with terrible rheumatism or something, and I told him he didn't have to give me his seat, but he didn't pay any attention. Probably, he wasn't doing anything of the kind; he probably didn't want to hang around if some kid was going to be sitting down and yammering and disturbing his quiet staring. He didn't pay any attention to me, didn't even look at me, but walked off down the incline to the highway, and I supposed he was making for the tavern.

By comparison with the old man, Mr. Root was spanking clean and even smelled of Aqua Velva, or maybe it was Old Spice, for there was a faint aroma of alcohol and cloves. I only knew about men's lotions from studying the cardboard displays in Souder's Drug Store. I frankly thought it was a little sissy, and took note of the fact that the Sheriff never smelled of cloves or alcohol, just soap.

Mr. Root was wearing a nice blue shirt, really starched up, and wide red suspenders. I asked him if he was waiting for a cab or going someplace.

"No, I ain't. Just thought maybe I'd go over to Greg's for my dinner later on."

Greg's was the worn-out tavern over there, and I couldn't imagine having dinner in it. The most I'd ever get was a cheeseburger (if I was starving) and a Coke. Will and I liked to go there so he could play the pinball machine. He hit them up and slapped them something awful, until Greg had to shout at him to stop.

"Ain't seen the Wood boys," said Mr. Root, looking around and behind him to the dirt path that led away from Britten's, the one that the people who lived back in that direction took to get to the store.

He seemed to think we would be forever meeting here and making plans. "No, I haven't seen them today, either."

"You read about they found that woman over at Mirror Pond? Said she must of either shot herself or got herself shot by somebody. If you can countenance *that*." Slowly, his mouth worked around his plug of tobacco.

Mr. Root was the type to read *The Conservative* cover-to-cover, even the personals. But I also figured things slipped his mind pretty easily, for he was of an age where you probably like the past a lot better than the present. That was why it didn't really bother me too much that he would bring the subject up, as I knew he would, of course. It was the only hot news we'd had all year.

"Yes, sir, I did," I lied. "Every word. It was exciting—I mean, it was too bad." I tossed in that business about reading "every word" just in case he did remember a lot of the details. Now he would not feel it necessary to fill me in on whatever I didn't want to know.

He said he agreed, and how terrible it was, and asked, "You think it all had something to do with that little Devereau girl?"

I was really taken aback; I hadn't expected *that* kind of question. I wrinkled up my face at him. "Why?"

"Well, they both of 'em drowned in the water around here. Maybe she throwed herself in."

For some reason, my heart lurched, for there was something of the truth in what he'd said. Mr. Root, not having (I guessed) a very complicated mind, just took one event all those years ago and one right now and, because there were one or two similarities, just punched them out and put them together, like fixing clothes to a paper doll, and overlooking the enormous differences. I was sort of stunned. I said, "Well, but . . . the police said she was *shot*."

"Yeah. I guess. Paper don't tell you much." He sat, leaning forward, forearms across his knees, like a slightly younger version of the stubble-bearded old man who had just left.

I was glad to hear the paper didn't tell him much. I chewed the inside of my cheek and debated tossing out a detail or two, testing to see if he'd agree with them or not. "Someone said she was from Hebrides." I was working up to mentioning Ben Queen.

"Where all'd they hear that?"

"Said they got it out of the paper."

He shook his head. "Well, they didn't. Police never said where she's from because they don't know."

I felt disappointed. I wanted the dead woman to be from any place at all except Cold Flat Junction. But, of course, I was sure that detail hadn't been in the paper, either. "In there they said"— and I turned to nod towards the store—"it was someone named Louella somebody. From Hebrides. It was Luke who said it."

"Luke." Mr. Root snorted and dragged his hand across his mouth, as if the saying of the name made him want to wash it out. "Lot he knows. That Luke Hazel fellow, he always wants you to think he knows more'n anybody. Wasn't nothing like that in the paper. Police said plain as day they *did not know who she is*." He emphasized those words.

"I remember now it said that."

"Said it mighta been accidental but 'foul play cannot be ruled out.'" Mr. Root repeated this slowly.

"That's what it said, 'foul play cannot be ruled out.'
I guess they'll have to do a whatchamacallit—an
autopsy?" He turned to look at me to see if I agreed.

I tried to look wise.

"Who do you guess they'll get to do that, then?"

I shrugged. "Dr. Baum, I suppose."

"Well . . ."

As if I'd only just thought of it, I snapped my
fingers. "You know what I think? I think we just
should take a ride over to White's Bridge. Maybe
the Wood boys can take us in their truck."

I was surprised when Mr. Root shook his head.
"Their trucks is in Cabel Slaw's shop, being worked
on."

"Both of them? Both trucks?"

Mr. Root turned his head to the right, away
from me, and gently spat a stream of tobacco. "Yeah,
so they said. Funny, ain't it? When one goes bad,
so's the other."

I sighed. That sounded typically Wood-like. I
was so disappointed, for it seemed the perfect solution to getting a ride.

Mr. Root and I sat there for a few quiet minutes,
as I watched the old man, who'd crossed the highway
and was still creeping up the hill towards Greg's.
There was a sadness that clung to old people like
cobwebs—Mr. Root, Miss Flagler—something
sticky that a person could keep wiping at, but that
wouldn't wipe away. I was reminded of the unused
rooms above the kitchen that once were servants'
quarters, now just storage space and hardly ever vis-

ited, except by me. I would go in them for no particular reason and wedge my way between wooden chairs stacked, legs up, on tables, washstands, dressers with swing mirrors, all layered under dust, joined sometimes by misty stretches of cobwebs or delicate spider webs. Cobwebs clung to the window frame that the sun would hit and whiten and a draft of air would lift, so that being lifted and let fall they were like shreds of cotton or silk, taking on a material weight, and I found this beautiful but unbearably sad. I would be stuck there watching the corners and windows of those rooms, sometimes shadowy and still, sometimes light and moving. It would be like the sunlight striping Spirit Lake, or the mist and fog rising from its surface. And I imagined cobwebs clinging to my mother and Mrs. Davidow, even as she sat on the salad table swinging her legs. And it was like a web of mist that had hovered for a long time and had finally come down, settling quietly. Through the cobweb layer they talked and even laughed and fluttered the cobweb veil like the draft seeping in through the window cracks in the unused rooms upstairs. I guess it wasn't enough that something be beautiful, not enough at all. For the light would fade and the air draw in to a suffocating closeness.

Was it always like this, to grow old? I sat on the bench and studied the ground at my feet and felt sunk. Not that my life was anything to write home airmail about, but at least I was not old. But I was sure I would not be one of the ones to escape this fate, if anybody ever did.

After a while, I brought my mind back to the problem. I thought about what the one called Jude had said that had sent me flying out of Britten's.

"How long you been living here, Mr. Root? In Spirit Lake, I mean?"

He enjoyed this question, obviously, for he sat back to scrunch up his face and really meditate upon it. "It'd be twenty-six years come next September. That's right," he added, as if I were challenging him, "twenty-six years."

So he'd been here a long, long time; but he'd said he'd never known the Devereaus, and the whole affair would have had nearly another twenty years to die down by the time he came. So my question was probably safe. "You ever hear of a man named Ben Queen?"

This was even more enjoyable to him, for he could truly pretend to put on his thinking cap. I didn't think he knew anything about Ben Queen (which, the way I was going, made him safe to ask); but in casting about for the name, he just might come up with something else, something related. I was totally caught off-balance when he said:

"Ben Queen. Queen . . . Now there's someone I used to know married a Queen, I think." He smiled shyly. "I was kinda sweet on her my own self. Sheba Otis, her name was then."

I was surprised. "She married a Queen? Which one?"

"Can't say." He sighed. "Her name's Bathsheba,

but she never liked that much." He turned to look at me. "That's one of them Bible names."

I stared, blinking. I hardly knew how to reply. Then I asked, "Well, where is she? Or where do the Queens live?"

He spat out tobacco, carefully turning his head away from me. "Don't know, anymore. I ain't seen Sheba in a good fifteen years or more."

And he stopped with that. Why did adults do this? They could yammer on about nothing at all for hours on end and then say something terribly important and just clam up.

"Where *did* she live, then?"

He crooked his head sideways, pointing down the highway. "Vista View, when I knowed her. But she moved."

I sat there feeling really frustrated. Out on the highway, Axel rode by in his empty cab. He honked and waved and we waved back. Even from up here on the bank, I could see Axel was grinning. He was always grinning. I guess I would be too if I didn't have to take anyone anywhere.

When I asked Mr. Root the time, he looked at his watch and shook it, held it to his ear, finally said it was near three o'clock. If I was going to go into La Porte, I had two and a half hours before I had to get the salads ready. It was too bad I hadn't tried to flag Axel down, but he wouldn't have stopped. I would have to walk.

Forlornly—at least it felt so to me—I walked

back to the hotel, scuffing up gravel and bits of hard
earth. And to make matters worse, I remembered
Ree-Jane's birthday was coming up. That meant a
present, that meant all kinds of stuff—a special dinner, probably a party with what Ree-Jane called her
"older friends." I could just go into Souder's and get
a bottle of dusty old cologne. I wondered what Will
and Brownmiller would do. Probably make up a skit
or something. And then a few steps farther along I
stopped. Her car! Hebrides! Ree-Jane liked Will and
even Brownmiller. If *Will* asked her if they could
use her car, Ree-Jane just might let him. Brownmiller
was one year older than Will and old enough to drive.
Well, almost. He had a permit, but he was supposed
to have a licensed driver with him. But Ree-Jane
didn't have to know that. Will and Mill could lie if
she got suspicious. They could lie the wallpaper right
off the wall. I walked on with more spring in my
step. All Will would have to do is tell her he wanted
to go to Hebrides to pick up her present and could
they borrow her car?

Will and Mill were hard at work on one of their
"productions," which took up every waking minute
of their lives except for those Will had to spend
bellhopping. He was very good at his job, mostly
because he was so flirty. I don't mean just with girls;
he was flirty with everybody he wanted something
from, whether a tip or a ride to town or getting fancy
old clothes out of my mother's trunks that he could
turn into costumes. (The only person who seemed

to have his number was Aurora, but then she had everybody's number, so that didn't count much.) Or persuading Mrs. Conroy to let Brownmiller stay up later than his bedtime. Poor Mill. Imagine being sixteen years old and still having a "bedtime." Here was I, four years younger than Mill, and I didn't even have one. I don't recall my first reaction to Brownmiller's name. But I often wonder what some parents can be thinking of, saddling helpless little babies with first names that could only ruin their chances for a decent life. However, knowing his mother Edna, I guess I wasn't surprised.

No matter how many times he got something out of me with his flirty ways, Will could still make me think he was sincere and truthful. I was the one person who knew Will was *never* sincere or truthful, and if that sounds contradictory, well, that just goes to show you how he could take people in. I suppose he was sincere with Brownmiller, but then Mill was his co-producer, and I guess he was forced to shoot straight with Mill. Or perhaps it was that Mill was so much *like* my brother—not in looks, for Will had it all over Mill there; not in talent, for Mill had much more talent than Will; but in their love of scheming. Probably that was one reason they produced such clever shows.

I thought about all of this on my walk from Britten's to the hotel, wondering if I could get them to undertake this White's Bridge trip in Ree-Jane's car. I had high hopes that they would, simply because it was a scheme, not because they'd want to do me any favors. I liked to believe that Will would undertake this scheme because he'd give anything to put one over on Ree-Jane. But Ree-Jane didn't count any more than anyone else. That is, Will was so busy in his own mind with his own ideas, he hadn't any mental space left over in which to loathe Ree-Jane. Unlike me, whose mind was lazy and had plenty of free time to devote to loathing.

So tricking Ree-Jane wouldn't be payment enough. No, he'd probably exact some promise from me to play one of the really little roles in their production that no one else would play. Two summers ago, I'd had to play Igor in their production of *Frankenstein*. It was horribly embarrassing, to have to clump across the stage as a hunchback. But I had to admit, the effects were very smart. Will was extremely bright when it came to electricity and trapdoors and anything that involved somebody hanging in midair. He seemed to have been born knowing all of that.

Halfway down the dirt road that led through the back acres of the hotel grounds, I heard screaming. Short, kind of gulping screams coming from the direction of the big garage. The reason I didn't start running in some rescue attempt was because I figured Will and Brownmiller had Paul in there and this was all part of their extravaganza.

The garage was huge. At one time it could house as many as twenty cars, back in those days when the

Hotel Paradise was considered quite swank. Now it wasn't used for much except as a theater, for which you could believe it had been intended originally once you got inside and saw the stage that Will and Mill had built at one end and all of the folding chairs set up for the audience. The big doors were of course closed (the rehearsals always being a deep secret), so I had to knock. No one answered. I heard all sorts of shuffling around, sounds like huge objects crashing and low laughter, and now all was silent. This was so irritating that I started pounding. With all of that noise, did they really think they could fool somebody into thinking no one was inside? Yes, probably. Will and Mill seemed to think they inhabited an extra world, one that ran alongside of mine, and to which they escaped whenever they wanted. Their world did not operate by any of the laws of ordinary people.

I just kept on pounding. Finally, one of the doors opened about an inch and I could see one of my brother's eyes. "What?" was all he said.

"I want to talk to you. Both of you."

The one eye stared for some time and then the door closed again and I heard what sounded like chains and big pieces of furniture being shifted around. There was no real lock on the doors, so who knew what they'd rigged up. The door opened wide enough for me to walk in. I was right about Paul. He was down there on the stage hopping around.

"Why's he all covered in flour?"

Will and Mill exchanged looks. "He's in the production," said Will. "It's part of his role."

I just bet it wasn't. I knew Paul always wanted to be in their productions, and would beg and beg, but they never let him. "He's probably only here for you to drive him crazy."

Brownmiller shoved his thick glasses up his sharp nose and tittered. He had one of the most tittery laughs I'd ever heard.

Will simply smiled as they exchanged another look. "No, this time he's got a real role. Come on, we're busy."

I told the two of them my plan. In addition to working a scheme on Ree-Jane, another aspect of it that would tempt them dearly was that it involved the recent murder. "I thought we should all go and take a look at the murder site. The cops can't seem to get anywhere, or at least they're not saying . . ."

Will was chewing his gum in a ruminative way, the way he always did. He said, "Sam DeGheyn's pretty smart."

But I could tell he was considering. It was no use my trying to work my flirty ways on them, because I didn't have any. And they hated pleading, I knew, and that was fine with me, because I hated it too. I watched Will slowly chew and I watched the light from a spot they'd rigged up high on the roof bounce off Mill's glasses. They were interested, all right, even if it did mean carting me around. Mill really loved that white convertible of Ree-Jane's.

They exchanged another look and Will nodded. "Okay. But don't come with us when we ask her."

Not that I wanted to, but still I asked, "How come?"

"Just don't." He shouted to Paul that he could go back to the kitchen.

# TWENTY-THREE

It worked like magic, and I was really sorry I hadn't watched them in operation. I sometimes thought Ree-Jane had a crush on Will, even though he was two years younger. He was quite handsome (having got whatever looks there were in the family), and he was a completely accomplished liar. Or it might be nicer to say "fabricator." But it all went along with his being able to enter and exit his other world whenever he wanted.

So there we were with the top down and Ree-Jane's convertible guzzling gas. That of course was one understanding; they'd have to replace the gas they used. I hoped she didn't check the mileage, for I'd heard the Sheriff telling Maud once or twice that a check of the mileage showed someone had driven farther than he'd said. Donny probably. I had a notion Donny made more use of the "official ve*hic*le" than was absolutely police business.

It was truly enjoyable flying down Highway 231, Mill and Will in the front singing one of Mill's made-up songs, or rather made-up words to one of the Tabernacle hymns. And I hummed along as we finally bumped the car over White's Bridge, beyond which lay Mirror Pond.

Mirror Pond. When I'd been contradicting Suzy Whitelaw's description, the pond had seemed pretty ordinary. But looking at it now, after all of the working over it in my mind, it took on quite a different aspect. Lonely, creepy, even dangerous. It was bigger than what I'd call a pond, for it was probably sixty or seventy feet across. It was edged with goldenrod and black-eyed Susans in addition to the tall grasses and was prettier than I remembered it being. The water, though, was sludgy in its stillness, nothing like Spirit Lake, where the water always seems to be moving, lapping around the lily carpet, light and almost breathy.

There was a darkness here that seemed to collect in the shadows like rain before a storm. Or it might just have been my imagination. But it was certainly colder in these woods than it had been when we were driving. I shivered and tried to figure out just where the woman's body had been found.

We'd stopped the car under the rotted overhang of a falling-down gas station with an old bubble pump. I thought it a peculiar place for one, although twenty or even ten years ago the pond might have been some sort of junction. Besides a continuation of the road we'd come on, there was another, a dirt road that showed signs of once having been graded and that ran off into the trees. On one of the pines, wooden arrows with names and numbers painted on them by different people pointed inwards. It was a common way for families to give directions to their houses or summer places, but I was surprised all the same to find out the place was even this populated: "Vichy" was one name. Then there was "Butternut" and "Randall" or "Randolph"—it was hard to tell because the paint was worn. Anyway, there must once have been enough people living here to keep a gas station in business. What I was mostly interested in was whether this old road could possibly lead all the way to Spirit Lake or join up with another, narrower one—something that made a path to the house. I decided to walk it a little way just to see.

Will and Mill were crouched at the pond's edge, talking. I called to them I was going to walk for a few minutes into the woods here, and did they want to come along? I wasn't surprised when they declined, for I supposed they would want to use my absence to cook up some way of scaring me to death.

As I walked the road, the day did not so much get darker as *grayer*, gray light like a solid wall, and really cold. I saw another arrow, this one pointing off to the left with one of the names painted on it, and through the thick trees I could make out a house, or a cabin, ramshackle. I wondered if people still lived there, for I neither saw nor heard anyone.

That is, until a voice right behind me asked, "You the *po*-lice?"

I whirled around and stared into the clouded eyes of a man so old and wispy he looked like someone had stopped in the middle of making him. I was too surprised to be scared. No one in his right mind could take me for police. "Me? No. Who're you?"

"I kept tellin' that fella, that lawman, to listen to me, but he wouldn't. Little weasel-faced fella not much bigger'n you. Hell"—here he swiveled his

head nearly in a half-circle to spit some tobacco—
"hell, you ain't nothin' but a kid."

I nodded. My mind was clicking over. The
"weasel-faced" man must be Donny, and this was a
surprisingly good accounting of him. I would file
this away for when I needed it. Donny could be so
high-and-mighty when the Sheriff wasn't around.
"You mean he never came back to talk to you?"

"I'm a Butternut. We been around these parts
since time began."

Looking at him, I could believe it. But he was
going to get off the subject, I could tell. People who'd
been around that long always wanted to begin at the
beginning in the way of the book of Genesis, which
I'd once heard the Methodist minister start up about
from the pulpit once. "Oh, you're one of the Butternuts! I heard my parents talk about you."

If eyes so clouded could light, I think his did.
"Asa Butternut, that's me."

"What was it you wanted to tell the deputy
sheriff?" I hoped that would lend me a bit of authority, even though I wasn't the police.

"It's that there woman they found at the pond."
He raised the black briar stick he'd been leaning on
and jabbed it in the direction of Mirror Pond.

Eagerly, I asked, "What about her?" But he
wasn't telling me anything. I said, "Look, I can go
get the po—*po*-lice for you if you'd just wait right
here." He looked like he might dissolve away, so I
said it again. "Will you wait?" When he nodded, I
ran back up the road.

Will and Mill were so eager to be law-enforcement officers it was downright shameless. I danced around like I had to pee, telling them to be sure to put their sunglasses back on; that way, they might get away with looking old enough. Brownmiller, with his stingy, narrow face and sharp nose, might even get away with being the deputy. I couldn't imagine the old man's memory was all that good. We all marched down the road.

"You ain't in uniform," said Mr. Butternut.

"Plainclothes," snapped Will.

Mr. Butternut squinted up his eyes and pecked his neck closer to them. "Where's your i-den-ti-fi-ca-tion?"

I had to hand it to Mill: he whipped out his wallet and shoved his driver's permit right into Mr. Butternut's face, which was probably why the old man couldn't tell what it was. You'd have thought Mill had been banging on witnesses' doors most of his life from all his forwardness.

Will, unfortunately, didn't have one. But he always carried a little notebook, and he slowly removed that from his rear pocket, and stood there chewing his gum and looking deadly in those black sunglasses. He asked Mr. Butternut for his name and address (though we were standing right in it, so to speak), and Mr. Butternut told him carefully, spelling the name out.

"There's Butternuts lived here for a hunnert years." He reflected. "Two, mebbe three hunnert."

He spat tobacco again. "My daddy's name was Lionel. And his daddy before him was named—"

"Mr. Butternut!" Will slammed into the middle of these memories like a truck colliding with a train. "Did you know this woman?"

"What? No, I never knowed her—well, I ain't seen her, so how'd I be able to tell? I just thought the *po*-lice, they'd like t'know about these here cars, or maybe it was trucks, out here that night."

"What about them?" Mill asked. He looked unhappy because his voice cracked. It often did.

Mr. Butternut was looking and sounding pretty aggravated. "Ain't nothin' *about* them, just they was here. Drivin' down this here road, one of them, and ain't no one lives down here now but me."

I started doing my one-legged dance again, excited as I was, and forgetful that I probably shouldn't be sticking my non-*po*-lice nose into the conversation. "Where's this road go, anyway? Does it go as far as Spirit Lake?"

Mr. Butternut squinted up at the sky. "Well, I expect maybe it does. Or nearly. For Elmer Randall, he used to live down it, and that was a couple miles away, at least."

Will glared at me, or at least I assumed there was a glare behind the glasses. I was not to stick my nose in. "Did you see these vehicles?" Good Lord, he sounded just like the Sheriff. "Did you get their license numbers?" What a stupid question. If Mr. Butternut couldn't even tell these two were kids like me, how would he ever read a license plate? Even if he'd a mind to, and I doubt he had.

"Hell, *no*, I ain't seen no license plate! And it was pitch black, too, and I was inside my house"— he swung the briar stick off to his right and jigged it around like a fencer being careless with his sword—"and I *heard* this here engine sounded loud enough it was a truck, and then I come out on my porch and saw these lights. And before that I thought I heard noises like more'n one car up by Mirror Pond. Thought maybe it was some of them kids with them dirt bikes, you know."

"A dirt bike doesn't have an engine." Will hesitated. "Depending," he added, obviously uncertain of his facts.

"Well . . ." Mr. Butternut shrugged and started humming a tune.

"That's all?" asked my brother.

Mr. Butternut just kept humming.

That was all, we supposed. At least I'd found out there might be another way to Spirit Lake. And that Mirror Pond and the White's Bridge road had once been a crossroads for a lot of people. The lay of the land, so to speak.

Will and Mill thanked him and said they'd be in touch.

Mr. Butternut kept humming. I didn't think he'd be much in touch with anything.

We all piled back into the white convertible,

for we'd been gone longer than it would ever have taken us to get to Hebrides.

"What about the present? We've already been gone nearly an hour more than it would have taken to shop in Hebrides."

Will said, "There's a bait-and-tackle shop up the highway here."

Mill gave one of his sneezy, blubbery laughs and Will joined in, pounding on the glove compartment and choking with laughter.

We stopped at the bait shop—I could hardly believe it—and the two of them piled out and went in. They were still laughing. I lay down in the backseat, smelling the new leather smell of the buttoned back and thinking about Mr. Butternut. Within less than five minutes they were coming out of the shop, carrying a small bucket and a glass bowl. They were still laughing.

"What's that?" I looked at the bucket.

They didn't bother answering. They often didn't; it was as if I were invisible. "I *said*, what's that?"

Brownmiller swung the bucket over the seat and I looked in; there were five or six tiny fish. "These aren't anything but guppies!" I said.

"They're Starfire fish," said Will.

Mill said, "Angelfire."

"Angel's Teeth."

I said, "Oh, for heaven's sakes. You're going to just make up some story about them, aren't you?"

My brother turned and smiled. He did not answer my question, though, for he said, "You've got to play this part in our production." His smile was pinched and mean-looking.

I had promised I would just to get out to Mirror Pond. "What part?"

"We need a deus ex machina."

"A *what*?" I tilted forward from the backseat, propped my chin on the front one. "What in God's name's a 'Do-X machine'?"

Mill explained. "It's someone in a play, mostly in Greek, and usually a god, that just suddenly appears out of nowhere and comes down in a cloud to save the hero or whoever's there. Usually he's on a swing. Or a chair on pulleys. He—or she—rights the wrongs, ties up the loose ends, saves the day, you could say."

I tried to act as if this were absolutely impossible. "Stop being silly. I'm not coming down on any chair on pulleys."

"You said you'd act a part. Well, that's the part."

I sniffed, crossed my arms tight across my chest, and said, "Coming down out of a cloud. That's the stupidest thing I ever heard." And then I recollected Paul and sat up so hard I nearly fell over the side of the car. "A cloud! A *cloud*! You're not throwing flour all over *me*! Paul can be your damned Do-X machine!"

We sped on with them laughing and me yelling and the guppies sloshing.

# TWENTY-FOUR

Syrup pitchers in the morning, bread plates at noon, salads in the evening—these divided my day like larks, hilltops, and God did for whoever wrote that poem I can't remember. I was good in English, but vague about poetry, as I was about most things that didn't immediately relate to my own problems. I still felt unprepared to confront the Sheriff, or even to go into the Rainbow and try and ask Maud what she knew; I wasn't ready for the whole truth yet.

I decided to go to church.

St. Michael's is the Roman Catholic church in La Porte, and I sometimes pass it on one of my several routes. And I also sometimes stop there to think. For that purpose, St. Michael's is superior to the Abigail Butte County Library, for in the library people move about and talk and pages of books and magazines rustle and rattle as people sit by the periodical racks reading things like *Vogue* and *Popular Mechanics*. Also, there are hardly ever less than a couple of dozen people in the reading rooms, but St. Michael's is nearly always empty. The most I ever saw, mid-afternoon, was two or three people, and they, of course, were very quiet. Sometimes I wondered about this: why something as important as God took up less of people's time than *Popular Mechanics.*

I myself have never wanted to be saved (unless the only alternative is being damned), because I do not know what it means. I have run into a few "saved" people here and there, like Helene Baum, who says she's a devout Methodist (which sounds peculiar); and also some of those camp-meeting Christians over across the highway. These "saved" souls are too noisy for me. I'm sure that there must be some quietly "saved" people around town, but I wonder if one of the things about being "saved" is that you never know it. For instance: I bet the Sheriff is saved; but I bet if I asked him he'd just give me a peculiar look: *Huh?* One of the few times religion ever came up at the hotel, Ree-Jane told me that if I wasn't baptized (which I wasn't) I would be damned. That if I was to die right then (I'm sure she wished it) I would go to hell permanently. Forever. Ree-Jane, of course, had been baptized. She talked about it the same way she talked about having better clothes than I had, or more boyfriends. (Who didn't?)

When I was in St. Michael's once and Father Freeman walked by, I asked him about this, about going to hell if you're not baptized. Was it true? It was a good question, for it was merely a point of information and wouldn't engage him (or us) in a long, weird conversation about God or Jesus. Father Freeman looked at me for quite a long time and then looked up at the figure in the window and then back at me. For a minute I thought I'd stumped him, which

I certainly hadn't meant to. Finally, though, after a lot of thought, he said "No." And smiled and walked away. Although I hadn't really been worried, still I was a little relieved, until I realized I wasn't sure just how I had put the question. It had taken him, see, so long to answer, my precise words had got lost somewhere. Had I said "Does that mean I'm damned?" Or had I asked "Does that mean I won't be saved?" If the first, then "No" was a clear answer. But "No" to the second question could have meant two different things. I thought of asking him again, but I figured that would be a poor thing to do, seeing how long he thought over his answer.

I am of no religious persuasion (which is how adults talk about it), even though my mother and Mrs. Davidow say they are Episcopalians. Yet they hardly ever go to church. My mother *never* did, in my memory. But this is understandable, for Sunday is the busiest day for the dining room, and she's trapped between hotcakes and sausage in the morning and roast beef and oven-browned potatoes at one o'clock. Once in a while, Mrs. Davidow puts on a small hat with a little veil and drives to town to church. But if I were God and had my choice between my mother in the kitchen and Lola Davidow in the front pew, I know which one I'd choose.

I like St. Michael's Catholic Church more than the others, probably for the same reason the Catholics do. It's a lot fancier. There's much more to look at than in the Methodist church right across the street. If you get bored, or if it's a rainy, grim day, there's much more in St. Michael's to take your mind off things. Beginning with the stained-glass windows, which are truly beautiful. The other churches have them, too, but St. Michael's are taller and more involved and deeply colored. I move from one window to another, move nearly all around the church, with my notebook and pencil or ballpoint pen, pretending to be taking notes. What I'm really doing is thinking, but I don't want anyone to get the impression that I'm there to worship anything. If Father Freeman passes by, I tell him I'm doing research, which he finds extremely interesting—I think he's pleased that my topic is the Virgin Mary or the Apostles (there are twelve of them) and does not press me for details.

It would, of course, be easier to sit down in one of the pews to do my thinking, and once in a while I do, but try to avoid this, as it might give the impression I'm praying. I don't have many friends my age, and if that ever got around town, I wouldn't have any at all.

Sometimes, Father Freeman is up there at the altar in his white robes doing something or other, even though there's no real service going on. Or other times, he passes through the church in his black suit, smiles and says hello, and asks about my mother or Will. He never asks me what I'm doing in church, *never*, which I think is simply remarkable, as any other adult (except for my chosen few—the Sheriff, Miss Flyte, Maud, the Woods) would ask "Hello-what-are-*you*-doing-here?" and expect an answer.

But Father Freeman just seems to accept me as easily as holy water. He's like the Sheriff (though not as good-looking). And this makes me feel, really, very comfortable. Father Freeman acts as if we're all part and parcel of the same one thing. I wonder sometimes what the one thing is.

I got the idea that if I could concentrate long enough on one thing, whatever it was, I might figure it out, figure out its secret. Concentration is not as difficult for me as it is for most people; I spend a lot of time down in the Pink Elephant, concentrating. Usually, it's on a page of my notebook or my diary or some short story I'm writing. I can stare at the damp, pink stucco wall before me only half-aware of the pattern of shadows made there as the wind that comes in under the badly fitted wooden door stirs the candle flames. Sometimes my mind seems to go blank, as if the draft is passing through it, too.

For a long time, I carried a stone around in my pocket, this being the "one thing" I would concentrate on. I stared at it for minutes at a time, and it was true that my mind did empty out with the looking. It emptied out, but nothing came along to fill it up again. But I kept looking at that stone and nothing happened. Had I expected it to change shape? Or maybe glow? I would put it on the table and rest my chin on my folded hands—coming down to its level, you could say—and watch it. Sometimes I took it into St. Michael's and sat down with it in a back pew. I think I hoped it might get a blessing in some roundabout way, just by being in church. Once, when

I was standing before the stained-glass window of St. Francis feeding the birds, and staring down at the stone, Father Freeman saw it. He asked if he could look at it more closely. Naturally, I said yes.

He said, after inspecting it carefully, "That's a nice stone."

"Thank you," I answered, taking it back.

So it didn't get a blessing; it got a compliment.

A year ago, when I was in the library, I read a book, or parts of it—it was such a strange book I don't think the writer really meant you to read it all if you didn't want to—and I remember it now because of the stones in it. The reason I read it at all was because I happened to see it on the shelf, facedown, with the author's face staring out from the photograph on the back. I looked at him. His face was thin and his hair stood up and he looked terrified. I figured this book was for me. As it turned out, it wasn't. I hardly understood a word. It was strange, to say the least. The main character was pulling himself along the ground using crutches as hooks. The story was weird and also funny in parts, even though I had no idea what it was about. It was kind of like laughing at a funeral. What brought back the memory, though, was that at the end he had a pocketful of stones—pebbles, more—and he sucked them. But he made sure he sucked them in a pattern, not sloppily, like the way I eat popcorn. For some reason, this struck me as the last word in . . . concentration? No, it was the last word in whatever could be done with a stone. That's as far as I got. It did not have any purpose, and that was what was important.

Maybe that was my mistake: I was trying to get something *out* of my stone. It would have been nice to have been able to bat this idea around with somebody, and Father Freeman was probably the right person, but I didn't know how to bring it up. I should have been thinking about other things than stones; I should have been thinking about *every* other thing, I guess.

All of this, I think, had something to do with the Girl.

After my walk into town, I was too tired to move along the windows and pretend to be taking notes, so I just sat down at the end of a pew. Sitting down could be dangerous, for I might relax too much. "Relax" is not exactly the word, either. It was more like folding into myself. Like slowly collapsing or shrinking, much like the Witch of the West in Oz when Dorothy tossed the bucket of water on her. I didn't think I was a wicked witch, but it did feel as if I were deflating in some way, as if the air was just *whishing* out of me, only it wasn't air; it was more like everything I knew. At my age I didn't know a lot, and couldn't afford to lose a little.

## TWENTY-FIVE

Funny how my feet, which I had told to march me straight into the courthouse and down the hall to the Sheriff's office, carried me right past it.

My feet walked me across the street and past Candlewick, then slowed at the window of the Oak Tree Gift Shoppe so that I could admire a thin silver chain with a tiny heart suspended from it, then around the corner for the long block of parking meters and past Souder's Drug Store, where again I stopped, this time to look at the thickening dust layer on the Aqua Velva advertisement, then to Second Street and past the dime store where Miss Isabelle Barnett does most of her shoplifting; then past Stemple's dark and creaky British haberdashery. I carefully noted each and every one of these establishments, for at each I ordered my feet *go back go back go back* to the courthouse. But my feet went about their own sly business just like Miss Isabelle Barnett's hands.

Finally, they pulled up in front of the Rainbow Café. I realized that I had been horribly thirsty way back there in St. Michael's, parched from the feeling of what it must be like to be dying of thirst and to be offered nothing but a wet rag tied on a stick. It made me feel ashamed that all I could think of was a large-sized cherry Coke. So I did not immediately go inside, but stood outside the window in a state that Father Freeman might call repentance. After a minute or so of repenting, I went in the door to get my Coke.

But before I did, I looked through the steamed-over window, where I could make out Shirl sitting on her stool and working the cash register and probably her mouth, for it was open in a wide O and aimed towards somewhere in the restaurant. She turned and must have made me out through the dissolving moisture, for she rubbed a wider place in it and glared at me. I don't take this really personally, for Shirl glares at anybody under twenty, including Ree-Jane. This is something Ree-Jane *does* take personally and one reason she never goes into the Rainbow to sit. The other reason is she's a snob. She'd never sit at a counter with the Wood boys or Dodge Haines. Sometimes she goes in to buy doughnuts and Danish, which she takes right out again.

I'd think Shirl would be a little pleasanter to me, because she wants my mother's recipes, and when she can't get them, she tries to imitate or even steal them. Now, if *anybody* on God's green earth knows what's in my mother's dishes, it's me, for I often watch closely as she cooks, not with any idea that I can later on be a cook like my mother, but wondering at what point the rabbit will pop out of the hat or the silver coin slide from behind an ear. So one of these days I was going to clue Shirl in about being nice to me. *I* was the one who knew my mother didn't really add a cup of cold coffee grounds to her Chocolate Feather Cake; *I* was the one who knew that you shouldn't toss bits of rum-soaked banana peel into the fabulous Banana Baba Pie. But Shirl went right along treating me as if I had no value. Too bad. Let her keep on tossing cold coffee grounds and banana peels in things and see how far she got.

The Rainbow is most crowded at noon and six o'clock, but there are always customers from the moment it opens at seven a.m. until it closes around eight or nine. Even now, just a little after four, some of them were eating big meals. These were farmers, I supposed, from Paradise Valley, maybe. I couldn't imagine eating my mother's rare roast beef and oven-browned potatoes at such an off-hour. It was as if you wouldn't be holding the roast beef in high enough regard if the moon hadn't risen and the stars come out before you sat down to it. But then I reminded myself that I didn't get up at four a.m. and go to bed at eight, either; and didn't have to do a lot of hard labor in between out in the fields.

When I entered, Shirl was calling down the counter, "Well, why'd she go to White's Bridge for, then?" in that noisy, argumentative voice that irked people so much. "And you tell me how you go and shoot yourself in the chest? Huh? I never did hear of anybody shooting theirself in the *chest*."

At the end of the counter, a big-muscled man— probably one of the truck drivers who liked the place—flapped his hand at her, I guess shutting down her argument.

Shirl just went on arguing with herself as people came with their bills and toothpicks in their mouths and she punched the cash-register keys like a crazed typist.

I knew the Rainbow Café people would be talking about the dead woman, so it wasn't as if I'd chosen it as a place to hide from the news. The wire basket that held the Rainbow's supply of *The Conservative* was empty, and papers were spread on the counter or crinkling and rattling in people's hands. I felt it was pretty daring of me even to walk in here (although not as daring as it would have been a few hours ago). If the counter stools had not been full of broad rear ends, I'd have taken one, though I prefer a booth. There were two empty booths, but, of course, Shirl was there overseeing things. Still, I noticed Miss Isabelle Barnett was permitted to take up a booth on her own. This didn't mean that I could. So I stood there scratching my arm and being embarrassed I was alone and without a place to sit. Dodge Haines turned and gave me a sort of evil grin and Miss Isabelle offered me a little wave, fingers closing and opening on her palm.

Thank heavens Maud was there and saw me and motioned for me to stay put. Charlene was behind the counter, standing with her plump arms folded over her big bosom and laughing; pretty clearly, the customers had been served. Chicken-fried steak was the special, and the truck driver and Dodge Haines were eating it with sides of green beans and mashed potatoes.

Maud called down to Shirl that she was taking a break. In another minute she held up a tall glass of Coke and smiled and signed that I was to follow her. What she was doing was inviting me back to the Reserved booth to sit with her on her break. In fact, I guessed she was taking a break just for my sake. Shirl did not like this, but after all, if Charlene or Shirl herself wanted to share the Reserved booth with their friends, they were free to do it, and so was Maud. Shirl just didn't like the idea that some kid was allowed to sit there.

As we passed Miss Isabelle, she looked up and gave us both a glimmering smile and I noticed her earrings—cheap, bright blue, like chips of porcelain overlaid with a sprinkling of silver, something like the silver dust on some of Miss Flyte's fancy candlesticks. It wasn't hard for me to figure out where the earrings had come from.

Maud and I sat down and I saw *The Conservative* lying on the table. Maud set her coffee cup on a corner of the front page, but she didn't seem aware of the newspaper. She didn't bring up Suzy Whitelaw's account, either. After setting down her cup, she lit up a Camel and waved the match into the aluminum ashtray. I started in on my cherry Coke and she turned to peer around the corner of the booth and then turned back again. She asked, "You seen Sam today?"

I sucked Coke through my straw and shook my head.

She sighed and looked back towards the door again. "Usually he comes in after lunch, at least."

Maud looked peculiar—that is, sad. Because she'd been so nice about taking her break now, I felt compelled to say something that might cheer her up. Without realizing what I was doing, I said, "Probably he's busy over at White's Bridge." Quickly, I dropped my head and sucked up Coke, afraid I'd really started something.

But I hadn't. She merely said, "I guess," in a vague sort of way, and went on smoking.

Maud was never a gossip, never one to make a juicy meal out of some tidbit that came her way. Still, this dead and maybe murdered woman was more than a "tidbit." After turning the matchbook in her fingers awhile and continuing to look sad, she picked up the paper. It was bound to happen at some point, what with everybody in here probably talking about it. She appeared to be reading the article—I supposed that was what her eyes, traveling over newsprint, were taking in. Finally, she set the paper aside. She looked unhappy, but I don't think this was because of the stranger lying in Mirror Pond. Maud tended to be moody—not mean, just moody. The Sheriff had pointed this out to me several times. She didn't talk about what was in the paper, probably because I'd given the impression I'd already read it and knew all the details. Maybe I did; maybe there weren't many.

As much to break into her blue-devil mood as to hear myself talk, recklessly I said, "People are saying they know who she was."

Dismissively, she flicked her hand. "People are stupid, too."

"Well, in Britten's store someone said it was this Louella Smitt."

Her eyebrows crowded together over her nose. "Who's Louella Smitt?"

"This man said she's from Hebrides." I didn't go into what Jude had said about her being "Ben Queen's girl," I guess because I wanted to check that out somehow first.

"Police don't know *who* she is or *where* she's from. So whoever said that's just showing off. Unless, of course, Sheriff Dee-*Geen* has been running at the mouth."

When Maud was mad at the Sheriff, she started calling him by his last name, as if putting distance between them. It made me want to laugh, almost. But I said, "He never does. Maybe Donny does, though." But she just started flicking through the paper again, uninterested in Donny. She was mad because the Sheriff hadn't been in to the Rainbow to talk about what had happened.

"She's certainly not from Hebrides," Maud went on, squinting down at the paper. "Somebody would have identified her by now." She bent her head even closer. "And no one could tell *anything* from this picture—"

*Picture!* My heart stepped up its beating to a wild kind of whirr.

"—which the paper never should have printed anyway. You can't even tell what color her hair is, it's so wet and muddy. That Whitelaw woman never did have good taste." She shook her head. "All they really have to describe her is her dress. It says, 'a light cotton dress, with a flo—'"

Quickly, I cut her off: "Mrs Davidow says there wasn't any identification, nothing to tell who she was, not even in her handbag." I blurted this out fast to get her off the subject of the cotton dress, possibly "flowered."

"Hmm. I don't remember—oh, here it is. That's right, it says, 'No clues as to identification were offered by the white vinyl handbag—'"

I breathed more easily. The Girl would never have been carrying a white vinyl handbag.

" '—found some distance from the body. Sheriff DeGheyn—' What's he know?" Maud made a face—" 'speculated that it might not even have belonged to the dead woman.'"

*What?* The purse not belong to the victim? The presence of that handbag was the only thing that had made me certain it *wasn't* the Girl, for she hadn't been carrying anything like a white handbag. I became so agitated, I grabbed the newspaper and started reading. That was what he had said about the white handbag, true. Then I started at the beginning—even taking in the blurred picture of a facedown figure who no one could possibly have recognized from the photo—and read it straight through.

And learned nothing at all new, except that "inquiries" had been made of "all of the residents in the immediate area, without result." This had been done in case the person had been looking for someone who lived there. The dress itself was described as a "flower-print dress." But after I thought about it, I realized that covered the clothes of every woman in La Porte who wasn't wearing a solid color, like Helene Baum, who always wore yellow. All of the other details were exactly what I'd picked up by listening to people. And there really *weren't* any details to speak of.

I sat back feeling betrayed. It was possible to read this three-column account and come away from it knowing no more than if it had never been written. Here I had been playing cat-and-mouse with the newspaper, padding quietly around it, careful not to show too much interest or look it directly in the face. I had spent hours trying to avoid it.

I had gone to all of this trouble to keep from knowing and then found out there was nothing to be known. I should have been disappointed. Instead, I was strangely relieved, for I felt a weight lifting. People babble; they babble just to hear themselves, as if it proved they were really there. They even go along with other people's babble.

Maud had risen to go to the counter when someone there called her, and I sat staring out of the window for a moment, watching the trees on the other side of the street perform their magic trick of separating from the building they shielded. Then, suddenly I realized it was five-fifteen and I'd better get a move on or the salads wouldn't be ready.

## TWENTY-SIX

Ree-Jane was in the kitchen, pinch-hitting for Vera, who was sick. That made me laugh, the notion that Ree-Jane could take over for the be-all and end-all of waitresses. No one ever insisted Ree-Jane wear a waitress uniform like the rest of us; she was permitted to wear her own clothes, just as long as she wore one of the small organdy aprons. I hated those uniforms; they were starched white with short sleeves and flat mother-of-pearl buttons. We all looked like nurses with aprons. Vera, naturally, wore long-sleeved black, for she was the head waitress and had to be different. Ree-Jane let it be known that, as she was substituting for the head waitress, that meant *she* was in charge of who each of us would wait on. Since each of us had our regulars, and Vera had most of them, that meant Ree-Jane was going to be doing a lot of work, which was fine by me.

Whenever Ree-Jane works in the dining room, she's always dressed up and made up, since she considers these stints to be public appearances. She doesn't exactly carry the food in; she *models* it in and through the dining room. The path between the tables becomes her runway. She puts on that model walk of hers, the toe going down just a fraction before the heel, which results in an affected gliding motion. She will set down a salad or the little condiment tray with one hand on her hip and then do a quarter-turn with some shoulder action, as if she were showing the diners the back of her designer dress. All of this sort of kills two birds with one stone, given Ree-Jane's list of will-be-famous-fors, since she plans on being both a Powers model and a dress designer. Put that together with the photojournalism and the stint in Hollywood, and you can see Ree-Jane's going to have a busy life. All of these careers would, of course, come before she married either the English count or the Russian prince (or, I suggested to her, Mr. Nasalwhite, and then she could be Queen of Bohemia). But dining-room modeling was going to get her into a New York City stable of models, and from there it was but a hop, skip, and jump to the silver screen.

As there was only one source I knew of for information about Ben Queen, I had to work out how to tackle Aurora Paradise that evening. I didn't want to wait another whole day for the mid-afternoon doldrums. In between designing salads (*my* claim to fame) and slapping napkins in hot roll baskets, I managed to get a tall glass and pack it with ice that I chipped off the huge block in one side of the icebox. I filled this a quarter-way up with orange juice, dropped in a teaspoon of sugar, and buried a couple of maraschino cherries in it. Naturally, in the course of this operation someone asked me what I was fixing, and I just mumbled something unintelligible. I had learned long ago that people ask questions or make comments and don't care if the other person really answers as long as the other person makes an answering noise. So, if anyone saw this glass next to the block of ice, I'd mumble something else about it, such as wanting it for my dinner.

I would have to wait for a lull when my customers would all be chomping away and not in need of more water or butter, and this would have to coincide with Lola Davidow's filet mignon dinner, which I hoped she'd eat in the dining room instead of the office. I had seen her rooting through the freezer for her personal food stock—grapefruit and filet mignon, which she salts away like diamonds in a safe.

I could see her over in the office now, as I was loading salads on my tray. The window in the side of the office faces the kitchen's screen door, so that people can, if necessary, call back and forth, though it's quite a distance. From over in the kitchen, I could see she was trying to call to us, first waving, and then cupping her hands around her mouth. I went to investigate. What came across the blowing, uncut grass was the shouted message that *the dumbwaiter was broken*!

A stroke of luck!

At least it started out to be. The dumbwaiter occasionally breaks down, and no wonder, what with all the passing up and down of bottles of gin and pitchers of old fashioneds and cocktail nuts, and of shirred eggs and chicken dinners and dirty laundry. When this happens, it's Vera who has the honor of carrying dinner up to Aurora Paradise, Vera being the only one pleased enough with herself that if Aurora decides to lob some insults her way, well, Vera doesn't even notice. I remember hearing her say that Great-Aunt Paradise was "such a kidder." I could just imagine. My mother can't leave the kitchen at dinnertime to take up her tray, and Lola Davidow isn't about to walk up three flights of stairs, and certainly not after her pitcher of martinis.

Anyway, there being no Vera present, I quickly offered my services. My mother was busily fluting some whipped cream around the edge of an Angel Pie and said all right, but I should be sure to see that everything was on the tray.

And *then* Ree-Jane stuck her nose in. *She* was, after all, taking Vera's place, and she assumed that she should be the one to perform this task. I knew she didn't really want to; it was enough for her that I *did* want to—that would make her jump right in and offer to do it herself. My mother looked up and quickly let her eyes slide between me and Ree-Jane and then, with a tiny, tight smile, told Ree-Jane she could do it. Over my protests, my strong protests. But my mother refused to argue about such trivial things and told me to see to "Jane's" guests in case they needed anything while she was gone.

I fumed inwardly. Outwardly, I yawned and shrugged and picked up a Parker House roll.

Aurora's dinner tray was ready. Ree-Jane raised it up like a flag of victory with its load of fried (white meat of) chicken, shining mashed potatoes, peas as green as the Emerald City, a steaming carafe of coffee, and a slice of Angel Pie. Pleased with winning, she sailed off.

I sailed right behind her with the Pyrex coffee pot to refill the guests' cups and after doing that, put it back on the hot plate and did a quick step through the dining room that was nearly a run. Since Ree-Jane had gone through the music room to the staircase in front, I skipped up the back staircase and ran down the upstairs hall. She had had just enough head start to get up to Aurora's rooms about two minutes before me.

The caterwauling had already started by the time I reached the second floor, and by the time I got to the *third* floor, Aurora was shrieking as if she'd been set on by thieves wearing stocking masks. There were little animal-like, weepy cries coming from Ree-Jane.

". . . the hell are *you* doing, you bleached-out . . . ?"

A mumbled, whining answer from Ree-Jane.

". . . salt and pepper, you blond idiot?"

Another whined reply.

Then came a crash and sobs—I surely *hoped* they were sobs—and Ree-Jane protesting in a reedy voice.

I was hunkered down in a well of shadows at the bottom of the fourth-floor steps, rocking with silent laughter. Now there was scuffling. Maybe Aurora had finally gone berserk and was going at Ree-Jane with her cane or even her pocket knife, slashing the smooth, empty face. I had an image of Ree-Jane in later years, heavily veiled because everyone called her Scarface Davidow. As the ruckus continued, I looked up at the ceiling wanting to thank God for all this, but thinking Father Freeman wouldn't approve. So I thanked something vague up there, my fist in my mouth to keep back the laughter, drowning in my own saliva and tears.

Finally, the feet came pounding down the stairs and I could see through the staircase dowels something sail through the air and hit Ree-Jane on the head. Aurora screamed that next time she'd throw a whole chicken if she ever saw her peroxide head again.

Weeping and cursing, Ree-Jane ran past my shadow hideout, clawing at her hair. "Bitch! Crazy old fucking bitch!" and she turned the corner and ran down the next flight and, I imagined, on to her room to repair the damage done to her person. I crept up to the landing to see what missile Aurora had thrown. A chicken wing. I left it there.

Naturally, I wanted to be right on hand when Ree-Jane reappeared in the dining room; I took the route this time down the front stairs and through the long reading room and the music room. Calmly, I walked in, whistling under my breath. The dozen-or-so diners were still eating their chicken or baked fish. I was refilling water glasses and trying to ignore Miss Bertha's demands for hot rolls, when Ree-Jane came gliding into the dining room with her little toe-down-first walk. When she went through one swinging door to the kitchen, I went through the other, and heard Mrs. Davidow, who was readying the grill for her filet mignon, ask her if Aurora liked her dinner. My mother was piping another ring of whipped cream around another Angel Pie. We were always running out of that, for it was very popular, and people were known to ask for seconds.

Ree-Jane was casual, even breezy, as she assured everyone that Aurora thought the food looked delicious. "But she's so clumsy, she dropped the tray all over the floor. I guess she'll have to have some more, but I don't have time to—oh! Filet mignon! I'll have one, too, for my dinner." She ran her index finger right through my mother's bowl of whipping cream and licked it. My mother glared. Ree-Jane went on to say, "And she thinks I look *just* like Lana Turner."

Oh, that was too much. I bent over, arms folded around my waist as if I had to pee. Ree-Jane asked me what was my story, and I straightened up and suggested I take Great-Aunt Aurora more chicken.

Ree-Jane flashed me a really mean smile and said, "Yes, why don't you?"

"In a minute I will. Right now, I'm busy with Miss Bertha." And I ran to the icebox, took out the ice-filled glass (only slightly melted), set it on a tray, and calmly entered the dining room, where I broke into my quick-step again, and again ignored Miss Bertha's demand for hot rolls. I picked up speed as I went through the wide dining-room doors and broke into a run (holding the glass steady on the tray) in the music room and on through the reading room to the back office.

Here there was, of course, the usual cocktail-hour debris—a ruin of peanuts, pitcher, olives lolling by the pencil holder, lemon peels small as fingernail clippings on a plate. I scanned the shelves: Smirnoff, Early Times, Wild Turkey, a small bottle of fruit-flavored brandy . . . but no Southern Comfort, damn! I debated, shrugged, poured a little bit of the brandy on top of the orange juice, poured in some Early Times, filled it up with Wild Turkey, and floated the freshest of the lemon peels on top. I plucked up a cocktail napkin and ran up the two flights of stairs, depositing the glass and tray in the same shadowy place I'd been hiding in. Then, lickety-split, I retraced my steps right back into the dining room, where I attracted no attention at all, except from Miss Bertha, who was still yelling for hot rolls. It would have been too much to expect Ree-Jane to do any table waiting after seeing her mother preparing filet mignon. Mrs. Davidow was now sitting at the family table cutting it up and caring for nobody or nothing as long as she had her steak and her glass of whisky.

For the few minutes I'd been gone, Ree-Jane must have been talking about the Paradises. She leaned across the serving counter, her pointy chin in her hands, supervising my mother's preparation of the lobster tails that she was apparently having instead of gruel. No ordinary fried chicken, no fish for her. Mrs. Davidow's store of filet mignon must have gone dry; either that or she wasn't sharing

with Ree-Jane, who was now insisting on drawn
butter as she put down the Paradises. Well, I had
to hand it to her: a chicken wing in her hair and
she was acting as if she'd been in total command
of the Aurora situation. I felt something almost
approaching admiration, which I quickly stomped
on.

"She's mental," said Ree-Jane of Aurora, "but
I guess the whole family must have been, and that's
really too bad—I mean, you marrying into a family
like that—why, what you must have put up with!"

My mother gave her an evil look and plopped
the lobster tails on a plate. "Nothing to what I put
up with now," she said, and I thought I saw dry ice
coming out of her ears.

"Well, the guests are awful, that's true. Where's
the drawn butter?" And she peered all around, as if
maybe Walter had it back there by the dishwasher.

I myself had gone behind the serving counter
to take down a warm plate from the ledge over the
stove (as my mother would not be caught dead serving up hot food on cold plates), on which I first
placed a napkin and then arranged a gorgeous piece
of chicken breast on that—the napkin to soak up any
little hint of oil—and beside this I set a small dish
of mashed potatoes.

Ree-Jane was still insulting my mother's intelligence by saying, "And the hotel's still *named* for
her. I mean, 'Hotel Paradise' is kind of silly at this
point, isn't it?"

I knew, of course, what name Ree-Jane favored:

the Davidow Inn. But she didn't dare say that, seeing how she and her mother have only been hanging around for five years and the Paradises for more like a hundred. I hummed as I made a little dent in Aurora's mashed potatoes and poured melted butter into it.

"Something like, oh, 'The Willows,' that would be nice."

My mother lit up a cigarette and tossed her a dangerous glancing look. "The last time I looked, they were oaks."

"You know what I mean—*where are you going with my drawn butter?*"

I merely slipped away with Aurora's fresh dinner, slapping through the swing door with the tray held high as Miss Bertha shouted for hot rolls.

## TWENTY-SEVEN

"Cold Turkey." I told Aurora Paradise what I'd named it after she'd sipped the drink. "There wasn't any Southern Comfort left."

She took another sip and smacked her lips. "Pretty good. Not as good as the Cold Comfort, though. You left out the gin."

"There wasn't any gin left, either." Did she think I ran a liquor store?

"Who're you kidding? Lola Davidow probably never ran out of gin in her entire life."

"Well, she's drinking vodka now. And the bottle was empty."

"That stands to reason." She settled back to drink her Cold Turkey and ignore her dinner.

The room was the same; I was beginning to think I'd dreamed it all. The Bible was still displayed, this time open to a page I bet she never read. The walnut shells were lined up (for suckers like me). The steamer trunks stood open, as well as a couple of suitcases, with clothes and scarves and jewelry strewn about as if Aurora had been rummaging in them. I hadn't noticed before, but the dresses hanging in the steamer trunks were more like evening gowns or party things, quite fancy with lacework, embroidered with seed pearls, or strung about with dazzling black sequins. I wondered what sort of life Aurora Paradise had lived to have such clothes.

"Who's that crazy blonde that sashayed up here pretty as you please with my dinner? Who gave her permission? What nerve!"

"You know her. That's Mrs. Davidow's daughter. It's Jane Davidow." I left off the "Ree."

"Oh, lordy! Another one of *them*? Impostors! They're after our money!"

I was surprised to hear her call it "our." "Well, they're out of luck, because my mother doesn't have any."

"*Paradise* money. Your mother ain't a Paradise. Here, cut this up. I've got rheumatism." As if to prove this, she slowly opened and closed her fingers.

I knew nothing was the matter with her hands; she just wanted to bark orders at me. But she sat there stretching out her fingers, rubbing them as if they pained her. Today they were dressed in black crocheted mittens decorated with the tiniest satin rosebuds imaginable. I picked up the knife and fork and pulled the white meat from the bone.

"Where's my peas?"

"On the floor, just where you left them." Fortunately, the food had landed with the tray underneath it, so that the upset dishes had spilled onto its surface. Minimum cleanup, probably for me.

She looked astonished, but I knew it was all fake. "*Me?* I never did! It was that bimbo that threw the dish at me!"

We locked eyes, with mine, I hoped, looking

shrewd. Finally, her own glance slid away. It pleased
me very much, being able to outstare Aurora Paradise. Looking out of the window, she started humming to give me the impression she wasn't even
aware of my presence. I finished cutting the chicken
into bite-sized pieces as she switched from humming
to actually singing. It was "Alice Blue Gown" and
her voice was awful, raspy and nasal and off-key.
But she seemed to think it was wonderful, for she
clasped her hand to her chest and raised her chin
and fairly bellowed

"When I first *waaan*-dered down into *tow-en* . . ."

"Your dinner's getting cold!" I had to raise my
own voice over this caterwauling.

As if she'd never started singing in the first
place, she stopped all of a sudden and jabbed her
fork into the mashed potatoes. "Lots of butter. Good."

"It's drawn butter." I stood there—never having been invited yet to sit down—scratching my
elbows and letting her eat for a moment. Then I
said, "I was wondering about Rose. Tell me more
about her."

"Rose who?" she asked, mouth thick with potatoes.

I sighed heavily. "*You* know who. You're the
one who mentioned her in the first place. Rose
Devereau."

Daintily, she plucked up a chicken bite between

thumb and forefinger and popped it in her mouth and chewed and ignored me.

I persisted. "You said she played the piano." I was holding Ben Queen in reserve, like one of the aces in the Bicycle deck.

She went on popping chicken in her mouth, after which she pulled the napkin from her collar and wiped and wiped her fingers for no reason at all except to irritate me and keep me waiting.

Elaborately, I pulled the front page of the paper from my pocket and unfolded it. "Well, I guess you don't want to hear about the dead woman they found over by White's Bridge. In Mirror Pond," I added. As she looked at me bug-eyed, I refolded the paper and went over to pick up the tray of spilled food, as if I meant to leave.

"What dead woman? Who?"

"Some lady the police say could have killed herself. With a gun."

She leaned forward, eager for details. "Suicide?"

"Probably it wasn't. Probably, it was *murder*." I started for the door.

One thing about Aurora Paradise was, nobody had to spell out "blackmail," she being an old hand at it herself. "Come on back here!" She pursed her lips, as if thinking hard. "Well, now. Rose . . . Oh, yes, that Rose Fern Devereau. Played the piano and Isabel sang. Could hear it all the way across the lake."

"You told me." I wondered how she knew it

was Rose Fern (which I thought a very pretty name) playing the piano. Aurora left a lot of stuff out; either that or she made it up.

"Well, *Isabel* thought she was a big-time opera star, when *I* was always the one with the voice." She broke again into "Alice Blue Gown," and I let her sing a few bars. After all, she was at least on the general subject. She stopped and said, "But Isabel sang at the Chautauqua, so she thought she was something—*ha!*"

"Chautauqua" had always been a special word for me. I paused in my search for information to let my mind play over it. The word had about it the suggestion of magic, as if an enormous circus had set up its tents to dazzle Spirit Lake. It was no tent, though, but a permanent amphitheater put up somewhere around the turn of the century and most of it still standing, but disused, across the highway up the high bank in an acre or two of cleared space across from the Hotel Paradise. This huge theater would be demolished eventually, for the wood was termite-ridden and rotted and part of it had already undergone a slow collapse. Will and I had been told not to play there, it being dangerous; of course, we did (in our playing-together days), danger being the most attractive ingredient of any activity. The Chautauqua was a long-ago annual summer event, luring quite famous people, mostly singers and musicians. I have seen faded brown photos in one of my mother's dresser drawers and in old albums of women in huge hats and flowing gowns, fancy Victorian finery, much like the dresses in Aurora's steamer trunks.

I would really like to have seen it, that Chautauqua; and if I couldn't see it I wished I could have it described. All I had was the album down in the Pink Elephant, which I would leaf through, careful of its coarse black pages. The snapshots we take today are so clear and sharp and full of color. But it is the past that I want to see the colors of. Why does the past have to be such a blur, so muted and fuzzy around the edges? I don't need the color to be in a picture taken yesterday. I don't need to see, in snapshots, the blue of Ree-Jane's silk dress, not when I can see Ree-Jane in person (unfortunately). But what were the colors of those dresses at the Chautauqua? I would really like to know. I paint them in my mind sometimes as I study the album: pale yellow, smoky blue, and even jet black. I paint none of them bright or garish, although I guess there were as many bright greens and violent reds and purples as there are today.

And that led me to thinking: so it's a compromise. If I don't know what colors the gowns were, I can paint them any way I want. It would be what I wanted, but it wouldn't be true. Or maybe it would be, but how would I know? Maybe it is this that makes the past mysterious; I wonder if that makes it dangerous.

"So Rose played the piano," I said, in a prompting way.

"That's right. And crazy Isabel sang."

I wasn't getting much further. "Someone told me Mary-Evelyn played the piano."

"Maybe. I wouldn't know." She was polishing off her Cold Turkey and blowing through the straw to make gurgling noises in the bottom of the glass.

"Well, don't you think it was a really weird life for her?"

"Who?" She kept up the noisome gurglings, even louder, just to irritate me.

"Mary-*Evelyn*. Living with all those grown women the way she did."

She was smacking her lips and jiggling the glass. "I wouldn't mind another one of these."

I sighed. It was near-impossible to keep her on track. Already, she seemed to have totally forgotten the death/suicide/murder reported in the paper. People like her are hard to bargain with because they keep forgetting what bargain a person's trying to make. "You'll just have to wait."

"No I won't, Miss Smartypants. I'll just get that Lola to make me one."

"She doesn't know the recipe. I'm the only one that does."

That stopped her. She narrowed her eyes at me. "Well, you can bring it when you bring my dessert. I want Angel Pie."

"Aren't you interested anymore in this woman that was murdered?"

She made flipping motions with her hand—*be off, be off.* "You're just making that up."

"*No*, I'm not." I pulled out the newspaper and thrust it toward her.

She "*hmmph*ed" around and said, "Can't read this without my specs." Then she patted the pocket of her steel-gray dress and looked vaguely around the room. "Where are they? Who took them?"

Disgusted, I said, "Oh, *here*, I'll read it to you," and snatched the paper back. From her self-satisfied little smile I could tell that that was just what she was after. It was really annoying still to be trying to worm things out of her after eight o'clock, when I hadn't even had my own dinner. Thoughts of lobster and steak drifted into my mind, betraying me, baiting me, which was pretty silly, as it would have to be my birthday before I ever saw anything like lobster or filet mignon. I started to read the article with concentrated attention. I gave it my best dramatic reading. But I hadn't got through the first paragraph before Aurora interrupted.

"My God! Who wrote *they-aat*?" She sort of keened this word out, as if she were wailing from a mountaintop.

"Suzy Whitelaw-Smythe. She calls herself that, with a hyphen."

"You mean that awful Whitelaw girl? One used to go with anything in pants?"

I wondered just how old Suzy Whitelaw-Smythe was. But of course Aurora could have been talking simply about twenty years ago, not two hundred, which I often thought she probably was.

"I guess so," I said happily, delighted that here was someone who not only had some kind of writing taste but who could cough up some gossip about Suzy Whitelaw that I could later bandy about when Ree-Jane was within earshot.

"Good God! I guess she went and dropped her knickers for that lewd old Edsel Broadwinters if he'd put that tripe in his paper."

I didn't know who she was talking about. "I don't think it's his paper anymore. The publisher's Mr. Gumbel." I shoved that comment about knickers dropping to the back of my mind to be thought about later. The important thing was identifying this woman, and Suzy's reputation would have to wait. And as much as I'd like to get into a discussion about her writing style, that would have to wait too.

"Hell, *you* could write better'n that."

"I know."

"That's enough to make me vomit. 'Moonlit tranquillity'? Why, everybody knows Mirror Pond's nothing but a mudhole. Go on. I hope it's not all like that."

I was thoughtful. Maybe appealing to Aurora's sense of her superior knowledge of everything since kingdom come might help. "Well, you're right. It's really bad writing. But try to ignore the way she says it. See, the trouble is, *nobody* knows who this woman is. Not even the Sheriff—"

"That Sam DeGheyn, is that the one?"

I was truly surprised the name meant something to her, especially since the Sheriff hadn't been around since Aurora was in knee-socks and, hence, wouldn't count for anything in her life. I said, "Yes. He's the Sheriff. Sam DeGheyn." It always made me just a little breathless to speak his name, and I rarely did, except to Maud in the Rainbow. It seemed quite natural there. "He doesn't know who she is," I repeated. "It's a real puzzle."

Aurora's eyes narrowed in what I took to be concentration. I hoped she could keep her mind on the story. "Hmm. Go on, read the rest."

I did. I made sure I was clear about the description of the blond woman—her looks, her apparent age, her clothes.

Aurora sat looking out the window, though there was only blank dark out there. Then she picked up her Bicycle cards and slowly riffled them. She said nothing.

I was still standing, of course, for she never invited me to sit down. And I was getting tired. She sat there with her eyes still on nothing, shuffling cards in a sort of slow-motion way, her mind not seeming to be really on the cards but on the newspaper story, her lips moving in and out in the same way I'd seen a couple of fat-mouthed fish do in Will's murky fishbowl. I was exhausted with hunger (not that that was unusual) and standing all this while, so I varied my position by turning my ankles in and standing on the sides of my feet in the way I'd done when I was little. I held the tray first under my arm, then moved it flat against my chest, a chest I was beginning to be anxious about, thanks to Ree-Jane's sly comments about me "showing." (In the Creation story, Ree-Jane would definitely be the snake in the garden, slithering through the dewy grass, standing on her tail and telling people things they were happier off not knowing.)

My feet hurt like the devil, being stood on in that way, which made going back to my earlier posture almost a relief. I was amazed that Aurora was seriously thinking all of this over, amazed to the point I wondered if she really *was*, or if she was instead only thinking of how to cheat at cards.

Until she said, "Who's got a picture? There's got to be a picture."

I frowned. "You mean—of *her*? The dead person?"

"Well, I don't mean of you, Miss Smartypants."

There was no real nastiness in what she said; it was her habit of talk. "There's the one in the paper, but you can't tell anything from it. I don't know of any others," I told her.

"That Sheriff does. He's probably got plenty. See, they *always* take a photographer to the crime scene to record the way the body is. And all that. They are *very particular* about that." Slowly, she started laying out her cards in a row.

"But the Sheriff wouldn't give *me* one, for heaven's sakes! He wouldn't give anybody one!" At least, I couldn't imagine that he would.

"Steal one, then." She said this quite calmly as she moved a red jack to a red queen.

"What? *Steal* one?" Was she crazy? Well, yes, she was, but I'd always known that.

"You want to know who she is, don't you?" I didn't answer, and she looked up from under her neat gray eyebrows at me. "I pretty much know, but I want to be ab-so-*lute*-ly sure before I say."

I sputtered. "But—but—why can't you say now?"

"Because you'll blab it all over town." She started to hum.

I felt like throwing the tray at her. "I will not!"

Humming, she skidded a black ten over to the jack. She moved her mouth in that fishy way, not answering.

I just stood there, my fingers nervous on the tray, tapping. "Well . . . but I can't . . . what if I can't . . . get one?" The notion of stealing something out of the Sheriff's office appalled me. Not the stealing part. I was never all that honest. But from the *Sheriff*?

Then I wondered: how did the man who came into Britten's store know to say the dead woman was "Ben Queen's girl" unless he'd seen either the body or a photo of her? You couldn't tell enough from the picture in the paper. Maybe I should be talking to him, only I didn't know him from Adam and he didn't look too child-friendly.

"You going to steal that picture?" Aurora snapped.

"No."

"Coward."

"You just want me to start a life of crime. You want me to get in trouble."

"Fat lot of good you'd be at it, miss." She slapped a jack of diamonds on the queen of hearts.

What was maddening about all this was that I didn't know how much truth there was in what Aurora said. Was she only pretending she had a notion of who the woman was? Just to get me riled? I chewed my lip, fuming. Maybe what I should do was bring out what I'd overheard in Britten's. That it was "Ben Queen's girl." I could easily have done that, but I didn't. I don't know why. I think it is because I never want to know the truth about things too soon. I don't want it coming up like a sudden sun and blinding me. Better to have it trickle out over time. That was my belief. *But*, I thought, I could say a man in Britten's said he *knows* who it is and not tell her exactly what he'd said. But she was too smart for that kind of blackmail.

"What are you standing there for?" she asked. "And don't think you can bribe me, either, with that Cold Turkey." She slipped a ten of spades on the red jack and shoved her glass towards me.

"I just like watching you cheat at solitaire. You can't play red cards on red cards, everyone knows that rule."

She pressed her lips together hard. Then she said, "Well, these are the rules my own daddy taught me." Prissily, she went on as she pointed to the ace, king, queen, jack—a mix of hearts and diamonds overlapping in a row. "The same color goes on all the face cards. . . ." Now her eyes drifted over to the end row, where a ten of hearts lay over a jack of diamonds. "*And* the tens. Tens through aces, red on red or black on black. Deuce through nine, it's red on black and vice-versa." Her hand waved me away.

"*Really?*" I made my tone sarcastic. "Then what's that ten of spades you just slapped down doing on a *red* jack?"

She riffled the deck and thought a moment. "Ten of spades is wild, didn't I say that? Ten of spades is the one wild card, and it can go anyplace."

What a *liar*! Fuming, I snatched up her empty glass and turned and marched out of the room.

I heard her yelling at me, "And don't be too long over your dinner, either—you're getting fat!"

At the top of the stairwell, I wheeled around and stuck out my tongue, shaking my head hard back and forth, as if such motion would send my tongue flying away, straight through the wall and right into her old back. I then stomped, as hard as I could, downstairs. All three flights, stomping.

I saw Lola Davidow was gone from the back office, and even before I had my dinner, just to get it over with, made the Cold Turkey pretty carelessly, tossing in stuff from four bottles, fishing a few floating ice cubes from the restocked bucket (must have been a party in here after dinner), and poured in an extra-big measure of bourbon. I did not want to go back up to the fourth floor, that was sure. I opened the door to the dumbwaiter and looked it over. It seemed to be all right. It wouldn't have surprised me if it had never been stuck, and Mrs. Davidow, after her eleventh martini, only thought something was wrong with it. I plunked the glass on it, yanked the rope, and sent it rumbling and creaking up to the fourth floor. As it rattled on up, I pounded on the wall. That was the signal, and I pounded to hell-and-gone.

That night I lay in bed in the blue darkness of my third-floor room, hearing the distant strains of a radio or a phonograph. Music, somewhere.

I lay there comfortably filled with chicken legs and mashed potatoes with pools of butter. My mother never makes gravy wells in mashed potatoes, the sort you see cooks do in diners and low-class restaurants. She considers that to be awfully "common." Now, beef gravy *could* be poured over the mashed potatoes accompanying a hot roast beef sandwich, since that dish was all "one." But my mother never serves hot roast beef sandwiches, considering them to be "common."

Not-being-common could take the place of any of the Ten Commandments in my mother's Bible. "Thou shalt not be common" is as important as the commandment about lying or stealing (the ones Aurora never read) or cheating or killing. Every one except, maybe, honoring thy father and thy mother. My mother's definition of "common" was very complicated. Basically, it has to do with how much education you have or how well-bred you are. My mother does not have much education, but she is bred to the bone. Not-being-common ("common" doesn't have an opposite word, certainly not "*un*common") means— usually—you are well-bred or well-educated or both. Walter is an excellent example (to my mother's way of thinking) of "common," for he is neither of these, in addition to being a little retarded. Walter is so "common" he's barely worth considering as an example. All of the kitchen help would be, naturally, "common." *Even* (I sometimes suspected) Vera, although my mother would never outright say this. Vera probably hovers on the verge, walking the razor-edge of commonness. *But*, on the other hand, there are people who simply didn't fit into the general definition. Marge Byrd, for instance, who you would think would be "commonized" pretty much by bringing half-pints of whisky into the office in brown paper bags. But no. Marge reads too much to be common, and since my mother reads a lot, they're always comparing notes. And there were many fine points, too, to this idea of "commonness."

I lay there thinking this over, trying to sort out the "common" from the rest, and began to wonder if it was simply that whoever my mother personally likes is *not* common and whoever she doesn't is. But that doesn't give my mother credit enough for making fine distinctions. She would never be so crude as that. What it really is, probably, is that my mother has as many rules for cooking and commonness as Aurora does for playing solitaire.

I turned this over for some time, sleepily, and

thought I was dreaming when I heard the singing. I opened my eyes and pricked up my ears.

"When I first *waaaan*-ered down into *tow-en* . . ."

was wafting down the hall, coming down from the fourth floor. The Cold Turkey had really done its job.

## TWENTY-EIGHT

Vera was still sick, so that I had to take over her regulars at breakfast, in addition to Miss Bertha, who is always at her worst at breakfast. There are too many things to choose from. Besides the usual ways of cooking eggs, my mother has dreamed up a lot of others. I always hate to have to list "shirred" among the egg dishes, for no one ever seems to know what that is. And they are always wanting an exact description of things like "Omelette Florentine" (not that I blamed them). It always makes me snigger to see "omelette" on any menu other than the Hotel Paradise's, for in any other cook's hands it's not much more than scrambled eggs. My mother's, on the other hand, is high and humpy and soft as clouds, for she whips the whites to a meringue gloss before adding the yolks. And when she fills the omelette with one of her mixtures, it's a sight to behold. Why one of those food magazines isn't beating a path to the Hotel Paradise to take pictures, I have never understood.

Anyway, I tried to imagine Vera actually being sick, but had a hard time doing it. I could not think what "disease" could take hold of that whiplash body and reduce it to sniffling or emitting little gasps of pain or shivering with fever. Ree-Jane, naturally, having waited on tables last night (after which she must have gone out on her mysterious date with the Unknown), could hardly be expected to do anything but sleep in this morning. So that left Anna Paugh and me to wait on the dozen tables.

It was especially difficult this morning to keep my attention on the choice between dropped biscuits and corn cakes and orange muffins, for I wanted to get down to the Pink Elephant and make my plans. I made some mistakes (which wasn't unusual), most of them landing on Miss Bertha's table (which also wasn't unusual). I had brought her a California Omelette, lovely vegetables oozing out of its folds, which she swore she never ordered. When she banged her cane and yelled for attention, I disappeared into the kitchen and told Anna Paugh to take over. Fortunately, she was good and easygoing, not yet bent out of shape by the Hotel Paradise.

It used to be, when I was very young, we had a half-dozen live-in waitresses who occupied the rooms right above the laundry room in the wing where the kitchen was. To get to these back rooms, you had to walk up the darkest, narrowest stairs I've ever seen. At the top is a landing, and to the right, the six rooms, three on each side of a cramped hallway. Several feet beyond the head of the stairs the hallway dog-legs, making two separate sets of rooms along two different hallways. On this wider one to the left, there are more rooms, eight or ten, that other help used long ago. The way the rooms were arranged, it was as if the Waitresses occupied their own separate space.

I really loved the Waitresses. I have always spent more time with the hotel help than with the guests' kids; most of them are uppity and expect they should always win at croquet and other games just because their fathers pay to stay here.

My mother must not have known how much time I spent with the Waitresses, up in their rooms, talking and laughing, for they would surely have been considered "common." The Waitresses (for I thought of them as a unit, a group) were young, I guess, but when you're only six or seven, a woman of twenty seems as old as Egypt, and just as romantic and unreachable. Unreachable only in the sense that I could never imagine myself growing to that height or age or prettiness, for they were all very pretty, with similar carved-ivory faces and gold or red or ebony hair. Saturday nights were especially fun, because sometimes they would put records on an old phonograph and dance around. They would dress me up in one or another of their "evening gowns" and dab a little lipstick on me. I remember especially a midnight-blue dress, tulle and sequins, that I thought was the most glamorous dress imaginable. Or at least that's what I think now; I don't know what I thought then. But I do remember how I loved dressing up and dancing around. We would all dance around up there over the laundry room.

I say there were half a dozen waitresses, but I'm not really sure; there might have been four, or even eight. There might have been only three. It must have been because they all seemed to *enjoy* things

so much, and were so gay, that they appeared in my
mind as a "flock" of girls, like flamingos huddled
together in one of the paintings-for-loan hanging in
the Abigail Butte County Library. Or the ballet dancers in one of the other paintings—a very famous
picture, I think—that shows the dancers in satin and
tulle, limbering up, a couple of them with legs raised
up on that bar thing. The Waitresses were as brilliant
as flamingos and as limber as dancers.

And the Waitresses belonged to the days before
our playhouse, way up behind the hotel, burned
down, and I never knew why, or what Will or I had
done (if anything) to cause it; to the days before my
dog got killed just where the hotel's gravel drive
meets the highway, and I saw the car coming and
started to run across the highway but was held back
by someone or something; to the days before my
father died.

It's as if the Waitresses had a kind of magic to
them, like an ability to pull flowers out of hats or
endless lengths of brilliantly colored scarves out of
sleeves. It was as if they protected me from something, maybe the way a magician protects you from
seeing empty space. Away comes the screen and
where there once was empty space, now there's a
vase of roses or a bluebird.

And though they probably left one by one, I
think of them as disappearing all together. I see all
of them or I see none of them.

When I'm sitting in the Pink Elephant (as I
was doing on this morning after breakfast) with my

notebook and my Whitman's box of snapshots and stuff, I remember the Waitresses. Now, they're a memory. My head feels heavy and I drop it on my arms. I think: If memory is this painful now, what will it be like when I'm twenty? or forty? Thirty more years of memories to weigh me down, more and more things to lose. For at some point they would all be memories: Miss Flyte and Miss Flagler, the Wood boys, Maud. The Sheriff. *This* seemed so unthinkable that my head jerked upwards, like a puppet head, worked by strings.

More and more things to lose. And what comes in their stead, what comes to replace the Waitresses, is Vera, like a steel rooster, long-necked, gray, and strutting into the dining room. And it seems impossible that things could have changed so much. Impossible the Waitresses were gone and the midnight-blue tulle dress gone with them.

# TWENTY-NINE

After sitting in the Pink Elephant that morning, thinking unhappy thoughts, I finally got around to making my plans. I decided, first, to go into town to the courthouse. I didn't want to take up the time with walking, for by now it was nearly ten o'clock and I was due back by noon to serve lunch. Waiting on tables broke up the day something awful.

I went to the back office and called Axel's Taxis (first looking around to make sure Ree-Jane wasn't within earshot), and the "dispatcher" (with only two cabs, I couldn't think why Axel needed a dispatcher) said she'd send Delbert out as soon as he got back, which would only be a few minutes, as he'd just taken Miss Isabelle Barnett to the railroad station and she could hear the train coming now. (Everyone in town who ever called for a cab knew the business of every other passenger.)

I told her I'd rather have Axel himself, though it was nothing personal against Delbert. Naturally, I said this just to see.

"Oh, he's out on a call, honey, won't be back for a while."

Well, I could wait. (I wouldn't, but I just said this.)

"Axel's all the way to Hebrides, hon, won't be back for a good long time. Delbert can come get you real soon—well, speak of the devil, here he's just pulled up."

I sighed and thanked her and wondered why it was she never told the business of *Axel's* fares, who they were, where they were going. Maybe because *she* never saw them, either.

Delbert let me out at the courthouse, and I went in and lurked around for a while in the hallway, there by the water cooler, prepared to squash myself back into its shadowy alcove should the door to the Sheriff's office open.

I heard his voice, kind of a deep rumble. I also could see a dark outline, blurred, on the pebbled glass of the door. I figured he was coming out, so I shoved myself back in the alcove. For once (for once in my *life*) it wasn't him I wanted to see, at least not now.

Finally he emerged, and from between wall and water cooler I watched him walk away through the courthouse entrance and down the stone walk until he'd become a black sunlit silhouette. Then I walked across the marble foyer (the courthouse was quite fancy) and into the office.

Donny and the other two deputies were looking busy, and both of the secretaries were typing away. One of the girls looked up and smiled around her chewing gum, which she cracked (as if that meant "Hi") as she kept on typing.

Donny himself was sitting at the Sheriff's big

desk with his feet planted up on it, trying to look important. He was studying something, frowning over a batch of what to me looked like photographs. As I went up to him I could see that's what they were, though I could only see the backs of them.

I went a little cold. Police pictures.

He looked up over the tops of half-glasses that made him seem much older than the Sheriff, although I knew he was younger. He eased a photo from the front to the back of the several in his hands and told me Sam was out.

"Oh." I tried to sound disappointed. "Know where he is?"

"Rainbow, I guess. Said he wanted some chili."

I'd just had, two hours or so ago, corn cakes, link sausages, and an egg over easy; still, my stomach heard it: "chili." I ignored the call. "I guess you're all really busy—I mean, since you found that woman's body in Mirror Pond."

"Uh-huh." Now he was slapping a photo face-down on the blotter within my fingers' reach. I pulled back my hand.

Donny is like most adults: he doesn't believe in really having a conversation with a kid. So I'd have to weasel any information out of him. Which was what I seemed to like to do anyway. I frowned over that insight. "Okay." I made a movement to go, purely fake, and then said—as if I'd just got this bright idea—"Say, you know a man in Spirit Lake named Jude? I don't know his last name. But he knows you." That was a lie; it was another one that said he knew Donny.

He looked as if he was rooting around for the name and then shook his head.

"I went to Britten's store yesterday to get things for the hotel, and he was there."

"How's your mom, anyway?"

People never failed to ask after my mother, which I liked. Hardly ever did anyone ask after Mrs. Davidow. "She's just fine, thank you. Anyway, this Jude person was saying he knows who this woman is. Was."

Donny frowned. "Who?"

"He said . . ." I chewed my lip, hesitated, just as I had with Aurora, to say "Ben Queen's girl." "I guess I didn't actually hear the name he said. But what I wondered was, well, this Jude wasn't *there*, was he? I mean, the only ones there were you all." My eyes swept the room to take in the other deputies, who were talking to each other and not minding us. "So how would he know? That picture in the paper wasn't good enough."

Donny's eyes strayed to the ones in his hand.

I had guessed correctly; they were photos of the dead woman.

"Nope." He gathered them up, placed them carefully in a manila folder marked with a number, and then placed the folder in the deep file drawer of the desk. "You don't recall who he said?"

"No. Just someone's—'girl.' "

He was leaning back, very much in an I'm-in-charge way, hands locked behind his head, one big shoe sole against the desk's edge.

"Girl *friend*?"

"Well . . . maybe, you know, 'daughter.' Like 'boy' could mean 'son.'"

He thought this over, frowning. "You saying you think maybe this Jude fellow is im-pli-ca-ted someways?"

I was shocked. I stumbled back, holding up my hands as if to ward off something awful. "No, no. I didn't mean anything like that! That wasn't the only person that said he knew who she was." I dredged for the name. "Louella Smitt, one of them said. And *he* said he heard it at the courthouse."

Donny got wide-eyed. "Well, whoever he was *didn't*. We can't talk about cases. People just like to make things up, makes them feel important."

"That's what I say. That's what I thought." I was glad we were off my "implicating" Jude.

"They were saying the description in the paper wasn't all that good, too." That was a lie, but the truth wasn't getting me very far. "One of them said she was younger than the paper said. And blonder." I held my breath.

Donny was unstripping a stick of gum. "Don't know how they'd know that."

"I don't know, either. Only, I did sort of get the idea from somebody else she wasn't young. And not all that blond."

He shrugged. "Depends what you mean by 'young.' Or 'blond.'"

I couldn't win.

"Depends what you mean by 'young' or 'blond.'" I was eyeing the Sheriff's half-eaten bowl of chili when I said this.

He looked at me long enough to pry my eyes up from his bowl. "You want the rest of this chili?"

"*No.* It's not even lunchtime," I said disdainfully. I was irritated he was not responding to my comment. Maud and I had been discussing the article in the paper.

"Why would she want your cold, leftover chili?" Maud said this snappishly. She was in a mood.

"She likes chili," was the Sheriff's mild reply. He smiled.

Hardly ever did he rise to the bait of anyone's bad temper. I don't know how he managed this, for some of the things Maud and I said should have driven him to distraction. Well, *Maud* said.

Maud said, "Good Lord, I can get her some *hot* if she wants it."

"I don't want it. It's not lunchtime. I don't see how people can eat lunch so early."

"I never had breakfast," he explained.

"How can you eat chili for breakfast?"

"So are they working over there?" the Sheriff

asked me, ignoring my criticism of his breakfast. "Or just pretending to?"

I had told him I'd come from the courthouse. I didn't tell him Donny was sitting at his desk, big as you please. I *did* tell him that I had overheard "someone" talking about the newspaper account and saying it wasn't accurate. But remembering Donny's saying "implicated," I said I couldn't remember just who it was. That's when I'd tossed in the young-and-blond comment.

"How young *was* she?" Maud asked. "You're not saying."

"I know." The Sheriff rooted in his pack of Camels for a cigarette, found none, crushed it up.

Maud didn't offer him one of hers, I noticed. Payback for being secretive. "Probably you can't tell age."

His mouth twitched the way it did when he was trying not to smile. "About your age, maybe. Hair about your color, I guess. How young and blond's that?"

A wave of relief swept over me before I realized he'd just said this to kid Maud.

"The trouble is," Maud said, looking at me, "Sam doesn't know any more about her than he did two days, nearly three days, ago, and he doesn't want to admit it, so he's pretending everything's a secret." She pocketed her cigarettes, patted the pocket, and blew a little smoke ring.

"Uh-huh." The Sheriff looked behind him, sort of levering up to see over the top of the wooden booth, as if things might be more interesting up there with Shirl and the regulars at the counter.

"Well, you *don't* know any more, do you?" She was really irritated because he wouldn't tell her.

"While the investigation is in progress, I can't talk about things." His smile was maddening to Maud.

I said, "What I wondered about this man who said he knew who she was, was: How would he know unless he saw pictures of the body?"

Maud rubbed her arms. "This is giving me the shivers."

"Maybe he knew her, maybe he knew the person he thought it was." He frowned. "And you can't remember him or where you heard it?"

I shook my head as I stared at him. It was such a simple explanation. All the while I had been looking at it from one end, not realizing there was another end. It was not that he was identifying her from seeing either her or pictures of her, but that he was assuming it was someone he knew who fitted the vague description because *this someone was gone or missing*.

It was like a revelation.

Maud got up and went back to the counter, and I'm not sure I said goodbye or anything, I was so deep into imagining. I imagined this Jude saying to someone: "I ain't seen Ben Queen's girl around for several days." And this someone answering, "No, but there was a woman they found dead over to White's Bridge there sounds just like her." I needed to find this Jude. I had got the idea he didn't live in Spirit Lake, from the way the other men acted like he didn't often come to Britten's.

"Want to do the meters with me?"

The Sheriff's voice startled me. I came out of my trance and focused. "Meters? Oh. No, I can't. I've got to get back to wait tables."

He'd got up, put a few dollars on the table, and was hitching his holster around. "You need a ride?" He looked at me out of eyes that seemed to get bluer by the moment. He smiled.

"Uh . . . no, I . . ." The thing was that I wanted to stop at Britten's store and I didn't want to have to explain why. I had *never* turned down a ride with the Sheriff—never. "I'll just get one of Axel's Taxis."

The Sheriff positioned his hat, sort of snapped the brim, and smiled at me again. He left the Rainbow.

I thought for another moment about Jude and then looked at my hand. Why was I holding a spoon? I put it down. I looked at the Sheriff's bowl of chili. Empty. I'd been eating what was left.

He never said a word.

That was the Sheriff.


In the taxi (driven by Delbert) to Spirit Lake, I had practiced what I would say, but I had been planning on saying it to the old regulars who had been there yesterday. There was no one in Britten's except Mr.

Britten himself, which would make my task nearly impossible. Mr. Britten was not much of a talker at the best of times, and I'm sure he didn't connect me with the best. He liked to bury his hands under his brown cardigan and look at me over the tops of his black-rimmed glasses, ducking his head down in order to look up over them, as if he couldn't trust me not to try and take a swing at him.

That's the way he was looking at me now— very suspicious, wondering what I was doing back. I would have to invent, now, something my mother had told me to pick up. "Bisquick," I said.

"Must be doing lots of baking. Two boxes just walked out of here with Walter."

That was always how Mr. Britten described the sale of groceries: as if they operated on their own. No one actually *bought* them; they "walked out" or "danced out" or "fought for space on the shelves," so that I sometimes had a picture of cans and jars and sacks and boxes doing all sorts of things, the store shaking with ferocious activity.

"Walter's already *been* here? Already? Why, *I* was told to come get the Bisquick!" I just rolled my eyes and shook my head as if no one at the Hotel Paradise could remember his proper chores except me. I sighed, walked over to the long glass counter, and took some time looking at the candy and gum. "I'll have some Teaberry, I guess."

Mr. Britten didn't like having to move even an inch for the likes of me, so his walk was pretty slow and grudging. He frowned over the packet he plucked from the rows of gum and then handed it to me. I plunked change on the counter. Slowly (for I was giving myself rethinking time) I unwrapped a stick and folded it into my mouth. Then I asked him, "My mother was wondering if that man named"— I tried to snap my fingers in an effort of remembrance— "is it Jude? The one who was in here yesterday?" No indication yes or no as he just stared at me out of his flat brown eyes. "Well, she was wondering if he was available."

"For what?"

"I'm not sure." I wrinkled up my forehead as if trying to remember.

"Don't know him." Mr. Britten punched the cash register and gave me back my four cents change.

I stood there chewing my gum and feeling disappointed and was about to give up when the screen door banged and there was one of the men from yesterday's conversation!

"Mornin', Bryson," he said. Politely, he nodded to me, too, as he put down a dollar on the counter.

"Lucas," said Mr. Britten abruptly. Then he turned to the shelves behind him and slipped down a curled-up packet of Mail Pouch tobacco and put that on the counter in exchange for the bill. I guess it was Lucas's standard chew. Martin's was a little like the Rainbow Café in this respect, where Shirl and Maud knew more or less how everyone took their coffee—black, cream, sugar—and just set it before them.

"Anything else?" Mr. Britten glowered at me

over his glasses. He always acted as if I'd come to hold up the store.

Now I had to reintroduce my subject. "You don't know if this *Jude* lived in Spirit Lake?" Lucas had walked over to one of the wooden chairs, and I raised my voice a little so that he could hear. He did. He opened his mouth to comment when one of the *other* of the three men walked in ("Mornin', Bryson—mornin', Luke") and took the other wooden chair. This was the one they called Bub.

Luke indicated me and said to his friend, "She's askin' after Jude. She wants to know does he live in Spirit Lake."

All eyes were now focused on me, which I didn't much like.

"No, he don't," said Bub, unfolding his paper. Why give out information to a kid?

Luke said, "Lives over in Hebrides, don't he?"

Bub shook his head. "Over to Cold Flat Junction."

I took in my breath sharply. Arrows flashed on and off in my mind like the sign above Arturo's Diner, pointing to Cold Flat Junction. For a moment Bub and Luke quarreled over where Jude lived. I broke it up by saying, "And she—I mean my mother—said Mr. Jude did some work for her once."

Luke shrugged. I think he might have been irritated that I seemed to know more about Jude than he did. I didn't belong in here, after all; I wasn't one of them.

Bub was friendlier, apparently eager for talk

with anyone who came along, even me. "I seen you in here the other day, didn't I?"

Mr. Britten said, loudly, "This is Jen Graham's girl, from over at the Hotel Paradise."

Whenever Mr. Britten decided to talk, it was always in this butting-in way. When you didn't want him to.

Luke looked at me, wide-eyed. "You ain't ever Miss Jen's girl?"

I nodded and sighed, knowing Jude would now be forgotten, and so would Cold Flat Junction.

"Well, I'll be! I used to work for your daddy, when you was a little bitty thing." He measured off air the size of a mouse. He turned to the other man. "Hey, Bub, you used to work over to the Hotel Paradise, too, didn't you? Fifteen, maybe twenty, years ago?"

And then they started swapping remembrances, which started at the Hotel Paradise and then extended to the whole of Spirit Lake. And it was just like a train coming down the track, stopping at this station and that station, picking up facts like passengers and suitcases and trunks, getting heavier and heavier because they were both so full of memories of the last twenty years that they both kept refining ("No, that weren't *Asa* Stemple, it was *Ada*. It was Ada packed up and went off to New York City. Now Asa, he . . .").

I left.

*    *    *

My mother was miraculously absent from the kitchen when I ran in twenty minutes late. It was empty except for Walter, in the dark by the big dishwasher. Also, there were signs that Vera was back again, for her coal-black full-dress uniform was on a hanger, covered with Whitelaw Cleaners (no relation to Suzy, the star reporter) plastic. It must be the really good uniform, for Vera washed and ironed the others herself. And that must mean a big dinner party tonight.

I hated the thought of that, as I would surely be called upon to act as Vera's slave; she would be in the limelight, setting the plates before the guests, and I would be back in the shadows, carrying trays and handing off dishes to her. It was like those Dr. Kildare movies where the Great Surgeon is allowed at the operating table and the unimportant nurse is standing back and slapping instruments into his hand.

I wouldn't even have seen Walter if he hadn't said hello. It was like a pocket of shadows back there, a place where you could stand and be nearly invisible. Since there didn't seem to be any hurry about lunch, I decided to help Walter, something I hardly ever did. But I thought I should make up for pretending he was all wrong about the Bisquick. I picked up a towel and took up a dish. This way, I could both be helpful to Walter and invisible to Vera, should she walk in.

Walter smiled his half-moon smile; the corners of his mouth went nearly to his ears.

"I could have got the Bisquick, Walter. It's too bad you had to make a trip."

"That's okay," he said pleasantly, his hands slowly moving a sudsy cloth over a platter too big for the machine. Dishes were either too big or too small or too good, or pans too stuck with food. The dishwasher was near-useless.

"No, but I mean it. I was just up there and I could have picked it up. You shouldn't have to run back and forth."

"I don't mind."

"Well . . ." I put a certain grumpiness in the word to let him know *I* appreciated him. Which I didn't.

Vera came through the swing door then and went about doing busybody Vera-things, needful things-to-be-done just popping up all around her like bright weeds springing through the floor planks. I could hear clinking and china rattlings down at the other end of the kitchen as she went from table to cupboard to tray like a bee pollinating. Then she hefted the laden tray and returned to the dining room and I moved again to wipe the platter.

"I guess she's not sick anymore," I said, noticeably sad. Walter didn't like her, either, though he never would have said this.

"Says she still is."

"Why's she back, then?"

"Says it's a big dinner party tonight and she's ob-li-ga-ted."

"She wants the tips, that's what."

Walter chuckled.

Since no one considered Walter very much except when they wanted to blame someone, I suppose it wasn't strange that I didn't much think about him and about his life. But now I wondered how long Walter had been in Spirit Lake. I asked him.

"Near my whole life long."

And then I recalled Walter lived not far from Britten's store. I'd once or twice seen him in there, just standing around, not participating, but sort of standing around smiling. "You hang out at Britten's, don't you, sometimes?"

"Uh-huh." He handed me a pot.

"You ever talk to a man named Jude?" I could ask such direct questions of Walter because Walter never wondered why I was doing something. Walter just wasn't curious, or figured it wasn't his business. So it was almost like talking to myself.

"Jude, uh-huh. He comes into Britten's onced a week, just about."

I stopped wiping and stared. All of that trouble and here *Walter* knew the answers? Excited, I asked, "Who is he?"

"Jude Stemple. Lives over to Cold Flat. Comes onced a week to Spirit Lake to do work for Miss Isabelle Barnett. I used to do yard work for her until I got a better job."

Was he talking about the Hotel Paradise? I didn't ask. "What's he do?"

"Fixes things. He's putting lattice up around her porch. I guess he's like a carpenter, some. He's real good, some say."

"And this Jude Stemple lives in Cold Flat Junction?"

Walter nodded.

That day, I was lucky. There was only Miss Bertha and Mrs. Fulbright to wait on at lunch. Everyone else had either checked out or gone off somewhere. An hour and fifteen minutes after my talk with Walter, I was down at the Spirit Lake railroad station, sitting on a bench and waiting for the 1:53 to Cold Flat Junction.

This time I bought a ticket.

## THIRTY

Had I really thought the Girl would appear there, again, on the platform?

I suppose I must have, for I was disappointed as the train chugged to a halt and I saw the platform was empty.

It was a very short ride to Cold Flat Junction, eighteen minutes exactly, not even time enough for the conductor to punch my ticket. I could have got by without buying one. It's annoying to be honest and law-abiding and not get the credit for it, not even have people notice. But I felt a little better when I discovered, upon studying the square of yellowish cardboard, that the date was so blurred you could hardly see it. I tucked it in my change purse with some plan for its future use. I snapped the purse shut and put it in my pocket.

Before Cold Flat, there was only the one stop in La Porte, and that was only a few minutes beyond Spirit Lake. It was truly enjoyable being a passenger on the train instead of one of the people standing down there on the platform. It was as if it gave me some God-like view. I pressed my face against the glass looking out, knowing that even if someone there knew me, my face behind the glass of a train window wouldn't register.

Not even on Helene Baum—for there she stood,

gawking up, her hand shielding the eyes behind her butterfly glasses. I assumed she wasn't going any-where, since it was *her* dinner party tonight. She must have been scanning the train for whoever she was waiting for, and she was frowning anxiously as if the person might be looking out and deciding upon seeing her that he or she would rather not get off. Helene was wearing one of her yellow dresses and a yellow cardigan around her shoulders. I couldn't stand her, but I felt kind of sorry for her, with that look on her face that people allow themselves when they don't know someone else is watching. Unguarded, I guess you'd say. It was the sort of look that people wear in movie theaters, looking up at the screen.

Finally, a heavyset woman wearing tons of cos-tume jewelry stepped awkwardly down the little metal stairs the conductor put there. Now, Helene's expression changed into a showy smile. They sort of charged towards each other, in that clumsy way of people who feel they're supposed to hug but don't want to touch, so that arms never quite make it around waists or shoulders, and kisses are planted on empty air. They chugged off, and so did the train.

Fifteen minutes later, I myself was on the little metal ladder the conductor flipped down from the car to the platform. The conductor nodded and smiled pleasantly, unaware that someone was getting off his train with an unpunched and blurrily dated ticket. I said goodbye and smiled back.

No one else got off and no one was waiting to

get on, which didn't surprise me. No activity at all was taking place on the Cold Flat Junction platform. After the train roared off and its clattering wheels went quiet in the dim blue distance, I walked slowly along the empty platform, stopping to marvel at the turreted and towered station building. I looked in all of the windows, cupping my hands around my reflection to peer inside. I don't know if I thought the view would change from window to window. Having done this, I moved to the entrance, which had dark and beautiful molding that formed an arch above my head, with a half-moon of ruby-red stained glass over the doorway lintel. I stepped inside, hesitating the way a person would going into a church he didn't really belong to.

Actually, it was more like the light and dark of a movie theater. An empty theater, at that. Six long, solid wood benches stood back-to-back in a neat row across the waiting room. Three walls were also lined with benches. In the fourth wall was the ticket seller's room and window. No one was behind the ticket window, which seemed to be closed; a piece of wood had been placed in front of the semicircle opening in the glass, and a tan blind pulled partway down to announce absence. I could see, back there, the bottom half of a rack of a neatly arranged rainbow of tickets, as if these colorful destinations were always in demand. There was no sign saying where the stationmaster had gone, or if he would return. But the station was so well kept, there had to be a keeper.

On the bulletin board there were schedules,

those complicated lines of tiny type and little arrows
going up and down that probably nobody could
understand. But I supposed there was the same train
I had taken before from Cold Flat Junction back to
Spirit Lake as before, the 4:32. I now had nearly two
hours here in Cold Flat and could still get back in
plenty of time for the Baum dinner-party preparations.

Outside the station, I sat down on the same slat-
back bench the Girl had been sitting on when I saw
her. I needed to make up a plan. At lunch I had been
too distracted to think, between Miss Bertha's lunch
and my own. Ham croquettes with parsley sauce and
corn fritters naturally got my undivided attention,
and dessert had been Floating Island, which alone
would have driven out thoughts of anything else.

What I wanted was to find either Jude Stemple
or (but this seemed almost too lucky) the Queens.
And I wanted to plot out how I could get information
about him or them. I tried to keep my mind centered
on a plan, but it kept being drawn to the land beyond
me, out there across the railroad tracks—bare and
colorless and hardly even blistered with outcroppings
of vegetation. There was scarcely a tree until far off
began the dark line of woods. It was so far away,
not even squinting my eyes could separate one tree
from another. The distance and the light made the
wood a uniform navy blue. Between the station and
that line of woods, all was blank and empty. The
land looked savaged, as if Indian tribes had thundered
through here and scalped it, and whatever people

there were, and whatever buildings had up and retreated to the other side of the tracks behind the railroad station, as if it were a fort.

I sat there staring at the emptiness for longer than I meant to, feeling the land sucking me in. Cold Flat Junction had that effect, at least on me: it wasn't pretty like Spirit Lake, which was lush with big trees and where you could crush whole carpets of wildflowers underfoot; nor was it ugly like Dubois, twenty miles away, where the paper mill was and the houses were always coated with dark dust and the whole town smelled putrid. Cold Flat Junction just looked wiped out and anonymous. Only part of that look was the landscape; the other part was the strange quiet over the place, and that was because the town had come about from the promise of the railroad to give Cold Flat life. But life had never happened.

Cold Flat Junction didn't have a center: no "main road" lined with stores, just a few scattered ones, like the diner and the filling station. There were the white clapboard schoolhouse and the church, and Rudy's Bar and Grille that I'd seen before, and the post office, but there wasn't any central point. It was as if Cold Flat were waiting for something to give it shape. There wasn't a courthouse, and I didn't recall seeing a police station, either. I knew the Sheriff got called to Cold Flat on a regular basis to break up fights and so forth, which was probably the only form of entertainment they had, and which probably took place mainly in Rudy's Bar and Grille. There wasn't even a movie house; that alone would have wiped the place off my map.

As I walked a runnel of path made by people who'd tramped down the earth to a smoothness between the station and "town," I thought about how I was going to get my information. Remembering all of the arguing in the diner when I'd asked about the Tidewaters, I didn't think it would be hard to get people to talk; the problem was getting them to agree. I didn't want to be too direct; I didn't want to just come out and ask for Jude Stemple. So I was trying to make up another first name that would throw people off that it was Jude I wanted to talk to. I wanted a name that probably didn't exist among the Stemples—which was why I discarded Bob and Tom and so forth. As I came closer to the Windy Run Diner I was rejecting most names. Names from the Bible were good, but my knowledge of the Bible being what it was, I had to really think hard to bring any up.

I was right outside the Windy Run when I finally settled on Abel (Cain being too famous and too unpopular). A gust of wind coursed down the narrow road, blew my hair in my face, and sent leaves and sandwich wrappers and circulars skittering around the steps. I went through the louvered door and up to the counter, where I sat down and pulled a menu from between a sugar jar and salt and pepper shakers. I read it over, top to bottom, seeing "Louise Snell, Prop." at the head.

Louise Snell must've wanted everyone to know

she owned the diner. Then I replaced the menu, and without trying to seem interested, I glanced about the room and recognized a few of the dozen or so people sitting there. I recalled the woman with the thick glasses, and the heavy one named Billy. Also, the couple in one of the booths looked familiar. But then, it wasn't strange that they'd all be here, since it was the same time of day as before. Customers did that in the Rainbow, too. You could pretty much guess where the Wood boys would be at noon, or Miss Ruth Porte every evening at six, or Dodge Haines at three. I guess it makes you comfortable, knowing where you'll be at a certain time and in a certain place. I know it does me. Clockwork habits make me feel safer.

There really must not have been much going on in Cold Flat Junction, for the waitress remembered me. "Well, hi there, sugar. Your folks get their car fixed up okay?"

A gravelly voiced man down at the end of the counter shouted, "If it's Toots worked on it, probably it's still up on the lift." He thought this was terribly funny, and so did a couple of others in blue cloth caps. Toots must be the garage mechanic, I supposed.

I didn't care to be so well remembered, but I just said yes and studied the menu. I decided to order a hot roast beef sandwich to see if it was really as "common" as my mother said. I couldn't even remember having had one before. I asked for a Coke, too. I hoped the waitress wouldn't ask me any more questions, for I couldn't remember exactly what I'd said in here, except for asking about the Tidewaters. And I hoped they didn't remember that, as it might seem strange that here I was again, asking now about the Stemples. I decided not to say anything until after I'd eaten my sandwich and give them a little while to get used to my presence. And since nobody brought up the Tidewaters, and whether I'd found Toya, I was fairly sure they didn't remember. What they did was cast glances my way, but pretty soon they even got bored with doing that and went back to asking for refills on coffee. The heavyset woman asked Louise about "Betsy"—had she got over that cold? Louise answered no, she's still sick and missing school. Betsy, I decided, must be Louise's daughter.

I read my paper placemat so I'd have something to do. It was a collection of pretty easy puzzles, such as join-the-dots. I looked up when I heard a series of clicking noises. There was a partially open door off beyond the counter, and I saw the end of a pool table and a skinny kid in a white T-shirt with the short sleeves rolled up, I guessed to show off his muscles, what there were of them. He held a cue stick upright and was smoking a cigarette in quick jabs. Another boy came into view, then, and he was taller and even skinnier than the first, as if he'd been pulled, head to toe, like taffy. I hadn't noticed the poolroom when I was here before; maybe the door had been closed. The noise came from the clicking of the billiard balls.

It was then that the waitress, Louise, set my hot roast beef sandwich before me. Steam gusted from its surface in a way my mother would have approved of. The sandwich was lathered in dark gravy, which was also poured over the floury-looking potatoes and into a deep little well in the center. It looked really good for something "common." I ate and watched the boys in the poolroom, only occasionally flicking glances towards the other customers around the counter, especially Billy, for he was the one making the most noise. Billy would reach out for Louise whenever she passed on her way to the kitchen or the coffee maker. She'd slap his hand away and he'd laugh as if this were the funniest thing. Well, it was the same way Dodge Haines and a couple of others acted in the Rainbow around Charlene and Maud. I guessed it must be standard diner-café behavior; it must be that a lot of men don't feel manly if they just sit and drink their coffee and talk—they have to grab the waitresses and act like comedians. I had never seen the Sheriff stoop to grabbing and patting. That was a comforting thought.

When Louise came to take away my empty plate (how could I have eaten it all?) and asked me did I want some fresh rhubarb pie (my mouth puckered at the thought)? I told her no, thanks, and asked if she knew anyone named Abel Stemple who I'd heard lived in Cold Flat Junction.

"Abel Stemple? Now let me think." She screwed up her face and looked towards the ceiling in a cartoon version of Somebody Thinking.

Billy got into it, as I thought he would. "You say *Abel* Stemple, little lady?"

(I hated being called "little lady.")

"Ain't no Abel Stemple. I never heard of no *Abel*; did you, Don Joe?" And he turned to one of the men wearing a blue cap.

Don Joe scrubbed and scraped at his whiskers, coughed, and said no, he never.

Billy then asked Tiny, the other man in the other blue cap, who shook his head and kept his eyes on the counter. Billy was pretty much taking possession of the name now, and he sort of rolled it out to each of the others in the diner, as if it was one of the billiard balls. He seemed happy, relieved almost, to have this task of making sure there wasn't an Abel Stemple in Cold Flat Junction. He confirmed this fact with each of the customers.

"You sure that's the *name*?" he asked of me. "You sure *Abel*'s the name? We got Stemples living here"— and he rounded up a lot of head nods and people saying yes, they did, and that's right— "but no Abel, I don't think."

So I pretended to uncertainty. I scratched my head and squinted up my eyes in an effort of remembrance. "Well, I *think* it's Abel. I must be wrong. Maybe it was . . . Abner?"

Billy shook his head decisively, sure of his ground now, sure that I was asking after Stemples that had never been seen to walk this earth, and I was dead wrong.

"Only Stemples I know lives down a ways on Lonemeadow Road," said the thick woman sitting between Billy and me at the counter. Light reflected off the lens of her glasses, so that I wasn't sure she was looking at me. There was that same road again, and I hoped it wouldn't remind them I'd also been asking about the Tidewaters. Funny, but I'd all but forgotten completely about Toya Tidewater.

That started a disagreement, just as it had over the Tidewaters. But that was all right, for it took attention away from me. No one had asked, or seemed to care about, why I wanted to know. Even though this was eating up precious time (it being now a quarter to three), I let them argue. There were, I thought, plenty of Stemples to go around. Another bunch of them lived, according to the man and wife sitting in the booth, over at Red Coon Rock. Then there was a family of ten (Louise thought) on a farm just off Sweetwater Road, and she talked about most of the ten as she wiped and wiped the counter. But it was Billy who put his foot down that I most likely wanted the Stemple that had the place in Flyback Hollow.

Well, he was right, for in another second he said, "Jude Stemple. At least, Jude can tell you if there's an Abel, but take my word there ain't and never was. Not in Cold Flat Junction, there ain't. Maybe it's a Stemple packed up and left. Still, I been living in Cold Flat all my life and I expect I'd of knowed if there ever was an *Abel* Stemple." His look at me was hard and narrow, as if I'd called his memory into question.

Again, I pretended to consider. "You know, maybe that's the name. Where's Flyback Hollow?"

(Billy had pronounced it "Holler," which momentarily confused me.) I hoped no one would perk up and ask me why I wanted to know.

But they were all too interested in giving directions, and all disagreeing as to where this Flyback Hollow was. I thought, good heavens, with Cold Flat Junction being as small and depopulated as it was, I couldn't imagine everyone in it not knowing every square inch. Finally, though, Billy commanded them all to be quiet and told me that I was to go along Windy Run out there, down past Rudy's bar and right along to where the school was and then to go off in a kind of westerly direction until I saw Dubois Road, and to keep on that for a ways until I came to "the Holler."

I balled up my paper napkin and thanked them all very much and slid off my stool.

"Where you from, dear?" asked the woman in the booth. I was afraid someone would. I couldn't remember what I'd said before, so I told the truth and said La Porte, and that kind of brought down the house.

"You *are*?" said the heavyset woman at the counter. "Why, Billy, that's where they found that dead woman!"

"I guess I know where they found that woman, God's sakes. I happen to know the *po*-lice over there. That sheriff you got—DeGhyne?—I knowed him for years."

"Oh, stop talkin' just a minute, Billy, and let the girl speak," said the heavy woman.

Louise's eyes had gotten really big. "Go on, sugar, and tell us whatever happened over there. I mean, did they find out if that woman got murdered, or what?"

Again, I screwed up my eyes and looked blank. "What woman's that?"

# THIRTY-ONE

I was glad that I had my money out with my check, so that I could simply slap it down by the cash register (the cashier was the same one, and he was still reading a comic book) and bang out the door calling back "Thank you, thank you," for they all looked a little dumbstruck to hear a person, even a kid (since kids were generally supposed never to know what was going on around them)—to hear that *anyone* who was living around where a body was found (maybe murdered) would not have heard about it. I could see, in my hurry to leave, that mouths were beginning to form questions and hands were beginning to motion to me.

I couldn't understand this. La Porte was, after all, only fifteen or twenty minutes away, and why, if this was so fascinating to them, didn't they just all pile on the Tabernacle bus and go there?

But then I thought no: They wanted news; they sat around and waited for news; they *hoped* for news. But that didn't mean they were going to go out and *get* news. They did not leave the Windy Run Diner to search out news, no matter how fascinating. It was like what we called, or used to call, Living Pictures. As I scuffed along the road called Windy Run, kicking up pebbles, I was thinking this. It was such a strange notion, I stopped in front of Rudy's Bar and Grille and frowned over it. Living Pictures was something we used to do in school when I was little and in the first or second grade. What would happen was, a child (or even two, depending on the picture) would be dressed up in costume, for instance, to look like the Blue Boy or some other famous subject in a painting. The child would sit or stand inside a huge box, which was supposed to be the picture frame. This box was covered on one side (the audience side, for it was an entertainment) with some sort of gauzy material that you could see through, but as if you were seeing through smoke. Living Pictures was quite effective.

What I thought now, though it was a strange notion, was that all of the people inside the Windy Run Diner might have been in one of these Living Pictures. It was all like what is called, I think, a "tableau." They talked and moved, that's true. But there was this strange feeling I had that whatever they did, they didn't do in the outside world, that being the world beyond the Windy Run Diner. And so they would not leave the diner to go out and get some "news," no matter how interesting it might be. I thought about this staring at the plate glass window of Rudy's.

Rudy's was a clapboard house with a tilted front porch and signs in the window advertising "Dogs—Burgers—Suds," another big sign about the county fair in Cloverly (a much bigger town with a fairground), and a blue neon tube formed into writing that said "Beer—Eats."

I walked on down the road, then, and noticed a sign on my left that had an arrow pointing the way to Red Coon Rock (home, I understood, to some branch of the Stemple family). I looked off in that direction, past square houses, and beyond them, across the flat, beige landscape. Where in that land would there ever be an outcropping of rock, at least enough to earn it a name? Near home, we had a place called Chimney Rock, which was farther up in the mountains and was a great, huge slab of rock surrounded by other huge rocks. But for the life of me, I couldn't imagine more than stones and pebbles out there where I was looking now.

Soon I came to Schoolhouse Road and saw the place where Mrs. Davidow must come for the Hotel Paradise eggs. Henhouses sat in rows in the backyard. From this distance they looked like plantings in furrowed earth. I could hear the hens, too; warm clucks wafted on chilly wind, kindly clucks, slow and easy like old people over tea, like Miss Flyte and Miss Flagler (who probably wouldn't appreciate the comparison).

Not very far from the henhouses was the schoolhouse where I had played pick-up-sticks with the silent girl, the pick-up-sticks champion. The playground ran along the side of the school, and in it now stood a boy, maybe seven or eight, alone there, his arms wrapped around a basketball or volleyball. Since he was standing near the high-up hoop, I guessed he must have been trying to toss it through, but not now: he stood perfectly still there with the ball hard against his narrow chest, looking at me.

In another moment, a woman in a dark dress came out of the door at the rear of the school and stood at the top of the stone steps. She was too far off for me to make out anything about her, except for the black dress that looked out of place against its background of white school and pearl-colored sky. With her hand shading her eyes, she looked all around, as if searching for someone. I thought she must be looking for the boy, but she gave no sign of it as she looked in his direction, and he, anyway, was looking still at me. At last she dropped her hand, but still stood there looking around; and then, finally, she turned and walked back through the door, which I could hear shut softly behind her.

And it was like that as I walked farther—I mean, as far as the few people I saw were concerned: I didn't see any of them up close, but rather sitting on stoops, or walking, or maybe by their cars, or a child here or there playing with something I couldn't make out. But they seemed to be people always holding you at a distance, like the dark blue line of the woods, far off.

I came to the end of Schoolhouse Road and walked along one that didn't seem to be marked. The only house I passed was a big one with yellow shutters sitting on a large lot and with flowerbeds, which was unusual for Cold Flat Junction. There were climbing roses growing up one side of the door

and ivy half-covering the other side. Some flat boxes
of tomato-plant seedlings sat on the porch.

I didn't have the time, really, to be dawdling
about this way, lingering before schools and houses.
Already it was three o'clock which gave me only an
hour or so before I'd have to be getting back to the
station. I found the Dubois Road sign a little farther
along and just kept walking its dusty, unpaved length
until what few houses there were fell away, to be
replaced by a couple of rusty mobile homes with
rusty tricycles overturned in the front yards. After
that there was nothing for a while except, ahead of
me, trees and undergrowth. I was surprised by the
trees, for in my gaze across toward the horizon, the
trees surrounding all of this flat land appeared to
have been much, much farther away. Here, though,
was a little pocket of them—oaks and maybe sumacs
(I knew nothing about trees)—that stretched back
and got thicker, with branches overhanging the narrow road that got harder and more rutted. It must
have been difficult for cars to go back and forth.
Finally, I came to a hand-lettered sign in the shape
of an arrow, whose whitewashed paint had mostly
worn away. It said Flyback Hollow. So this was it.

Billy had mentioned that not many people lived
in this part of Cold Flat, and I didn't come to any
house at all in another five minutes of walking. Then
off to my right I saw a small gray shingle house,
and in another three or four minutes came on a queer
place that had originally been a log cabin and now
had a shingled wing added on to it. It stood on what

must have been an acre or more of land, but it was hard to tell where the land ended, what with the trees behind it. On the sinking porch lay a mongrel dog, who looked up when I came along and perked its ears, but made no sound. It was probably old. There was a lot of junk out in front—two-by-fours, boxes of building stuff—and I thought this must be Jude Stemple's, as it looked like a lot of carpentry might be going on. I heard the slow, regular *thwack, thwack* of wood being chopped, and followed the sound, and the picket fence, around in back. And there was Jude Stemple, chopping firewood.

It always looks to me as if men are really angry with the wood they're chopping, and hate it. The way he brought the axe down on the stump, with his face red and frowning, you'd think everything horrible that had ever happened to Jude Stemple had collected itself here in this block of wood on this stump.

The fence was between us, but it was a low one that I could easily see over and talk over. I stood there for a moment, watching. Then he looked up and saw me and wiped his forehead on his checkered shirt sleeve, and went right back to chopping again, as if anybody my age must be invisible.

I called out, "Excuse me!"

Again, he wiped his face, this time taking out a big handkerchief. "Yeah?"

"Is this Flyback Hollow?" I took a slip of paper from my pocket, which was only an old check from the Rainbow Café, but I pretended to be studying it, as if information were written there. When he answered yeah, it was Flyback Hollow (like Billy, he said "Holler"), I went on: "Where do the Queens live? A family name of Queen?"

He shook his head, studied me for a moment, then came a few sullen steps closer to the fence. He was still holding the axe, so I was just as glad the fence was there. "Queens don't live in the Holler no more."

"Really?" I frowned over my scrap of paper. "I was told they did."

"There's a couple of Queens live back there"— and he nodded toward the road I had just traveled— "on Dubois Road. Big house with yellow shutters to it." He went back to whacking at wood.

I could hardly believe it! I'd found the Queens! A couple of them anyway. I forgot to be cool and casual and asked in a rush, "Which Queens are they? Which ones?"

My question must have sounded too eager, for he came closer to the fence. Biting off a plug of tobacco, he asked suspiciously, "Who wants to know?"

I thought it was obvious I did; but being only twelve, I didn't rate as a person. I considered. I said, "My grandmother." *Great-aunt* was just too complicated. "Her name's Aurora Paradise."

He stopped in his chewing. "You mean from Spirit Lake? You mean from over there to the Hotel Paradise?"

I doubted he would know Aurora enough to go

checking up. "That's right." All I had to do now was work around to Ben Queen.

"What's she want to know for?"

Actually, I thought that was kind of nosy, but couldn't say so. "Well, I'm afraid I'm not prepared"— now, where had I heard this expression?— "to di-vulge that information."

"No?" He drew himself up and mimicked my voice. "Well, I ain't prepared to di-*vulge* where the Queens is, neither." He turned and started back to his block of wood.

Oh damn, oh damn. I had taken the wrong tack and didn't know how to go back and wipe out what I'd said. Someday, I was going to get the Sheriff to give me lessons in getting things out of people. I thought about him for a moment. Then I said, almost gaily, "Okay, thanks anyway, I'll just tell the Sheriff and I guess he'll come and talk to you." Quickly, I almost skipped away from the fence, casting a glance back over my shoulder.

That stopped him dead.

I kept on quickly walking until I heard him shout, "Now, you just hold it right there, Miss Lickety-split!"

I obliged. I turned around.

"What's all this about a sheriff?" His tone was belligerent.

"Nothing. He's just a good friend of my grandmother. And she—" I paused to think, but was pretending to get a pebble out of my shoe. "My grandma Aurora"— that certainly stuck in my throat—"she's afraid maybe this dead woman the police found over near White's Bridge, that she might be the woman my grandma knew. . . ." My voice trailed off.

For some reason, his annoyance seemed to have eased off. "Yeah. I read about that dead woman."

I couldn't understand, though, why he wasn't asking me what I was doing here and questioning *him*. Why would any sheriff be sending *me*? Did I look like a deputy? I wondered if he was guilty of something, for he seemed to relax a little when I mentioned the dead lady, as if he was relieved it was some other business that didn't concern him.

"They don't know who she is. Like I said, Grandma's afraid it's this friend of hers. This former friend."

"Huh." He didn't sound very interested. But he'd moved closer to the fence and was eyeing me now with suspicion. "How old're you, girl?"

"Fourteen." I pulled myself up out of my socks. Most people thought I was older than twelve.

Now, he was finally getting around to asking me what I was doing in Cold Flat Junction.

"Came to visit someone," I answered without thinking.

"Yeah? Who?"

Desperately, I searched for names. I squinted over towards the porch. "That your dog?"

Slowly, he spat out a stream of tobacco juice. "Sittin' on my porch, I guess it must be, don't you? So who'd you come to visit here?"

Suddenly, the scene in the Windy Run Diner

flashed across my vision. "You know Louise Snell over at the diner?" I hoped he didn't; I didn't want him comparing notes.

"Sure, I know her."

"Oh. I came to see Betsy Snell. You know, her girl." I hoped to heavens that Betsy Snell didn't have anything wrong with her that meant people couldn't visit her—like being in an iron lung or something. Apparently not, for Jude Stemple merely gave a disinterested little snort. I continued by saying, "So my grandma asked me, if I was coming to Cold Flat anyway, would I stop off in Flyback Hollow and see if I could talk to the Queens. About this dead woman." I shrugged, as if I too were indifferent to the whole errand.

He thought for a bit, looking at me, but now without suspicion. "So which Queen does your grandma think this is?"

"Serena. Serena Queen." How had I ever come up with that name? In my whole life, I'd never heard of a Serena, Queen or otherwise.

He shoved his checkered cap back on his head, wiped his forehead with his arm, and then resettled the cap. "I never heard of no Serena Queen." But he seemed genuinely puzzled, and to be thinking this over.

I was relieved to hear that, at least.

"Maybe that's one I don't know." He was fingering a cigarette from the crushed pack in the pocket of his woodsman's shirt. I wondered if he intended to smoke and chew at the same time. Then he said, after framing his hands around a struck match and sucking in on his cigarette, "Anyways, that ain't who that dead woman is."

I chewed the inside of my lip. "It isn't? Oh. How . . . uh . . . well, how do you *know*?" I wanted to be careful not to act as if I was challenging his knowledge of the Queens. But he didn't take offense.

Blowing out smoke and looking off towards the trees, he said, "That's Ben Queen's girl, sure as God made little green apples."

*Ben Queen's girl.* I stood there as a whippoorwill somewhere hit its mournful notes. *Ben Queen's girl.* By now the words had taken on the chanting sound of prayer. *Holy Mary Ben Queen's girl Mother of God Ben Queen's girl.* They were potent, like magic, even though at the same time they weren't at all conclusive. The words didn't decide anything, or answer the ultimate question.

"You mean his daughter?"

"Uh-huh." He drew in on his cigarette and then let go with a hacking cough.

For a moment I felt sorry for him. Trying to tread lightly (for my sake, not his), I said, "Then was Ben Queen's daughter blond and . . . middle-aged?"

"Forty or so, I expect. But the blond come out of a bottle, you ask me."

So the dead woman couldn't possibly be the Girl, not if he was right. The Girl couldn't have been more than twenty or so, and her pale hair had never come out of any bottle, not unless they bottled moonlight somewhere. The relief I felt made me shiver so much I had to wrap my arms around myself. Jude could be wrong about this woman's identity, but I didn't think he was. And he hadn't actually answered my question "How do you know?" So I asked it again.

He answered, "Because the lady I'm talking about left here for La Porte five days ago, got on the Tabernacle bus over there by the Cold Flat post office, and ain't been seen since."

I was wide-eyed. The way he said it made it all seem fraught with danger. "Well, but . . . I mean . . . listen, how come you didn't go to the police?"

I was afraid then I'd offended him, but he only shrugged it off. "Why would I? That's in La Porte, not Cold Flat, and I figured they already knew who it was."

"The Sheriff doesn't, at least not the last time I . . . I mean, not when he was talking to my grandmother. That was just yesterday. There wasn't anything that identified her, see."

He smoked some more, leaning over the fence. "I don't see how it's my job to go talking to no sheriff in La Porte." He was getting defensive.

"I don't either. No, I don't think it is either. It's those Queens you'd think would tell him. Why do you suppose they haven't said something to the police? If she's been gone five days?"

He shrugged and knocked off ash from his cigarette with his little finger. "Queens is kind of weird. Who knows? Maybe one of them did her in." His chuckle was ghoulish.

It hit me that I'd nearly forgotten the woman was probably murdered. I shivered again and plucked my sweater sleeves down over my hands.

He said, "I can't figure out this Serena, though. I can't place her."

"Oh, I probably got it wrong. Then who's the woman you think they found?"

"Fern Queen. It must be Fern, to my way of thinking."

I was astonished, though I don't know why. "Rose Fern Souder Devereau," that's what Aurora said. Rose Fern had run off with Ben Queen, so if this was his "girl," then the name "Fern" seemed natural enough. After her mother. I just stood there, thinking about the Devereau house on Spirit Lake.

Without any prompting, Jude Stemple went on talking. It was if he'd been waiting to talk for some long while, like in a fairy-tale, being at last released from a charm, and it didn't make any difference I was only a kid. Adults do that with me—start talking, I mean. It's very strange. Sometimes I think talking to me must be for them like talking to themselves. I don't know whether or not to compliment myself over this, though.

"The Queens, or leastways some of them, they live in that big house with the yellow shutters. You must of passed it coming along Dubois Road."

"I passed it. With the roses growing up it?"

He spat out more tobacco at the same time he dropped his cigarette butt and ground it out. "That's it. Now, this Serena, what'd she tell you about her?"

I wished he'd forget about Serena. "Nothing much." And I chanced it. "Does Ben Queen live there?" I hurried on to explain my interest by saying, "I think Grandma mentioned him."

"Ben?" He frowned at me. "Ben's not been around for twenty years."

He must be dead. I don't know why my heart sank at this thought. But I didn't let it show. Casually, I asked, "I wonder what happened to her mother. I mean Ben Queen's wife."

He looked at me very directly. "You do a lot of wonderin' for a kid." He was quiet for some moments, and then said, "Rose was near forty when . . . she died. That's going on twenty, twenty-one years ago. Rose Fern Queen." He shook his head, smiling, and his pale eyes were clouded over. "That was one pretty woman, Rose Queen. Prettiest woman I think I ever seen. Too bad Fern never got her looks. Thing is, no one could be as pretty as Rose." Jude Stemple looked terribly sad, as if he'd lost something. It was all very strange. Then he leaned the axe against the fence and said, "I'm goin' in to get me a beer. You want some pop, or what?"

I nodded, stunned that he was making this now a social occasion and including me in it.

He called back over his shoulder, "You go on round to the porch there. That dog, he don't bite."

So it looked like we were even to sit down by

way of continuing our visit. I walked around to the
front of the house and up to the porch, where there
was only one wooden rocker. I sat down beside the
dog, who flapped his tail around in his version of a
wag, I guessed. I rubbed the old dog's back and he
seemed pleased with the attention, half-rolling over
and stretching, his front legs partly off the edge of
the porch and his head dangling there. I often wondered how animals (cats especially), could get themselves into such uncomfortable-looking positions,
but appeared not to be at all. My hand's movement
on the dog stopped a minute while I wondered if I
should envy animals. It would be a relief not to want
things, like white meat of chicken or buying clothes
from the Europa. Or it would be a relief to be a cat
and loll on a kitchen chair in a beam of sunlight and
not have to pay attention to Vera shouldering trays
and bossily calling out "Coming through, coming
through!" But the other side was, if I were a cat I'd
never be able to go to the Orion movie house and
eat popcorn from a pink cone and watch a rerun of
*Waterloo Bridge.*

Jude Stemple was back with his beer, a bottle
of Black Label, and with my soda. It was Orange
Crush, and I told him that was my favorite. It was,
too. I liked Orange Crush because of the brown bottle—dark brown and slightly ribbed up and down. I
loved that bottle, which was like no other pop bottle.
Almost all of them were plain clear glass.

Instead of taking the rocker, he sat down beside
me on the porch step. I hoped the interruption caused

by getting the beer and pop wouldn't mean we'd have to start our conversation all over again with a lot of small talk, as people seem to do; they always seemed to have to remeet and get up a lot of small talk before they can continue along the line they've been discussing. Fortunately, this wasn't the case with Jude Stemple. Once having mentioned Rose and Ben Queen, he seemed deep into his subject.

"Now, Ben Queen took off when he wasn't much older'n you. Went out west somewheres— Nevada, Arizona, one of them. Come back when he was around twenty. Didn't have much schooling. Didn't have a trade. My guess is Ben lived by his wits. And his looks. Real handsome." He stopped to take a long drink of beer and wipe his mouth. "Let me tell you, good looks, they'll get you a long, long ways in this world." Then he turned to look at me and frown, as if he figured I wasn't going far. "The women just followed Ben Queen around like puppies. So somehow he gets to know Rosie Devereau. Rose Fern Devereau. Devereaus lived over your way, over to Spirit Lake."

(As if I didn't know.)

"Well, he ups and marries her, or at least I as-*sume* so. But they had to run off, for her family, though I never knew them, they were awful high and mighty from what people said, and didn't much care for the likes of no Queens. I'll admit some of the Queens was damned peculiar—excuse my French. It's Ben's brother and sister-in-law lives in that house on Dubois. I guess he's all right, but she's a damned busybody. They grow their own produce out back—"

"I saw some tomato plants."

He nodded. "They got them a big old garden out back—lettuces and asparagus, cabbages, you name it."

"Did you know the Devereaus?"

"Rose's people? I never did know them. Wouldn't find no Devereau comin' to Cold Flat Junction." He picked at the label on his beer bottle.

"Didn't she ever talk about them?"

"Not that I ever heard."

"But what about Fern? I don't see how someone wouldn't report she's gone."

He let out a guffaw. "Probably they think maybe she run off and don't care much, if the truth be known."

I guess something in the way he said that stopped me from asking why. I had a funny feeling if I had asked it would have put an end to the conversation. But it was getting on late and I couldn't be forever skirting around issues, so I did ask, "You never heard anyone mention Mary-Evelyn Devereau?"

He thought for a moment, looking off through the trees, frowning. "I do seem to recall something about an accident. It must've been thirty-five, forty years ago."

I told him what had happened to Mary-Evelyn and he nodded, yes, that's sort of what he'd heard. And he clucked around about its being real sad.

I was disappointed he didn't know more about Rose. Then I said, "I guess you know about everybody in Cold Flat Junction." He said yes, nearly. "I wonder, did you ever see—" I stopped. I don't know why I didn't go on and ask about the Girl. But I didn't.

We were quiet, and the old dog was snoring lightly. I followed the direction of Jude Stemple's gaze, off towards the tops of the high branches coming into leaf, where gray light fretted the outlines. The sky was a shade darker and I looked at my watch. I had twenty-five minutes to get to the train. "I've got to go!" I sang out, jumped up, and did a dancing step backward.

Jude Stemple straightened up and said, "Well, it was nice talkin' to you. But don't you go back and tell that there La Porte sheriff all I told you, hear?"

I stopped dead, thunderstruck. "Well, but—"

He was shaking his head no, no. "Now you promise me that, hear? After all, it's none of my affair."

Not tell the Sheriff? How could I not? I swallowed, hard. Yet Jude Stemple looked so—I don't know—*downtrodden*, or miserable, that I just went ahead and nodded. I thought maybe he was lonely. I guessed a person would have to be, to be hanging around talking to me all this time.

I felt really uncomfortable thinking I might be walking around with this parcel of knowledge that I couldn't deliver. Especially knowledge the Sher-

iff—of all people—would want. I consoled myself
by thinking that surely he'd know by now who the
dead woman was.

Jude Stemple seemed able to read my mind, the
doubts in it, the uncertainty, and he was looking at
me long and hard. He gave me a sharp little nod, in
answer to my own nod, as if we were sealing a pact.

I started off and then turned back just for a
moment. "What did she look like? Rose Devereau,
I mean."

For a few heartbeats, he bowed his head, then
looked up, as if thinking deeply. "Like I said, she
was beautiful. Real pale blond hair she had—it
looked like that light up there on those little leaves."
He nodded upward toward the light filtering through
the branches. "And kind of lakewater-gray eyes that
was always changing color. She was tall and slim
and so pale and blond, why, she was almost transparent." He had risen from the porch and was dusting
off his pants and shrugged. "Well, I ain't much of
a describer."

Yes, he was. He had just described the Girl.

I think I had known he would. From Rose to
Fern to the Girl. She had to be Fern's daughter.
Sure of the answer now, I asked: "What about Fern
Queen's own kids? Where are they?"

He shrugged. "Fern didn't have no kids." Then,
giving a smile and a little wave, he turned and walked
back through the door.

I stood there, staring after him, rooted. *Fern
didn't have no kids.* Probably I'd be standing there

still, I was so surprised, except I had to get to that
train.

Since I wasn't dawdling, twenty-five minutes was
time enough, but not to stop and make a survey of
the white house with the yellow shutters. I noticed
the seedlings were gone from the porch. I also noticed
that no one appeared to be behind the curtains.

When I finally reached the railroad station I had
five minutes to spare and sat down on the same
bench. I went back to gazing off across the empty
land where nothing moved and nothing changed.
Time had stuck in my throat like one of those popcorn
kernels that drive you crazy when you're watching
a movie. You can't reach it with your fingers; you
can't swallow it. It just sticks and then you forget
about it and then it disappears.

I was so sure I had made the connection and
had been able to trace the Girl back to a beginning.
Now to find I hadn't was a bitter disappointment.

Or was it?

What had kept me from asking someone—the
Sheriff, at least—about her? What had kept me from
describing her to someone like Dr. McComb after
I'd seen her across the lake? And what had kept me
from asking Jude Stemple if he knew such a person?

Even when I heard the train coming from a long
way away, I still sat there, staring off at the horizon,
where the late afternoon light fretted the blue line
of woods. Cold Flat Junction seemed to me not so

much a place as the memory of a place. This upset me no end. For now she seemed like the memory of a Girl.

The train rounded the bend way down the track, sounding at that distance as mournful as the whip-poorwill in Flyback Hollow. I got up, creaky as an old lady, and crossed over the wooden planks to the other side, where there was another bench.

Louder and closer, the train seemed to be picking up speed, but was actually slowing down, still some distance away.

I looked across the tracks now to the bench where I'd been sitting just a moment ago. In my mind's eye I saw myself sitting there; it was very strange, like an afterimage left on your eyeballs when you glance away from a blinding light.

I sat there until the train roared in and cut me in two.

## THIRTY-TWO

I was back again among the salads. I could hardly remember the train ride, or getting on and getting off, or my walk along the boardwalk back to the hotel. I remember stopping a minute or so to sit on one of the covered benches in cold shadow where the boardwalk crosses over the rocky stream. I think it might have been built there so that people could take shelter from the rain.

I sat on the boardwalk for so long that it was nearly six when I appeared in the kitchen, where there was a lot of noise and activity, the sort that always went with a dinner party. I could never understand why a dinner party of perhaps ten or twelve people caused more excitement and anxiety than having fifty guests all sitting apart and at separate tables. The salad bowls were filled with chunks of iceberg lettuce and the plates of onion and pepper rings and tomato wedges were sitting on plates ready for arrangement. These had already been sliced by Anna Paugh, who, I sometimes feel, thinks it very unfair that I always get stuck with the salads. Anna Paugh is truly nice and nothing like Vera, although she's probably just as good a waitress. Anna is small and wispy, where Vera is tall and (I think the word is) "imperious." Special salad plates had been set aside for the Helene Baum party. These were deep green glass and each now held a Bibb lettuce. Lola Davidow was handling the French dressing ladle and talking about the Bibb lettuces as she always did, as if they were emeralds, or had been rooted out of the ground by a pig's snout, as my mother said truffles were. I've never seen a truffle in my life and wish I'd never see another Bibb lettuce. It was all right with me, though, for nothing had to be done to the precious little things, nothing added except for French dressing from the crock. And this task was not to be entrusted to me, but was, as I said, given over to Mrs. Davidow herself, as if she were the only one with the talent. The real reason she undertook this was because she had to feel she was necessary to the success of a dinner party, which, of course, she wasn't. My mother was all geared up for the dinner party, smoking more cigarettes than usual, and calling orders out, and lecturing us to remember: if the food didn't get in there hot, it would be the cook (meaning her) who got the blame, not the waitresses (a lot *she* knew). On these occasions, part-time help was called in. Mrs. Ikleberger acted as "undercook"—why, I couldn't imagine. All Mrs. Ikleberger does is churn around and get in my mother's way, so that my mother is always shoving her out of it. Mrs. Ikleberger opens her lunchroom beside Greg's tavern in dead winter and serves lunches to school kids. Will and I would eat there on those rare occasions that we stayed here through the winter and went to the Spirit Lake grammar school. She was a cheery woman to have around on those cold, cold winter days when the snow was so deep it sucked our feet down into deep pockets and the frigid air seemed to turn all we saw in the distance to a smoky blue.

Right now Mrs. Ikleberger was making her usual noise with clattering pots and pans and shouting to Walter to bring over washed ones, which of course he did, though it seemed to take him an hour to remove himself and the pot or pan from the roving shadows and cross the dozen feet between dishwasher and stove. Dinner parties meant too that even Walter had temporary help. This was Paul's mother. It was interesting listening to Walter and her talk; I would hang around the dishwasher sometimes, just for that. No words ever seemed to get beyond her tonsils; it was as if they didn't travel up to her teeth and tongue. Walter, because his words came molasses-slow, sounded a little like her. They were a perfect match and got along well together in spite of their troubled talk, or maybe because of it.

Sometimes she brings Paul with her, much to my mother's dismay. He calls my mother "missus" and every ten minutes is standing with his chin just reaching the serving counter, plunking a big plate down and asking, "Missus, can I have dinner?" Every once in a while his mother yanks him away and boxes his ears and threatens him with awful punishments, but Paul doesn't appear to mind. He doesn't pay any attention, either. So a lot of his time is spent

tied to a wooden chair out on the back porch, where
he likes to pick the threads out of his brown shoes
until the shoes fall apart.

This evening I stood there in a spell of noises,
seeming to be hypnotized by the salad makings.
Actually, I barely saw them, for my mind was back
in Cold Flat Junction, moving between the station
and the Windy Run Diner and Flyback Hollow. In
one way, I felt I had found out an awful lot; in
another way, not much. For I still couldn't be *sure*
that the dead woman was this Fern Queen (although
it sounded extremely likely). No one at the hotel had
as much as mentioned the woman, so I assumed that
her identity was still unknown around La Porte. It
amazed me that this dead woman hadn't yet been
identified in a place as small as La Porte and a place
even smaller like Cold Flat Junction. People must
not have the sense they were born with. Here was a
woman who left Cold Flat not to be seen again for
four or five days, and here was a woman turned up
dead outside of La Porte nearly four days ago. They
both answer to the same description. My Lord, how
smart do you have to *be* to put two and two together?

The only answer to that was that the Sheriff
(who is certainly smart enough) simply didn't know
anyone was missing and that the Queens had never
reported it. Maybe they thought Fern had just gone
off on her own. Maybe the Queens did not read
newspapers. I told myself that I wouldn't be breaking
my promise if all I did was to tell the Sheriff I'd
heard that a lady over in Cold Flat Junction was

missing and not tell him *how* I'd heard it. And then I realized that I really *had* heard it in Britten's that day when I'd first seen Jude Stemple.

I felt relieved, thinking about this. I started slapping onion rings on the iceberg lettuce for the "ordinary" salads and felt just as glad that my role tonight would be merely as Vera's "helper." And Miss Bertha, who I had to wait on as usual, for she demanded it. You'd almost think she liked me, but I knew that wasn't the case; she just didn't want to have to get used to yelling at somebody else. Anna Paugh would be serving all of the other guests; there were four other reservations, which would mean about ten or fifteen people.

Naturally, I had already looked over the preparations to work out the menu—meaning what I would get to eat at the end of it all. Roast lamb, oven-browned potatoes, and green peas. To put it that way, though, is something like saying a sunset is red, blue, and yellow. It does nothing by way of describing exactly how the three things appear individually (the crusty edge of the browned potatoes, for instance), and certainly not how the colors mingle and melt into one another. To my mother, a meal must be "composed." Broccoli never is to be eaten with lamb or roast beef. Nor browned potatoes with chicken. Tomatoes must never appear with pimiento. Things like that. It is, as I've said, an ART. That was the evening's menu, and the only choice I would have to make (as would the diners) would be between brown gravy and mint sauce. That sounds easy, but then so did that Solomon-and-the-baby business, until the details were revealed. The brown gravy was as smooth and glowing as the newel post at the bottom of the lobby steps; the mint was fresh and picked from a huge wild acre of it out behind the icehouse. (Since Mrs. Davidow came to the Hotel Paradise, there is considerably less of it around. She is extremely fond of mint juleps in the summertime.) My mother told me once that all she does to make her mint sauce is to crush a handful of mint and add water, vinegar, and sugar. Anyone can do it, she says. Oh, wrong, wrong, wrong. For some reason, if my mother fills up a cup with water and pours the cup into a glass or a jug, something happens to the water. It is like a woman passing through a room in a long gown of silk and chiffon wearing some ethereal perfume. Even after she passes, a bit of the silk train can be glimpsed on the doorsill, and the scent floats back.

She is like a sorcerer. Unfortunately, I am not the sorcerer's apprentice.

While I thought about Cold Flat Junction and mint sauce, the salads somehow got composed and removed to the dining room. One couple had turned up and Anna Paugh was moving back and forth serving them. Where Miss Bertha was, I didn't know. Maybe she'd had a stroke. I tried to banish this hope. And the dinner party was late. My mother fumed; Vera regally smoked a cigarette and adjusted her high starched cuffs. To my mother, a dinner party being late was some kind of heresy. Food, she said, dried out. I never saw any evidence of this, but to her immaculate eye I'm sure it was the case.

Miss Bertha, who most of the time was completely unconscious of what went on around her, always seemed to know when she was least wanted and would be the most trouble for people and came into the dining room right before the Baum party. They were so close on her heels she might have been the Baum flag bearer.

"That old fool!" exclaimed my mother, banging a pan of hot rolls down on the counter. Then she said, "Find out what she wants, quick! And then just slap it down in front of her!"

I sighed. "Quick" and "Miss Bertha" never did go together, but I could understand my mother's desperation. Now I would be drawn away from the Baum dinner and helping out Vera. Vera (of course) announced that she "could manage," as if it made absolutely no difference whether I was around or not. Then Anna Paugh bustled through the swing door and said that she would wait on Miss Bertha, whether Miss Bertha liked it or not, because I was absolutely necessary to the smooth running of the Baum party. She didn't use those words, but she certainly conveyed that idea. Well, I thought that was wonderful, and Vera could have killed Anna Paugh.

Vera shouldered her way into the dining room through the swing door with her tray of consommé bowls held high on one palm. I followed with the Bibb lettuce salads. Helene Baum was trying to rearrange her guests and no one was paying any attention to her. They were all drunk, naturally, and none drunker than Lola Davidow, who had seen to it that the rest of them followed her jovial lead. Mrs. Davidow was right there, grabbing another dinner service for herself off a nearby table, and starting to squeeze herself in between the mayor's wife and Ken King, the pharmacist, who was laughing and yelling at the top of his lungs down the table to the doctor. It amazes me how Lola Davidow can get away with inviting herself to people's dinner parties, but she's done it more than once. No one seems to care. It's true that Mrs. Davidow can actually be good company, and I suppose that people like to appear to be open-minded and cheery and up for an adventure.

All of the other reservations had descended on the dining room at exactly the same time as the Baum party and Miss Bertha. As good a waitress as Anna Paugh was, she could not be at all the tables at once, so that eventually the diners were sending out little silent signals to me (since I appeared not to be doing much but standing at attention over the Baum table), either trying to beckon me over with little waves or mouthing silent requests—"water, water," "rolls, rolls"—as if they were perishing in the desert. Miss Bertha, however, was not silent. She trumpeted down half the length of the room. I ignored them all.

It was halfway through this dinner that I realized several of the Baum guests were exchanging comments and theories about the dead body found in Mirror Pond. I picked up the water pitcher and edged closer to the table, presumably to refill water glasses but really to listen. All that was clear was that the Sheriff and his men still hadn't been able to identify the woman, and wasn't it the most incredible mystery?

Unfortunately Helene Baum chose this interesting moment to take her life in her hands and complain that her lamb was overdone. The talk about White's Bridge and the dead woman was deadened by the quarrel that broke out between Helene Baum and Mrs. Davidow over the lamb. Instead of quietly and quickly sending the lamb back for whatever reason, Mrs. Davidow told Helene that the lamb was *perfectly* cooked, that Jen always roasted it for exactly the same period of time. Naturally, Helene kept on complaining. It wasn't pink, she said; it wasn't *rare*. When she had it in Paris, it was *rare*. She started showing it around and holding it aloft as if for the judgment of God and the president of France. If Vera had been there at that moment, instead of in the kitchen, she would have made mewling, apologetic noises and offered to get a lamb-replacement. I'll say this for Lola Davidow: no one was going to criticize my mother's cooking when *she* was around. So since no one was going to do anything but fight about it, I snatched the plate from Helene Baum's presenting hand and hurried off to the kitchen.

There was nothing overcooked about the lamb at all; it wasn't supposed to be served rare. Even I knew that. My mother said it could give you the same disease you could get from underdone pork.

Helene Baum always claimed something was wrong every time she came to the hotel, for she was jealous of my mother and her cooking. I set the plate on the surface of the black iron stove to heat up. Vera and my mother were hovering over the dessert table, apparently doing something complicated with the pies.

Just then Mrs. Davidow stormed into the kitchen, red-faced and fit to be tied, as Helene Baum was still going on about Paris and spring lamb. She told my mother about the complaint.

"Rare? The damned fool wants *rare* lamb?" My mother reached around to a shelf that held empty canning jars and banged one down on the pastry table. "Here, take her a jar of trichinosis."

Lola and Vera laughed and so did my mother. It was a good lesson in not wasting anger on damned fools. But there was still Mrs. Baum's dinner to be dealt with. What I did with the plate was to add a fresh half of roast potato and neaten up the pile of peas. I intended simply to make the plate look like a whole new dinner.

I did this mechanically, as my mind was really on the dead woman and Fern Queen. I was the only person, besides Jude Stemple, who suspected they were one and the same. As I spooned fresh hot gravy over the same old lamb slices, I wondered about my promise to Jude Stemple. Had I really, officially "promised"? I didn't think so. I hadn't actually *said* "I promise." But it was no use; I couldn't convince myself. Granted, I was often pretty careless with the truth, but it was one thing to make up convenient little stories and another thing to break promises. As I plucked a sprig of parsley from the parsley bowl and dropped it on the gravy, I was feeling noble.

Back at the Baum table, Mrs. Davidow was still smarting over the "undercooked lamb" accusation, and when she saw me place the fresh plate before Helene, she raised her eyebrows. For all that we didn't get along most of the time, Mrs. Davidow and I often operated on the same wavelength. I wiggled my eyebrows at her, in answer to her own eyebrow movement, and as Helene Baum pronounced *this* lamb properly cooked, I rolled my eyes and Mrs. Davidow answered with some eye rolling of her own.

So the dinner proceeded through dessert, with Vera whisking around the table placing a piece of Key lime chiffon pie, elegantly decorated with whipped cream, before each guest. Poor Anna Paugh was charging about between her five tables, and Miss Bertha was still yelling at me. I continued to pay no attention.

When the dinner party was over (or over enough for me to leave, as they were still carousing with brandy snifters), I had my own dinner (mint sauce like liquid emeralds), and at nearly ten p.m. I was sitting in the Pink Elephant with my notebook open before me and my chin in my hands, staring at my most recent rented painting. It was a restful, watery-colored garden scene by one of those French painters whose names all begin with M, and who the part-time librarian said was her very favorite painter. She told me all about him, but five minutes later I forgot. I wondered what that meant for my future education. There was another French painter who lived and worked at the same time and whose name (which I also forgot) was almost exactly the same as this one's except for one letter. And the second one also painted in those watery colors, with tiny little strokes and dots. Now, I wondered how anyone in his right mind could be expected to keep those two M-painters separate—or even why I *should* keep them separate. I wondered if it might not be a hoax, and it was all one painter.

All of this was merely distracting me from my real problem, about how not to tell the Sheriff about Fern Queen. And even Fern Queen was only part of a wider mystery. I sat at the green painted picnic table sleepily trying to figure it out.

"Fern didn't have no kids." That's what Mr. Stemple had said. I reached for my Whitman's box and removed the snapshot of the Devereau sisters taken out in front of the hotel with Mary-Evelyn in the foreground, standing slightly apart. Was Rose not there because she had run off with Ben Queen by then?

*Why* were people's memories so bad? My mother hardly seemed able to recall anything about these important people of forty years ago, even though she could tell stories about her family and my father's and long-ago guests at the Hotel Paradise and residents of Spirit Lake that stretched back practically to the beginning of time. I'd heard her tell these stories, sitting out on the front porch late summer evenings with her glass of tawny port and Mrs. Davidow with her highball, with the smoke from their cigarettes sifting upwards, blue in the dull gold of the porch light overhead where dead moths were imprisoned in the white globe. My mother would remember so very clearly those past times, while Mrs. Davidow would rest one arm along the porch railing and carelessly tap her cigarette over it, sending the ashes sifting down to dust the rhododendron bushes. They would both laugh gaily at these recollections, for they were indeed quite funny.

As crazy as Mrs. Davidow drove me most of the time, on these front-porch evenings when my presence did not seem so much a burden to them I honestly wished their pasts had joined further back, which sounds strange, coming from me. If five years of having Mrs. Davidow around was awful, why would I wish for fifty? Well, I don't know. I mean to make it clear that I'm talking about Mrs. Davidow, *not* Mrs. Davidow and Somebody Else. The Somebody Else never hung around for these porch talks, anyway. The past bored her. This was probably because she wasn't in it. But I was never bored. Such nights were as smooth as the tawny port in my mother's glass, and the light was close to its color. I would sit there rocking and listening and wishing I had been part of this past.

For my mother was a great storyteller, in addition to being a great cook. Probably, she should have been a writer. At the very least she should have been a society hostess in some huge and fancy city, like New York or Paris. She should have hosted those gatherings (I forget what they're called) where artistic people would all drop by of an afternoon or evening for drinks and talk and leave little white cards on silver trays. My own life would then have been much different, I guess, although it was difficult for me to picture myself living it: would I move through the crowd with plates of tiny sandwiches or hot crab puffs (assuming my mother would still be making them), listening to words and laughter tinkle like those little spoons on demitasse cups?

But then I wondered: if all evenings were to be brimful of "sparkling repartee" (as I believe it is called), then how much would I value those rare nights on the porch with the crickets droning into the summer silence?

Because of my mother's storytelling abilities, I couldn't figure out, sitting here now in the Pink Elephant, why she didn't seem to remember clearly the details of Mary-Evelyn Devereau's death. Maybe she just didn't want to.

Sleepily, I stared at the snapshot, bringing it right up to my eyes to better make out the faces. And I remembered the photograph left hanging on the wall in the Devereau house. They had been much younger then, but easily identifiable as one or another face in this little snapshot.

I rested my chin on my arm and slowly turned

the snapshot, my fingers on its edge, as if I were looking through a kaleidoscope. Perhaps I thought this action might rearrange the surface. Of course, it didn't. Sideways or standing on their heads, the Devereau sisters looked out at me in their dark clothes and with their changeless expressions, silent as the tomb. *Fern didn't have no kids.*

If the Girl wasn't a blood relation of Rose and Fern, where in heaven had she sprung from?

My eyes mere slits of sleepiness, I could see down the table to my stack of books. With the hand not holding the picture, I pulled a Nancy Drew towards me and looked, sideways, at its torn cover. There was Nancy with her flashlight and her aghast look. Probably she'd stumbled on a clue as big as a giant's footprint.

I closed my eyes. There were no clues.

## THIRTY-THREE

I woke into eerie pink darkness, wondering where I was and what all the commotion was overhead. Up there was the dining room and part of the kitchen, and the noises, I realized, were breakfast (I hoped not lunch) preparations.

Groggily, I shook myself awake and saw one hand was still clutching the snapshot and the other had been lying atop the Nancy Drew book as if it were a holy missal and as if all through the night my sleeping mind had kept searching out clues. At the other end of the table, the hotel cat was curled in a doughnut, having managed to get into the Pink Elephant somehow. Cats could dissolve, I'd decided long ago, and re-form themselves on the other side of a wall.

The hammering sound continued off and on, and I had the fanciful notion that Miss Bertha was up there thumping her cane. Probably, even after I was buried, Miss Bertha's table would sit on top of my grave, and she would pound her cane at me and yell, *Get up, get up, and bring me hot rolls!*

I was all cramped and had to shake myself and jump around to get some feeling back in one arm and a leg. Then I crept to the door (hoping the day wouldn't hear me, I guess), pulled it open a crack, and looked out. Early morning, quite early. I relaxed and opened it all the way. Everywhere ground mist, like quilts and cobwebs, stretched and clung. It lay evenly over the tall wet grass, the acre of mint, and then vaporized upwards to drift in branches. Far off across the mint acre and up an incline, the line of woods was utterly shrouded in fog, making ghosts of trees.

I always thought it was beautiful, on those accidental occasions when I witnessed such morning scenes, and each time I vowed to get out of bed an hour before I had to in order to appreciate it. But sleep won out over nature (as most things do), so it was only by stumbling on it like this that I saw the mist-covered road and the fields and the muted gray shapes that would become the icehouse or the chicken coops when the fog dispersed.

The cat had woken behind me and apparently seeing me standing in the door of the Pink Elephant, slipped through it. As I said before, cats can get in and out of anyplace completely on their own, but just let a human show up and you can bet that person will have to hold the door. It walked on ahead of me. Since it was probably only a half-hour before I'd have to appear in the kitchen anyway, I didn't want to bother going back to my room. I went directly to the kitchen. There were four ways into the kitchen, two doors on each side of the wing and two in back, one through the laundry and one all the way around by way of the enclosed porch (where I hoped Paul wasn't still tied to his chair). That door was the least likely one to cause comment if Vera was there, or anyone question why I was early, so I walked around toward it. We (the cat and I) walked the dirt road up and around the laundry room. I liked looking down and seeing my feet lost in fog. It fascinated me, too, that all I could see of the cat was its big gray tail ahead of me, weaving through the ground mist, its body otherwise shrouded. On the flagstone walk that led to the kitchen door, the tail swerved off through the grass, taking its own early-morning route, maybe up to the big garage to chase mice.

Pushing through the door, I wondered why I had been so particular about which way I entered the kitchen, and why I thought I would be questioned. I could have fallen through the roof and no one would notice, invisible as I was, like feet in fog.

Breakfast was short, thank heavens, and would have been shorter if I hadn't had to listen to Miss Bertha complaining about last night's dinner. "The rolls were cold and that little wasp-waisted waitress didn't know what in hell she was doing. . . ."

I stood there with my tray tucked under my arm and my eyelids heavy as lead. Then sweet old Mrs. Fulbright tried to calm Miss Bertha down and told me that they did prefer having me wait on them as I was so good and so familiar with their wants. I admired Mrs. Fulbright for turning the whole harangue into something complimentary. She was almost as diplomatic as the Sheriff.

And what I was going to say to the Sheriff was uppermost on my mind.

After my own waffle-and-sausage-patty breakfast (which did a lot to revive me) I was hanging around the front desk, debating walking into town. I was too tired for walking and decided to call Axel's Taxis again. Right after I hung up, I discovered Ree-Jane had been sitting in one of the easy chairs hidden by the huge rhododendron pot, for she rose and came over to the desk, still flouncing through her fashion magazine, as if raising her eyes to look at me would be too boring. She said she wanted to go into La Porte, too, but her convertible was in the garage. She looked at me accusingly and added that something had been wrong with it ever since Brownmiller had driven it to Hebrides. As long as I'd called a taxi she'd go with me. Not asking, telling.

"What're you doing up so early?" I was furious with myself for getting caught by her. Ree-Jane usually never got downstairs before ten.

It was only a quarter to nine, and she answered me by saying, "Sam wants to see me." Then she sighed as if this were ever so tiresome, the police calling her in.

"The Sheriff does?" I was flabbergasted. Of course, she could have been lying. "Why? How come?"

That was her opportunity to give me a smirky,

secret-keeping little smile, one corner of her bright-red-lipsticked mouth hooking up. "It's confidential police business."

Knowing how nobody's confidence could ever rest easy with Ree-Jane, I prodded her by saying, "It's about the dead woman." I made an absolute statement of this, as if I were sure.

She dropped the magazine, clearly irritated. "How do *you* know?"

"How do I know?" I thought quickly. "Because the Sheriff wants to see me, too."

Her red mouth tightened in anger. "He's supposed to see me at nine o'clock."

Casually, I looked up at the regulator clock, ticking uncaringly above us. "Well, you're going to be late."

Ree-Jane opened her mouth to say something she probably thought would be scathing, but just then we heard gravel spit and a horn honk, so the taxi had arrived.

We plucked up sweaters, jackets, money (I would of course be stuck with the fare: "But you were going in anyway . . .") and we went out onto the porch. Delbert yelled a friendly greeting and we clambered in and I asked him where Axel was. I always asked that.

"Oh, Axel got a call from some of them lake people wanted to go to Meridian."

"They must really be rich to hire a taxi for that long distance," I said.

"I guess. Axel, he likes the long runs. Axel just

loves to drive. It's why he started his own taxis. He's a real good driver."

I would never know.


Ree-Jane stared straight ahead and didn't speak to me, for she was still smarting with the knowledge that I too had been called in by the Sheriff. I wondered why she believed me. But I still had the problem of needing to think while Ree-Jane's mere presence was sucking all of the brain oxygen out of the air. I decided to test out on Ree-Jane what I might say to the Sheriff. "Helene Baum and those people last night said the police didn't know a bit more about the dead body. I mean, who she was."

"Don't ask me," Ree-Jane said, bitterly.

I at least could tell from that she didn't know any more than before, because it was a sure thing she'd have milked anything she *did* know to death. Delbert heard this and of course he had his own opinions, which he was pleased to share with anyone who'd listen.

I didn't.


At the edge of town, I guess Ree-Jane's curiosity got the better of her, and she asked me what Sam said he wanted to talk to *me* about. (I just hated the way she called him "Sam.") "I don't know. I'm supposed to meet him at the Rainbow Café." I said this in case she mentioned to the Sheriff that I'd claimed I was supposed to see him at ten o'clock. That way, the Sheriff would just assume I probably meant we would run into each other at the Rainbow and maybe check the parking meters, as we often did.

Life needed too much quick thinking.


Delbert dropped Ree-Jane at the side of the courthouse, and I could just as easily have got out there too, but that would have suggested I didn't have my own equally important destination. Which I didn't. I just had Delbert drive down the hill and around the corner and drop me across the street from the courthouse.

I got out on the other side of the street in front of the Oak Tree Gift Shoppe, thinking that it would be nice to join Miss Flyte and Miss Flagler for their morning snack. Miss Flagler's white kitchen was a cozy, restful place for thinking, as I often did while the two of them were talking. The cat helped my thinking, too.

One reason I loved the Oak Tree was because it was so small and shabby—"shabbily genteel" was what my mother called it—and because it always smelled of lavender and "eau de rose." I looked into the pretty bay window, whose display always appeared much the same, though I know Miss Flagler changed it, for I'd seen her leaning in and arranging jewelry from time to time. But there were always the same sorts of things: silver hearts on narrow chains, gold lockets, silver rattles tied with ribbons, a tray of birthstone rings, little silver bears (which served no purpose I could see). The necklaces and pins sat in white boxes on cotton squares; bracelets and silver chains were draped on display tiers covered with a waterfall of dark blue velvet.

The sound of the tinkling bell died away completely before I heard shufflings in the room at the rear. It occurred to me that as I had several dollars in my change purse, it would be nice to buy a present for Anna Paugh, whose birthday was a few days away. My mother was going to make her a cake (something my mother did for all of the help), and there would probably be a little party in the kitchen. Anna Paugh always wore pins, I'd noticed, so that's what I was looking for when Miss Flagler came through the curtain. She seemed glad to see me. I told her what I wanted and we both searched through all of the pins. There was a silver one of three cats in a row with tiny jewel-like eyes, chips of some blue-green stone. Anna Paugh loved cats, including the hotel cat, and I knew she had several at home. So that's the one I bought, and I watched Miss Flagler wrap it in silver gift-wrap paper with a lot of narrow silver ribbon. Miss Flagler really loved silver.

"Miss Flyte is coming for coffee," she said. "Wouldn't you like some cocoa?"

Since that's what I'd come for, I quickly said yes, and we went back to the kitchen, where Albertine, the cat, was lying fat and furry before the cast-iron stove. She shivered herself awake and, seeing me sitting down in the buttercup-yellow chair, jumped up on the shelf behind and directly over my head and started sniffing my hair. A plate of fresh buns was sitting on the white table and Miss Flagler told me to help myself, but I said I would wait for Miss Flyte. I probably wouldn't have been so polite if I hadn't been full of waffles and sausage.

By the time Miss Flyte came in through the side door, with the scent of candle wax clinging to her cardigan, Miss Flagler was pouring the steaming cocoa into a mug. I stirred it quickly (to avoid the skin) and added two marshmallows. The three of us sat there peacefully drinking and eating buns while Albertine chewed the crown of my hair. Miss Flagler told Albertine to stop, but of course she didn't.

I brought up the subject of the woman found in Mirror Pond, thinking that they might have heard some interesting rumor. "But the Sheriff doesn't know any more about her, about her identity. Well, I think that's really strange. It's been nearly four days. Wouldn't you think the police would at least know who she *is*?"

Miss Flyte agreed that yes, it was indeed strange.

But Miss Flagler, after a short silence, started talking in an odd, roundabout way. "You know, I think sometimes we become . . . well, *stuck* inside a problem." She said this and looked at me and looked away. "For some reason, we keep moving around it or inside of it. Or not really moving at all, but fluttering." She frowned at her cup as if it were difficult to explain what she meant.

"Like moths, you mean," said Miss Flyte. She was never far from thoughts of candle fire. And then she added, "Obsession." Miss Flyte liked words like that. She was romantic. "The way moths circle around flames, or beat their wings against a lamp," she went on.

Miss Flagler seemed to be thinking this over as she ran her fingers over the rim of her teacup in a way I had seen a tea-leaf fortune reader once do. "Obsession . . . no, not precisely. *Attraction* is more what I mean. Yes, attraction."

I frowned. What was she talking about? I didn't see how she could be talking about the Sheriff's problem with the dead woman.

She said, "Certain problems just *attract* us. They're *attractors*, they're like magnets. And once drawn to them, you can't quite . . . stay away." She held her hand out as if she were trying to reach for words.

Ordinarily, the two of them just chirruped away about everyday affairs. But Miss Flagler seemed to be off on something deeper. Miss Flyte must have thought so, too, for she nodded and said, "That's deep. That's very deep."

"I'm not saying it well. It's what I mean by getting stuck. Or trapped."

It was making me uncomfortable, this "attractor" business, and I said, "Well, but it's not the *moth's* fault if it gets trapped." I felt I should make this clear, in case there was any blame to be handed out. I studied the bottom of my mug and felt anxious. "Anyway, how does a person get *un*stuck, then?"

Miss Flagler shook her head slightly. "I don't know. I don't know."

That wasn't much of an answer. Impatiently, I asked, "But what *kinds* of problems are you talking about?"

She thought for a moment. "I guess inner problems. Yes, inner." She tapped at her chest with a fisted hand.

*Inner problems.* I relaxed a little bit.

Except for how to get rid of Ree-Jane, I didn't have any of those.


" 'I'm not at lib-er-ty to tell you,' " Maud said, mimicking the Sheriff.

After the difficult ideas Miss Flagler had been trying to express (and making me nervous in the bargain), it was a relief to hear Maud not searching for words at all.

She went on. "Do policemen really say that? 'I'm not at liberty'? I think he's just putting on he's a TV cop, just to annoy me." She lit a cigarette and waved out the match.

She had been talking about the Sheriff's response to her question. He'd come in a little before ten, about fifteen minutes before me (worse luck), downed a cup of coffee, and taken off "like a bat out of hell," or so Maud described it, as she struck one palm against another and slid the hand straight out to indicate, I guessed, bats screeching out of hell.

"You want some chili?" she asked. "They just made some fresh."

I told her I'd just had sticky buns and cocoa over at Miss Flagler's, with her and Miss Flyte.

"You have more of a social life than I do."

I was studying my fingers, splayed on the table as if it were piano keys, pondering over what Miss Flagler had said. I asked Maud: "Do you think people can get stuck in their problems?"

"I'm not sure what you mean."

"Oh, it was just something Miss Flagler was saying. Something about a person can get so attracted to a problem that they can get stuck in it and can't get out."

"Miss Flagler said that? I'm surprised. She's so quiet." Maud was thinking about this and peeling a bit of pink nail polish from her thumb.

"Miss Flyte said she must mean 'obsessed,' but Miss Flagler said no, she meant the problem was an 'attractor.' That's what she called it. An 'at-trac-tor.' "

Maud debated, frowning. "I guess we all know people can get totally immersed in their problems. But that doesn't sound exactly like what she means . . ." and she raised her eyes and her hand much as Miss Flagler had done, palm upward, as if maybe God would help out. But we both knew he wouldn't, of course. "Maybe it's that you could get 'stuck' in a problem if it had especially serious consequences for you, personally."

What I liked about Maud was that she didn't just dismiss a question and didn't ask *why* you were asking. For all of her sarcasm (mostly around the Sheriff) she took things seriously.

"What were you talking about when she said this?"

"The dead woman." I cleared my throat. I didn't want to talk about Miss Flagler's comment anymore, as it was getting my nerves up again. "Where did the Sheriff go, if he was so excited?"

"Excited? I didn't say he was excited. Just as stony-faced as ever." She blew a smoke ring.

Surely Ree-Jane couldn't have told him anything important, could she? Maud answered that tormenting question without my asking it. "All he said was it was regarding a missing person."

My head snapped up; I sat rigid. *"What?"*

"A missing person."

"Well, but *who*?"

" 'I am not at *lib*-er-ty,' et cetera, et cetera." She shrugged. "I don't know who or where." She inclined her head toward the jukebox. "That sounds like something Jo Stafford would sing. 'But I can't remem-*ber* where or when,' " she sang. Maud had a really pretty voice. Then she started in again on her thumbnail, peeling off another scrap of polish. "Donny came running in to get coffee and doughnuts from Shirl and then ran out again and jumped in the squad car."

That was interesting. Donny was a blabber-mouth. So was Shirl. I raised myself up to look down towards the cash register. Shirl was there as usual, sitting on her high stool. It was a little after eleven o'clock now, and I said in a rush that I'd have to get back to the hotel and wait tables for lunch and I asked Maud for a check. She didn't want to give me one, but I insisted. I said I was afraid someday she'd get in trouble giving me free Cokes. No, I insisted. Maud just shrugged a little, smiled, and wrote up a check. I took it up to the front, said hello to Shirl, and placed the check with my money on the rubber mat. After gazing in the glass case at the rows of doughnuts, I said, "My mother says you make the best doughnuts in a hundred miles." Actually, my mother made the best doughnuts and she knew it.

But Shirl was all smiles. "Well, tell her thanks."

"Okay, I will. I think maybe I'll get a couple doughnuts and take them across to the Sheriff and Donny. I have to talk to the Sheriff."

As she plunged her fingers onto the register keys, Shirl said, "Ain't no use doing it now, hon. Donny was in here less'n an hour ago and took off like he was greased. With Sam."

"No kidding?" I frowned hugely. "But I was supposed to see him. Where'd they go?"

"Cold Flat Junction." Shirl plopped some change on the rubber mat.

I knew it. Jude Stemple was right.

*I just knew it.*

## THIRTY-FOUR

If it hadn't been for having Miss Bertha and her three meals a day, I'd have taken my bag of doughnuts straight to the courthouse and just sat there until they came back. But as it was, I headed instead for Axel's taxi stand. Between there and the Rainbow Café I had to pass the Prime Cut, and I saw, through their big plate glass window, Ree-Jane sitting in one of the three beauticians' chairs, getting her hair combed out. I had totally forgotten about Ree-Jane and her courthouse errand, and for a minute I considered going in and asking her, but that would only have told her I was really wanting to know something, which would be, of course, a good reason for not telling me. She only enjoyed telling me what she thought I didn't want to know.

There she sat, chattering a mile a minute to Alma Duke, Beautician (written in chalk-white letters down in the right-hand corner of the window). Alma Duke owns the Prime Cut. Alma Duke is without doubt the biggest gossip in La Porte, bigger even than Helene Baum or Mabel Haines (which is really saying some-thing); and Alma Duke, like most gossips, gets it wrong most of the time, because it would slow their tongues down if they ever took the time to get it right. Getting it right meant at least hesitating long enough to check your story out or get your facts straight.

I thought how horrible it would be, being a beautician and all day long catering to women's vanities. I noticed Helene Baum was in there, too, almost hidden under the big globe of a hair dryer. She was sitting next to Mayor Sims's wife, and their mouths were also moving a mile a minute, their magazines forgotten in their laps. How they could hear one another with all of the noise of those hair dryers whirring, I couldn't imagine.

I moved off and plodded along Second Street (in what Ree-Jane called my duck-footed walk) and was lucky enough to find a taxi sitting outside Axel's.

But not lucky enough to find Axel, of course.

And I was also lucky to find only Miss Bertha wanting lunch; not even Mrs. Fulbright was there, for she had gone off with her nephew (to be with human beings for a change, I guessed). The dining room was completely empty except for Miss Bertha, which was just the way she liked it. She could order me around; she could yell across its vast space as if it were a canyon; she could thump her cane. She could do all of this over nothing but a club sandwich, which she said she never ate and didn't want; she wanted something hot. My mother said, "Take her a bucket of boiling water, the damned old fool!" Walter just thought that was a scream, and his shoulders shook in soundless laughter as he wiped his dishtowel around and around on a big serving platter.

So Miss Bertha, in protest, took her club sandwich all apart, one layer after another, and made me listen to her complaints about the wretched ingredients in it, until toast, chicken, lettuce, ham, tomato all lay in a mayonnaise shambles on her plate. I just stood sucking back yawns until she released me to the kitchen for her chocolate sundae. "And none of that damned thin Hershey's syrup, either! I want fudge sauce!"

Well, I couldn't say I blamed her when I thought about my mother's hot fudge sauce.

Several times after lunch I tried screwing up my nerve to call the Sheriff's office, but I found it too hard to be casual in a phone call. It's not like appearing in person, where you can pretend you've just met by accident, just "bumped into" someone in the Rainbow or out doing meter checking.

I was rocking in one of the slat-backed chairs on the side porch, thinking of my problem, when I spied a white car way down on the highway turning into the drive. I remembered that Ree-Jane was picking up her car from the garage. I didn't want to put up with her preening over her convertible, so I left the rocker rocking just as the white convertible was bumping halfway up the potholed drive. I walked from the front down the hall to the back door and up the flagstone path.

My immediate problem was getting someone to go along with me to the Devereau house. I didn't think the Woods and Mr. Root would be up to a second trip, but you never knew, so I decided to go along to Britten's and see if any of them were around.

This route took me up behind the big garage where Will and Mill were messing around getting their summer production ready and in which once again I would not star. There was always competition coming from a cousin or two who, being rich, thought that meant they must be really talented, too. But the only one with real talent is Brownmiller, who is the most incredibly talented person I've ever met. He can play anything from a comb to a piano concerto; he can write songs and even the plays that he and Will produce in the summer. It was Will who solved the name problem by shortening "Brownmiller" first to "Miller" and then to "Mill," so they could be known as "Mill" and "Will." (I personally think that "Miller Conroy" sounds like a writer, or artist, or musician. And he is all of those.)

So Mill and Will were in there, planning whatever the next lavish production would be, Mill pounding an ancient upright piano and the two of them singing some song he had written (on the spot, probably) and both of them hardly able to get through it for laughing so hard.

I stood outside the big garage, picking at the peeling gray paint around the door. No, I thought. There must have been a reason why I hadn't asked them to accompany me before when I went to the Devereau house, and now was no different. They would play tricks on me all the way there—not really unfriendly, but tricks still: things like hiding in the woods or pretending they saw things that they hadn't. And in the Devereau house it would be worse. I'd been around the two of them long enough to know they loved practical jokes. Sometimes they were funny; sometimes they were plain silly. One of their favorite things to do was to get the hose and hide behind bushes and turn the hose on Paul when he went by. Paul was so dumb he thought it was a game.

I did not continue on my way to Britten's store, either. Instead, I went back and around to the Pink Elephant and collected my homemade butterfly net and box and set off for the lake.

What was in my mind was a hazy notion that this time I should go alone.

So I stood in the exact same spot in the marshy grass with my butterfly net and the empty box at my feet, staring across the sheer surface of the lake. It was very calm today, gray like slate. I suppose I thought if I looked hard enough and long enough, everything would come again, it would all repeat itself. I would see the Girl standing over there in her white dress, stock-still and looking right at me. But I didn't see her, though I waited for a very long time, until it felt almost as if the muddy water I stood in was seeping through my old rubber boots to my sneakers.

I left the net and the box beside it to pick up again on my way back. I guess I had brought them only as props, the sort of thing Will and Mill use to set a stage. I walked here to the spring and sat on this same stone wall for a few moments, collecting spring water in the tin cup that was always weirdly there, for it was a wonder to me that someone, some boys, didn't steal it just for the sake of taking something. But then I realized that this wasn't a place people would be likely to come to; it was too overgrown, too out-of-the-way, too much *trouble* just for an idle hour or two of playing. It just wasn't *interesting* enough. Unless you were like me.

It was that way into the woods, the dark and tunnel-like recess that I studied over for some minutes until I worked up my nerve. If I hadn't gone through those trees once with the Woods and Mr. Root, I'd never have been able to do it on my own. I still might not be able to go the whole way to the house.

You would never have known it was broad daylight in among those trees. Light barely filtered through the overhanging branches, as thick in winter as in summer, for most of them were conifers with limbs spread wide as tents. It was the sort of silence that people call "unearthly." It wasn't like the silence of the hotel lobby midday, or the side porch, or the Pink Elephant. It was a different silence, as if the last layer of disturbance in the air had been removed, peeled away; the last rustlings of leaves, the last faint birdcalls gone. I walked steadily, without looking back or even around very much, until I reached the edge—the clearing and the house.

I breathed easier and headed around behind the house to the kitchen door.

It was all the same in the kitchen—the candles, the porcelain table, the musty sour smell still clinging to the empty refrigerator with its listing door. The dry, moldy smell of dead leaves gathered on window- and doorsills seemed stronger than before, probably only because I had had the Woods and Mr. Root to distract my senses then. I walked through to the living room or front parlor or whatever the Devereaus would have called it and looked around in the twilit gloom. The piano, the heavy armchairs—all the same. Perhaps I thought my mental picture of the room had been defective somehow.

I moved over to the wall on which hung the single photograph, the one of the Devereau sisters as girls—teenagers, maybe. That I now knew this, that I could now attach a name to this face, for some reason made me feel choked. Now she had a name. Not only that but I knew things about her. Yet, Rose hadn't figured in Ulub's story—or at least I didn't *think* she had figured in it, since with Ulub it's hard to tell. In his playacting, there had been only *three* sisters sitting around the kitchen table, three sisters on their awful midnight errand through the wood. The events Ulub had recounted to us in his story (if Ulub was to be believed) had happened the night before Mary-Evelyn was found in the lake. So Rose must not have been here then.

"Run off with Ben Queen," Aurora had said. Rose must have already been gone.

The photograph hung beside a huge sideboard, wood so dark it was nearly black. It was from the "Empire" period; I knew this because there was one almost exactly like it in the hotel dining room. We kept silver, placemats, and odds and ends in it for setting up tables. I started opening drawers. Mostly, I was looking for pictures. There had to be some, I thought—another old photograph, snapshots such as the one given to my mother. That showed they took pictures, at least. I started with the biggest drawer in the center. It held linen napkins, not starched to a slickness like the hotel's linen service did them, but soft and limp, almost silky, and creased yellow where they'd been folded for so long. There were tablecloths too, probably to cover the round table in the center of the room that they might have used on Sundays for dinner, or sometimes for tea, when they didn't eat in the kitchen. I pulled out all of the drawers; there were more napkins, tarnished napkin rings, silvery pads to place under hot dishes to keep from marring the wood. These were all that I found. Carefully, I rearranged what I had removed and closed the drawers. Then I went over to the desk, which also had the chunky look of "Empire" about it, and checked out all of its drawers. There was nothing but some old empty envelopes, scraps of receipts, old advertisements, even a menu on which "Hotel Paradise" was written in spidery letters. It was quite old and I saw that food was a lot cheaper then. I refolded it and put it in my pocket. On my way upstairs, I passed the phonograph standing beside the porch door and stopped to look through a stack of records. Someone named Lauritz Melchior I thought I recognized, for I think my mother had listed him as one of the well-known singers to join the

Chautauqua in those far-off summers. A lot of the records were French, songs whose titles I couldn't read by singers I had never heard of. I guessed the Devereau sisters were well-educated.

Upstairs, I began my search of the bedrooms. Three of them were much the same, double beds, one with a fourposter covered with a quilt and lumpy with mothballs. I imagined these were the three sisters' bedrooms. The beds had their mattresses rolled up and mothballs stuffed in them. It was more the way that summer people close down their houses for the season than it was the way for people who leave forever. It made me wonder: did they intend to come back? The sisters were in their forties then; by now they must be dead, or else in their eighties or even nineties. I opened the bureau drawers, empty but for a few newspaper linings. The newspapers were interesting; they were the same old *Conservative*, except that here the name was printed differently, written in the sort of curly letters I sometimes saw on chocolate boxes, such as my Whitman's box. Another room at the end of the hall was not much bigger than Mary-Evelyn's. Its long narrow window overlooked the woods, and if I stood a certain way, I could glimpse the lake and, on its far side, the stone bridge. It must have been Rose Fern Devereau's room.

Mary-Evelyn's room was the nicest, for it had near-fresh-looking candy-striped wallpaper, not the faded peony pattern dripping down dirty-looking brownish backgrounds of the other rooms. The yel-

low and white stripes looked good with the blue
furniture. There were the dormer windows looking
out over the lake and, of course, the little balcony.
I raised the window, lifted my legs over the sill as
I had done before, and sat looking out across the
lake. Clouds had gathered and the sky was graying
over; I looked up just in time to catch a raindrop
right near my eye. Still, I sat there and let the drops
rain on me for a while. They were slow in coming
down and without any force, and I liked watching
the surface of the lake when it rained, the pockmarks
made by the drops that set it moving slightly and
shimmering. When it began to fall in earnest, I
crawled back inside.

The mattress wasn't rolled up on this bed; it
was covered with a pale-yellow and white chenille
spread, drawn up and tucked neatly beneath the pil-
low as if someone expected to sleep in it tonight, or
soon. Not even the mice had got to the spread, though
I would have thought the design of interlocking circles of white tufts would look pretty tasty to mice.
I hesitated to go through Mary-Evelyn's things. I
guess I knew how furious I'd be if someone did that
to me. But this was the only bedroom that still looked
a little lived-in, and since there were a few articles
still sitting on the top of the white dresser—a brush,
a mirror, a bottle that might have held some kind of
perfume—I thought there was a possibility I would
find something helpful.

I was right, too: the drawers still held things
like underwear, rolled-up socks, pajamas. There were

no T-shirts or shorts, but there were several carefully folded blouses of very fine cotton, white eyelet, and even some lace at the collar. But aside from the clothes, the drawers held no secrets, such as diaries or pictures or anything. I shut them and went to the wardrobe. The clothes inside were still in excellent condition. Pine chips on the hangers and the strong odor of camphor also might have held off the mice and moths.

There was a plaid woolen skirt and soft pastel sweaters and dresses. What dresses! They were unbelievably elegant, and I was used to the Europa dress shop, too; I knew what I was talking about. Many's the time I'd had to be the audience for Ree-Jane modeling the latest fashion, with her unnatural gliding step and her hands bent stiffly at her wrists or on one hip as she twirled around, stopping, posing, smiling artificially over her shoulder. I was also the cheering section for Mrs. Davidow, though she didn't walk around in Ree-Jane's show-offy way that made me want to throw up; she merely stepped smartly from the dressing room, turned this way and that before the mirror, yanked her girdle down and made various adjustments. The point was, I had seen the most expensive, exclusive garments within a hundred miles of the hotel being modeled and purchased and heard long conversations between Helen Gay Struther and Mrs. Davidow about bias cuts, gores, tucks, and pleats. Enough to know really good sewing when I saw it. And I was seeing it now, as I held out the tiny-pleated skirt of a pale yellow dress, accordion pleats that would lie perfectly flat and neat until the wearer of it moved and then the skirt would swirl about. There was another one of a beautiful shade of greenish blue, very plain except you could see how well it was cut, and the material was petal soft. There were eight such dresses, ranging from the plainer green one to an incredibly fancy party-dress of ice-blue taffeta, down the front of which marched an intricate row of buttons and loops of the same material. I fingered the materials of each of these dresses and thought it must be the finest of its kind: the rose-gray wool, the deep blue velvet were so *melting*; the smooth taffeta the color of the delphiniums that encircled the garden at the front of the hotel.

I picked out the plainest one, the green one that looked most me, removed my T-shirt and cotton skirt, and slipped it on over my head. Over the bureau was a mirror that I tilted to see all of me that I could, and I looked quite nice. I bent closer to the mirror to see what the green (which was the shade of one of Mrs. Davidow's liqueur bottles) did for my eyes. It made them much greener. Once, I had told Maud my eyes must be shrug-colored, for every time I asked someone what color my eyes were, the person would just shrug ("Oh, I don't know . . . blue? green? brownish?") and shrug again. Maud had said this was absolutely ridiculous; anyone could see my eyes were "hazel" and extremely pretty. It was a relief to know this. And it was true my eyes changed color depending on what color I was wearing. Although, since most of my clothes were T-shirts, and white ones, my eyes didn't change much. Now they looked really green from the dress. I stood back, admiring myself, picked up the brush, and ran it through my hair. Even my hair lost that "tan" look, looked blonder with this green dress on. Of course, I have always pretended I don't care about clothes, which is what it was—pretending. I would be teased unmercifully if I ever let on I did care. Clothes are for girls Ree-Jane's age. And size, and looks, and model walk. For someone who can show them off. I know I've been told *that*. I looked down at the green dress and smoothed the skirt, which was cut on the bias so that it flared at the bottom. It was the kind of dress I might have had if anyone had ever bothered about my clothes.

Then it struck me, as if for the first time, as if I'd never known it before (which I always have, but only on the thin top layer of my mind), that I was not even to *consider* having such a dress. Not this one, not any of the ones in the Europa. And I wondered: Why? Why was I not even to think about standing in one of the Europa's dressing rooms, pulling the little curtain across the space and trying something on? Why, for my birthday, couldn't Mrs. Davidow and my mother have put their heads together and then told Helen Gay Struther to keep an eye out for a dress for me on one of those "buying" trips she did? I couldn't answer these questions. So I decided to keep the dress on for the short time I was here in this house. Or maybe I would try *all* of them on. I was wringing my hands, working myself into a snit, and then decided it would take up too much time to have one, or to try on all the dresses. Instead, I went over to a chest that sat at the foot of the bed. It was also painted blue and looked very much like my own worn pink toy chest, which I didn't use anymore, of course, but looked in occasionally only to check the contents to make sure Ree-Jane hadn't been messing with them.

The chest, too, was almost full. There were stuffed animals (some moth-eaten and mouse-chewed); game boards; puzzles of nature scenes, like "Winter Wonderland" or "Flowers-A-Bloom," which were pretty sickening; several dolls. I checked the games, found Monopoly and my all-time favorite, Mr. Ree. I sat cross-legged on the floor (being careful of my dress) and opened the board, which displayed one floor of a big house, showing all of its rooms as if the roof had been sliced away and the players were looking right down on them. Tucked neatly in the box were the round tubes on which little molded heads could be fitted. These were the people the players became. Then there were the tiny weapons—knife, gun, axe, rope—which would fit into the tube. It was the cleverest game I had ever seen, the one with the most intricate design. There were also three sets of cards: one for each of the six characters, one for each murder weapon, and one called "refreshment" cards. These had colorful pictures of cakes and drinks and sandwiches on them—another reason why I like this game.

I fixed the little heads to the tubes and lined them up and sat looking at them all. It is no wonder this game is popular, for it has the feeling about it of a family living in a house. Even though the people here aren't all that closely related, still, they all live together comfortably, until, of course, one of them decides to murder another of them and Mr. Ree has to be called in. I picked up each of the tiny weapons and placed them in my palm, studying them. The only thing I hadn't considered using to kill off Ree-Jane was an axe, and that was because of the gruesome mess and the blood probably landing on me. I sat there humming and imagining the rope around her neck and her twisting in the wind; I could hear her gasp and choke as the poisoned cup of something fell from her hand and her face turned blue; I could hear her scream as the knife went into her back. It was pleasant, sitting there with the rain on the roof and thinking these thoughts.

But I finally put the weapons aside, rested my elbows on my knees and my chin in my hands, and studied the people: Mr. Perrin. Miss Lee. Aunt Cora. Niece Rhoda. Butler Higgins. Beatrice. These names are quite wonderful, but Niece Rhoda is my favorite. Niece Rhoda is too sweet-looking to be the guilty party, too pretty to murder anyone. It disturbs me to think she might get herself murdered. I took out the character cards, wishing the Woods and Mr. Root were with me so we could play a game.

Humming again, I put the top card, Mr. Perrin, in front of his tube and head. The next card was

Artist George—but there was no Artist George tube
or head. I looked through the box and found no sign
of him. I wondered if he'd fallen out of the box to
the bottom of the chest, so I took out enough of its
contents to see what was down there, to feel around
for him. But I couldn't find either the head of Artist
George or his tube body. That was disappointing. It
meant the family wasn't complete. And then, turning
up the cards, something surprised me enough to forget the missing Artist George.

Each of the other four cards had another face
pasted over the card face. Cut out of what looked to
be a photograph was the face of one of the Devereau
sisters (Isabel, maybe, though I couldn't keep them
straight) smack over Beatrice. And over Miss Lee
was the face of one of the others. The third sister
had been carefully cut out and pasted over Aunt Cora.
And there was a fourth glued over Niece Rhoda. This
cutout was very pretty and very blond. I could only
suppose this was Rose Fern Devereau.

I had seen her three times. I mean, I had seen
her likeness. The face looked exactly like the girl on
the platform in Cold Flat Junction. The girl walking
down Second Street. The girl who watched from the
other side of the lake. The Girl.

It really took my breath away. Of course, the
face in the photograph downstairs resembled her, but
younger; and here, shorn of the other faces ranged
around her, the face of Rose Devereau shone out, its
white-blondness as near identical to the Girl's as
could be. I got up, went over to the bed, and, being

careful not to muss the dress, lay down, holding the Niece Rhoda card in my hands, staring at it and wondering, frowning in thought, yet my mind blank except for the recollection of the Girl. I looked from the face on the card to the face in my mind: on the railway platform in Cold Flat. On the sidewalk in town. Across the lake. It was like looking at slides. *Click. Click. Click.*

I lay the card facedown on my chest and folded my hands over it. I looked up at the ceiling and the swimming pattern there of shadow and light made by the reflection of the rain tracking down the windowpanes. I was tired, or my mind was, with all of this searching and thinking. The rain came down in that pleasant, monotonous way that rain does sometimes, as if it hadn't anything better to do with its time. It was restful, despite my mind's turning and turning with thoughts of the two faces, or the one. As I stared upwards at the whirlpool of shadowed light, I felt hypnotized. Once Will had tried to hypnotize me by getting me to stare at a spot on a white ceiling. Will had read a book on hypnosis and naturally chose me as his practice victim.

Will had failed, but the swirling rain pattern was succeeding: I felt myself being slowly drawn into the swirl up there as if all sorts of nagging, ordinary thoughts were falling away—annoyances and busyness, such as Mrs. Davidow's awful bursts of temper, Miss Bertha's demands, salads waiting to be made, Vera's cuffs and apron crackling starchily. As all of these were blowing away like the filaments of thistles borne off on my breath's currents, leaving only the thistle core behind, I felt my own central self being pulled toward the center of the wavering lights on the ceiling. And I felt that all of the filaments were little lies, distractions, and not part of that central self. Into this clear place up there would float, on and off, the face of the Girl. I must really have been hypnotized (I thought), for I grew sleepier and sleepier, sleepy with all of this wondering. I felt I could lie here forever, hypnotized or entranced. I scarcely noticed the cold of the house, though my arms were completely goosebumped. It was the sort of still cold which (I had heard) ghosts cause, the sort of cold where there are no drafts, no air currents to stir and chill a person. But I do not believe in ghosts or that houses are haunted. I am afraid of a lot of things, but not that. I am too practical. Also, I have never been sure ghosts were ever anything to fear: I held more with the notion they were sad and sadly haunting places they could never leave because of that sadness: on a stairway, or in a library, or by a window looking always out to sea. To tell the truth, I wouldn't have minded at all if Mary-Evelyn's ghost had come here and we could play a game of Mr. Ree.

I thought of all the dresses hanging in the wardrobe and realized I could come here to the Devereau house whenever I wanted, every day, if I chose to, and put on one of those dresses. I could wander around, I could play with the things in the toy chest, I could sit on the windowsill and watch the lake, I could even bring sandwiches and Orange Crush over. Why, I could even bring blankets and sleep here. No one would notice at the hotel what I was doing after dinner was over and all the guests went away. Then what floated into the white spot on the ceiling up there was an image of my mother's candied yams, the ones with pecans crumbled on top, that she served with baked ham, and I decided I was not hypnotized and could get up.

Which I did, and sat yawning on the edge of the bed, still holding the card with the glued-on picture. I realized I had been just dreaming away about myself and forgetting the mystery of Rose Devereau and Ben Queen's girl, Fern.

I got up, slipped the dress over my head, and carefully returned it to its hanger, buttoning the top button to secure it there. I left the room and went downstairs. The rain had stopped and the sun come out, suddenly brilliant on the water. The phonograph standing beside the door to the porch was the sort that sits in its own wooden case and has a handle you turn to make it go. I pulled open the little door set in the mahogany case and found some more old records. They all seemed to be in French, and I recalled my mother or Marge Byrd saying the Devereau sisters were extremely well-educated and spoke foreign languages. I slipped one of the records from its sleeve and cranked up the phonograph. The needle was pretty old, for the music came out scratchy for a while and then settled into some really sad-sounding song with a background mostly of violins. I opened the inner door to the porch (for there was still a screen door) so that the woods around could have the treat of a little music. For a few moments I wandered about the room, looking at horsehair chairs and sofa and footstools and still searching for photos or diaries, though not quite so intently since I had found the Niece Rhoda card.

I had missed the piano bench when I was looking through drawers, so I lifted its hinged lid, not expecting to find anything, which I didn't, except for a lot of sheet music. Aurora's favorite, "Alice Blue Gown," was right on top. I opened it and looked at the notes. I was useless as a musician (which was why I admired Brownmiller so much, as he played everything by ear), but I did remember simple notes and could tap out a song with one finger. So I raised the big lid on the piano, propped it open as if I were about to bless a concert hall with my playing. The record on the phonograph had come to an end and the needle was scratching away on the inside, so I went over and removed the arm. Then I was back at the piano, sitting down at the keyboard. I punched out "Alice Blue Gown" and even sang some of it. I tried to play a chord with my left hand, but that didn't sound any too good, and I was glad Brownmiller wasn't there to hear it. I played "Alice Blue Gown" twice (liking the sound of my own voice singing), then grew tired of it and went back to the inside of the bench again for some more music.

The old sheet music swam around beneath my hand. A lot of these pieces, too, were in French. I picked out several and tried to make out the titles, which of course I couldn't, except to note that "amour" appeared in a lot of them. Some of them looked vaguely familiar, though, and my eye flicked over to the phonograph and the inside of the cabinet which held the records. Apparently, the Devereaus had been very fond of these French songs, because the records and the sheet music were, as far as I could make out, similar. I saw the title of one piece of sheet music was the same as the name of the song I had just been playing on the phonograph. I thought it would be nice to play my one-finger pieces with accompaniment and so I went to the phonograph to replay the record that matched my music. I wound and wound the handle and resettled the needle on the record, then raced back to the piano.

The French singer and I had a good time for a while. It was lucky the song was so slow—mournful, I realized when I actually stopped to listen. The voice came out of the phonograph suspended in air, as if there were nothing to support it, as if it were disembodied. Some of this of course was its foreignness. Since I couldn't understand the words, I couldn't attach any images to them. There were only the words—syllables, sounds. This slow French song was the only thing to break the silence of the shadowed parlor, and with the slow movement of cloudy light across the rug it was just—lonely. And as the voice continued, it became a crushing loneliness. My body grew heavy with the weight of it. It was as if the stone lady standing watch in the garden had come in and sat down beside me, leaning her weight into mine. Finally, the song stopped, the statue rose to return to her dead garden, and I could move my fingers again.

The silence was almost worse than the song. So I went back and played the opening notes again. The needle was scratching on the inside of the record. I was about to get up and move the needle when I happened to look through the screen door.

The Girl was standing out there, inside the rim of pines, just beyond the clearing. Over the rim of the pines across the lake the fiery sun looked about to go down in a blaze. Then the room got colder, and the woods darker, and she turned and walked away.

# THIRTY-FIVE

I do not go off the deep end about fate or God or astrology. Ree-Jane, on the other hand, takes to heart the horoscope column in the *Conservative*. It's pretty safe to believe in, since the only future it foretells, no matter what sign you're born under, is a good one. A great one, to hear Ree-Jane talk about her many future romances, the handsome strangers who will go with her on all of the exotic trips she will be taking, luring her away from all of the careers she will be having.

Ree-Jane reads all of this aloud to me, and, of course, reads me my horoscope, too, even though I've told her I don't believe in it. I am at times cruelly honest with myself (although I don't make a habit of it), and I must admit the reason I don't believe in horoscopes and Ree-Jane does is because hers are a lot happier-sounding, lighter and brighter than mine are. Her sign paints a picture of a future that will have her twirling down the nights and days in a white net evening gown aglitter with sequins. (I see it clearly because just such a gown is hanging upstairs in her wardrobe.) But I see myself in my own future wearing thick glasses and mouse-brown sweaters and being incredibly intelligent and looking down my nose at silly pleasures like dances.

So Ree-Jane also likes to read my horoscope to

me because *my* sign always leans toward things like doing good works, being loyal and self-sacrificing— in general, qualities found in nuns and saints, people like Joan of Arc or someone willing to die in an anthill for God. (I have never heard of God stepping in and taking over in cases, like Job's; I guess He's waiting to see if you're really serious, but by the time you prove it, it's too late, anyway.) Even though my own horoscope was lacking in love, money, and fame, it was still complimentary. Still, Ree-Jane managed to turn it into something really awful. She kept on about my fate, and what she called my "karma," and how I couldn't escape it.

The reason I bring up astrology and horoscopes is because in Spirit Lake there is a fortuneteller by the name of Mrs. Louderback. Mrs. Louderback is said to be pretty noble herself, because she does not charge for her services. Not officially, that is. She is willing to accept "offerings," so naturally those people who accept her services "offer" her something so as not to appear cheap. I don't want to sound spiteful about Mrs. Louderback (or "cynical" might be the word, though it only means smooth spite), for Mrs. Louderback, I've heard, is a really nice person who uses her kitchen to tell people their fortunes and for which the "offering" is generally two dollars.

And, after all, who else did I have to consult with? To tell the story of the Girl and anything to do with her—Mary-Evelyn, the evil sisters (which is the way I'd come to think of them), the house, Jude Stemple —this story would fall on deaf ears.

No, not deaf exactly, but people would certainly laugh at me. When I saw them in my mind, standing in a circle with me inside, and all of them laughing (including even Will, who ordinarily wouldn't, but whenever he was around the others he'd kind of "catch" their mood), I also saw this: that they weren't really laughing out of spite (excepting, of course, Ree-Jane). It was more as if they felt it was their right. My mind would flood with a jumble of images when I thought about this. I saw war-painted Indians whooping in a circle around a fire, calling forth whatever their gods were, or their spirits. I saw people surrounding a goat, fixing pots and pans on its back, then herding it into the hills.

Someone *had* to be It. Someone *had* to be. This was not really a punishment; it was more like karma.

Going back to Mrs. Louderback: I'm a practical person. I don't believe in ghosts, spirits, devils, angels, monsters springing from dark closets, and so forth. I don't mean I *test* my unbelief. I don't do things like going into vacant houses on Halloween or walking through cemeteries. But that, again, is simply being practical.

The way Mrs. Louderback works her hobby is for a person to make an appointment for certain afternoon times (as she has her housework to do just like everybody else) and *not* tell her who it is calling. This struck me as strange, since she probably knows everybody in Spirit Lake on sight. Maybe you aren't supposed to tell your name to ensure that she won't in the meantime check up on you, like finding out things that happened in your past so that she can then pretend to guess at those events. I don't think Mrs. Louderback would cheat in that way, anyway; why would she rush to find out what went on in any of the pasts around Spirit Lake or La Porte? Helene Baum is, I have heard, one of her regular customers. Imagine hearing all about the boring past of Helene Baum. It was probably hard enough to face her across the kitchen table right now in the present.

Ree-Jane went to see Mrs. Louderback several times and always came back looking like the cat that swallowed the cream. I gave up asking her what she'd found out, because all she'd say was that it was wonderful but refused to give me details. Mrs. Davidow also went to her. My mother never did. Mrs. Davidow tried to get her to go, not wanting to appear silly by herself.

I was afraid Mrs. Louderback would think I was a kid pulling a joke on her when I called for my appointment, but she didn't. She told me I could come at four-thirty.

I spent the day being very nervous. I was afraid of the future. I had heard that Mrs. Louderback would not tell anyone of a truly bad future happening, such as dying next week. That made me feel a little better, but then I was afraid I would just read something bad into her expression if she turned up a suspicious-looking card. I had seen the tarot cards because Ree-Jane (naturally) owns a deck. Unlike Mrs. Louderback, Ree-Jane is always happy to flip over Death and Damnation cards predicting my future. In Ree-

Jane's readings of my future, I would burn at the stake without the reward of people thinking I was a saint and worshiping me. I'd just burn. Naturally, Ree-Jane was lying, for no one's future could *always* be the gloomy picture she painted.

But the cards themselves I thought to be fascinating and some of them quite beautiful. It surprised me to find out the meanings for a few of them: the Hanged Man, for instance, who meant something like "rebirth" and not (as I imagined) death from hanging by your foot.

Before my appointment with Mrs. Louderback I went to Britten's store, legitimately this time, as my mother had told me to pick up a box of cornstarch for tomorrow's Floating Island. It wouldn't be needed until then, so I didn't have to run back with it.

Mr. Britten looked at me over the tops of his black-framed glasses, suspiciously, as always. But since there was no one in the store who looked like a source of Ben Queen information, I didn't linger over the display cases or hang around the shelves. He knew to put the cornstarch on the Hotel Paradise account, which might or might not get paid before Doomsday. Lola Davidow is very good at juggling bills.

Outside, Mr. Root was occupying his end of the bench. The Woods weren't around, though. He greeted me with a wink and a nod, then looked all around, as if we belonged to the same secret society and he didn't want anyone else horning in.

"I thought maybe," he said, nodding towards the highway, "when that bus pulls in, you know, that there church bus, that maybe I could ask a few questions." Mr. Root turned his head to the side, away from me, and spat out tobacco, quite delicately. "Thought I might find out whatever happened to Sheba—you know, the one that married one of them Queens? You think maybe we should go back to that house? You and me and the Wood boys?"

He meant to the Devereau house, of course, and I never knew when I might want company, so I told him maybe we should, a little later. After we sat there for another while, Mr. Root soberly chewing and apparently thinking hard (to judge from the furrows in his forehead), and me looking at the woman on the cornstarch box, I decided it was time to be starting for Mrs. Louderback's. She lived on the other side of the village, across the highway, and down several streets, but it would only take me ten minutes to walk it.

"You be careful now," Mr. Root said.

I thanked him and went down the embankment in front of Britten's and across the highway. There was never much traffic on it. I passed by Greg's rickety restaurant where the pinball machine was, and the lunchroom next door to it where Mrs. Ikleberger served up her potato soup in winter. That was all of the "business area" Spirit Lake had. Britten's store across the highway, and Greg's and Mrs. Ikleberger's. I walked along between rows of big old Victorian houses and smaller, neat cottages, like Marge

Byrd's which had a lot of lattice and climbing flowers across its front. The garden looked weedy, but Marge Byrd wasn't the type to leave off reading a good book to go out and pull weeds.

I was let in to Mrs. Louderback's house by some woman—family or friend, I supposed—who told me just to go on into the parlor and that Mrs. Louderback would see me in a few minutes.

The room I entered was cool and dark. It reminded me of Dr. McComb's house, stuffed with furniture and piled high with shadows. Framed photographs were grouped on one large round table that was covered with a runner of darkly patterned material; the overstuffed chairs were so close together that the arms touched. I wondered if she needed to provide for a lot of people at once, as in a doctor's waiting room.

But I was the only customer at this time and I was relieved. One thing that had inhibited me was running into Helene Baum, for instance, someone who would blab all over town that I was seeing the fortuneteller. I had already decided that if there were other customers there, I would make it appear that I had only come to deliver the box of cornstarch. I was embarrassed by the thought of anyone else knowing.

Mrs. Louderback is a heavyset woman in her fifties or sixties or seventies (those ages looking pretty much alike to me). She has a lot of gray hair that she wears in a coil, extremely clear skin, and eyes with such pale irises I can't tell their color. You

know right away from her expression that she must
be very kindly. On this occasion, she was wearing
a bib apron over a cotton housedress, and out of the
apron pocket she drew her deck of cards. It was all
very homey. We sat down at the kitchen table, which
was covered with a red-and-white checked cloth, and
on this I set my box of cornstarch. Then I removed
it and set it down on the floor, in case it would cause
confusion in the spirit world. She knew me, she said,
and called me "Jen Graham's girl," which surprised
me, as I was so used to people thinking I was Lola
Davidow's. I could never understand this, for my
family had certainly been around a lot longer than
the Davidows. One reason might be that in the last
five years, my mother didn't go into La Porte to do
the shopping. Mrs. Davidow always did, and she also
went to social events when my mother was just too
tired out from all the cooking. So it was the Davidows
who got "seen" around town. This, as I have said,
caused people to confuse me and Ree-Jane, which
naturally made me nauseous.

The cards she drew from her apron pocket were
worn from all of her years of telling fortunes. She
split the deck in three and told me I must ask a
question. Whatever question I wanted.

*A* question? *One* question? Questions shot
through my mind. Who was the Girl? What had
happened to Mary-Evelyn, really? Had Fern Queen
really been murdered at Mirror Pond? Would Ree-
Jane come to a horrible end? (That last question
jumped in, unbidden, among the others. I certainly

had no intention of wasting my question on Ree-Jane.) I just sat there, my eyes so hard shut they ached.

She told me that, for instance, I could ask if my life would be a happy one, or if I'd be rich, whether I'd succeed in my work or my profession, whether I was "headed in the right direction"—things like that.

I stared at her and frowned. What? Why should I waste my question on things like that? I wasn't headed in any direction I knew of. I thought Mrs. Louderback's examples were, to tell the truth, pretty dumb. But she wasn't going to wait all day. And it popped into my mind that what was very important at this point was, Should I tell the Sheriff what Jude Stemple had told me? This surprised me, this question. I was mildly shocked that of all the possible ones, I found this to be the one I should ask.

Must I ask this question out loud? She said I could or not. Only if the cards got confused, then perhaps I'd say it out loud.

"If the cards got confused," she'd said. It occurred to me that Mrs. Louderback was leaving herself a lot of leeway. She had a pretty good thing going, for she was not responsible for the outcome. It was the cards themselves. I did not think this was at all dishonest; I just wished that I could walk into the kitchen late for making salads and when my mother or Vera started in on me, I could say that the cards got confused.

Not wanting to involve the Sheriff, I told her

I'd just ask the question in my head. She didn't mind at all. She told me I was to restack the cards, which I did. Mrs. Louderback slowly turned up three cards: the Queen of Cups, the Hanged Man, and two orphans. Well, that's what the card looked like to me: a boy and a girl walking in a bad snowstorm dressed in raggedy clothes. It was hard to believe anything good could come of this card. But it didn't surprise me I got it.

Mrs. Louderback looked at my cards intently. Her lips moved ever so slightly, as if she were trying to put into soft words what she saw as the meaning of these three. She said, "Now, that's very interesting." Suddenly she asked, "Has something terrible happened to you? Have you had . . . have you put up with a lot of—"

I was in suspense about myself and leaned closer to the table. My chest dug into its edge, for the chair I sat in was low for me. "A lot of what?" I prompted her, afraid maybe she was sailing off into a world where I could not follow.

Her brow creased with her hard thinking. "Difficulties. Pain. Blame." She frowned as if she just couldn't find the right word, so made do with "Having to do for yourself?"

Oh, boy! If she knew the Davidows she wouldn't be asking that question. If she had to get back and fix salads (keeping my wrist below the table, I checked my watch) in a half-hour, she wouldn't ask. I nodded. "Yes."

Mrs. Louderback looked honestly concerned

and I was fearful she might have stumbled on one of those bad-news interpretations she always kept to herself. Like death. I shivered in a rash of goose pimples. No, I decided, that really wasn't it; it wasn't that she didn't want to scare me with what she'd seen in the cards. It was more a look of confusion. She really seemed to be overcome by some force.

This wasn't any seance (she'd made clear), but she certainly seemed to be gripped by something. She was silent for a long time. Her eyes, looking over my shoulder, weren't focusing on anything but empty air, yet she seemed to be *seeing* or *hearing*. She told people she wasn't a medium, but I was beginning to wonder. Maybe she did have the power to invade the spirit world and didn't even know it. That could be tough on a person. I turned around just to cast a glance behind me. Of course, I didn't believe in spirits and so forth, but it never hurt to check. Over the sink was a window, and it was as if on the other side of the clear glass she'd seen a face or a figure or something; yet the clear glass, one pane burnished by sunlight, was empty of anything but the day. She made a sudden gesture with her hand as if to shut something out, or wipe it away.

But now she gave herself a little shake and went on. "This means hardship"—and she placed one finger on the orphans-in-the-storm card. I could have guessed that. "But it means that there are going to be things to overcome to get where you want to go. It won't be easy, but you'll be much, much better off for its not being. You'll come to a state of greater clarity. You'll learn a lot from things getting in your way, obstacles to overcome. You'll be better off than someone who gets whatever she wants, and gets it without half trying."

(I wondered if Ree-Jane had just been here.)

She was looking at me closely. "You're very resolute."

"Resolute." Did that mean the same thing as "resolved"? I didn't want to ask.

But then she explained. "You never give up."

"Oh. Well, people tell me I'm really stubborn." "People" being Mrs. Davidow, Ree-Jane, Vera, my mother.

She actually seemed irritated by these "people." "*No*, you aren't! That's not what the card means at all. Not giving up is *not* the same as 'stubborn,' so whoever tells you that better go think again."

I was enormously pleased by this, by her being so sure I wasn't just "stubborn." Did I never give up? I couldn't think clearly of situations where I might have given up or not. But what about the Girl? It was true I wasn't giving up on *her*. "Resolute." I kind of squared my shoulders. I was glad I'd come.

But before Mrs. Louderback could start in on the Hanged Man—who looked really interesting— I saw I only had fifteen minutes to get back to the hotel. I told her I'd have to be leaving, thanked her, and took the two dollars out of my pocket and handed them across to her. She smiled and took one of the bills. "We didn't do the whole reading, and I always do an hour. One dollar's plenty."

It was hard for me to believe Mrs. Louderback would do this for a whole hour, because it was clearly tough on her. I asked her about that.

"Oh, not always, no. Most people's not got an hour's worth of gumption in them. They're boring. You're not. You're not one speck boring. Anyone says you are's a damned fool!"

"I'm not?" These words were music to my ears.

She shook her head slowly, determinedly, eyes shut.

Again, I shoved the second dollar towards her, and she cocked her head. "I told you, one's plenty."

"No, it isn't. And I'm *resolute*."

Mrs. Louderback put her head back, laughed, and pounded on the table. It was like I'd said the funniest thing she'd ever heard. "Okay, thank you very much."

I picked up my cornstarch and we walked to the door. She told me she hoped I'd be back for the rest of my reading, and I said I would.

The woman who'd let me in had disappeared. I wondered if things did that around here.

Walking along under leafy branches that splashed coin-shadows on the pavement, I suddenly realized that Mrs. Louderback hadn't once treated me like a child to be talked down to. It was as if I had as much right to ask my one question as anyone in Spirit Lake or La Porte. Mrs. Louderback then would be grouped with Maud and Miss Flyte and Miss Flagler, with

Dr. McComb and Mr. Root and the Woods. And the Sheriff, of course, but he made up a group of his own.

I thought again about my question. I stopped there on the walk with the leaves over my head shivering a little in the light wind and wondered if that was the real reason, not wanting to tell what Jude Stemple had made me promise I wouldn't. Refusing to betray a promise *sounded* good. It even sounded noble. Prissy-good, more like. It was the sort of reason you'd come up with to cover up the real reasons that you didn't want to admit. Or, to do myself justice (something I did far more often than being "cruelly honest"), maybe it was correct to say it was part of the reason, but not all of it. I walked on slowly, then stopped again outside Marge's cottage, for I had this cloudy notion—it was very dim— that the real reason I didn't tell anyone what Jude Stemple had said, or what Ulub had said about the Devereaus, and especially about the Girl, was . . .

I shook my head and chewed my lip, looking towards Marge's windows with the sun on them making them shine as if she'd pulled down blinds of radiant light. The reason I didn't tell anybody what I'd seen or heard was that I didn't really *want* anyone to know. Was all of this like having a huge secret? If you give away a secret, even if it's your own to give away as you like, would it rob the secret of its power? Or should I say, its magic? So I wouldn't want to tell anyone, not even the Sheriff—

*Especially* the Sheriff, I should say. He was

very smart. He'd investigate. He'd track down the Queens behind their yellow shutters. He could even find *Her*.

She would be in peril.

That sounded like a fancy way of saying it, but I felt it was true, though, again, I wasn't sure why. I felt she should be allowed to go on looking for whatever she was looking for.

## THIRTY-SIX

Even when I was doing the salads, I could not keep my mind from going back and forth, back and forth, between telling and not telling. Keeping silent I had always thought a good rule of thumb, but I hardly ever practiced it. I guess I was too much of a busy-body. I know *not* keeping silent was what got me in hot water with Lola Davidow. I could not help returning her tongue lashings with one or two of my own, which sent her into a whirlwind of rage.

But keeping this particular silence was different. Although I was running them together in my mind— Fern Queen and the Girl—so that telling about one meant telling about the other, I had to admit that they weren't necessarily connected. Not *necessarily*. But I knew they were. They didn't have to be in the telling. If that was so, then I was left with a much lesser problem: how to tell the Sheriff about the Queen house and about the dead woman and her relationship to the Cold Flat Junction Queens—how to do this *without* telling him about Jude Stemple saying it.

I stared down at the rows of salads—sliced tomatoes tonight—and tried to bring back exactly what Jude Stemple had said. *Exactly* what. I frowned. This could be the way to a solution. I pictured us both back there, me and Jude Stemple, back in Flyback

Hollow, listening. I would change from being back in the Hollow to being here in the kitchen, studying the salads and debating whether to put a slice of black olive atop the crumbled egg or to finish the salad off with some chopped parsley.

Walter had stopped his broom to look at the salads and kind of nod. Then he started sweeping again, unnecessary sweeping, since the floor was already as clean as a whistle, but since there were no dishes yet to wash, my mother had told him to sweep. Neither my mother nor Lola Davidow could stand it if Walter wasn't working. It was like the end of everything, like their entire livelihood was being pulled out from under them, if Walter ever stopped to rest. It made me really mad.

I smiled at Walter and sprinkled one salad with parsley. I looked at another on which I'd put a slice of black olive on top of the crumbled egg. I was looking from one to the other when Vera turned up behind me like a black specter. Her high, thin voice made me jump. Walter jumped too, I noticed (and it was hard to make Walter react). Vera was holding her empty aluminum tray up on the tips of her fingers, trying, I guess, to make the point that all she had was an empty tray and why weren't the salads fixed? She wanted to know, what did I think I was doing, putting that crumbled egg on them, anyway? I thought for a moment and then calmly told her that I'd read this whole article in an old *Ladies' Home Journal* saying that hard-boiled egg, especially mixed with either olives or parsley, was wonderful for clearing out impurities of the blood. I added that Harold (he was her husband) should probably try it. I knew it irritated the life out of Vera for me to refer to Harold by his first name, which is why I always did that. It also irritated her that everybody knew Harold was just an old geezer of an alcoholic and a hypochondriac to boot, not really sick at all, except for whatever "impurities" got into his blood by way of Wild Turkey, and that he was not really sick at all. So while Vera had to go out and wait tables, Harold just stayed in bed complaining to the four walls. It was my guess he probably jumped out of bed and made straight for the Wild Turkey the minute Vera left.

Vera was trying to think up a good retort to this *Ladies' Home Journal* article, but she couldn't, so she settled for frosty looks and starchy movements as she clattered six salads onto her tray.

Walter was now leaning on his broom and laughing his weird laugh, like someone just rescued from smoke and fire or from near-drowning, sucking air into his lungs and letting it out in a *har-har-har* way. Walter never said anything mean about anyone, but you could tell he despised Vera, and told me he thought my salads were "purty," and I rewarded him by asking which decoration he liked, olive or parsley. "Both," he said, so I sprinkled paprika on one and lay the olive on top of it. I agreed with him that the colors looked good.

*     *     *

After dinner and after dark, I was down in the Pink Elephant, still trying to call up just what Jude Stemple had made me promise. I thought hard. Had Jude said, "Don't tell anybody about Fern Queen," or had he said, "Don't tell anybody *I told you* about Fern Queen"? Those were two entirely different things. I *thought* it was the second, but I wasn't sure. I tried to work it out logically: it wouldn't really make any difference to Jude if someone told the authorities that the dead woman was Fern Queen, would it? And someone must have finally reported the missing woman, or the Sheriff wouldn't have gone hightailing it to Cold Flat Junction. Wasn't what worried Jude that he'd be dragged into it? I fussed with the collection in my Whitman's box as I thought this over. Surely, the important thing was to understand the *intent* of what a person said, rather than just his words. Being perfectly honest, I had to admit that Jude Stemple's intent was for me to keep my mouth shut. Well, I didn't see how I could. But I wondered why, if he felt so free to say that in public, he'd wanted me to promise not to tell where I heard it. It must be that he'd told me a lot of other stuff, too. All that about the Queens.

I yawned. I doubled my fists, one atop the other, and leaned my chin on them. My eyelids kept shutting, and I must have slept just for a moment until a little snore jerked me awake. My chin was still on my balled-up fists, but I raised my eyes to look over at my rented library picture of the bridge across a pond full of lovely flowers. I told myself that it was

like Spirit Lake, but of course it wasn't. It didn't
look haunted.


*Difficulties. Pain. Blame.* Mentally, I pictured the
Hanged Man and the orphans-in-the-storm card. And
I decided these cards don't tell your future at all; I
think they tell you What Is, or maybe I should say,
What You Are. They do not tell you what to do.
They do not tell you where Aurora Paradise has her
money buried, or where Lola Davidow has the crate
of whisky hid. They do not tell you if Ree-Jane will
die a miserable death, though you can hope so.

    *Difficulties. Pain. Blame.*

    But I was resolute, Mrs. Louderback had said.

    Resolute. I wouldn't give up. That was a com-
forting thought, even if I wasn't getting any good
advice from those cards of hers. But then I thought:
there would be no reason to be resolute if all you
had to do was ask the cards for advice, and they
would give it. Maybe I only *thought* I wanted help
or advice in making up my mind. Probably, when it
came down to it, I didn't want advice at all. For I
always hated being told what to do, even by orphans
or the Hanged Man.

    Life was hard, but I was resolute.

## THIRTY-SEVEN

The next morning I called Axel's Taxis and was told that Axel himself might be coming out my way to deliver some goods and that if he did, he'd pick me up. I knew of course that Axel would do no such thing and that it would be Delbert driving. When the dispatcher asked me where I wanted to be dropped off, I told her the courthouse. I had made up my mind.

I had decided that it really wasn't right to keep information "vital to the investigation" (which was the way I'd heard such things described) to myself. Although I knew the Sheriff had gone to Cold Flat Junction two days before, and I bet it was about the dead woman, there was still no telling whether it was the Queens who called the police, or someone else, who didn't know much, maybe even the First Union Tabernacle preacher. So it would certainly save the Sheriff time if I were to tell him what I'd learned from what Jude Stemple had said.

I was not bound to tell the Sheriff about the Girl, though. That would save me a lot of explaining about my first visit to Cold Flat, and going with the Woods to the Devereau house. There was no earthly reason to drag in Mr. Root and the Wood boys and take the chance that somebody in the Sheriff's office would come out here and grill them. It would proba-

bly be Donny throwing his weight around and pretending they were all suspicious characters for going
over to the Devereau place. He'd pretty much try
and leave me out of it, though, even though I was
the ringleader, because the Sheriff would not take
kindly to Donny's treating a child like a possible
criminal, especially me. There were advantages to
being a child. The police didn't think you had anything to do with a murder case, and also you could
get into the Orion for half-price.

I ordered the taxi for ten a.m., which would
allow me time to wait on anyone coming in late for
breakfast. Breakfast is supposed to be from seven-
thirty to nine, but my mother will still cook if some
guest wants to be served. This annoys me. Dinner
is the same way, but Vera and Anna Paugh go home
around nine p.m. If guests show up for a room and
want a late dinner, my mother obliges, which means
I have to oblige too, as there isn't anyone else to
wait tables. Except Ree-Jane, and God forbid anyone
would have the nerve to ask *her* to oblige.

So this morning would have to be the one morning Miss Bertha decided to be late for her breakfast.
You could have set a clock by her and Mrs. Fulbright,
usually. Still, "late" for them was just a little after
nine, and that was all right; not even Miss Bertha
could take more than a half-hour or forty-five minutes
to eat her breakfast and complain.

Which, of course, she did. The orange juice was
watery, the corn cakes soaked up too much syrup,
the sausage wasn't spicy enough. This really irritated

me, for usually she squawked about just the opposite: my mother put much too much pepper and spice in things. It was all so ridiculous; they were the same corn cakes and sausage as she'd always had, year after year. Mrs. Fulbright told her to stop making trouble for people, but Miss Bertha just sat rigid, her arms lapped around her like a little gray mummy, shaking her head. I took the plate she'd pushed away back to the kitchen and banged it down on the serving counter. My mother said just to send her in another plate of cakes and sausage and tell her they were made specially. There were sausage patties sizzling on the black griddle, sending up gray threads of smoke. My mother was taking off her apron, unwinding the ties, which she usually wrapped twice around her waist, the apron being so big. She told me she had to go out to the front desk and talk with Mrs. Davidow about the linen delivery and that in two minutes I was to turn the patties over and cook them on the other side. I could grease the other griddle and use the batter in the bowl. "You know how," she said. "Just take her in fresh cakes and she'll think I made them especially, the old fool." Then she strode off through the side screen door and along the little wooden walk towards the office.

I was pleased to cook the breakfast; I liked being put in charge. While the sausage grease popped, I rooted in the icebox for the can of green chilies I knew was there, and which my mother used sparingly in a hot sauce for some Italian dish. I removed one to the chopping board, took the big knife from an

earthenware bowl and chopped the chili in tiny bits.
I pressed some of these into two sausage patties
before turning them over. Humming away, I carried
the batter bowl to the griddle and spooned out the
corn cakes. The batter was thick and grainy. My
mother's corn cakes would have been my favorite if
it hadn't been for those buckwheat cakes. Or the
waffles onto which she would drizzle fresh fruit
syrup.

The sausage was done and when the corn cakes
bubbled up I quickly turned them over with a spatula
and let them cook just a minute on the other side. I
reached down a plate from the ledge above the stove
where they sat warming and slid the cakes onto the
plate with two patties. The rest of the patties I carefully lined up on a paper towel to drain off the grease,
as my mother always did.

Then I carried Miss Bertha's plate into the dining room. It was nine-thirty-five by now.

Miss Bertha didn't hang around the dining room
long after she got a mouthful of that sausage, which
was fine by me, for my taxi would be arriving in
twenty minutes or so. I was careful to remove the
plate to where Walter was slowly wiping a platter
and scraped the sausage into the garbage. I did this
in case anyone decided to investigate. Walter was
grinning, for he knew something was going on. Who
wouldn't, with Miss Bertha yelling someone was
trying to kill her? I told Walter I'd tell him all about
it when I got back from town, but right now I was
in a big hurry, and also, I could hear my mother

walking through the dining room. She had an unmistakable way of walking, and I recognized her footstep. I quickly told Walter I'd appreciate it if he didn't happen to mention I cleaned Miss Bertha's plate. That just made him grin more, his flat smile nearly splitting his face in two. Walter just loved to be in on a secret.

My mother marched into the kitchen saying that Miss Bertha was throwing a fit, the old fool, because the sausage was poisoned. She had a way of banging pots and pans around when she was annoyed, the way an artist would probably throw his brushes against the wall if he didn't like the way his picture was going. Then she picked up one of the remaining sausage patties from the paper towel and bit off a piece.

"It tastes perfectly all right to me; it tastes exactly the same as yesterday's. Here—" She broke another patty in two, walked over to the dishwasher, and handed me and Walter the halves. "Doesn't it taste the same?"

We both chewed and considered. I said, "Of course it does."

Walter said, "Uh-huh, same as always. Real good."

My mother threw up her arms. "If all three of us think so, then she's obviously loony."

My mother was very democratic that way.

"And she says she's not going to eat *one more meal* in this place. Which should be good news for *you*." She smiled at me. "You won't have to wait tables at lunch."

A bonus! All I'd wanted was to get my ten o'clock taxi. I never expected a bonus.

Then Walter said, giving us his slow smile, "I guess she thinks only *her* patties was poisoned." He gave his sucked-in laugh. I glared at him. "Too bad I went and throwed the rest of her breakfast away," he said, winking at me. "The old fool."

As I climbed into the cab, Delbert squinted his eyes, as if that would help him hear better. He asked me what in tarnation people was yelling about in the hotel and I said I hadn't the least idea and I'd like to go to the courthouse, please. I ignored his comment about having taken me there just a couple of days ago and was I in any trouble? He thought this was hysterical.

Just to see what the answer would be, I asked him what happened to Axel. Didn't he have things to deliver somewhere in Spirit Lake? "Oh, Axel done that," he said. "Early on this morning. He would of come got you, only he had an emergency call from up there at Buena Vista."

I wasn't really interested in any emergency the people who owned Buena Vista might have; they were all falling down drunk most of the time and having to be taken to the hospital. As Delbert talked on, I looked out of my window at the open field where some of the older La Porte kids came to race their ancient, beat-up cars. Bronze in the sharp sunlight, the dirt showed old slicks of oil and grease in between the puffballs and straggling black-eyed Susans that managed to sprout where there was grass left to do it. It made me mad to think that whole field would be covered with wildflowers and grass if it weren't for the boys with their ugly shrieking cars. I also saw tire-sized patches of grape hyacinths and I wondered if Nature wasn't stronger than I gave it credit for being. I remembered the woods around the lake, the way the underbrush, the stout vines, and the thick-trunked trees had taken over the road where a person used to be able to drive a car, and the flat paths that had once been a way through. The Devereau house, which had once seemed to be the very center of that side of Spirit Lake, looked as if in a few years' time it might be invisible to the eye, where the heavy-leaved branches would overlap and cover it like dark green water, and it would sink.

I was thinking these thoughts all the way into town, with an added thought for God as we passed St. Michael's on the right. I was jolted out of my thoughts when the taxi pulled up to the side of the courthouse, and Delbert told me, Here you are! as if it was pretty clever of him to know where it was. I got out and paid him the fare, plus a quarter tip, which pleased him. Then I ran on into the building. Having made this decision, I could hardly wait to get everything off my chest.

\*   \*   \*

"Sam ain't here." Donny was sitting behind the Sheriff's desk again, sounding pleased to be delivering disappointing news.

"Where'd he go?"

He looked at me for a long while, making up something even more frustrating to tell me, then said, "Police business." He leaned way back in the swivel chair and clasped his hands behind his head, rocking slightly, just to let me know he had taken over.

"I've got to talk to him. It's important."

"Well, talk to me. I'm in charge till he gets back." His smile was so insincere it was rancid, like cold grease.

I looked as if I was considering telling him, which of course I wasn't. "I guess I can wait." I walked back to a short row of hard chairs and sat. I knew he hated me watching, especially as he hadn't anything important to do. He would have liked me looking and listening if he'd been on the phone with the mayor or even the governor, or if he'd been telling off somebody about a violation. Except for Donny and me, the place was empty; there wasn't even the secretary or the file clerk for him to pretend to be busy with. After a while of me staring and him picking up and putting down sheets of paper and pink memo slips, I guess he couldn't stand it any longer, me being there and seeing he really didn't have much authority over anything.

"Sam's over to Cold Flat. Probably be gone all afternoon."

I caught my breath, but outwardly appeared

cool. "He was just there a couple of days ago," I said, adding, "So were you." It would irritate Donny to pieces that I knew this. It did. He glared at me. I slid off the chair said goodbye and thank you and left.

Sometimes when I want to think I go into the Candlewick, just to browse around and look at Miss Flyte's "effects." They are often wonderful, and she likes having people come in, even if they aren't the buying type. That is definitely me.

The sun never seems to make a direct hit on Miss Flagler's plate glass; it only manages to paint a seam or a ruffle along the side or the bottom edge. This is because Miss Flyte lowers a narrow awning over the window which cuts the light partially off from both shops.

Inside, it is shadowy and, with the lighted candles, almost spooky. It would be a fire hazard to have a lot of candles burning, so these are either protected by glass globes or wall sconces or otherwise surrounded by something which is not flammable. She likes to place candles between facing mirrors to give the effect of wavering flames, reflected endlessly; or to surround them with a three-sided mirror and get something of the same effect, this time tripled.

Miss Flyte was not there today, so Bonnie, the stock girl and general helper, was behind the register. She was looking at a magazine, wetting her finger and slowly turning pages as if it was one of those

ancient manuscripts with jewel-like decorations. I
forget what they are called. She didn't pay any attention to me (people don't like kids in shops) until I
asked her where Miss Flyte was. She answered without even looking up that she was at Miss Flagler's.

I did not really need to see Miss Flyte for anything in particular; it was just nice to know if she
was as usual and not sick or anything. I walked
around the shop, enjoying it as I always do, except
for Bonnie being there. It's hard being in the presence
of someone who wishes you'd go away. It's as if
the other person could reach out a dark hand and
take the shine off your pleasure, as the narrow awning
outside stops the light from falling on that strip of
visored pavement.

Bonnie was still reading her movie magazine
and fingering a strand of lifeless hair and paying no
attention to me. I moved towards the smoky-dark
rear of the shop, where Miss Flyte had arranged some
very tall, thin candles and a couple of chunkier ones
on a mirror half-surrounded by polished tin with a
sort of roof of some darker metal. It looked almost
like a miniature amphitheater, such as the one in
Spirit Lake. Now, on the mirror she had placed tiny
metal figures, smaller than toy soldiers; these were
skaters. Men in scarves, women in bonnets and long
full skirts, boys in caps, and little girls with muffs.
An old-time skating scene. But what was the biggest
surprise was the way the different-sized candles
made their "effects." The high, thin ones pointed

their lighted wicks up to the dark roof and made stars; the chunkier candle had a thicker wick and made a wavery, uncertain moon; and the ropy wick of a very low candle must have been spliced and feathered out, for the threads gave off tiny flames that sometimes blended, sometimes separated, and looked for all the world like a campfire.

Imagine going to all of this trouble! I was awestruck. Yet, given Miss Flyte's reputation, I shouldn't have been surprised.

The gently flickering lights almost hypnotized me, just as the reflection of the water on the ceiling in Mary-Evelyn's room had done. It was equally hard to explain. It was as if a lot of things of no importance that were cluttering up my mind began to burn away like bits of dark ash lifting from burning newspaper, floating up and off. Things like how annoying Miss Bertha was, or Vera's waiting on only the best customers, or even Mrs. Davidow's temper tantrums. What was left was the small but still burning core, and it was the core that was important, and all else was ashes and cinders and I was not even to waste a thought on it. My state of mind was strange; it was bright and empty like a room full of light. I watched this lighted-up space to see what would come into it. I wasn't surprised when it turned out to be the Girl, just standing there looking at me, first as near as she'd been on the station platform, then as far away as the other side of the lake. My mind felt very clear, as if everything had been swept away so that she could be free to speak. Of course she didn't. Clear as my mind was, it couldn't force words from her.

She faded, and the next thing to occupy that space was Jude Stemple and me, sitting on his porch in Flyback Hollow as we'd sat that day when he told me about the Queens.

*Fern never had no children.*

I looked into the fluttering candlewicks and frowned.

*Fern never had no children.*

The explanation hit me, the answer kind of slammed me in the stomach because it was so simple: How did Jude Stemple *know*?

I don't mean he was lying, for I suspect he really thought he knew; but Fern Queen could have gone off somewhere and had a whole litter of kids, for all he knew. Hadn't he said how Fern "went off" and then'd come back and after a while just go off again?

This was a lesson to me to believe in the evidence of my own senses, and not just what other people said. Mr. Stemple had sounded so positive, but he'd never seen the Girl, and I had.

I was surprised to find it was almost noon when I left the Candlewick; I'd been looking at Miss Flyte's "effects" for over an hour. I really must have been in a kind of trance with these thoughts of Fern Queen and the Girl. *Her* girl, I thought, again with a little shocked feeling.

I was thinking all of this while walking from the Candlewick to the Rainbow, the next street away, past the Orion and Souder's. I was so lost in these thoughts I guess I snubbed Helene Baum, for I turned when I heard her call my name from Souder's doorway, where she was just going in or coming out. Was I getting so stuck-up I no longer spoke to people? That's what she called out, right down the street, in case anybody else wanted to wonder if I was getting stuck-up too.

I didn't care.

It was pretty clear the Sheriff knew, now, about the missing Fern Queen, and that it was the missing Fern Queen who'd been shot and left to lie in Mirror Pond.

I stood staring for a minute or two into the Rainbow's plate glass window. I sighed with a kind of contentment despite my new knowledge. For it was lunchtime, and I wasn't at the Hotel Paradise listening to Miss Bertha complain. Standing there, I had a couple of sharp stomach spasms. I wondered if I felt guilty about the sausage patties. No, it was because I was thinking about the chili and oyster crackers that I could see Charlene setting in front of the Woods.

Maud was behind the counter making a milk shake when I walked in. She waved and smiled. Shirl greeted me with a grunt, as always. She was positioning lemon meringue pie in the display case.

Both Ulub and Ubub said their version of hello

and acted excited that I was there. Ulub got off his stool and took the one next to it, and it was clear they wanted me to sit down between them. Most of the people at the counter were turning to look at who or what had got the Wood boys talking. Well, kind of talking. That I could excite anyone by my mere presence made me feel like a celebrity as I calmly took the stool offered me and asked Charlene for a cherry Coke. But Maud was already pumping the syrup into a large Coke glass.

"Good Lord," she said, setting the glass in front of me. "You out of stir?"

I was surprised when Ubub heaved with laughter at that. The Woods weren't dumb. It's too bad other people didn't realize it. I laughed along and told her, "There wasn't anyone there for lunch." I sipped my Coke, glad to be a celebrity for once in my life.

"Well, come on back and sit with me. The cook just made a fresh pot of chili."

Chili was better when it wasn't just cooked, better after it had sat for a day to blend the seasonings. Not many people seemed to understand that. Actually, I wasn't really so hungry; it must have been all of that thinking I'd done. Maybe I had too much on my mind for chili. "Not right now," I said. "Maybe later."

Politely, I waited for another five minutes for Ulub and Ubub to finish their own chili, since I didn't want them to think I was deserting them for something better. When they'd wiped their paper napkins across their mouths and balled them up, I told them I'd be seeing them soon. Both of them smiled big smiles and nodded.

Maud sat down beside me and said, "You must be sick as a dog, turning down chili. Or is your mother making something special for lunch?"

"It's always special," I said, seriously.

Maud looked at me for some moments, smiling, but in an odd, hurt kind of way. "I bet Chad never says that about *my* cooking." She lit a cigarette.

I didn't see Chad much around La Porte because he was usually away in school. And he spent some of the vacations with his father. I had always felt there was something very painful in all of this for Maud, especially being away from Chad, just as there was something painful about the Sheriff and his wife, Florence.

"Donny was saying the Sheriff went to Cold Flat Junction." I wondered if he'd told Maud anything.

"I believe he found out who she was," Maud answered.

"The dead woman?"

She blew a thin stream of smoke sideways so as not to get it in my face. " 'Day-ed'? When'd you start talking like that? Sounds like *you've* been hanging around in Cold Flat Junction. 'Day-ed.' "

"Who is she?"

"He didn't say. Maybe because he wasn't certain, or because he'd have to tell the family first."

I was glad that now I didn't have to worry about actually identifying Fern Queen for the Sheriff. Now I wanted to devote my thinking time to how to get back to Cold Flat Junction and into that yellow-shuttered house.

# THIRTY-EIGHT

It did not surprise me that Miss Bertha was the reason I missed the train to Cold Flat Junction the next day. When her spaghetti and meatballs were served (this being the only dish on the lunchtime menu), she started in. First she told Mrs. Fulbright the meatballs were really that leftover poisoned sausage; then she raised her voice even more and told me; then she actually wrenched her way out of her chair and, bent over her cane, went to the door of the kitchen and shouted the news at my mother.

Finally, everybody got her settled down again, but by then it was after one and I would never be able to get down to the Spirit Lake station. I suppose I would have been more disappointed if I had worked out a plan. Only I hadn't. I was stumped. Nothing I thought of, like knocking on the Queens' door and saying I was collecting for the County Cripples, was very convincing. And it would have to be something that would get the Queens talking about the Devereaus and about Ben Queen, too.

But my mother's spaghetti and meatballs did a lot by way of cheering me up, and after I'd eaten it and cleaned up Miss Bertha's table (where she'd hidden her meatballs in the sugar bowl), I felt better and decided to walk up to Britten's. Not only had the spaghetti made me feel better, it had started my brain humming again, and I had an idea about how to get to Cold Flat Junction.

Mr. Root was sitting on the bench, but Ulub and Ubub weren't there. I was disappointed. I asked Mr. Root if he'd seen them, and he said no, not that day.

"I was hoping we could all go to Cold Flat Junction. They've got their trucks."

"Yeah, they do. What you want to go there for?"

I didn't want to tell him all I wanted was a ride from somebody, so I said it had to do with the Devereaus and I needed them to help out. I guess that sounded pretty mysterious, as he just kept looking at me and I knew he was trying to work this out.

Glumly, I had listened when the train went through; glumly, I sat there sucking on my cheek, thinking.

And then a miraculous thing happened. Father Freeman probably wouldn't have called it a miracle, especially since it came from the First Union Tabernacle church. It was the bus. The bus from Cold Flat that came twice a week and then went back to Cold Flat.

While my plan was forming, it let off one person and then drove on. But I knew it made another stop— over there at the camp meeting ground just across from Greg's. I'd have plenty of time to get over there.

"Mr. Root, I'll see you later. I'm going over to get the bus."

"Well, but I don't think they let you on, you're not one of theirs."

But I was nearly flying down the bank to the highway while he was still talking. I heard him call out if he saw the Woods he'd tell 'em I was needing 'em.

In the hubbub of people leaving the big prayer meeting, no one paid a bit of attention to me going into the tent. There were a lot of kids running around (and getting smacked up the side of their heads for it). I just plucked up an extra prayer book—or whatever the little black book was that was lying on a folding chair—and then went out and stood with the others waiting for the bus. I'd say there were twenty-five or thirty-five standing around, talking among themselves. Occasionally one or another glanced at me, but not at all in a suspicious way, merely indifferent to me, or, from the ones who'd taken their religious training seriously, looking friendly and giving me a smile or two.

I looked holy and listened closely to whatever talk I could and decided Maud was right, for they did have a way of saying words like "say-ed" for "said" and even said "tooken" when they meant "took." Unless they did mean "took *and*."

". . . an' I done tol' her my mama's vis-ut-un . . ."

"Visiting" was pronounced as if the person drew in her breath and sucked in the second syllable with it, so it kind of got stuck in the back of her throat.

I tried it out, "vis-ut-un," kind of like a little hiccup. Or swallowing the second syllable.

I'd been concentrating so hard on this interesting way of talking that I barely registered the bus was standing there and I was at the door to it. I stepped up to where the lady driver was.

"Why, hullo, hon, I ain't seen you before," she said. "You never come over on the bus, did you?"

I cleared my throat and said, "No, ma'am, I never did." I kept my voice kind of high and singsongy. Before she could ask—and I knew she would—I said, "My name's Rae Jane and I'm cousin to the Queens. You know them?"

"Course I do. What—"

People were jostling to get around me, so I tried to bunch myself back where I wasn't in their way. I said, "Well, it ain't the Queens I'm vis-ut-un, it's folks live in Flyback Holler."

The driver was saying hello, hello, to people who boarded and not giving me her full attention, which was fine with me. I just kept on talking. "Like I said, I'm vis-ut-un the Stemples. They live in Flyback Hol-*ler*." For I wanted to make sure she caught the way I said that.

"Um-hmm. Do your folks live . . . where?"

"Oh, my mama and my daddy's day-ed." I looked down at my shoes. A lady who'd just said hello to the driver heard me and glanced at me with a sympathetic shake of her head before she passed on to claim a seat.

The driver patted my arm. "Now, honey, never

you mind, you just take yerself back to the back there and have a nice ride."

"Thank you. Most kindly." I tried not to skip to the back of the bus.

Well, about five miles out of town they started singing "I Once Was Lost in Sin," singing and clapping, and I, of course, sang along with them, although the only version I knew was Brownmiller's "I Once Was Lost in Gin," dedicated to Lola Davidow, so I had to be careful. Mill and Will were always going to the camp meetings to listen to the hymns so they could go back to the Hotel Paradise and Brownmiller would make up new words. It was a good rainy-day pastime for them when they weren't otherwise engaged. I was grateful they'd done it, too, for that made the hymns familiar to me. At least the music was. Between the two of them, Will and Mill, it was like a single wildfire imagination that, once a twig of it was lit, would spread and suddenly burn the whole place down. I liked to warm myself in it, but I could never compete and always got the worst roles in their plays. They only let me play pigs and dogs and Igor—things that weren't supposed to speak properly.

The singing in the bus ebbed and flowed around me as we bumped along. I happened to look out the back window where a spewed-up cloud of dust made me think I surely must be seeing a mirage. For in its cloud I could swear I saw a pickup truck. It was.

I went back past the last row of seats to stare out of the window and saw one of the Wood boys' trucks just down the road. I squinted through the dust cloud and was able to see a license plate with ULB on it jigging up and down. Oh, good grief, Ulub was following the bus. With the sun making a silver skin across the windshield I couldn't tell if it was just Ulub ... and then I saw behind that another dust cloud and there was UBB.

I slumped down in my seat, really irritated that I'd gone to so much trouble just to get a ride on this bus, and then here they came when I didn't need them. But I had, after all, told Mr. Root (and I bet he was with them, too) that I wanted a ride, and so they thought they were doing the right thing. Probably, they thought they were protecting me, too, watching over me. That anybody would want to protect me was a totally new idea, and I guess I felt grateful.

But what was I to do with them once we got there?

There was the Windy Run Diner. Ulub and Ubub loved the Rainbow, so I supposed they wouldn't mind having coffee in the Windy Run. I recalled seeing big swirls of sweet rolls with butter icing on one of those domed cake plates on the counter. They'd love those.

What about Mr. Root? Probably he wouldn't want to just sit—

And I sat up straight all of a sudden, as if the bus had hit a rut. I recalled that talk I'd had with

Mr. Root on the bench outside Britten's. He'd known a Queen, a woman named Sheba. And who was to say that this woman might not be the same as one of them who lived in that yellow-shuttered house? Who was to say she might not be this old friend of Mr. Root's? As the bus bumped off the highway onto the Cold Flat Junction road, I thought about this.

Cold Flat Junction was as empty of people as before. The bus drove along the street that divided the town and turned left into Schoolhouse Road, where I saw the church steeple glaring white as one of my mother's meringues. The two trucks pulled up to a curb a little distance away. As I stepped down from the bus, a few people grinned at me and patted me as if for encouragement, as if one more sinner saved, and I thanked them. Then I cut off towards the pickup trucks, both sitting there belching smoke out of their exhaust pipes. Mr. Root was in Ubub's and they both seemed really excited, as if this were an adventure. I said I'd go get in the cab of Ulub's truck and they could follow us to the Windy Run Diner. Ubub's face split in a big grin the minute I said "diner."

Ulub said something indecipherable as I slammed shut my door and directed him to the diner. He seemed even more pleased than Ubub had. As we drove onto the unpaved road that was Windy Run, Ulub started singing something weird. I really had to admire him for being made so happy by something as unimportant as the prospect of eating in a diner. I sighed and shook my head. I guess I was just too used to Ree-Jane wanting to be the Countess of Kent.

Louise Snell was cutting up with the two men who looked like truck drivers, but I still didn't see any trucks out there, so maybe they lived in Cold Flat. It made me nervous going in there again, for Jude Stemple could well have mentioned that I'd said I knew her daughter, but when she saw me she came right over and, with a big smile, said, "Well, hello."

"Is this your dad?" She was wiping down the counter in front of us and nodding towards Mr. Root. I thought he looked kind of old to be my dad, but maybe not. I explained that these people were my friends from La Porte.

Mr. Root seemed pleased to have been mistaken for my father and beamed as he pulled a menu out from between sugar shaker and napkin holder. Ulub and Ubub did the same, though I wondered if I should order for them, since they always were used to Maud just setting things in front of them. I told them the sweet rolls here were really good and Louise nodded hard.

"Homemade," she said.

They looked at each other and nodded.

"You want coffee, I expect," I said helpfully.

They nodded again.

Then I said to Mr. Root, after I got my Coke, that maybe the Queen he knew a long time ago might be one of the ones living here in Cold Flat. Oh, he doubted it, he said, and I said, well, but maybe. We went back and forth like this for a minute or two until I got him thinking and talking about how sad it was, time passing, and old friends being missed, and so forth, until Mr. Root was getting pretty sad. And to top it off, I said that these Queens might be related to the dead woman and might have something to do with Mary-Evelyn. Well, that convinced him, although I could tell he was pretty shy about just walking up to what might be a stranger's door and announcing himself.

I insisted on paying, but Mr. Root told me my money was no good today, and we left the Woods happily munching their sweet rolls and said we'd be back in no time, there was someone Mr. Root wanted to visit.

He was still worried that either these weren't the right Queens or no one would remember him, or other reasons for not doing this, as we walked out of the Windy Run Diner and down its few steps.

So I told him I'd do the talking. Which, of course, I didn't intend to, as *I* wasn't Sheba Queen's old friend.

## THIRTY-NINE

Mr. Root said it had been over ten years since he'd been to Cold Flat Junction, close as it was to Spirit Lake. But he remembered a lot of things as we walked along and seemed pleased at the remembrances. He said as we passed the general store that Elmer Fry, who'd once owned it, had been tossed in jail for having two wives. Mr. Root thought having two was punishment enough, and did the law have to go and add to Elmer's suffering by giving him a jail sentence?

We passed the schoolhouse, and came to Dubois Road, and I asked him if he knew Jude Stemple. Yes, he did, but not very well. And then he asked me just what was it he was supposed to do at the Queens. I explained that he could just talk with them about anything, but preferably try to get them remembering. Remembering particularly about Rose Devereau.

"You think she knows something about that little girl, that Mary Ellen Devereau?"

"Mary-Evelyn. And my great-aunt Aurora says Ben Queen ran off with Rose Devereau."

"Ah-ha!" he said, mashing his fist into his palm as if he'd just made all these important connections.

And there was the house, kind of springing up in our line of vision, old banana yellow shutters, and paint peeling all around the window moldings and off the porch railings.

Mr. Root paused on the weedy walk and slowly shook his head. "If it's Sheba lives here, well, I ain't seen her in—"

"Fifteen years, I know. Come on." Afraid he was going to get droopy or even start crying, thinking about the old Bathsheba days, I wanted to get him inside.

Well, I needn't have worried about people recalling people, for when the thin, sharp-featured woman dressed in a muslin print came to the screen door, her mouth dropped open and she fairly wailed: "Elijah ROOT! In all my born days—"

She never finished that, but slapped the door open, nearly hitting me in the face and just clapped her rough hands one on each of his shoulders and shook him a little. They were about the same height, but she was more sinewy.

"Sheba, you hardly changed a day!"

That was certainly a big lie, and I stood there and listened to a few more before Mr. Root (whose first name, I'd only just found out, was Elijah) kind of turned me to her and said, "This here's a friend of mine from Spirit Lake said she'd always wanted to come to Cold Flat and never got the chance and would I bring her?"

Grown-ups could lie without turning a hair. But that was all right, for Sheba Queen acted like I was a special friend and invited us in and said she'd get me some of her home-baked molasses cookies and lemonade. I never looked forward to getting food in other people's houses, knowing it just couldn't compare in any way, shape, or form to my mother's.

We stood in the cool dark hall papered with horrible brown-and-green vines or something as she whisked through a parlor calling to a man who'd been hidden by the big wing of his chair that he should take us out to the porch.

Which he did, introducing himself as George Queen, Sheba's husband. He seemed nice enough, but kind of gloomy and sad. He had a soft, uncommanding voice, and we all trooped out to the porch. Mr. Queen and Mr. Root took two rockers, pulling a third over for Mrs. Queen. I sat on the wooden swing so that I was behind them. That was all right with me; I could listen better.

Mrs. Sheba Queen came back with a tray full of lemonade glasses and nearly black cookies that I held out little hope for. All the while she kept telling lies about how young Elijah looked and how he still had that wonderful smile, and so forth. Mr. George Queen apparently had not known Mr. Root back then, so could neither confirm nor deny, but smiled pleasantly and nodded his head. Maybe his gloom and his faraway look was because of Fern Queen's awful death. But Mrs. Sheba Queen was pretty cheerful; it struck me as strange that she was chattering brightly away, as if she didn't know Ben Queen's daughter, her own niece, had been murdered. But she must know. The Sheriff had been to Cold Flat about a missing person twice, and must have told the family of the tragedy.

Mr. Root brought it up. He did this by way of extending his sympathy to them in their hour of grief. I think George Queen was truly grieved, for he had to turn his face away. But she was just putting on. I could tell from the way she made so much of now what she hadn't given a thought to before. I didn't judge her for not being sad or even shocked over Fern's murder. I only judged her for putting on this act.

But none of that was important; Mr. Root had got them—or at least her—talking about the Devereaus. For she started sniffing in that prim way, that self-righteous way some women do when speaking of those they don't like.

And she did not like Rose Devereau.

"We told him he shouldn't ought to marry a Devereau girl. Crazy, every one of them!"

I had stopped creaking the swing and held it at a slant with my feet on the porch floor. Frozen there.

Mr. George Queen spoke: "Now, now. Ben was pretty wild, Sheba, we both know—"

"We know nothing of the kind, George Queen! That's all gossip." Whipping her face around like a rattlesnake, she said to Mr. Root: "Ben just ought not to have married that girl, he'd ought to have kept on with Lou, that's what!" Helpfully, for Mr. Root's sake (they'd forgotten I was here), she added, "Louise Landis. Did you know Louise? Well, she was Ben's girl, and even then when she was no more'n eighteen, nineteen, you could see she had sense. Real growed-up for her age, and she'd've settled Ben right down. But no, he had to have that crazy Rose Devereau."

George said, thoughtfully, "Real beautiful, Rose was. Just as pretty . . ." His voice trailed off.

I was glad he'd defended her. Even though I thought Rose Devereau should never have left Mary-Evelyn like she did.

"And that little sister of hers, one that drownded . . ." Sheba frowned in an effort to recall her.

I sat right up to listen, but her voice fell again to a whisper. I strained to hear.

". . . Can't remember her name . . . Mary something—"

"Mary-Evelyn." I said it out loud without even thinking.

They all looked at me, Bathsheba turning to peer around the back of the tall rocker.

"Well, for heaven's sakes, child, how'd you ever know that? It's been forty, fifty years back." Turning back, she said grimly to the two men, "Less said about *that* business, the better." She gave a quick nod back in my direction, adding, "Little pitchers . . ."

I stuck my tongue out at her back. You could almost see the self-righteousness sprouting like wings from her narrow, muslin-covered shoulder blades.

"Poor, poor Fern," she whined. She had taken

the handkerchief she'd tucked into her sleeve band and was blowing her nose as if she'd been crying. Which she hadn't. There was more low-voiced talk and I heard, "It was no more'n she deserved!"

I sat forward. *What* was? Than *who* deserved? Did she mean Rose? Or Fern?

Mr. Root slid me a glance. "Now, what was that, Sheba? What do you mean, there?"

Oh, bless Mr. Root! I wanted to clap.

"Well, Elijah, you living in Spirit Lake, so near and all, surely you must've heard about Rose. It was all over the papers."

"No, I never did. See, I might not've put two and two together, not knowing all this history you're telling."

George broke in, "Telling wrong, too." He sounded disgusted.

"No I am not. It's just you always sided with Rose Devereau against your own brother!"

"You know that ain't true, Sheba! That ain't the way it was." He slapped the arm of his rocker. "Anyways, siding with Rose was siding with Ben. You just don't want to believe that. Only thing they ever didn't see eye to eye on was Fern."

That set Sheba Queen off again with her "Poor Fern"s.

George Queen just flapped his hand at her in a "be quiet" gesture. "Poor Fern my eye." He said it so soft I wondered if anyone heard it except me.

"You always sided with Rose about what to do about Fern. Rose was against Fern, her own daughter!

She wanted to send her to some institution . . . 'cause
she was too lazy to care for her."

"You don't know nothin' about it, woman."
George sounded angry enough to spit. "Ben Queen
never sided against *any* member of his family,
Sheba." He lowered his head, rested it in his hand,
and shook his head slowly back and forth, as if
he'd rid it of some old misery. "How you can think
either of them was against Fern, I don't know. It's
as well she's dead. Finally." His voice was heavy
with sadness.

Sheba was halfway out of her chair with rage.
"Your very own niece, you say that about your own
*blood*!" And just for something to add to his crime,
she pointed at me. "De-*nounce* your own kin before
strangers!"

For heaven's sakes! I wanted to say. Sheba was
one of those grown-ups who liked to drag kith and
kin and blood ties across your path like dead skunks.
It was to make you sit up and take notice and clap
your hand over your heart. *That's my kin!* I spent a
moment wondering what "kith" was.

But George Queen wasn't having any of that.
"*You* know what trouble that child was! Must've
gone with every man in Cold—"

Now Sheba was all the way up, waggling her
finger at him. "Don't you never say that, George
Queen! Not now she's dead. *Murdered* is what police are saying."

In a low voice, George said, "Chickens come
home to roost."

I should have been working out in my mind what all of this meant instead of sitting there enjoying hearing grown-ups fight. Sheba yelled at him again, but he didn't answer.

I was sitting so far on the edge of the swing I was tilted nearly to the porch floor. But then Sheba's voice dropped to a whisper as she leaned herself nearly right into Mr. Root's face and kind of grabbed at his forearm with clawlike fingers, and then I could hear nothing clearly, only this savage whispering. Then I thought: the scandal. This is the scandal Aurora spoke of. I watched Mr. Root, who was sitting forward too, and could tell he was really concentrating on what she was saying, probably trying to memorize it to tell me later. I was so pleased with myself for bringing him along I could hardly sit still. I never would have got this information by myself, for it was obviously thought to be unfit for childish ears.

But Mr. George Queen apparently wasn't worried about my ears, for he was getting more and more impatient with her telling this story and finally broke right in and said: "It's neither one of them to blame! Neither one. Ben *never* would've done that!"

"Well, I'm glad to hear you defend your poor brother for once," she said primly.

"It was somebody else. I always did say it was somebody else."

"Don't be silly. There wasn't no one else that'd have reason to. She drove him—"

"Oh, stop saying that, woman! You don't know what you're talking about. He loved her and that's a fact. And there was too somebody else could've done it."

"Stop it—just you stop it now!" What he'd just muttered seemed to get her madder than anything. She nearly got out of her chair to say something back, but thought better of it and sat down again. Rocked, rocked as if she wanted to rock all the way to perdition. I wondered if *she* was in that line of women Aurora said stretched "all the way to perdition and back," the ones that had a case on Ben Queen. It sure sounded like it.

In the silence that followed, Mr. Root finally cleared his throat, then, with a kind of exaggerated look at his watch and at me, said, "You best be gettin' back to the Hotel Paradise, I guess."

I could have hit him. Everybody was just getting down to business, and he had to interrupt. But then I felt ashamed of myself, for I saw by my watch it was much later than I'd thought. "Yes, I do have to get back."

The Queens seemed surprised I was still here, for Mr. Queen started a little, and said, kindly, "It's nice seeing you, young lady. I know your mother. Used to take my produce truck over there to the Hotel Paradise. Me and Ben. Years, that's been."

And he looked out over the porch railing and into the sun, casting deep shadows across the dusty road. He must have been remembering better days, days when he was happy with his brother. I concentrated hard, willing Mr. Root to ask, "Where is Ben?"

But he didn't, so I did, taking my roundabout

way. "Well, I'm sure my mother remembers you and your brother, too. Where'd he go? Is he here?" I looked around, trying to sound as if I wouldn't be surprised to see Ben Queen step through the screen door at any moment.

George Queen opened his mouth to answer, but was cut off from doing it by his wife. "Now, never you mind, dear." She gave me a maddening, unmeant smile and him a hard and warning look.

So irritated I could have spit, I said, politely, "Thank you for the lemonade. And cookies." I had bit into one and sunk the rest in my pocket to throw away later on.

Mr. Root rose and hitched up his pants the way men do and shot out his hand to George. He said goodbye to Sheba, who was still steaming from what George had said. But she tried to be polite and told Mr. Root not to wait so long between visits, for heaven's sakes.

We left them standing there on their porch, waving.

As soon as we got out of their sight, I stopped, pulled at Mr. Root's sleeve, and demanded, "Well? What'd they say?"

He was fingering a cigarette from the pack straining his shirt pocket and striking a match to light it. I guessed this was so he could feel important, knowing things I so much wanted to know. But I didn't mind. Really, he deserved to be able to keep me in suspense for a minute. I hopped from one foot to another, unable to contain myself.

"Well ..." He drew in on his cigarette and stared off down Schoolhouse Road. "Well ..." He cleared his throat and finally said, "That's some story." He drew in on his cigarette again.

I gritted my teeth but refrained from saying anything.

"What happened was near twenty years ago. Rose Queen got killed." He paused.

"Killed? How did she get killed?"

"Well, she got murdered. Now ain't that something?"

My mouth dropped. Rose Devereau was *murdered*?

He went on. "Seems they found her one day out there in the backyard down by where they kept the layin' hens, all bruised and bloody. Somebody'd took a knife to the woman ..." He stopped, shook his head.

I took a step back, shaking mine, too. I couldn't find my voice to say anything for a minute, and then I asked. "Well, but who ... ?"

Still shaking his head, as if it'd happened in his own family, he answered, "They say it was Ben Queen done it. I don't mean *they*—" he hooked his head back toward the Queen house—"believe it. No, they don't believe Ben was the one. But he got jailed for it. Went to prison. Had a trial and all and went to prison."

I just stared. My mind was so full of questions, I hardly knew what to ask.

Mr. Root went on. "What some people *said* was, it was another man, probably some trash Rose

Devereau run around with behind Ben's back." Mr. Root held up his hands as if to ward off my questions. "That's all she told me. I guess Sheba thought Rose just brought it on herself, whoever done it to her. Sheba must not've liked her much."

Was *that* ever an understatement, I thought for a moment. "How come Fern Queen was over in La Porte? Did you ask Sheba that?"

Mr. Root nodded. "Said Fern said she was going there to meet somebody." Mr. Root shrugged. "That's all she knew." He shook his head. "I guess she met somebody, all right."

"Then it had to be somebody Fern knew." I was stunned by this: two murders in one family. I turned all of this over in my mind while looking down Schoolhouse Road. How could Ben have ever killed Rose? How could Rose have been running around with "trash"? It didn't make any sense. From what Mr. George Queen said, Rose was crazy about Ben and Ben was certainly crazy about her. I guess I could see why, too.

I could see in the distance down Schoolhouse Road the little swings in the schoolyard turning in the wind, the chains twining around each other the way they do, the way I used to make the swings do by shoving off with my toe so I could go dizzily around. I think I let this take up the slack in my mind so I wouldn't have to let pictures in of Rose Devereau and all that blood.

But then my thoughts untwined and I asked, "And that's everything she told you?"

He nodded and said nothing.

I groaned. It was almost worse than not knowing. How could all the people I knew have forgotten such a terrible thing? There must be somebody—

"Mr. Stemple!" I started pulling at Mr. Root's shirt sleeve. "Come on!"

"Where? The Wood boys, what about them? And you said you had to be back at the hotel—"

I didn't care if I was late to do the salads; it wasn't important. "Mr. Jude Stemple—you said you knew him a little." I pulled him along a step or two beside me. "He lives right down there in Flyback Hollow. He knows the Queens. He'd know what happened."

Jude Stemple and his hound dog were there, sitting on his front porch, just like I left them. It was as if he might have been waiting for me to return and continue our talk. I was flattered, I must admit.

He looked up from the piece of wood he was whittling and called out, "Well, look who's back!" And his dog even got up and swished its tail.

I pulled Mr. Root up the walk and introduced him to Jude Stemple and his dog.

Jude Stemple squinted. "Ain't I seen you out there at Britten's store? On that bench out front?" He snapped his whittling knife shut and invited us to sit.

"Mr. Root here wanted to visit the Queens because he knew Mrs. Queen a long time ago." Why was I telling Mr. Stemple these half-truths? You get in the habit, I guess.

Jude Stemple nodded and opened his knife again to cut off a piece of tobacco, which he offered to Mr. Root. They both sat for a minute chewing away, talking about Mr. Stemple's dog and about hunting. That could go on forever if I didn't say something, which I did: "You remember we were talking about the Queens?"

Mr. Stemple nodded eagerly. Living here in Flyback Hollow by himself, I imagined, he was more interested in gossip than he was in dogs and hunting. I just told Mr. Root he should tell Mr. Stemple what Sheba Queen had said, which he did, but with a lot of pauses and offering his cigarettes around and asking for a drink of cool water and so forth. This was to draw out his telling of the story. But he told it, finally. Jude Stemple thought it over.

"It's true what you heard. Ben Queen did go to prison for killing Rose. Jury said he was guilty, but the judge, he took into account it was one of them crimes of passion."

Mr. Root nodded. " 'Cream passionals,' that's what they call 'em in France."

"Whatever. I never believed it was that nor anything else to do with Ben Queen, though. Always thought there was something fishy there. And I'll tell you two reasons why: one was that Ben Queen was absolutely crazy about Rose. Never have I seen any man so taken with a woman after being married nearly twenty years. And he still doted on her. They had some fights, yes. But it weren't over no other man. That's just dumb." He waved this idea away. "For she loved him, too. I never saw Rose Queen flirting with another man long as I knew her. Not that I knew them all that well, but some. The fights they did have were about their girl, Fern. One that just got herself killed over by White's Bridge. Fern went missing for a couple days and I was pretty sure that dead woman was her. Anyway, Fern was queer in the head. Just . . . I don't know . . . just like she was *blank*, or something. Rose and Ben fought about what to do about Fern. Rose was more practical than Ben was; she said Fern'd be better off in an institution. Oh, Rose wasn't hardhearted; it was just that I guess that girl was wearing them down. If anyone was runnin' around with men it was her, and not more'n fourteen, fifteen years old. But then she hadn't good sense, like I said. Day Rose got killed, I heard Ben and her had this bad fight, though of course Sheba Queen'd never allow Ben was mad at Rose, I'll give her that, as that wouldn't have looked good at his trial, would it? But can you blame Sheba? Okay, they said he killed Rose, and the really hard thing was he never took the stand. Nobody ever heard him say otherwise, not 'I never done it,' or 'Not guilty,' not nothin'. Any talkin' done was lawyer talk."

Jude Stemple stopped talking. He chewed his tobacco and rubbed his hand up and down the old dog's back. I didn't want to disturb his mind, so I said nothing. I don't think he'd got to the second reason he'd mentioned. Then he did.

"Now, the other reason I don't believe Ben ever could have done it was because of the way the whole thing looked. Rose was out in back, went back to the henhouse to collect eggs. They kept chickens for eggs that sometimes Rose used to sell, and for the pot, too—"

I couldn't help thinking of my mother's pot pie.

"—but Rose, she couldn't ever kill them chickens, not even for their dinner. It had to be one of the others did that, mostly Sheba. Sheba could just take one of them old chickens by its scrawny neck and"— he twisted his fists, one atop the other—"or take the axe to them." Then he raised a hand as if it held an axe and brought it down on the top step, making a scrunching noise in his throat.

I could have done without that. "But what about the way you said it looked?"

"There was blood all over, there was half a dozen dead chickens, a couple with their heads cut off. Blood all over, a lot of it Rose's."

He looked at Mr. Root and even included me in his silent asking.

Mr. Root said, after aiming a hard, thin stream of juice at the ground, "You're saying that don't look like Ben Queen done it?"

Jude Stemple nodded. "That's right."

Mr. Root said, "Sounds like somebody must've

been awful mad. And you said he got real mad at her, didn't you?"

"Mad at a person's one thing. Killing everything in a country mile, that's another."

They both looked at me. I must say I was flattered they seemed to think my opinion was worth something. "Who else was there? I mean, did anyone else come under suspicion?"

Mr. Stemple chewed awhile, reflecting, then said, "I'll tell you one got suspicioned, real bad. That was Lou Landis."

I frowned. "The lady that used to be Ben Queen's girlfriend? But that would have been years and years before!"

Mr. Root and Jude Stemple exchanged one of those I guess you call them worldly looks and Jude Stemple said, "There's some women never get over a thing. Lou Landis never did marry." He nodded up Flyback Hollow Road towards some distant object we none of us could see. "Lived here ever since and never left. She's our teacher, maybe she's principal now, though with only three teachers all told there's not much to set one up over the others. Good with kids, though. Teaching, that just became her life. Never went with no one else, and, like I say, never did get married. Good looker, too, is Lou, even now."

I looked up the road towards a school ground I couldn't see. Could that have been her—the dark lady who walked out of the door and stood and just looked straight ahead of her? Miss Lou Landis. It's

funny sometimes the way things all seem to be connected.

"And then what?" I asked.

"Well, there was this investigation, of course,
and the sheriff—"

"Was it *our* sheriff?" I gasped.

He frowned a bit, puzzled. "Oh, you mean
DeGheyn. No, Sam DeGheyn wasn't sheriff then.
Another one ... can't remember that fellow's
name...."

I thought a moment and now *I* was puzzled.
"Wait a minute. If there was this trial it must've
been in La Porte! That's the county seat. And I
can't imagine people wouldn't remember it, like
Mr. Root here—"

Jude Stemple was holding up his hand for me
to stop. "But it weren't in La Porte. There was a
change of venue."

I frowned. "Change of menu?" I guess my
thoughts never strayed far from food.

"Not 'menu.' 'Venue.' That's where they have
a trial elsewhere when they think a jury'd be too
prejudicial in the place where the crime was commit-
ted." He spat tobacco juice. He seemed proud for
being so knowledgeable about venues. "Trial was
over in Meridian. Hundred miles away, that was.
Didn't last long, neither. But his lawyer got the other
lawyer to agree to manslaughter, that Ben did it in
a fit of temper. Something like that." Jude Stemple
sighed. Then he went on. "I think anybody'd really

think twice before they hurt Rosie Queen. Yes, I think even the devil'd give Rose Queen a wide berth. There was just somethin' about her, somethin' that kept bad thoughts away." He was looking up towards the tops of the trees now, up where the sun was going down and the leaves had trapped the red-gold light. "I recall one day seeing Rose walking along the Holler Road up there, a basket over her arm, for she was bringing eggs or something to sick old Mrs. Jessup. And she waved at me, halloo'd and waved, her arm up in the air, and I recall how—*bright* she was. Just *bright*. As if she was filled with the sun behind her back." Here he raised his own arm, the fingers of his hand spread against the sunlight, and I could see the blood in it, looking red-gold. As if he were waving back at Rosie Queen. "Rose was so light you could almost look right through her—" He stopped suddenly, embarrassed. "Well, anyways. I'm not good with words, never was."

"I think you are, Mr. Stemple. I think you're real good with words."

Mr. Root nodded, agreeing.

Mr. Stemple went on. "I just never in my life saw a girl as beautiful as Rose Devereau Queen. Never did. And she was still a girl, you know, even when she was near forty years old. I never seen her like again. I never have."

*I have*, I wanted to say, but of course I didn't. I was quiet in honor of Mr. Stemple's powers of description. But not for long. "What happened to Fern? Did she just go on living with Sheba and

George?" My mother always told me to never call unfamiliar adults by their first names. But by this time I really felt I'd known the Queens all my life.

"Fern, she went away for a long time. Sheba Queen's got kin out west someplace, and I think Fern went to stay with them."

"Out west" was almost as romantic-sounding to me as "Ben Queen." "So when she come—came—back, was she still touched?" I had no trouble at all falling into Cold Flat speech.

"Yeah, she still was. Fern got better when she got older; she got a little common sense in her. But she always did act queer."

I looked up to the tops of the trees where the sun turned the dark leaves now to a glassy greenness you could see through. I imagined them staying like this until autumn, when they would drift down and blow against one another so that everywhere would be the sound of wind chimes. I listened so hard to this glassy leaf-tinkling I lost track of Jude Stemple's talk. Until he said, "Now he's out."

I was puzzled. I stared at Jude Stemple. "What?"

"Ben Queen. He's out of prison."

# FORTY

For someone who swore that we of the Hotel Paradise were trying to poison her, Miss Bertha certainly managed to get in for her meals quick enough so as to give us plenty of chances at it. She felt it her due to take up a lot of my time rehashing yesterday's breakfast calamity. Also, she felt that she was now entitled to refuse the set menu entirely, and insisted my mother cook her something special. This did not sound very logical, as it's always those "special" dishes that have arsenic and so forth in them. She declined the pork chops and chicken. She wanted fish.

My mother was fit to be tied. She told me to go back and tell the old fool that she'd cook her a mushroom omelette, and if she wanted fish, give her one of Will's fishing poles and tell her to go down to Spirit Lake. My mother banged the pots and pans around on the stove and Walter nearly killed himself laughing. I, of course, had to bear the bad tidings back and forth between them and was feeling put-upon until I remembered this was really my fault. So I accepted my punishment and offered Miss Bertha the mushroom omelette. She declined, saying there'd be a death's cap mushroom in it, and toadstools for good measure. No thank you, *miss*. Poor Mrs. Fulbright, talcumed and pink-cheeked, was mortified that Miss Bertha could "blacken the good name of the Hotel Paradise." Miss Bertha countered by pointing out nobody was trying to kill Serile Fulbright, *were they*? So naturally Serile would stick up for the hotel.

It was about this time that Will came in with his great big smile and great big lie. He told Miss Bertha how wonderful she looked and announced he'd caught a fresh rainbow trout just for her. Would she like it almondine?

I stood there getting nauseous listening to him. But Will can do no wrong. Everybody trusts Will, and this always amazes me, because I am far more to be trusted than he is. Well, maybe not more to be *trusted*. I mean, I lie too, but for important reasons. Will just does it for fun.

Naturally, all of this wheedling attention worked on Miss Bertha like a charm and she said the rainbow trout would do fine, with just some lemon.

I stood with my arms wrapped around my tray wishing for something to get me out of this dining room.

For once in my life, my prayer was answered.

The dumbwaiter wasn't working again and Aurora was demanding *I* bring her up her before-dinner drink. When I took Mrs. Davidow's dinner out to the back office, she was shouting up the shaft Regina would take her up a drink and Aurora shouting back to keep that blond floozie off the fourth floor! I ran back to the kitchen to tell my mother. She could hardly contain her laughter, for I knew she couldn't stand Ree-Jane either, in spite of always giving her white meat of chicken. Walter overheard me and laughed his hiccuppy laugh.

Mrs. Davidow shouted out of the office window for somebody to come. My mother went out and listened to her and came back and told me Great-Aunt Aurora wanted me to take her her cocktail up and her dinner too. My mother said further, to Vera's astonished ears, that I could be excused from waiting tables any more that dinnertime, as I had to perform this chore. As a dinner party had canceled, that left only three tables of hotel guests, and Vera could easily handle them.

Vera would have to wait on Miss Bertha! She gave me a look that would have cut like my mother's meat cleaver as she whisked around the kitchen, so starched and clean she looked varnished.

Lola Davidow fixed up a small pitcher of Davidow martinis and placed it on a tray together with a stemmed glass—probably no substitute for a Cold Turkey, but I couldn't help that. As I went through the swinging door, Miss Bertha was refusing to have Vera wait on their table, said she'd trained me up to do it right, and she didn't want Vera messing up Miss Bertha's good schooling, that Vera wasn't a good waitress, not like me. I was through the dining room and hearing all of this to my extreme delight. Vera's colorless eyes blazed at me. With the small tray of martinis professionally balanced on one hand, I called to her, "Be sure to give Miss Bertha lots of hot rolls," and then made a dash, as far as the laden tray would let me, through the dining room door.

Aurora cast her eagle eye on the pitcher as I set it down beside her game of solitaire. I noticed that the cards were put down properly, red on black and black on red.

"Is this that Davidow woman's martinis? Where's my Cold Comfort? I told her you were to make me a Cold Comfort!" She slapped a black eight on a black nine and added, "So go make me one!"

"It takes some ingredients we're out of."

Suspiciously, she looked up at me over the rims of glasses set halfway down her nose. "Well, it ain't liquor you mean. This place is *never* out of al-co-hol-ic refreshment."

"No, but we're out of maraschino cherry juice," I said.

"Oh, for pity's sakes. Just leave it out."

I shook my head. "Can't, because it's part of the secret. It"— I searched for one of my mother's cooking words—"binds everything together. It *binds* the whole drink together." And before she could object, I said, "But after you eat your dinner, I'll bring you a special after-dinner drink." Since it could take hours for Aurora to eat her dinner, she fooled around so much, she'd probably forget all about it. "Or if I can't, somebody else can bring you some brandy or something like that."

She glared at me over the jack of hearts she was going to slap down on the queen of diamonds.

She was doing it just to annoy me, I knew. "Not that peroxide-headed tart, not her!"

"I was thinking of Will. He'd be glad to." Serve him right for that trout story.

"That smart-ass brother of yours? I don't want him within a mile of my place. And not that Conroy brat, either. I will never know how that busybody mother of his ever laid still long enough to do what it takes to have a baby." She swept all of the cards up and rattled them together in one dramatic gesture. Sometimes I could picture Aurora Paradise on one of those Mississippi gambling boats.

I was surprised hearing her talk about Will that way. I said Vera could bring up anything she wanted.

"That gussied-up plank of wood! My God, I don't know how your mother stands her. I don't see why *you* can't do it."

"It'll be past my bedtime," I replied.

Well, Aurora had the good sense not to believe *that*, but she said, anyway, "Let that man bring it up—at least he's got the sense not to talk my arm off. He can bring up my dessert and coffee, too, since I see you do not seem so in-*clined*." She bit the last half-dozen words off.

"That man"? Surely she couldn't mean Walter. I never even thought she knew Walter was alive; besides, no one ever asked for Walter. "You mean Walter?"

"I don't know his name, do I? Godsakes, ain't I got enough to do without learning all the kitchen help's names?" Briskly, she shuffled the cards, fanned them out, and shuffled again. "The one with black hair kind of falls forward."

"That's Walter. You mean he can bring up your dinner?"

"No, I mean the damned cat can bring it! Didn't I just *say* I wanted him to do it?"

"Okay, that's good."

"Just as long as I get my drink later, too, you hear?"

I heard.

When I told them in the kitchen Great-Aunt Aurora wanted Walter to take up her dinner, everyone was dumbfounded. Except for Walter. He just dried his hands on the kitchen towel and said he'd be glad to do it. I marveled at how smooth and unsurprised he was, and then I left.

# FORTY-ONE

This time I took a stronger flashlight, a lanternlike one that can turn the entire area you're standing in to a sick white light. It would be another hour and a half before darkness came, but I was ready for it. Dusk always seemed to last longer here than it did other places, hovering over Spirit Lake like a great gray moth.

As I walked, I looked across the lake to see the house blending into the trunks of gray trees, becoming part of the wood. It looked the same. Maybe I'd expected it to change with all of the new things I'd found out over the last few days.

I stopped here at the spring to get my usual drink of water and also filled up my water bottle. As I drank from the tin cup, I looked down into the tiled pool at the center of this way place, searching the bottom to see if anyone had tossed in any money. I must have been the only one who did throw it in, for I recognized my coins lying down there and none had come to keep them company. People hardly ever come to this spring now. Like my father, they used to, but not anymore.

I had lost something of my fear of the woods, having made this trip twice already. Still, to be sure the flashlight was working, I switched it on and off a few times to check the batteries. It worked fine. I picked up my old book satchel, in which I'd brought a triangle of coconut cake (in case I got stranded), and started walking.

For some time I walked through the stillness, with the only sound the soft squish of my feet on mulchy leaves, or, occasionally, the sharp snap of twigs breaking. As I walked, I began to notice that I felt proud of myself, and this surprised me. A year ago, even a month ago, I would never have considered such a trip as I was making. The Devereau place had always seemed such a sealed-up secret, and the woods impassable. But now both house and woods had become recognizable and familiar places; I was beginning to feel secure just knowing where the leaf-blackened path led. That made the surroundings less mysterious, and I could imagine a day when there might be no mystery attached to these woods and the house at all. That made me pause a moment to wonder if I had to give up mystery to gain security. While I thought this over, I decided to take a drink of spring water from my canteen. And as long as I was taking a drink, I might as well sit down and have some coconut cake, too.

My seat was a crumbling log right by the tree where Ulub had carved AL beneath a heart, and I wondered again if he had ever had a girlfriend. With my cake in my hand, I got up and peered at the heart and ran my finger around its roughly carved edge. It was kind of hard to imagine Ulub with a girlfriend. But, then, I couldn't imagine *me* with a boyfriend, either, so that was nothing against Ulub. I finished off the white icing and coconut shreds, picked up my satchel, and walked on.

I didn't really need the flashlight, for enough light trickled through the thick high branches. I heard the rustlings of small animals—or maybe milk snakes—in the undergrowth. And I heard a bird somewhere, and thought it might be a loon. It was all so still, and all so much the *same* as it had been before, I thought maybe it's a Living Picture that remains the same all the time—even when I'm not here—and only its quiet breathing makes it different from moment to moment. At last, I was walking across the clearing towards the house, the sun starting to fall through the trees across the lake.

As I opened the screen door to the kitchen I imagined I saw out of the corner of my eye something move. I held my breath. I thought it must happen that on one of these journeys I would see the Girl again. Whatever moved (if anything had, and probably it hadn't), it was a dark flicker of movement.

As soon as I was in the living room, I walked to the wall where the photograph of the Devereau sisters hung. I wanted to look at Rose again, thinking that maybe my new knowledge of her would work some change in her photo. But of course it didn't. Rose was pretty all right, truly pretty; but to understand why Jude Stemple had talked about her as he did, had said she'd had a "lighted look," for that you'd have to see her in person. The picture listed a little; I touched the frame and set it straight. Then I walked slowly around the room, touching each piece of furniture I passed, with some notion in my mind that this might drive out bad spirits or call up good ones. While I did this I hummed the French song whose words I couldn't understand but whose tune I couldn't forget. I stopped to look out the front window, where the sun cut a burning path across the lake.

Perhaps I expected the Girl would turn up again over there, but of course she didn't. I thought: It's so strange how all of these generations of people hung together. First there was Mary-Evelyn, then Rose, then Fern, and now the Girl. All of them connected. I turned from the window and went up the stairs to Mary-Evelyn's room.

I opened the wardrobe and carefully inspected each of the dresses. I wondered if the pale yellow one, so pale it was nearly white, was the dress Miss Flagler had described, the one Mary-Evelyn had worn to the garden party. With those satin-covered buttons, it certainly looked like a party dress. I took down the pink-dotted Swiss. I held it up under my chin and decided the color didn't do much for me. I returned it too to its hanger and reached for the delphinium-colored taffeta. I held it up before the dresser mirror and saw how it made my eyes look really blue, so I took off my skirt and T-shirt and tried it on. I turned and twisted in front of the mirror (hoping I didn't look like Ree-Jane doing it) and found the dress fit just as well as the green dress.

Then I went over to the toy chest and lifted the lid. I rested my forehead on the edge and peered into its dark blue shadows, wondering if there might not be something else in there that would tell me more about Mary-Evelyn. For with all of the information I'd got about Rose and Ben Queen, I still hadn't heard any more about her. When I was searching for the Artist George piece, I hadn't seen a notebook or anything; but wasn't there always something like a diary being discovered in mystery stories? I myself had a five-year diary with flimsy pages that I could lock with a key but never bothered to. I hid it in my underwear drawer.

There were three dolls in the chest and I pulled out the stuffed one, a doll with a long full skirt and yellow hair with a pink ribbon in it. When you raised the skirt or turned it over, you would find a black doll in a bandanna. I once had one of these when I was little enough to play with dolls. I spent a minute turning the doll over and up again, but couldn't decide which—the white or the black face—I preferred. I know I liked the checkered bandanna a lot more than the pink hair ribbon. I stood the doll against the chest and pulled out a train engine painted black with bits of gold and looking a lot like the train that came through La Porte. There were a few broken pieces of track, and I wondered if Mary-Evelyn had ever had a train set. There were some jigsaw puzzles and a deck of cards spilled around that I collected and put in their box. On the bottom was a real find: a Ouija board! It was something I'd always wanted but forgot to ask for around Christmas time. Ree-Jane had one, but of course I wouldn't play with her because she pushed the marker to wherever she wanted and then insisted it was done by the Invisible Hands. The Invisible Hands always had good news for her and bad news for me. If I had listened to the Ouija, I never would have got out of bed in the morning.

There were a number of books, too, several with their covers missing. I was surprised to see Babar stories, as they had been my favorites when I was a child. To make sure I had outgrown them, I chose one to read and lay back on the floor (carefully, so as not to muss the dress) and held the book above my face. While I read the story through, I studied the pictures closely, and then closed the book, sadly, for I found that it was true: I had outgrown Babar. So I merely leafed through the second book, not stopping to read much.

I barely noticed that a streak of sun had all but vanished from the page and left behind only a heavy pewter light. I returned the books to the chest, rooted down farther and found some doll clothes—a wine-red velvet coat and bonnet, but not meant for any of these dolls. I set the coat to one side and kept on looking. But there was no diary or notebook. And no Artist George, either. I thought this piece might have got buried beneath dolls and mittens and a couple of doll blankets.

I got up with the double-faced doll in my hands and went to the windows that looked out over the lake. Why had Mary-Evelyn's things been left here, this way? Perhaps the Devereau sisters didn't want to take any reminders of her. They might have wanted to blot her out. And yet, the furniture had also been left, and the pictures on the walls, the dishes and silverware, the music in the piano bench, the records of French songs. It was as if they expected to return at any moment; it was almost as if they'd never gone away.

I stood twisting the doll by its arms over and under—white face, black face; pink ribbon, bandanna—and wondering if the house had a cellar, when a flicker of movement outside caught my eye, or the corner of my eye. I went very still and turned my head very slowly in case someone was watching me. I could see no one. But I *had* seen a movement; this time, I was sure of it. I left Mary-Evelyn's room and ran down the hall to the end room that I thought must have been Rose's. Its single window gave out over the woods.

I looked down into the gathering dark. A man stood there. He was a few feet back in the woods and he was just standing, looking up. Quickly, I stepped back from the window. Clutching the doll to me, I held my breath, as if the tiniest motion could give me away. I knew who it must be, because he was the only one besides me who would be drawn to this house. Ben Queen.

Carefully, I took a step to the window. He still stood there. I heard Aurora's voice saying, "Never set foot in that house." How Ben Queen would come through the woods and stand and watch for Rose.

But maybe Aurora'd made that up so the whole thing would sound romantic.

He could have come the same way I did, but I didn't think so. I heard Aurora again: "Men like Ben Queen always find a way in." He stood there perfectly still, a frozen stillness, with his thumbs hooked in his jeans pockets. He wore a long coat, and a wide-brimmed hat, and a kerchief around his neck, so that he looked like he was right out of a western, one of those Saturday-afternoon westerns at the Orion.

Even in the dusk and with that hat shadowing his face, I could tell he was still handsome, though he had to be in his sixties. It was over forty years ago Rose Devereau had run off with him and she'd been twenty then, and Ben Queen not much older.

I tried to imagine how Rose Devereau had felt, seeing him there night after night, wishing her— *willing* her—to come out of this house, to leave her sisters and run away with him. It must have been like trying to resist a terrific force, a hurricanelike wind or tornado rattling the house, shaking the trees, spinning along the lake's surface. My stomach felt hollow, but not from fear. I can only explain it by saying I felt empty.

When he finally moved, I felt a shock, as if a statue had picked up and changed position. He walked the little distance to the house and then I couldn't see him anymore, because he was coming inside. I heard the kitchen door creak open, creak shut. I stood there, not knowing at all what to do. I

simply stood and listened to the sounds, slow foot-
steps on the floorboards, stopping and starting, then
other small sounds like the rustlings in the woods.
Then silence. Then movement. And then, after a few
moments, the music. He must have started up the
record player. I had left the French song on the
turntable, and that's what he played.

Very carefully tiptoeing, I left the room, freez-
ing as a board creaked beneath my foot. And then I
realized that he must have seen me anyway. Outside,
before I'd come in the house. He must have seen
me. He knew I was here. So all of this taking care
being quiet was kind of silly. So would hiding be.
If Ben Queen came looking for me, well, there wasn't
much I could do about it. I thought I might as well
go on downstairs.

But I still wanted to hang back. At the top of
the stairs I stopped, then sat. I could see him just
beyond the record player, standing and gazing out
of the door at the side of the house. He was smoking
now, a thin kind of cigar. As he brought his hand
up to his mouth, he turned his face, looked up the
stairwell, and went on looking, not saying a word.

For some reason, that look got me to my feet.
*Pulled* me to my feet might be a better way of saying
it. Even all the way down there to up here, it was a
powerful look. He was taller than the Sheriff. He
was handsomer too, something I thought I'd never
in my life see. But he was. I didn't see how anyone
that old could be that good-looking.

If he was surprised to see me, he didn't show

it. He stood there smoking his cigar, his eyes giving me a considering sort of look. I guess if you've lived a lifetime of surprises, you learn to hide your feelings when you meet a new one. Hearing him speak surprised me, though. I nearly jumped.

"Whyn't you come on down, girl?"

I did. Trying to be casual, I walked down the stairs.

When I was finally there, looking up at him, I guess he figured I wasn't going to be the one making conversation, so he said, "You live here?"

I shook my head, unable to find my own voice. I saw I was still holding tightly to the double-headed doll and tossed it onto a chair.

"Didn't think there was nobody lived here now." He looked me over. "That's a mighty pretty color on you. Matches your beautiful eyes."

He gave me a flirty look, the kind I see Will giving people, and I was a little breathless. Beautiful eyes. Not shrug-colored at all. I'd completely forgot I was wearing the taffeta dress. "There was a . . . party at the hotel; I dressed up." I don't know why I felt I had to explain things; it only got me in deeper.

But not this time, for all he said was, "You must like this place if it's better than a party."

I cleared my throat and said: "The Devereaus used to live here. They're gone now."

He didn't comment. Slowly he shook his head. He looked directly at me, then; his eyes were a winter gray, the color that Spirit Lake gets in December. It's a gray that seems to spread from the water itself to the grassy banks, the trunks of trees, up to the sky.

"Hotel? You're not from over at the Hotel Paradise, are you?"

I was glad I could surprise him, at least. "Yes. It's my mother's."

He was even more surprised and laughed. "My Lord, I know them over there. Knew them, I should say. Grahams own that place. I remember. What's your name?"

"Emma." It felt strange, my own name in my mouth, as if something about me had just come into being.

"I'll be . . . I'll be." He shook his head. "Long time ago." He looked away, and I knew from the direction of his gaze he must be looking at the photograph. "Long time."

"You're Ben Queen, aren't you?"

He did look a little surprised that I'd know that. "Reckon I am."

"You were married to Rose Devereau."

He didn't even nod this time.

"You just got out of jail, that's what I heard."

"You seem to know me pretty well. If you know all that, why ain't you scared? Being alone here with a stranger that's a convicted killer?"

"I—" I didn't know. "What—why did you come here?" I asked him.

"I could ask you the same question."

Well, I could see why they didn't get much out of Ben Queen at his trial.

He said, "You must be hellbent on something, to go through them woods out there alone." He nodded toward the part of the woods I'd come through, where the lake curved around. The night was coming on swiftly, and the trees out where he was looking shifted in a wind off the water like black feathers. I couldn't see the lake now except for a crescent rim. It was fading fast from view, disappearing part by part like that cat in *Alice in Wonderland*.

And I guess it was Alice that made me think of the Red Queen, how she galloped on her horse over ground that moved as she rode so that she was always in the same place. I don't know what it meant, but I felt like the Red Queen, and I really couldn't stand it, all the effort it took to stay in one place. I was taken by a feeling of terrible sadness and was afraid I would start to bawl, so I kept my head down and my eyes fixed on the floor, trying to swallow the ache in my throat. "I guess I am hellbent, all right."

"Makes two of us."

It was safe to look up now, I was back in control of myself, and I raised my head to see he had pulled out a book of matches and with his thumb struck one up, expertly, as if he were used to doing things in the dark. He put the flame to the tallow candles where they wavered and threw up cones of light on our faces. Being lit from below, we must have looked like a couple of jack-o'-lanterns.

Before I could think I said, "There's a lady they found shot over in Mirror Pond by White's Bridge."

He looked off into the darkness, not answering.

So I went on. "Isn't she some—relation of yours? That's what I heard."

He drew in on his cigar, let out the smoke before he said, "Her name's Fern. She was my daughter."

Saying it, Ben Queen sounded not so much sad as weary. The way I feel when I've cleared all the tables and they tell me there's six more for dinner. Just plain weary, as if some chore you'd supposed was over turned out to be endless.

He looked at me for a long time from the hollows of his jack-o'-lantern eyes. Then he said, "If it's any comfort to you, I didn't kill neither of them, not my daughter and God knows not my wife, Rose. But they'll be after me, of course. Sheriff here already is. Only he's looking in the wrong place." He struck another match on his thumbnail and raised it to the cigar, relighting it.

Then, to my astonishment—I was too surprised to be frightened—he pulled out a gun from inside his long coat, a little one not much bigger than the palm of his hand, broke the barrel, and tossed it on a table beside the sofa.

"There's the weapon. You want to turn me in? Might as well—I don't feel much like trying to get away." He shrugged and gave me a thin smile. "Times you just get damned tired. Excuse my language." He made me a stiff little bow that could have seemed like he mocked me, but I knew he didn't. My eyes riveted on the gun, this dangerous thing that he was tossing around with no more concern than I had shown when I tossed the doll on the chair.

"Found it near the bridge. Near that pond."

"Mirror Pond. You *found* it? Nobody's going to believe that!" That was one of the dumbest explanations I'd ever heard. And I said so.

He laughed, and his laugh was hearty and deep. "I reckon you're right. It is pretty dumb."

"But that means you were *there*; you were at the pond." My arms came out in goose bumps.

"It's getting late, Emma. I think I'd better leave and so should you, and I think you should let me walk you through the woods." He reached to pick up the gun, which he then stuck back in some inside pocket of the coat. "I'd go ahead and leave it except some kid might get hold of it." He moved over to the record player and lifted the arm, which had been sliding back and forth when the sad French song ended. "Come on, then. I'll walk you."

"Yes—but wait! I've got to change out of this— my dress." Before he could reply, I rushed upstairs, took off the dress, and put my old clothes back on. Then I ran down again. He was nipping the candle flames out between thumb and forefinger, and if it hadn't been for the moon, we would have plunged into total darkness.

I'll say this: it felt a lot better going through those woods with him than it did going it alone. Especially someone who seemed not to have any fear about him. He pushed low-hanging branches out of my way and made sure I didn't turn my ankle or fall over a root or a limb. And because he was so tall he could hold the lantern higher and give me a better pocket of light to walk in. Yes, it was nice to have someone making that trip with me. Especially Ben Queen. I expect people would have called me totally crazy for not being afraid of him—a strange man and one they said had killed a woman to boot— but I wasn't. I had so many questions I wanted to ask I had a hard time settling on any one of them. We walked in silence until he said, "It sure sounds as if you made quite a study of me."

I wasn't sure if I wanted him to think that, so I said, "Oh, it was my great-aunt who made the study. She told me some about you. She said the Devereaus didn't like you coming here to see Rose."

He laughed. "That's sure true enough." He nodded toward some distance behind us. "Back there about a quarter-mile there's an old dirt road I don't suppose anyone ever uses anymore. I'd just leave my truck there and walk through the trees. Sometimes I'd come around the way you said, but they'd know my truck, see it from the other side of the lake. I think those women were always looking out of windows."

We picked up walking again. I asked, "But why wouldn't they let you come in the house?"

He gave a gruff laugh. "Now, the reasons they gave out were I wasn't good enough for Rose Devereau. Cold Flat Junction people, they ain't exactly thought highly of. Another thing was, they said I was wild."

"Were you?" I was a little excited by this. I'd never had the chance to talk to somebody wild before.

"Sometimes I was. Drank too much, got in fights, played too much poker."

"That's what Aurora told me," I said without thinking. "Said you taught her how to play poker."

He stopped suddenly. "My Lord! You mean that woman's still alive? *That's* your great-aunt? My *Lord*! You talk about *wild*, Aurora Paradise could of taught me a few tricks. She's still there at the Hotel Paradise? My Lord." He shook his head.

"She lives up on the fourth floor." I was absolutely thrilled that Aurora had been wild, too, along with Ben Queen. "What kind of tricks?"

Ben Queen chuckled and pushed away some briars for me to pass. "Never you mind."

I stopped dead by the tree where the heart was carved. "People *always* say that to me."

He put his hand on my shoulder. "Settle down. I'll tell you one thing that you can hold over her head when she starts in giving you trouble, as I'm sure she does. When I was about your age, Aurora Paradise jumped buck-naked into this lake here in front of twenty people. Someone dared her, so she just threw off her clothes and did it."

We walked on. I was pleased. He was right; I could just bring that up the next time she wouldn't tell me something. We walked on, and I said, "*I* don't think Cold Flat people are to be looked down on."

"Oh, that wasn't those Devereau sisters' real

reason. The real reason was they didn't want Rosie to be happy. They didn't want *anyone* to be happy. You could tell it from their pinched faces and their tight corsets. They meant to keep her forever with them, miserable as they were. There's people like that, you know. But in spite of them and having to live amongst that cold clutter, Rose was still a happy woman."

I felt terrible again. Like I might cry, but angry, too. "Mary-Evelyn wasn't."

He stopped, looked down at me, and asked. "How do you know about Mary-Evelyn?"

"How do I know? It wasn't exactly a secret, was it? It was in all the papers." We had come to the opening where the spring was, and I didn't know if I was glad to see it or not.

He pushed his hat back a little, wiped his forehead with his forearm. He said, "Yeah. I expect it was."

Ben Queen looked around at the rocks, the tiled pool.

He nodded. "Let's sit down a minute. I wouldn't mind a cold drink." We walked across to the spring and he bent and let water run into his hands.

"Wait a minute, there's a cup." I got the tin cup from its hole and held it under the pipe until it was nearly full. He was sitting now on the ledge around the spring and I carried the cup over and sat down beside him. I passed him the cup.

After he drank, he passed the cup back to me, then fired up another match for a fresh cigar and asked, "You know what a scapegoat is?"

*Did* I? If there was one thing I knew, it was scapegoating. "I sure do. It's a goat they used to tie things on, like pans and pots. Then they make the goat go off and it's as if the goat's taking all of their sins with him." I scratched my ear. "Or something like that."

"*Exactly* like that. Well, little Mary-Evelyn was one. In some families, they just got to have one person to pass all the blame to. Because sometimes it's the only way the rest of them can get by. Either they're too blind, or too weak, or too stupid to see what they're doing. . . ."

I didn't much want to sit and listen to excuses made for the Devereau sisters. "So they stuck her in that boat and shoved her off into the lake—" I stopped suddenly. Is *that* what I'd believed? It was too horrible to think about, it really was. Out of the corner of my eye, I could see he'd turned his face to study mine. But I wouldn't look at him; I was angry with him. I was angry because he hadn't saved Mary-Evelyn Devereau.

"Why did they hate her so much? Why wouldn't they talk to her? Why did they send her to Cloverly?" I wasn't too sure about that last question.

"To where?"

"Cloverly. It means people not talking to you, shutting you out."

He turned his cigar in his mouth, made a noise deep in his throat.

I just brought it out, my anger. "Rose knew they did it! Rose must've known it. She should never have run off and left Mary-Evelyn. Mary-Evelyn was all by herself. . . ." Well, this time I just broke down and cried. I jumped off the stone wall and just walked around the spring, crying. Ben Queen didn't ignore me, yet he didn't say a word, and I was thankful for that. The tear storm only lasted a minute and then stopped, like the sudden cease of rain or thunder. Just stopped. I went over to the pipe that jutted out, bent down, and turned my face so the icy water ran on my eyelids.

I was pretty wet, and Ben had taken the neckerchief from around his neck and was holding it out. "Here, Emma. Come now and sit down." I did this, grateful that he didn't say the sorts of things grown-ups like to, such as I had no reason to cry; or, even if I had a reason, crying wouldn't do any good. "I'll try to explain," he said.

"Time someone did," I said, with a lot more starch than I felt. I was folding the damp neckerchief into a small square.

He smiled. "You're right there." He was quiet for some moments, considering this, as he studied his cigar coal. "But we was going to go back and get her. We was trying to work out a way to get her out of there. The accident happened just a few days after we left."

"You think it was an accident?"

"I surely do. That boat had a leak in it. Didn't studying up on it tell you that?" He sighed. "We meant to go back for her."

So she hadn't simply been abandoned. My anger

evaporated, and that same feeling of relief washed over me. More breath let out. But I said, sternly, "Well, it's too bad you didn't, because look what happened!" As if he hadn't looked; I guess he'd been looking for a good long time. No one said anything. I passed him the tin cup and he took another drink.

He rolled his cigar in his mouth awhile then let out the smoke. "It was bad, real bad. I thought poor Rose's heart would just break over that. For, you see, she blamed herself. Mary-Evelyn might just have thought no one could follow her, that those women couldn't find her if she was in a boat. At least that's what Rose figured—that maybe she'd row until she found a river. To go where, we couldn't say, if to go anywhere."

*To row until she found a river.* I felt relieved, as if I'd been holding my breath for days and only now could let it out. But again I felt angry. "Well, she'd never have done it if you two hadn't of run off and left her behind!" But my anger now was sort of manufactured; I believed they really would have got Mary-Evelyn out from under her aunts if they'd had the time. Then I remembered what Ulub had said and told Ben Queen. "They were making her go over to the boathouse!"

He frowned. "Most likely they were just looking for her, don't you think?"

"*Looking* for her?" I was astonished. And then I realized, Ulub could have misunderstood. He'd already left and he was watching from this side of the lake. How could he have distinguished lamps from candles, or how could he be sure Mary-Evelyn was with them? By the time he left the Devereau house, ran home, and ran back, Mary-Evelyn could have come around to this side of the lake. Indeed, all along I'd been depending on Ulub for information about the Devereaus and had turned what might only have been their nature not to talk much into this policing silence. I had to admit, too, that I'd loved that image of the three of them walking through the black woods, lighting their way with lamps or candles. I thought of Miss Flyte and her "effects." It was kind of Nancy Drew–ish. So if that kind of misunderstanding could apply to the Devereau women, well, why not to anything? All we had was either the evidence of our own eyes or that kind the Sheriff has to go on: footprints, thumbprints, alibis. "But why didn't those women call the police?"

"I don't know. Rose thought it was because they were so sure they'd find her or she'd come running back. They were too prideful to admit she'd run off, and Rose said they couldn't stand to be thought wrong; they would have hated to make their business public."

We sat in a pleasant silence for a few moments, me turning over and over the subject of the Devereaus. I hoped Ben Queen wouldn't mind me bringing it up, but Rose's murder got to be too much for me to keep silent. "People know you didn't kill Rose."

He nodded briefly, as if that settled it. "They're right. Too bad they weren't on that jury."

"Mr. Stemple—do you remember him?" Ben

Queen nodded, said he sure did, and I went on. "He says your friend Miss Landis came under a lot of suspicion."

Ben Queen waved that away. "Lou Landis was the kind of person could accept things that went against her. I never heard Lou utter one word against Rose. When we was married, she came up to both of us and sincerely wished we would be happy. Lou's a fine woman."

I thought of the woman in the dark dress, looking out over the schoolyard as if waiting for someone to come back. I lowered my head, for I might cry. It was all so romantic and tragic. I got control of myself—I always did—cleared my throat a few times so my voice wouldn't tremble, and asked, "But why didn't you even defend yourself? Why?"

"Guess I didn't much care what happened, not with Rose gone."

In a squall of anger, I half rose and said, "That's not fair! You had Fern to look after—you had a *child*! It's like you just *forgot* her and left her to fend for herself!" I sat down heavily, as if the burden of forgotten children were just too much for me.

Ben Queen turned to give me a long look. "You've thought about all this real hard, ain't you, Emma?"

I nodded. I realized I was exhausted with thinking about it.

He sat and smoked another few moments, then he said, "The one bad thing that ever happened to Rose and me was that our child was never quite right in the head. Poor Rosie, she seemed to blame herself because of her crazy family. *None* of them was right in the head, she used to kid around saying. Of course, that was just silly—Rose was about as right-minded as a person can get. She was right about Fern being better off in someplace she could have been helped and watched over. Fern did a lot of crazy things. She'd run off days, weeks at a time; she was promiscuous—you know what that means?"

"Oh, of *course!*" I had a kind of blind idea, something my mind couldn't see all that well. Was Ben Queen smiling? I didn't look. "Go on."

"Fern didn't want to go to this institution, although she didn't know what it was nor why her momma wanted her to go there. I didn't want her to go. But Rose was right. She was sure right."

I looked at his head, bent down, and the sadness seemed to rise off him like river mist and take me into it. I put my hand on his arm. "I'm really sorry, Mr.—Ben. I'm really sorry. It was—" But I stopped, because some things are better left unspoken or not spoken aloud. "It was Fern," I had been about to say. But why add to his woes by saying it aloud? Unhappy things brought out and said aloud had a kind of black magic working in them. Anyway, he knew I knew. It was Fern he'd been protecting. How terrible.

"Times I think some of us was put on this earth for no reason except to take the blame for others," he said.

"Like Mary-Evelyn," I said. "And you," I didn't say.

Ben Queen was looking up at the night sky. "She was one, that's sure."

We sat there in silence. And then I thought about the Girl—not that she was ever far from my mind. I screwed up my courage to ask: "Did your girl Fern ever have any children?"

He was shaking the tin cup as if he'd make more water spring from it, like magic. He turned to look at me, his expression hard and silencing. "Why are you asking that?"

I put off answering by saying, "Jude Stemple said—"

"Girl, you sure do have some strange friends." He shook his head.

I ignored that. "He said Fern didn't have any kids, but—"

"What makes you ask if she *did*, then?"

I felt a great upheaval in my heart; I felt another squall of tears like a cloudburst coming on. I did not want to tell anyone about her, though I didn't know why. But this was Ben Queen after all, and I thought he'd taken too much blame already. "Because I saw someone who looks just like Rose, your wife, did. Just like that picture on the wall."

At this he rose and walked over to the water pipe and just stood looking down at it, his hands jammed in his jeans pockets.

I don't know why saying what I'd just said

made me feel so fearful. It was like breaking a trust, or telling a secret you were bound to keep. And my punishment could be that the Girl would disappear— or worse, it would be like she'd never been.

For what seemed ages, Ben Queen stood studying the pipe embedded in the rocks, listening to the steady trickle of clear water. And then he looked at me and smiled in a ghostly way, saying, "I'd say maybe this girl you saw, or *thought* you saw, that maybe she was a figment of your imagination. You think that could be?"

I knew he didn't believe that. Otherwise, he'd have asked more questions about when I saw her and where, especially since I'd told him she looked exactly like Rose Devereau. So I knew he didn't believe what he was saying. What's more, I knew he knew *I* didn't believe it. Still, what I said was: "I guess so. She was just a figment."

We said nothing more about this, but still we sat for a while until Ben Queen dropped his cigar on the ground and got up. He said he had to be going.

I got up too. I did not want him to go and did not know how to make him stay.

Then he turned and smiled and touched his hat brim as he'd done before, as if saluting me. And what he said next was strange and surprising: "Now listen, Emma. If anyone starts asking you questions, as well they might, and if things go too hard on you, go ahead and tell 'em you seen me, and where." He smiled. The smile was to fool us into thinking it wasn't all that serious, none of it. But I knew and he knew it was: "If it goes too hard on you, turn me in."

I was too amazed to speak. *Turn me in.*

He touched his hat in a kind of salute, smiled, and said, "Pleasure talking to you." Then he walked away.

I stood there looking after him until he was soaked up by darkness, until I heard no more sound of twigs trampled or bushes rustling. But I hadn't finished asking him questions. For it wasn't enough. It wasn't *enough* to think it had all been unplanned and unplotted. I felt the mystery was leaking away and would leave me with nothing. Frantically, I started into the woods. *"Mary-Evelyn!"* I called after him. I ran a little way along the path we'd taken, calling again. But either he didn't hear me, being too far away by now, or heard me and didn't come.

"Mary-Evelyn." This time to myself.

## FORTY-TWO

I didn't sleep at all that night. At least, I knew I was staring up at the ceiling thinking about Ben Queen, and in the morning I was staring up at the ceiling, so I don't know what happened in between.

Groggy, I was dragging on my socks and shoes, thinking how Ben Queen seemed able to see underneath things, underneath words; thinking he was a lot like the Sheriff—

*The Sheriff!* I sat bolt upright, fully awake now. Oh, Lord! I was right back in it again, right back wondering whether to tell the Sheriff what I knew. Only this time, there was absolutely no mistaking if I *should*. Why was it, you get through making one decision, another decision comes along, and this one even harder? I guessed that was the way it was for everybody as they got older.

Except everybody didn't have to go downstairs and wait on Miss Bertha.

After I'd cleaned up the buttered toast Miss Bertha had managed to knock onto the dining room floor, along with her orange juice, which she claimed was canned and not fresh, I phoned up the taxi stand, was told Axel would come on out right away, and when the taxi came, it was, of course, Delbert.

I had been almost too tired to eat my own breakfast, except for a waffle and some of that canned orange juice, so by the time I got to the Rainbow (I wasn't ready for the courthouse yet) and smelled the chili, I was pretty hungry. Maud brought me a bowl and a little dish of oyster crackers and told me the Sheriff would probably be in soon for lunch, as Shirl had just made deep-dish peach pie, one of his favorites. I figured since I had my chili in front of me, I might as well stay. I'd have to face him sometime, though I didn't know what I was going to say.

Maud had her cup of coffee and her pack of cigarettes. She sat down beside me and lit one up.

I dropped oyster crackers one by one on my chili and watched to see whether they'd float or just stick. It was my chili test. If they stuck, that meant it was too thick. They floated.

"Does it pass the cracker test?"

I nodded. "I guess it always does."

"You look a little tired. They're working you too hard."

"It's Miss Bertha." I told Maud what had happened. She knew all about Miss Bertha.

"You're probably the only one who gives her the attention she wants."

It just amazed me, the way Maud could take throwing your toast and orange juice at a person as some kind of compliment.

She said, "Sam found out about that woman who was shot. Her *father* just got out of prison. Fifteen years he was in for killing her *mother*. Isn't that strange?"

I nodded, and broke more crackers into my chili.

"Well, at least Sam thinks he found out how she got there. . . . Are you at all interested in this?"

I looked up quickly. "Me? Sure I am. So how did she?"

"Took a train to La Porte. Then she got a cab out to White's Bridge. Axel drove her."

Maud turned just then to look toward the door, so she didn't see my mouth drop open. *Axel drove her.* Yes, I guess that's just as it should be. Maud had looked toward the door because the Sheriff was walking in. I dipped my head a little more deeply into my shoulders and slid down in my seat.

The Sheriff stood over our booth, and if he was looking at me, well, I couldn't tell. My nose was nearly in the chili. He said hello to both of us and stood there with his arm resting across the high wooden back of the booth. He asked Maud for some of the deep-dish peach pie.

She told him, "After you eat some chili or a roast beef sandwich or something. You can't eat only dessert." She got up and kind of ducked under his outstretched arm.

"Yes I can." He called over his shoulder to her back, "If you don't mind."

Then the Sheriff sat down across from me. There was a silence and I tried to think of something light-hearted to say. I couldn't.

"I went to Cold Flat Junction a few days ago. And again today. I was talking to George Queen and his wife. But you know them probably better than I do."

"You want some chili?" I shoved my bowl toward him. "It's four-star today."

"No. Thank you."

It seemed an effort for him to get out the "Thank you." He repeated it: "You know them, don't you? George and Bathsheba Queen?"

I stopped my spoon on its way to my mouth and pretended to be thinking hard. "Well, I know *some* Queens, I guess. . . ."

"You know *these* Queens. You were there day before yesterday with Elijah Root."

"Oh, do *you* know Mr. Root?" I crumbled some more crackers and drizzled them over my chili. "He likes to sit outside Britten's store with Ulub and Ubub. He can understand just about everything Ulub says. Mr. Root—"

The Sheriff raised his voice just a little to tromp on that. "According to Mrs. Queen, Elijah Root came to see her and brought along Jen Graham's daughter. That would be you, wouldn't it? Last time I looked, you were the only daughter Jen had."

I knew this was the beginning of a life of cobweb lies. Like up in the old servants' rooms, where those transparent and filmy cobwebs stick to you, and you don't see them coming. "I was sitting outside Britten's with Mr. Root. He said he wanted to go over to see this Mrs. Queen, who was an old friend of his. And I didn't have anything to do so I went along with him. You know, for the ride."

Oh, thank heaven I saw Maud coming back, for the Sheriff was already shaking his head. She

set a white dish of pie oozing peaches and topped
with ice cream before the Sheriff. I scooted over
farther, meaning for her to sit down. But the Sheriff
held his cup out to her.

"Mind getting me a refill?"

"In a minute, Mr. Stoneface. You should be up
on Mount Rushmore today."

I glanced up quickly at him. He did not look
angry. He just looked clenched, like a fist.

Maud walked off and I crumbled the crackers,
making a coverlet of the crumbs all over my chili.
I wondered if the Sheriff had questioned any of the
First Union Tabernacle people. But why would he
do that?

"George Queen said they talked a lot about his
brother, Ben."

"I guess so. I wasn't paying much attention."

"I bet."

The peach pie just sat there with the vanilla ice
cream tracking down the sides. Everything had gone
quiet, as if all the customers in the Rainbow Café
had suddenly stopped talking to listen. Someone had
plugged money into the jukebox and Patsy Cline's
voice cut through this silence like breaking glass.
Then Maud was back with the coffee pot. She poured
a measure into the Sheriff's cup and turned and
walked off again.

He said, "Ben Queen is the father of the woman
we found in Mirror Pond."

"You haven't got any *cream*! I'll get it!" I was
halfway out of the booth when he reached out with

his hand and pulled me back down. I saw that Maud had been called back into service by the men at the counter. I picked up another fistful of crackers and crumbled them. By now my chili was half crackers. I risked a quick glance up at the Sheriff and wished I hadn't. His blue eyes were icy.

"Ben Queen got out of prison a week ago. He was in for murdering his wife—"

"He didn't do it!" It came out in a rush, unplanned and helpless.

"He didn't?" Surprised, the Sheriff sat back. "Now, what makes you say that?" Then he leaned forward, halfway across the table, fixing me with those blue eyes. "Do you know something I don't?"

This was misery. I swallowed. "Well, it's just that plenty of people in Cold Flat don't think he did. His sister-in-law, that Mrs. Queen, said he just couldn't. And the same goes for his brother, George." I didn't bring Jude Stemple into it.

"It's understandable his own family would feel that way." There was another silence. "You going to tell me?"

I didn't even bother with the crackers anymore. I just said, with a little shrug, "Tell you what?"

He sat now with his hands kind of tented over his chin, so I couldn't see his mouth. I would have liked to think he was hiding a smile, but this time I knew he wasn't. I crinkled up my forehead in as huge a frown as I could and said again, "Tell you what?"

"I have the strangest feeling you know something you're not telling me."

His voice was soft, but his eyes were like that blue ice you see in travel pictures of Alaska or the Poles.

A small wail almost like the note that Patsy Cline was drawing out set up in my mind, as if wind blew through its cracks and crevices. *Oh no, oh no, oh no*. Was this what happened to friends? Could something come along and be more important than the friendship? I opened my mouth to answer him, but then I heard that other voice in my mind: *If things go hard for you, turn me in.*

So I closed my mouth again and looked at the table while my chili got cold and his ice cream melted.

Finally, the Sheriff said he'd see me later, and got up, and walked towards the door. He never asked me to check the meters with him.

I stared at his untouched pie and fell, like Patsy, to pieces.

# FORTY-THREE

I found the Artist George tube lying in the little stone alcove where we keep the tin cup. Strangely, I was not surprised. I unscrewed the head and looked inside, thinking there might be a message. If I were Nancy Drew, there'd be some kind of note. But I guess in real life, you don't get those kinds of messages.

Mary-Evelyn has always been there in my mind, as if she had just appeared at twelve years old, she and her aunts, all sprung up suddenly in my line of vision. They might have been born as I looked. It was as if the aunts had come into being with the misery or were the misery itself, or had brought it with them, like the blue devils, to heap on Mary-Evelyn's head.

Mary-Evelyn. In my mind's eye I see her moving through the black leaves in her white dress, in that slow-motion way people do in movies. I watch her get into the rowboat and watch her push off from the dock with the oar, which she then lets drop. Maybe she wanted to die. Or maybe she wanted to see if she could be borne up by water. To be borne up, borne up by anything.

I'm glad the name of Rose Devereau is cleared in my heart, for she was hard to hate. I guess all along I secretly liked her, which I couldn't help.

The strangest thing of all is that Mary-Evelyn's death—or her life, maybe—was finally avenged. It's as if the Girl was dropped down from heaven; the Girl was like one of Will's and Mill's do-X machines, dropped down from heaven to finally avenge Mary-Evelyn Devereau. I think Ben Queen knows why she did it. As for me, I can only guess that the blue devils got handed down to her because she was, in part, a Devereau. It might have taken two generations to do it; it might have been cowpoke justice, but as far as I'm concerned, it's at least some relief to see that even if it looks like wrongs aren't righted, well, finally they can be.

As I said before: when you think the mystery is solved, it just begins in again. What Mrs. Louderback called a "state of greater clarity"—that to me is very strange, because I would have said my life, up until two weeks ago, was clear as arithmetic.

However much I want to believe the story has a neat ending, I guess it doesn't. Turn the page, another story; another page, another story. I run my fingers along the print of this Nancy Drew book and imagine what it would be like to be blind and read braille. What it would be like to actually *feel* words. That must be what I like so much about the Abigail Butte County Library—the comfort of words.

The other thing I've come to believe is this: you only have two choices. You either drift out in a leaky boat or you turn the page.

I wonder where the Girl has gone, as I wonder where Ben Queen will go, if he gets away, and I think he will. In case I ever doubt myself and think it all must have been a dream, I still have the neckerchief folded in my pocket. I take it out now, wonder about him.

And I turn the page.

(continued)

Gabriel García Márquez, *Of Love and Other Demons* (paper)

Martha Grimes, *The End of the Pier*

Martha Grimes, *The Horse You Came In On* (paper)

Martha Grimes, *Rainbow's End* (paper)

David Halberstam, *The Fifties* (2 volumes, paper)

Katharine Hepburn, *Me* (hardcover and paper)

P. D. James, *The Children of Men*

P. D. James, *Original Sin* (paper)

Pope John Paul II, *Crossing the Threshold of Hope*

Pope John Paul II, *The Gospel of Life* (paper)

Dean Koontz, *Dark Rivers of the Heart* (paper)

Dean Koontz, *Icebound*

Judith Krantz, *Dazzle*

Judith Krantz, *Lovers* (paper)

Judith Krantz, *Scruples Two*

John le Carré, *Our Game* (paper)

John le Carré, *The Secret Pilgrim*

Anne Morrow Lindbergh, *Gift from the Sea*

Cormac McCarthy, *The Crossing* (paper)

Audrey Meadows with Joe Daley, *Love, Alice* (paper)

James A. Michener, *Mexico* (paper)

James A. Michener, *Miracle in Seville* (paper)

James A. Michener, *Recessional* (paper)

James A. Michener, *The World Is My Home* (paper)

Sherwin B. Nuland, *How We Die* (paper)

Richard North Patterson, *Degree of Guilt*

Richard North Patterson, *Eyes of a Child* (paper)

Luciano Pavarotti and William Wright, *Pavarotti: My World* (paper)

Louis Phillips, editor, *The Random House Large Print Treasury of Best-Loved Poems*

Colin Powell with Joseph E. Persico, *My American Journey* (paper)

(continued)

Ruth Rendell, *Simisola* (paper)
Maria Riva, *Marlene Dietrich* (2 volumes, paper)
Andy Rooney, *My War* (paper)
William Styron, *Darkness Visible*
Margaret Truman, *Murder on the Potomac* (paper)
Anne Tyler, *Ladder of Years* (paper)
Anne Tyler, *Saint Maybe*
John Updike, *Rabbit at Rest*
Phyllis A. Whitney, *Daughter of the Stars* (paper)

---

*The New York Times Large Print Crossword Puzzles* (paper)

Will Weng, editor, Volumes 1–3
Eugene T. Maleska, editor, Volumes 4–7
Eugene T. Maleska, editor, Omnibus Volume 1